A TIME TO SEE

A Time to See

S. J. Knight

C.M.P.A.

404 Shaftmoor Lane
Hall Green
Birmingham B28 8SZ

2009

First published 2009

ISBN 978-0-85189-185-9

ACKNOWLEDGEMENTS
Illustrations & Calligraphy – Paul Wasson
Additional Illustrations – David Knight
Cover Photography – Nigel Moore

Printed and bound in Great Britain by:

THE CROMWELL PRESS GROUP
TROWBRIDGE
WILTSHIRE BA14 0XB

AUTHOR'S NOTE

This is a work of fiction, not exposition.
What is not recorded, has been respectfully imagined,
but the Scripture alone is True concerning the words and deeds
of Jeshua the Nazarene.

For the rest, there was no Banayim – no Dan, no Anna.
But there were people like them.
They lived ordinary lives in an extraordinary time.
They were people like us.

S. J. K.

Chapter One

DAN could not believe he had missed out the last two sheep, but so it was. He had called to Holah, Golan, and Geba and got no further. Lop-horned Almon was always next, just before motherly Hephzibah. A sudden trick of the mind had slipped the name *Ammiel* to his tongue instead of Almon, and instantly his thoughts flashed – *Ammiel! – Johanan! – Loukanos! – Jeshua!* – before he realised that Hephzibah and Almon were plodding dutifully towards him, twitching their pendulous ears. Was that a reproachful look in their trustful eyes? Dan shook himself in annoyance and bent down to hug them.

"Come on, my darlings … Almon! Hephzibah! … Come to *Abba* …"

He rubbed their long noses repentantly. It was unforgiveable to have let his mind wander!

Dan loved them, all the more because they had been named and raised by his father, and were his legacy. Patient and reliable, these five were also the steadiest in the flock. Only the old Queen of Sheba, who was now Caleb's special care, was more precious … she and Dan's pet ram Moses, who seemed to think he was a dog most of the time, and was not impressed to be penned with the others when he so often served as his master's pillow. But though

Dan was no novice, this was his first solitary watch, and he was not taking any chances.

"Moses! Moses! Come here to *Abba*! You too, tonight … inside. Yes, in you go, boy …"

Dan grinned at the little ram's reluctance, gave the jaunty haunches an encouraging push as they passed, and dragged the heavy gate over the opening, dropping the wooden bars into their greasy-smooth sockets. Over the years, sheep, goats, cattle, and even nervous travellers, had found refuge inside these rough limestone walls. It was a tall, solid enclosure, generations old, a boon to shepherds and drovers on the south west slopes, who kept it in good repair.

Painstakingly Dan plied bow and tinder to start the fire, arranged his fuel, and checked his supply of sling stones, ready for the night. The summer shearing had past, the days were still warm, but the nights cooling. Sharp-fanged hunters would soon become even bolder, fattening themselves for the winter, and the smell of sheep would attract them. The flock was safe enough from wolves, but wildcats would climb, and only dogs or fire or a deadly slingshot would keep them at bay. Bears and lions could climb too, of course, though Old Caleb had always reassured Dan there were not many around in lush, cultivated Galilee these days – why, he had not seen a single one in years! Even so, Dan felt a tinge of apprehension added to the weight of responsibility. Caleb was a faithful master of the flock, but the animals were Dan's own inheritance, and tonight he, a half grown boy, was their sole protector.

While the light held, Dan inspected the walls of the fold. There were holes at the base where stones had been scraped free by eager, hungry claws. The last shepherd had spiked these gaps with vicious thorn bush, and balanced the loosened stones on top of the wall to alert him to scrambling paws in the night. But Dan put more faith in rock than thorns. Carefully he raked out the sharp spines and replaced them with blackened limestones which had ringed numerous campfires. The sandy edges crumbled to a tight fit as Dan pounded them into place. The boy wiped his hands with a sense of relief. Now the sheep were as safe as he could make them. Even so, he was glad that Samuel's Eli had insisted that twenty animals were more than enough for him to manage on his own for two days. So far, it had been uneventful, but the night would be the real test.

Dan sniffed the late afternoon air and looked at the streaky sky doubtfully, almost wishing he had Caleb's rheumatic knee which foretold rain. He was not as hardened as the old shepherd, and preferred to keep his head dry. He unwrapped the long strip of tenting around his pack, and tied one end to the top bar of the gate, holding the other end down with a few heavy rocks toppled from their sentry duty on top of the wall. They would hold well enough, he thought. The fold was in a sheltered hollow, there was no wind, and rain was not likely, but dew would be heavy. No doubt Old Caleb would have turned up his weatherbeaten nose at this luxury and pointed out that the hard trodden dirt in front of the gate would capture the wet, but his young apprentice scraped drainage channels around his makeshift tent, heaped up dried bracken for a bed, and hoped for the best.

Now Dan was satisfied with his preparations. At last he could eat his leathery bread and cheese, washing it down with water to which he had added a splash of vinegar. That was Eli's tip, and distracted from the muddy taste which the clay bottle had imparted. There were a few dried figs in the satchel, but these Dan tucked

3

into the smaller scrip at his belt for later, knowing their sweetness would be all the more welcome in the cold, stiff hours before dawn. He wolfed down the rest of his food without thinking, and then had to kick himself for not saving half of it for morning. It would be a hungry wait till Eli arrived at noon. Well, he wouldn't do that twice. Now, he could rest. He fed the fire, crawled under his shelter, arranged his blankets, and curled into his thick, felted cloak as the light was sucked into the western hilltops. Stars faded behind gathering cloud, and although it did not rain, the darkening air was soon damp and cold.

One part of Dan's mind was alert for his sheep ... and would remain so even while he slept. That was a skill he had long since learned. But the rest of it was free ... and this was his time for meditation ... the time when he attempted to pray, even as his father Ammiel had done, every evening, and every morning.

What did Ammiel pray? Dan's prayer began like his father's had, thanking the Eternal for the daily blessings, and asking for a safe night, but Ammiel had always ended with 'Show us Thy Messiah!' ... and though Ammiel himself had not lived to see it, that prayer was now answered.

Oh, what a time it had been! A time of excitement, of struggling to understand the signs, the prophecies, the stories and rumours! A time of disappointment when they understood that Prophet Johannes, the baptising Nazirite of Jordan, was only the herald and not the One they sought. A time when private tragedy had overtaken them so suddenly that even the Messiah faded from their minds. But finally, a time of clarity had come – a time of certainty, a time to hear the thrilling message from the Baptiser himself – "Behold the Lamb of God that takes away the sin of the world! This is He of whom I spoke!"

They had heard him say so – hundreds of them, clustered on the Jordan banks two years ago. Undoubtedly it was true. They had witnessed that unearthly moment for themselves. All of them. Cynical Loukanos, Anna, Dan and Johanan … and even Aunt Etta and Old Caleb, still wet and shivering from their own baptism … they had seen the thin dark man emerge from the dull waters. They had seen and heard … a shaft of light, a fluttering dove … a rock-shuddering Voice claiming "My Beloved Son!"… had stood motionless with hammering hearts as an intense, river-drenched workman passed them by, sliding his wet feet into scuffed, mud-slippery sandals, the squelching leather dark-sodden by the Jordan water streaming from his soaked tunic. He had lifted his dry cloak from the rock right beside them, and melted into the crowd … and they had seen his face, and knew that what Johannes proclaimed, and what the Voice had thundered, was truth.

This truth consoled them when Loukanos left them, abruptly. He had promised to stay until they saw the Messiah, but they had not expected him to take it so literally. Neither had they expected their newfound Messiah to disappear just as suddenly, and remain away for forty days. *Had not Moses done the same?* they encouraged each other. *Was he not to be 'a prophet like unto Moses?'*

They still clung to this truth in the face of disappointment when the Chosen emerged from the bleak desert, though without tables of stone, plans for a tabernacle, or cleansing whirlwind of judgement such as Moses had brought from the solitude of Sinai.

But where was it written what must happen next? Nobody knew. They could only wait with bated breath as the story flew around that the Promised One proclaimed by Johannes the baptising prophet was a nobody. The whole nation hummed with the news, and in Jerusalem the air fairly crackled with agitation.

Could this be right? They could more readily have believed that Messiah was Johannes himself – the ascetic prophet whose beautiful voice belied his rough clothes, who had stirred religious revival among the thousands of Israel, who urged good deeds, and a repentance so deep as to demand baptism, which hitherto had been reserved for Gentile converts! But there was no getting round the fact that Johannes was of the wrong tribe, and from the beginning had told them plainly, "I am not He, but I am his herald."

And so the people were faced with the Baptist's own startling declaration of whom their Messiah was – his own cousin! But the men were not alike. Johannes had stood out – the miracle child of ancient parents; a Nazirite, by his mother's caution, even from the womb; the austerity, the stark desert life, rough clothes, and food gleaned from the wild ... when he could have enjoyed the Levitical comforts of holy service, soft robes, and a good table. Such a choice inevitably attracted cynical murmurs of *Madness!* but nobody seriously believed it. After all, who could doubt his compelling voice, fearless teachings and bold ritual? Yes, Johannes had been a great man, clearly a man of God!

But the Saviour of Israel who came after him, was undistinguished by any of those things. He was only a thin, work-shabby man with a slur on his paternity, speaking the oft-mocked, clumsy dialect of rough-and-tumble Galilee of the Gentiles ... ungraciously called *Kabul*, a 'nothing' place, for centuries. Even more uncomfortably, the Chosen One hailed from a tired trade-route town, Nazareth, humbly crouching like an untidy dog in the greater shadow of Herod's newly rebuilt Sepphoris.

That the Messiah promised from the foundation of the world should come from such a place and be such a person – a man of no account, and no education – neither learned sage, ruler, statesman, or mature warrior, but a common tradesman! A threadbare, lowly woodworker, wearing aprons of leather and sacking … covered in dust and splinters … a wiry labourer with muscular shoulders, hard bare arms, calloused hands, broken fingernails and dirty feet like everyone else. An everyday fellow who was no glorious stranger suddenly revealed in shining splendour, but someone who had always been around, everyone's neighbour, the man you paid to make your shelves, or fix your door, or build your privy.

Even Dan himself had once met him – spoken to him – and thought little of it … when three years ago, he and Ammiel had bought Aunt Etta's precious walking stick in the dim little workshop with its sign 'Ben Netser'; where Jeshua and Jacob ben Joseph carried on their father's trade, where they sawed and hammered, sanded, polished and sweated, where they hummed or growled or sang according to the task's degree of difficulty, where they debated and teased each other in the way of brothers everywhere. Ammiel had coaxed sharp sawdust out of Jeshua's eyes with Anna's dainty handkerchief, and they had all laughed at Jacob's indignation when he walked into a pile of planks. Who could have chosen between the brothers, in any case? They were ordinary men, surely, even though it was whispered that they could trace their ancestry back to King David.

Dan shifted restlessly on his crackling bed as his thoughts flew through the past few years. The difference was hard to put into words, but even aside from his powers, Nazarene Jeshua was *not* ordinary. All that time, he had been patiently preparing for the moment he would be revealed as the Messiah. The stillness, the intensity which hung around him, was a potent attraction. But

7

he did not rally the people and lead them in battle, as many expected Messiah would; he led them by far stiller waters than the whirlpool of war. He talked to them peacefully, sat with them, even fed them, and tended their sick – *more a Shepherd than a Lamb*, Dan thought in confusion, admitting to himself that he had no idea what 'Lamb of God' meant.

Meanwhile, Jeshua taught the people, not rebellion, but peace. Like his weather-beaten cousin, Johannes the Baptiser, not once did he refer to a learned teacher, or give intricate dissertations on the *Torah* or hold forth on *Halakhah* – but he taught by swift, potent tales of the reality they best understood. Anecdotal teachings – *Haggadah* – were not new. They could be heard in any synagogue, where too often they were mere entertainment; airily brushed illustrations of the Law, so watered down that it frequently paled into invisibility.

But the Nazarene teacher never wasted a single, vivid stroke – his sharp life sketches of the fields and the sea, the market place and the fireside leapt boldly into relief, educating them to look behind the outward forms so hallowed by the revered scribes. His words demanded a response in the hearts of his audience who could suddenly see themselves as they were, and they flocked to him with a hunger never aroused by their betters. On his part, he observed no distinctions among men, eating crusts and vinegar with the poor, or meat and wine with the rich, with equal goodwill – uncaring that his acceptance of normal hospitality was contrasted unfavourably with the Baptist's abstinence, by the same men who had called Johannes a madman for abstaining.

The Sanhedrin in Jerusalem muttered and growled and snarled like hyenas around a fold, as the wrong man did all the right things. The Romans looked sideways at the squabbling and frowned impatiently – the Jews were always spoiling for a fight, and if they didn't look out, they'd get one.

Meanwhile the man who had once made tables, fed a multitude with a child's picnic lunch. The one who had fashioned walking sticks, caused the lame to throw theirs away. He who once repaired broken wheels and damaged chairs, now healed crippled bodies and lives with a word and a touch. The man who had laboured on doors and windows now let in light and hope to those whose minds had struggled in darkness. Thousands had seen, felt, and begged for his miracles of healing from the most dread diseases, the most staggering of deformities – Leprosy! Madness! Blindness! And in astonishment of heart some had even seen the dead raised – or so it was claimed.

Acceptance of the new prophet had been gradual, but had built to a kind of hysteria of expectation. Everywhere the Nazarene went, crowds followed like a swarm of locusts. Dan himself had been a part of these crowds whenever he had the chance, seeing bewildering things in the heady times when the whole land flocked to Galilee or Jerusalem or wherever they could chase after Jeshua the Nazarene and his men. Many a time he had stood on a hill watching a whole flotilla of small craft bobbing in the wake of a boat carrying the Teacher, the shores dark with people scurrying the long way round to waylay him ... but while even the lake fishermen had joined the man whom the Baptiser had proclaimed as the spirit-anointed Son of God, Dan was firmly tied to his sheep and his family.

Of course, once he had seen the miraculous for himself, he didn't need to be in the man's presence to believe what he heard. No-one, since the beginning of the world, had wielded such power to heal! Men who had begged were now labourers. Women who had been shut away were free to stand in the synagogue. Silent children could now shout and cry. Lepers had been examined by astonished priests and returned joyfully to their families. *Magic and sorcery and spirits of Beelzebub*, sneered the scribes. Did not even Pharaoh's magicians also do as Moses did? Was there not an imposter in Samaria performing similar tricks even now? Marvels and wonders were no proof of Divine power!

But the people didn't care – all they knew was that they were the grateful recipients of the impossible – that someone was doing for them what nobody else would – or could – do. Small wonder that everyone thronged to see him, to touch him, to implore his help, with many asking nothing but to hear him speak.

All through the land, Dan knew – everyone knew! – fetters of bondage were being struck from those who were imprisoned by disease and misfortune. Surely this was just the beginning! Surely this was just a foretaste of deliverance from the bonds of Gentile power! Dan struggled to make sense of the Baptiser's words about the Lamb of God taking away the sin of the world. Perhaps this had to do with removing the great sin of Roman occupation? *And since sickness comes from sin, perhaps this is why he is healing people first?*

In his confusion, Dan did not realise that he had his logic back to front, and tried to look further into the future. Once there were no more people to cure, perhaps then would the Nazarene push forward at last, to take that final step towards freedom for his people. Salvation from the iron grip of Rome! But there were *thousands* of sick and damaged people in Israel. Who knew how long it would take?

As the darkness and silence deepened around him, Dan's racing thoughts brought a tumbling whirlwind of unwelcome doubts and questions …

Though the Baptist had performed no miracles, and played no politics, he had been accepted by everyone, even Herod, as a prophet of God. He had equally touched those who seemed to be far above any spiritual need, and those who were so low as to appear beyond help. Johannes had prepared the people to hope for even more, and stirred great searchings of heart. He had gathered crowds, demanded repentance, required obedience, appealed for changed lives – he was as eccentric and uncompromising as Elijah – a man of mystery and authority. But now he had been imprisoned, and murdered by the State, which no Saviour could ever be.

And so they were left with the carpenter.

There was no doubting that for more than two years Jeshua of Nazareth had proven himself to be the man of God Johannes had prepared them for – so why the growing dissatisfaction and perplexity? The learned scribes, fierce Zealots, supercilious Sadducees, pragmatic Pharisees, educated priests – all had the same dismissive answer, delivered with a shrug. *The purpose of Messiah was Israel's Deliverance! So, where was it?* The land was still under Roman rule, Israel was still undelivered. Therefore, even if the people's hero *was* a prophet of sorts, he was certainly no Messiah!

Dan squirmed restlessly on his bracken bed. Sharp stems jabbed through the thickly woven woollen blanket as irritatingly as his unwanted qualms. Jeshua talked constantly of the Realm of God but was disinterested in kingship, and nothing had really changed. The mood was turning ... the rulers were more adamant than ever that the Nazarene was an imposter, and sought to discredit him at every turn. Was this the way it was supposed to be?

Surely it was no mistake, surely Jeshua was the one! But since the beloved Baptiser who had heralded him had been executed, even the common people were restlessly wondering when they would be freed from the relentless grasp of ungodly Caesar ... and the fervour was cooling.

Dan's head spun with the tumult of his conflict, and there was nobody to share it with. He huddled in his cold hollow in the darkness, straining his ears for sounds of danger, trying to make sense of all that had happened, and uneasily wondering what was yet to come.

Chapter Two

THE young shepherd rubbed his stiff, grimy hands together and stretched wearily. He had been sawing away with his bow until the string had almost snapped, and still the point of the whirling stick had not raised a wisp of smoke from the soft wood beneath. What a fool he'd been to let the fire die so early. He wasn't going to raise a spark with damp tinder in this clinging mist. Dan huddled deeper into his thick greasy cloak and blew on his fists.

He should have realised that any moist grassy hollow might trick him with a day-break fog at this time of year. Any shepherd worth his salt – a new expression for Dan and he grinned fleetingly over it despite his irritation – any shepherd worth his salt would have kept the finely chopped straw and shavings more firmly tied in their oiled leather pouch. Or better still, would have managed the fire properly. Well, the cold was nothing, and he deserved it. But predators respected only a flame or a sling, and right now it might as well be twilight. He peered cautiously into the gloom, glad of the well-built fold behind him, but uncomfortably aware that a determined wildcat could cause havoc within, merely by the threatening smell of its presence.

There was a thud of footsteps and the scrunch of a body through bush. Dan leaped to a crouch, snatching the slingshot from his girdle, already up and whirling the leather when a deep voice shouted, "Hold your hand, Dan!" and a stocky young man emerged from the mist.

"Hey, boy – where's your fire? I was lucky to find you!"

Shamefaced, Dan told him, and was thankful when Eli merely shook his head, setting to work with his own dry tinder and a flint.

"You should know by now, Dan – always expect the unexpected. Better to waste a bit of fuel than be caught without flames. And you should carry a flint. That bow's no good in this weather – ah! That's it."

Eli blew carefully on the tiny spark which leapt to his fine tinder from the expertly chipped flint, and a weak flame wavered into life. Dan soberly took the stone from his sling, wound the thong around the leather and tucked it away.

"Just as well I know your reputation with that sling," Eli remarked cheerfully. "Another breath and you'd have knocked my brains out."

Dan did not reply at first, warming his hands as his friend coaxed the fire into a blaze and began rummaging in his pack.

"Sorry, Eli," he said at last. "I didn't think you'd be here until noon."

Eli did not tell Dan that he had been quietly camped all night on the other side of the same hill, at Samuel's instruction. On his own first solitary watch, his father had done the same. He would tell Dan later – maybe next year. He shrugged good-humouredly as he untied a bulging cloth full of flat bread rolled with lentil paste.

14

"At least you were expecting the unexpected in *that* way … but sight your prey before you let fly. You don't want to kill a man – or a harmless creature."

Dan stared at the flames. "How do you know when to wait? Old Caleb says surprise is everything but hesitation can be deadly too. Anyway …" He stopped.

The young man looked at him shrewdly. "Anyway, when you're startled there's no time to think?"

"Yes." Dan poked the fire glumly. 'Startled' was a mild way of putting it – yearlings had been taken by a big cat two valleys away only recently, and they both knew it.

Eli grinned at Dan's tense face. "Who *isn't* wary with a pen full of tasty meat behind him and a countryside full of sharp teeth all round? You'd be a fool not to be."

He punched him lightly on the shoulder. "But don't worry, next time there's a mist I promise to sing loudly as I approach. Now, speaking of words like *teeth* and *tasty* – where's your food? Gone already? That's jumpiness for you – makes you eat – and I bet you didn't taste much of it either. I know that myself. Lucky I brought plenty."

Dan's compressed lips relaxed as Eli casually pronounced the customary blessing, and he fell on the breakfast offered him, with a good appetite. He *had* been jumpy since the fire went out – and hungry since finishing his few dried figs in the night, which only served to wake his stomach. Dan determined to be much wiser next time. He would pack a decent flint, take more care of his tinder, and – especially – bring extra food!

"Father thinks it's time you shared some more watches with Caleb," Eli told him with his mouth full. "He's sure to have some friend-or-foe tricks to teach you … and he's itching to get back to work."

"He's better?" Dan had been very worried about the old man.

"Extra Pressings says so, anyway."

Dan snorted. Caleb's over-frugal daughter would not want her father lying around her house wheezing and coughing and eating his head off like an outworn mule.

Eli grinned, and added casually, "And so does Anna bath Netzir. I heard two nights ago."

"Praise the Eternal!" Dan brightened at once. "If she says so, it is so!"

Eli nodded and wiped his short beard. "She's kept an eye on him, don't you worry, marching off to Extra Pressings with some foul nostrum of black elder, pomegranate and persimmon, ugh! She told her to pour it down his throat every few hours if she didn't want the cost of a funeral. That did the trick all right! Caleb swears he had to get well in self-defence. So you can stop worrying. Father says we're to move the flocks to the gleaned field outside Banayim – the feed is good and will do them till New Moon – Caleb will join you there, and you can visit home too, as much as you like. Now, aren't you glad you didn't knock me out?"

A scuffling from inside the fold announced that Moses was awake and wanted his morning treat. Dan pulled down his awning and pushed the barrier aside just enough for the shaggy little ram to squeeze through. Moses flopped between the two youthful shepherds, sniffing hopefully at their fingers. Dan pulled the long ears affectionately and fed him a woody apple core he'd saved from his dinner. Moses was lucky to get it. Had it been less shrivelled, hungry Dan might have eaten it himself by now.

16

Eli nodded towards the east, where welcome light was beginning to slide along the dark ground. Around them, spectral images were firming into substance as the mist thinned. Suddenly a whiff of breeze swirled into the hollow, scooping out all greyness to unveil the waiting day – brisk and sparkling, every leaf and blade of grass flashing in the sun. It was a signal for the morning to begin. Birds began a belated chorus, fussy ants emerged to fossick, spiders crept stealthily along dew-diamond threads to inspect their night's catch, lizards slunk out sleepily to soak up the warmth, and bees bounced around among the wildflowers, ecstatically foraging even those fallen to the ground.

Dan hummed cheerfully as he and Eli inspected the flock together before letting them out to graze. Hoofs, tails, teats, bellies, ears, eyes … pot of ointment at the ready. Dan loved the smell of it. It was bitter and pungent, but a window to the past. How proud he had been as a small boy to smear the stuff on his father's precious sheep! His mother (so Aunt Etta had told him) would wrinkle her nose and flap her hands to wave away the stink. Now, both parents were but dust and shadows – their likes and dislikes all one – yet while Dan's memories of his mother had long since faded, one sniff of the sticky unguent brought his warm, generous, auburn-haired father vividly before him.

"Over here with that, Dan."

"Holah, you careless old woman!" Dan scolded the shaggy animal. "Don't you know by now you can't eat bees?" He daubed her swollen lip. "That's the third sting this month! Now behave yourself today."

So Caleb was better – Anna herself had said so – and would meet him in the pasture which was so close to home. Dan would confess his blunders, Caleb would rebuke him, capping that with ancient admissions from his own apprenticeship – and Dan would not make the same mistakes again. The boy began to whistle happily. The weeks away from home, and his first solitary stint were both over sooner than he had expected – and there was also a private question he would only ask of the old man …

"But I can feel it with my tongue, Caleb!" Dan protested. Impatiently he tilted his face the better to catch the light glittering through the dark olive leaves. "Are you sure it doesn't show?"

The scrawny old shepherd lightly ran a bony thumb experimentally over Dan's top lip and sat down with a chuckle to rummage in the food satchel.

"I'll grant you it's there all right but it'll take a long time to impress anyone."

"Why not? Johanan's didn't –he had a moustache in no time and just look at his beard now! I still look like a baby beside him. I'm not *that* much younger. It's not fair."

"Well … see, he's black-haired from crown to chin, and that shows up nice and strong … much quicker than fair …"

Dan jumped up indignantly and tugged at his dark, cropped curls. "What do you call this then? Fair?"

The old man shook his head thoughtfully. "Your hair's black, lad, but it seems to me you'll end up brindled."

Dan sank beside him, alarmed. "Brindled?"

Caleb nodded as he pulled apart a sticky lump of dates and stuffed several into his mouth at once. He mumbled, "I reckon your beard'll favour your father, may he rest in peace."

Dan threw himself down in despair, and groaned. Moses trotted over to him anxiously, thrust his bony face into Dan's neck and nuzzled the despised light fuzz with loving bleats.

"No kissing, Moses!" Dan morosely pushed away his favourite while Caleb shook with laughter, spat out the date stones and began to sing, beating the time with his gnarled crook.

"My love loves me because I am handsome!" he croaked. *"My love loves me because I am wise!"*

Dan glared at him, but the old shepherd ignored it and warbled relentlessly on.

"My love loves me because I am hairy ...
And bearded clear up to my eyes!"

With Caleb not sparing much sympathy, Dan gave in. He sat up and pulled Moses' ears repentantly. *"**Red**-bearded clear up to my eyes!"* he corrected sarcastically.

Caleb clapped his approval, and the two of them yelled the improvised refrain together, making Moses skitter away in fright.

"I'm red-bearded clear up to my eyes! I am!
Red-bearded clear up to my eyes!
Oh, I'm handsome and wise and hairy,
And red-bearded clear up to my eyes!"

But Dan was not wholly reconciled to the prospect yet. Visions of his adult face haunted his imagination that night.

"Can you imagine it, Aunt Etta?" he said bitterly the next day as he sopped up the last of his soup with bread soft and hot from the cooking stone. "Me with an auburn beard!"

"It looked very handsome on your father," Aunt Etta said cautiously, trying not to let a smile enter her voice.

"My father didn't have black hair," Dan said crossly. "I'll be all mismatched like one of Samuel's ugly old crossbreeds."

Aunt Etta pinched the back of his hard brown hand. "Think of what you say, Dan," she said warningly as the door curtain lifted, but Anna had heard.

The tall woman stooped over her adopted son and dropped a kiss on his dark curls. She lifted his chin and looked at him with her steady, strange eyes – one brown, one hazel. Her hair – still quite short for a woman – swung over her shoulders as she leaned over. The seven braids, though rich brown under her knotted cap, for over half their length were oddly streaked with patchy colour, and thinned to mere wisps at the neatly bound ends. The full import of his words struck Dan. When he spoke, he had been thinking only of himself. How could he have forgotten Anna's eyes! Let alone her hair! Oh, and that she was half Greek as well! Poor Dan mentally kicked himself.

"Do you think of your *very* mismatched *Amma* as an ugly old crossbreed, Dan boy?" she asked him lightly.

"Of course not!" He flushed with vexation.

"Why not?"

Dan squirmed. "Well, it's just – you – that's all. I'm used to it – I don't even think about it. Anyway, what does it matter?"

Anna rumpled his hair affectionately and laughed at his exasperated expression. "Exactly so!"

Aunt Etta nodded. "Exactly so, Dan!" she repeated firmly. "We can allow a woman a bit more vanity than a fledgling man, eh? And if she agrees it does not matter to *her*, it certainly doesn't for you. But fret about it, if you like, Dan – worry will make you bald quickly and then the problem will be solved!"

"Be glad you're not a woman, Dan," Anna gave her lopsided smile. "At least a man's face is judged by his expression, not his beauty."

"Or the colour of his whiskers," Aunt Etta added drily.

Dan pulled a face. "Just as well, then – but be fair, Auntie – how would *you* like a red beard?"

The women exchanged looks, and then they were all laughing. Recovered, Dan leapt up, and danced a few strutting steps, snapping his fingers with a flourish.

"My love loves me because I am handsome!" He sang the old folksong boldly, and Aunt Etta fluttered her frayed eyelashes.

"Handsome!" she sighed, looking as love-sick as was possible for a fat old woman who'd had no practice at it.

"My love loves me because I am wise!"

"So wise!" Anna repeated solemnly and with a touch of irony.

"My love loves me because I am hairy!" Dan slapped his smooth chest. *"And red-bearded clear up to my eyes!"*

"Red-bearded clear up to your eyes! Oh yes! Red-bearded clear up to your eyes!" they sang back, laughing at Dan as he combed imaginary whiskers of impossible length.

"Oh! I'm handsome and wise and hairy,
And red-bearded clear up to my eyes!"

Dan growled the final notes as deeply as he could manage, making the women laugh again.

"Never mind the colour of your poor little infant moustache, Dan," chuckled Aunt Etta. "You will have a voice rich and dark enough to make up for it in a few years."

"But not just yet!" Dan answered gaily, stepping and hopping and humming like a bee.

Anna smiled at him. No, not yet. For a little longer he would still be a boy, with a boy's enthusiasm and a clear boy's voice, and sing the lovely high notes she could never manage. She was glad his irritation had passed, their rare evening together unmarred. The fire crackled noisily under the pot and spat colourfully around it. Anna looked up from her sewing.

"Dan, have you been putting thorns under the wood again?"

Dan grinned. "I like the sound – and don't they make pretty flames?"

Aunt Etta grumbled, "Ash in no time, and just a waste of kindling – you mischief, you ..."

She drew a breath for more, but Dan laughed and slipped outside for another branch or two from the neat pile in the courtyard. The night was cool and clear – not really cold enough to keep the fire so well built up, but Aunt Etta's bent old bones tasted frost long before anyone else's, and only heat kept the pain away from her curled spine. After long watches on the breezy uplands of Galilee, a warm room was too close for Dan's liking. He drew in a deep, grateful breath of the crisp, fresh night. The approaching autumn chill was welcome after a blistering summer when the air had fairly simmered. He glanced through the half-shuttered window as he scooped up the rough sticks. The women's shadows loomed on the plastered mud walls, Aunt Etta's like a humped tent, Anna's tall as a man as she stretched, flexing her fingers. They seemed to be clutching at the air. *A flailing body – hurtling through the night – screams – and a sickening blankness –* Dan blinked, shook his head, and picked up the dropped wood.

The nightmares had long since gone, but the flashes still happened, unexpected blows which left a fading ache.

Chapter Three

DAN brought in his load, made up the fire deftly and left the room again without a word. Aunt Etta and Anna looked at each other.

"Suddenly his mind is elsewhere," Anna commented.

"It's his age," Etta shrugged. "Silly one breath, sombre the next. It could be worse. Remember what Marta used to say? *First All Hair and Horseplay – Then All Legs and Loudness.*"

Anna smiled. "Well, not much hair yet, is there … Turn around, now – let's rub this heat into your spine."

She began to give the curved back its nightly massage. "Do you remember his father at that age, Etta? You were twenty years older …"

Etta, groaning and grunting appreciatively as the firm fingers went to work, raised her wrinkled hands in mock horror.

"Oh! Do I remember! It's as well you were not around to see your *dodi* then, my dear! With his angry skin, and nose growing too fast and lip sprouting fiery little whiskers – he was not a pretty sight – and not a pretty sound either! Honking and gargling and braying and clattering about like a young donkey with bellyache … and awkward as a camel besides."

Anna burst out laughing. "My poor, poor Ammiel! Oh you cruel, wicked sister to say such unkind things!"

Peal after peal of laughter drifted up to Dan as he lay on top of the little hill behind the house. Anna's distinctive gurgling which skipped up the scale and broke into an indescribable sound which reminded Dan of water over pebbles … mingled with Aunt Etta's slow chuckles which quickened like the slapping of sandals on running feet. He lay with his head on his arm, trying to trick himself into hearing another sound threaded through their voices – the full, rich laughter of an auburn haired man with gold lights in his beard, a man who ought to have been there with them – who had run gaily up a steep flight of steps one fatal night in far-off Jerusalem – and had been knocked into oblivion by a drunken fool lurching out of the darkness above.

Dan lifted his head from his arm and looked at the house below. In the moonlight there was no difference between what he saw now, and the past he remembered. The blackened ruins had been cleared, new walls built on the foundations of the old. Only the privy in the scrub was the same, though it was almost time to move it. Aunt Etta's herb garden and vegetable plot flourished again, the big shade tree had recovered from its scorching, the path to Banayim was once more retrodden. Everything looked the same as it had. Yet so much had changed. His family, for one thing.

Ammiel's death had denied Anna bath Asa of wifehood, but she had espoused herself to a higher love and now people called her Anna bath Netzir – daughter of the Nazirite vow – a separated one. Inspired to live joyfully, she would not be parted from her beloved's family. With their glad consent, Anna had claimed Etta and Dan as sister and son by adoption and enough time had passed for folk to cease to comment. After all, the woman could not be judged by the usual standards – educated! – unmarried! – half Greek! – a Nazirite! – whatever next? Well, in Galilee of the Gentiles, such oddities passed with a push, and she was a worthy woman, they confessed, whatever her peculiarities … and so the novelty faded and the tongues ceased to wag.

But – oh, the men had gone … first Ammiel, then Bukki, and finally Loukanos. Dan felt their absence still, though thieving Uncle Bukki was no great loss. It was just too much of a coincidence that the man should leave in disgrace and the house burn down immediately afterwards. Dan could never decide whether it happened through intent or carelessness, but he was convinced Bukki was the cause one way or another, and Anna's cousin Johanan agreed with him. Bukki's whereabouts did not concern Dan, though the boys had promised themselves to choke some answers out of him if he ever crossed their path again.

Long, dark Loukanos was another matter. He had been in Dan's life for such a short, intense time, and as suddenly as he had appeared, he had gone. Anna had wept when her brother left – almost as much as she had wept for Ammiel – but she would not reproach him, and neither would Aunt Etta. Dan burned over it.

"He was free to go, Dan," Aunt Etta reminded him gently. "You told him so yourself. And you know how he was fretting to leave."

"But he didn't just leave," Dan protested angrily. "He disappeared! Anna has written to Philippi time and again and heard nothing."

Aunt Etta sighed. "You know, Dan, there is always the possibility that some evil has befallen him."

This, Dan would not believe – and yet, what other explanation could there be? Over the last two years, he and Johanan had argued about it together, and when apart, had scrawled their way through as many ideas, excuses and suppositions as they could afford to post to each other, without finding a satisfactory solution.

"Uncle Asa still has heard nothing, either," Johanan wrote recently from Jerusalem. "I have asked all my friends in the bazaars to watch for him – but it seems Loukanos did not return here. If he is not back in Macedonia, then he must be travelling again. Perhaps visiting Egypt or Athens or somewhere he can learn even more to improve his skills."

But why had he not at least sent some word to his family? Her brother's silence added pain to Anna's anxiety, and Dan no longer disturbed her with fruitless questions. So the mystery gnawed silently at them all, until Dan resolved to thrash it out with Blind Mordecai the next time he went to Cana.

For nearly three years Dan had been chafing away the mornings at the Magdala synagogue, catching up on his schooling, but whenever the shepherds were near enough, the boy rejoined them, and so combined trade and education as best he could. In the meantime, he counted the days to every third New Moon, when Anna sent him to Mordecai to sharpen his thinking. The Magdala rabbi hammered the sacred texts into his pupils well enough, but the blind scribe taught Dan to see what was not written.

Mordecai was not in the courtyard of Anna's old home when Dan sought him, and neither was he on the corner where he once begged alms, and where he still sat in the evenings to gather news. Dan ran inside, calling to Old Dinah, who kept the house, just as she had when Loukanos was there.

Blind Mordecai's post as assistant to Loukanos had vanished with the man, but at Asa's insistence he also remained in the house – thankful for the generosity which gave him shelter, and a place in which to instruct any who came to learn the Holy Writings. Over the last few years the hospitable dwelling periodically had been choked with eager travellers following every step of the Nazarene, who had performed his first miracle only two streets away. But he and his men had not been in Galilee for some time, and today the place was peaceful.

Now Old Dinah paused in her warm kitchen and wiped a floury forearm across her sweating face, grinning toothily at Dan's inquiring look.

"Eh, young man, is it the third New Moon so quickly? *Shalom, Shalom* to you, indeed. How early you are – and how hot and dusty you look! Have you run all the way from the Sea? Well, here is the pitcher, so drink deep, and then you must eat!"

"*Shalom* – blessings and peace, Dinah," Dan gabbled and gulped the cool water gratefully. "I'll eat later – where is Mordecai?"

"What? No food after your journey, and you with the hollow legs? Is the world on fire?" An astonished Dinah paused in the act of setting a pile of bread and a pickle pot on the table. "Well, then, take it with you, if you are in such a hurry!" She tossed a cloth to him resignedly. "If Mordecai is where I think he is, you can share it."

Snatching the cloth, Dan wrapped the food, crammed it into his tunic and with hasty thanks darted into the street to find his teacher.

"Try behind the market place!" Dinah called to his shadow.

Market day was over. Bright sunlight bounced off the white, hard-trodden ground, which was strewn with wilted leaves, straw, animal dung and the usual litter from the cramped stalls, now dismantled. Bare of their flapping canvases, weathered beams stuck out from the thick limestone walls like spars from a shipwreck. Three quarrelsome dogs snarled and snuffled at a morsel in a corner. One lifted a dirty yellow muzzle to bare its teeth at Dan, who flung a warning pebble by way of reply, and the trio growled sulkily before snatching their titbit and loping away to worry at it in peace. The market place was quiet, but not for long.

The silence was broken by a garbled nasal droning answered by a murmuring voice. Dan peered around the back of the deserted enclave where a tumbledown old booth formed a rough shelter against the warm rock. It reminded Dan unpleasantly of the sagging creation on the housetop which Bukki had begun but never finished.

Bukki's booth was the one thing destroyed by the fire which Dan had not regretted. Now a plan suddenly began to form in his mind – that this year it should be rebuilt. And *he* would be the one to do it! A new shelter for the replaced house – a magnificent shady place which would forever banish the memories of Bukki's folly! The Festival of Booths was approaching – and if Johanan came for the holiday as usual they would soon have the temporary one thrown up, and then they could begin at once on the more permanent structure which would be a haven on hot summer days.

Johanan had always liked the idea of building something – in fact, it had been his suggestion to rebuild the old burnt house bit by bit, which had caused the two of them to start clearing the ruins, and led to the rescue of Aunt Etta's shelves, and finding the money Ammiel had hidden from light-fingered Bukki. Yes, Johanan would relish the project – it would be a lot of fun, and the shelter would stand as a memorial to their combined energies and skill! Anna and Aunt Etta would furnish it with bright, striped cushions and proudly show visitors to the cool shade in the evenings and casually mention that Dan and Johanan had made it all by themselves … Dan's eyes glowed with the glory of his ambition, but then abruptly he dropped out of his reverie with a thud, recalling that he was supposed to be finding Mordecai, and why.

He sighed. It had been a pleasant, though brief, distraction from the questions which were burning and biting away inside, and making him feel that he had swallowed a nest of ants. If Mordecai couldn't help him, it must be accepted that Loukanos was now just another of the blank, uncomfortable mysteries of life – such as the house fire, and Bukki. But that didn't bear thinking about – Mordecai must do something! – if only to soothe the agitation which Dan was weary of living with, but could not let go. Mordecai would at least listen; that, Dan was sure of.

There he was at last – half hidden by the shadows of the drooping timbers – sitting on the ground beside a dirty, bedraggled, unveiled woman, who drooled and twitched and writhed her twisted hands as she struggled with speech. Dan watched for a moment as Mordecai, his head bent intently, held up a hand.

"Wait – say that again – I could not catch your meaning."

Again the tortured sounds were wrenched from her lips, and to Dan's astonishment, Mordecai burst out laughing. Harsh braying sounds from the woman came through a wide open mouth, and the look in her eyes showed him she was laughing too. Surely they could not be sharing a joke?

"Mordecai!"

"Dan? Dan! I had not expected you so soon. Your legs must be growing longer, that you arrive before sundown."

Dan shook his head. His legs were not growing fast enough for his liking. "No, I left very early – Old Dinah said you might be here." He hesitated, and looked uncertainly at Mordecai's companion. "Shall I stay, or await you at the house?"

Mordecai put out his hand and tugged Dan's tunic.

"No, no, sit with us a moment, and then we will return together. I'm sorry I was not there to greet you. Yet, perhaps that is not entirely true, for now that you find me here, you can meet my friend. I have spoken of her many times, though you have not met."

Dan sat down resignedly. Mordecai had a knack for befriending outcasts – he and Loukanos both. Dan was not averse to this, but just now he wanted his teacher to himself.

Mordecai gestured towards him and spoke to the woman. "You have heard much of Dan, my pupil from Banayim."

There was an inquiring noise and Mordecai shook his head with a smile.

"No, not short for Daniel, though we do call him that whenever he is particularly wise! Just Dan, like the city. Dan, this is Sobek."

Beggar Sobek? Dan's mind was whirling. Impossible!

"The same Sobek you told me of last year? Who tells you all those funny stories about Market Days? The same stories you tell me?"

He had built a picture in his mind of quite a different person. Dan had assumed a wrinkled crone, for a start – sly, observant, garrulous – ready to entertain for a coin, and no doubt with limbs twisted in some way, as the name Sobek implied, but not like this! This woman's neck, her jaw, her mouth – even her tongue – seemed to fight every word she attempted to articulate.

Mordecai's face crinkled in amusement under his eye bandage. "The same. Take no notice of her manner. She is sorely afflicted in body, but she is not deaf, and her mind is lively."

The woman's eager eyes turned upon Dan, and she ducked her head in an awkward nod.

"*Shalom*, Sobek, friend of my friend." Rather automatically, Dan scraped up all his most polite phrases. "We meet on a good day. Blessings and peace to you."

Meanwhile he was struggling to readjust his thoughts, and wondering how Mordecai could understand her at all.

The woman's slack mouth widened in a smile which showed chipped, discoloured teeth, but her lips trembled and to Dan's surprise tears sprang to her eyes. She struck at Mordecai's arm with her clawed hand and uttered something.

"What did she say?" Dan asked curiously.

Mordecai patted Dan's shoulder. "Ah, Dan, Sobek is thankful for your courtesy. She is not used to it, as you might imagine."

Dan could imagine very well. He remembered now the times he had run to the market for Old Dinah and noticed a bone-thin, ragged creature on the edge of the crowds; which scrambled stiffly – and often uselessly – with other beggars for the market scraps. A creature at which boys might flick stones as thoughtlessly as Dan had shied at the ugly dog a moment earlier. She was part of the market-place, that was all, just as Mordecai had once been part of Blind Corner. He fumbled the bread and pickles from his tunic.

"I have food with me. Shall I give it to her, Mordecai?"

Mordecai tapped him warningly. "She hears perfectly, Dan," he reminded. "You don't allow that white hair of young Marta's to make her into an old woman, do you? Well, don't allow Sobek's speech to make her into a deaf idiot."

Dan looked Sobek in the eyes, surprised by their alert expression. Was it really possible this ill-smelling, deformed woman was no different to the cheerful, sensible young wife of Potter Ittai? He tried to imagine himself chattering to Marta herself as he held out his bundle.

"Old Dinah made this. Her bread is very good, and her pickles are too, though Aunt Etta thinks she uses too much salt. You may like them that way."

Sobek grinned her thanks as she clumsily dragged the package from Dan's outstretched hands. Mordecai laughed and got to his feet.

"She knows Old Dinah's bread and pickles very well, Dan. Be sure the bundle is untied, though."

Sobek's head tossed with effort as she forced out sounds slowly and carefully, spittle flecking her chin.

"Did you say *just right?*" Dan hazarded a guess, as he obligingly undid the knots and opened the pot. "Dinah makes it just right?"

The woman nodded, pleased, and they left her busy with the food.

"Kindly done, Dan," said Mordecai, walking briskly with a hand on Dan's shoulder. "Time, effort, patience – that's how we learn to understand."

"Not always," Dan replied with some warmth. "I've tried them all."

Mordecai slackened his pace. "Alas, Dan, patience needs a little hope to nurture it. And true patience cannot be hurried, more's the pity, for we always need it right now. Now before you unburden yourself further, let me remember my manners at least. First tell me, how is your mother? And your aunt?"

"They are well, and send their greetings – and they want you to know I'm no longer behind my age in school, even though I'm away much more these days."

"Ah – this is good news! You have diligently made up for the lost times. Few have that chance, or apply themselves when they do. I am proud of you, Dan, you have worked hard and long. Soon your schooldays will be over, but let's hope you keep learning all your life, eh? That's the true measure of a wise man. And don't forget, among those who think you are a Daniel, you have a reputation to uphold!"

Mordecai squeezed his pupil's shoulder affectionately as he trotted out the old joke, but Dan was unusually silent. The blind man felt his mood. Not rejoicing at his success? Something was gnawing the boy's vitals, that was certain. *Perhaps a sharp dose of calf-love? No, that would only make him absent – and there is some anger here, I think.*

Carefully Mordecai continued, "So it is not your studies then, which require this time, effort and patience to understand! What is troubling you, then? Is it about the Nazarene? I hear things are not good for him in Judaea."

"Not him – Loukanos," Dan replied shortly. Of course he was as keen as anyone else for news of the Prophet, but …

"Loukanos!" Mordecai repeated, surprised. "Why? Have you heard any bad news?"

"No! Nothing! Good *or* bad!" the boy blurted out. "Where is he? What is he doing? Why has he not written? Why has he deserted us?" Dan gave the wicket gate an irritated shove and it slapped open with a protesting creak.

The afternoon glare was softened under the thick tree in the centre of the empty courtyard where once Loukanos had sat painting strange pictures on wood, or rapidly sketching with charcoal on sheets of papyrus. There, Anna and Ammiel had pledged their betrothal, there Dan and Johanan had eagerly discussed the coming of Messiah, there little Rhoda had flitted cheerfully among them all, wielding her broom and opening the gate. Dan stopped short as the memories took hold, and Mordecai bumped into him.

"Have a care, young man – it would not look good for a blind man to knock you over. How the women would laugh!" He took Dan's arm consolingly. "Come now, be calm, my boy – we will find answers sometime, if we have the right questions – but you must eat first, and rest. Then while Dinah takes her afternoon sleep and gives us a little peace, we will do our work, and talk afterwards. I see you have a lot on your mind."

Old Dinah put her hands on her wide hips and shook her head at Dan.

"So the food I gave you an hour ago is gone, and here you are in my kitchen again! Are you already hungry for more of my good cooking? Aha, yes, I know – this is the real reason you arrived here so early today!"

"Now, why should that be?" Dan replied, somewhat loftily. "Don't you know I have two perfectly good cooks of my own at home?"

Dinah turned her back. "Well then, I can see you won't be needing this," she said just as loftily, whisking away a waiting pot of soup.

"I didn't mean it, Dinah!" Dan repented hastily, scrambling to the table. "I was only teasing! You do make the best chicken soup in Galilee – even Aunt Etta says so."

Mollified, Dinah waved her ladle at him warningly and pushed him onto the bench. After all, she knew where Dan's lunch had gone, and was glad of it.

"Eat then. And maybe I'll tell you some news, eh?"

"About Loukanos?" Dan blurted out eagerly.

"Ho! Master Loukanos, indeed – vanished like Enoch, that one! Of course not. No – about Rhoda."

Rhoda! Dan hadn't heard news of Rhoda for a long while. Anna's maidservant had been up in Jerusalem with Johanan's family for three Passovers gone, and Dan had not seen her more than once in that time.

"Is she well?" Dan asked guiltily, conscious that he had forgotten to acknowledge her last message. Johanan had shown surprising persistence in teaching the girl to read and write but it had been a long time since any of his letters had included one of her messy, breathless postscripts.

"She's well enough," Old Dinah sniffed, "but her mother wants her home. Back here in Galilee."

"Oh!" For a moment Dan felt a vague thrill. "Why?"

35

Dinah thumped the pot in front of them. "She's getting married."

"What? Rhoda?" Dan choked suddenly.

Dinah snorted. "Rhoda's mother. A widow these ten years, and now a bride again – at her age! A disgrace, I call it."

Mordecai raised a hand in protest. "What? Where is your charity, woman? A man for her family again after so long! What does her age matter? This is a good thing for them all, praise the Eternal."

Dan agreed indignantly. "Why a disgrace, Dinah? Why not a blessing?!"

Dinah poured soup into his bowl and shook her head at them knowingly. Wisps of grey hair waggled from under the close-tied cloth around her temples.

"Because she's marrying a Roman," she answered shortly. "She may even leave the land with him. And of course, she'll take Rhoda with her."

Dan's head swam so busily with dismayed thoughts that he forgot Mordecai had not yet pronounced the blessing over their food. He gulped the soup and it scalded his lips, his tongue, the roof of his mouth, and half way down his throat.

Chapter Four

"LEAVE the Land?" Dan spluttered, when he could breathe again. "How could anyone leave the Land *now*?"

"Why not?" Mordecai asked coolly. "Life goes on, no matter what. People marry. They plant. They build. They always have ... and no doubt they always will."

Sympathetically, Dinah handed Dan some cold water.

"Drink this ... if you have a throat left to swallow ..."

Dan obeyed but the burning was as much in his conscience as his mouth. *Somehow!* – even with all he had heard and seen, his passion about the Messiah had – *again* – leaked away into everyday life. What had happened to the urgency they had once felt? So much time had passed since that heart-stopping day beside the Jordan when they were all so sure that the Messiah had come at last. Yes, amazing things had happened, but Dan's own life had gone on no matter what, just as Mordecai said. Meanwhile, bold Prophet Johannes had been wickedly snuffed out of life, and who knew what must come next, or when? He sat dismayed and silent while Mordecai gave the blessing and started on his soup.

It was not until they were sucking the bones that the blind man wiped his beard and asked again.

"Why *not* now, Dan? Tell me what is wrong with anyone leaving the Land 'now'."

"Because we have waited so long," the boy replied slowly, trying to sort out his confused thoughts. "All that time of waiting and wondering about the Messiah – and then the message of the Baptiser – and finally he did come. And he's still here ... visiting every place, and working miracles, so it *must* be soon that everything else happens! If anyone leaves the Land now, won't they miss out on seeing the Deliverance?"

"Who knows how long the Deliverance may take?" Dinah sniffed. "Moses took forty years, and the Nazarene appears to be in no hurry either. Even King David took his time about claiming the throne."

"That's a worthy point, old lady," Mordecai said, impressed. "He had an unlikely start indeed – at first a hero, then an outlaw for years! – and even after Saul's death, there was a long civil war before the whole nation accepted him."

Dinah preened herself on the compliment to her mind and graciously ignored the insult to her looks. 'Old lady' was at least much more respectful than 'old woman'. It was true she was known as Old Dinah, but sometimes folk forgot it was in distinction to Young Dinah, her daughter. *And after all*, she consoled herself, *the poor man is blind!*

Dan slurped slowly at the dregs of his soup, still wincing as it went down his sore throat. "But it can't be like that," he frowned. "Messiah being an outlaw ... or taking years and years to be crowned ... and everyone fighting about it ... we are all united in wanting our King to deliver us ..."

Unbidden crept into his mind, frank words from a distant hot and dusty day when the family laboured together on rooms for a marriage which never took place.

"I know he is to be our King," Ammiel had said soberly. *"But will he come with trumpets? Or as my shepherd king David – hunted in the mountains, gathering the outcasts of Israel, until his time came to take the crown?"*

No, he had not come with trumpets, but thankfully, not as an outcast either. He had come with stirring words like Johannes, and miracles to help his people ... but so far, that seemed to be all ... and already, though he would never have believed it possible, Dan had even become accustomed to miracles. The first lame man to walk was something to weaken the knees. The first dumb man who spoke left you speechless. But the fiftieth was less remarkable, and the hundred and fiftieth was just another body to clog the crowd and delay the next man's turn, while the healthy had to wait even longer to hear the Teacher's latest words.

Dan told himself that it was just as well Loukanos had gone! Otherwise, he would be out of a job soon, with so many cures abounding ... and he'd have to stick to picture-painting, which, considering the mess he made of it, wouldn't keep him in shoestrings.

Dan had come to the table filled with frustration, but the shock of realising how dulled he had become concerning Messiah, had flattened the mystery of Loukanos – until this moment when it sprang up again, as annoying as ever. Now he felt doubly agitated, thoughts darting around like anxious swallows, imprisoned by blank walls of ignorance. *I don't know where Loukanos is. I don't know if he's even alive. I don't know how the Messiah will bring deliverance. Or restore the Kingdom. Or when. Or what comes first. I don't know enough about anything that matters.*

Old Dinah looked at the brooding young face and shook her head. "Of *course* it won't be like that, even if it does take a long time! If the Nazarene *is* the Messiah, of course ... an outcast? The very idea! Now finish your food and let me get on with things."

One of the 'things' so pressing was her midday sleep, but it was just as important as everything else, and Dan had enough composure left to comply without complaint. It was not until Dinah lay gently snoring in her chamber, and he was fretting over a long sum, that he expressed his irritation.

His folding wax tablets were almost covered in figures ... when the slowly scraping stylus oozed to a halt, whereupon Dan morosely dug the point in deeper and screwed up his face.

"Is it seven hundred and twenty-eight bushels?"

Mordecai sighed. "Young man, you are not concentrating. That's the second time today you have multiplied and ended with less than you began with, and I'm sure your messy writing is the reason."

"How do you know that?" Dan asked, the more crossly because he realised it was true. "You can't tell."

"Oh yes, I can, if you dare let me touch that wax! You can do this type of sum in your sleep, so you must be misreading the figures. Take more care, or you waste your time and mine. How can you get the right answers, if you don't work with the right questions?"

Dan gave an exclamation of disgust. "Questions! Sums are not the kind of questions I want answers to! There is so much I want to know, Mordecai! And it takes so long, and never comes in the right order!

"It's a painful process, eh, Dan?" Mordecai agreed. " But no learning is easily come by. Or if it is, we don't appreciate its value. Only when you have struggled for something do you prize it."

This was something Dan found hard to believe. If he had the answers he wanted, of course he would prize them – how could he not! He frowned.

"I don't see why it makes any difference. Hard or easy, surely just *knowing* is the most important thing. Isn't that what Solomon says? *Wisdom is the principal thing!* If only I knew more – about everything! What if we could just know everything instantly! If we could – oh, I don't know – if we could sort of *eat* a whole scroll – or drink in a whole library like water – and know all the laws, all the figures, all the books, all the knowledge! Wouldn't that be easier? Wouldn't it be wonderful?"

"No," Mordecai answered firmly. "You did not finish that quotation. *Get wisdom*, Solomon said, *and with all this getting, get understanding.*"

He reached for his pupil's work, and with a sudden gesture, flicked it clear across the room to clatter into a corner.

"Knowledge alone is nothing," he bluntly told an astonished Dan. "Of what use to man or beast is knowledge? You can't eat it. You can't shelter under it. You can't wear it."

He could not see Dan's face, but the silence told him. He waited for the inevitable question.

"Why am I learning, then?"

"Ah, why?" The blind scribe leant forward and tapped Dan's knee. "Forget the books, the Law, even the figures, for a moment, and think of all the learning you have which is not written anywhere. Knowledge of your sheep, for instance."

Dan hadn't thought about that as Knowledge. Of course it wasn't *written* – it was just – what he knew about. It was a surprising thought, but it pleased him.

"Yes?"

"How much do you know about sheep?"

"Well … a lot more than you … but a lot less than Old Caleb … I'm always finding out what I *don't* know about."

Mordecai nodded. "The fate of the 'prentice boy the world over, Dan. Remember the day Caleb had you deliver Sheba's triplets?"

It was a tale Dan had told proudly and often, how he had struggled under Caleb's instructions, how his small hand had finally done what the old shepherd's big fingers could not.

"My first delivery – and such a mix-up! Caleb had to tell me everything! But I know more now."

"Aye, I'm sure you do. Now, Dan, you said Caleb could not do the job himself that day. What if he had sat down, folded his hands and just thought mightily about all he knew."

"What? And done nothing? Or said nothing to guide me?" Dan was scornful of the very idea. "What use would that be? Sheba would have died – and her lambs."

"Ah! So what use is knowledge alone, without action?"

"Oh." Dan frowned. "Tell me some more."

Mordecai nodded. "Take figures. You're quick with numbers, I know – when you're not turning them into scribble. What use are they?"

"Counting sheep," Dan shrugged. "Keeping Old Zack honest at the market."

"What else?"

Dan looked at the pair of fine-grade scales on the shelf behind his teacher, their engraved bronze weights lined up neatly, remembering how Mordecai would lean his elbows on the bench and test the level of the balances against his bare forearms. Dusty jars, pots and measuring spoons sat tidily alongside, next to a heavy stone mortar and pestle. It had been a long time since they were used.

"When Loukanos had you compound his medicines," he replied slowly. "You needed numbers to weigh and measure things."

"Yes – or I might poison someone. So the knowledge of numbers, records, and measuring means you can repeat a compound exactly – every single time and no guessing. See here."

Mordecai felt for a box under the bench, and dragged it out. Dan pounced on it with interest, and began flipping through a stack of slim wax tablets, each deeply scored to inform the scribe's sensitive fingertips.

"What's on them, Dan?"

"Words – and figures – yes, I see – for your remedies. Here's one for sore throats ... another for boils ... inflammation of the ear ... fever ... toothache ..."

"Not my remedies, Dan. Your uncle's. I was just the instrument. This is his knowledge – sitting in a box. So when some poor soul came with a toothache, did Loukanos just hand him the box? Of course not. He wrote the instructions, yes, but then I set to work to weigh and measure and pound and mix – exactly, according to his word. So?"

Dan frowned. "So ... knowledge ... in a box – or in a shepherd's head – is useless ... on its own. It has to be acted upon. It has to be used, accurately."

"Exactly!" Mordecai beamed. "Knowledge is a tool – a tool for living, Dan. Remember that, and you will never go wrong!"

He felt for Dan's shoulder and patted it reassuringly. "It's good to seek knowledge, Dan. It is a good, and essential thing – we can't do without it. But mark this," he added soberly, "it is only the beginning. Knowing and acting – that is a marriage which will produce beauty and glory to God. Divorce them, and you are in trouble."

Dan made no reply. He pushed the box back under the bench, leaned back, and folded his arms with a sigh.

"You are not your usual self today," his teacher said shrewdly. "I said we would talk after some work, so forget my lecturing for the moment and speak of things closer to heart. There is the Nazarene, there is Rhoda – and you are distressed over Loukanos. Shall we begin with him? This is a belated grief for a man who has been gone so long. I asked before and you answered me well ... and though the subject is different, I ask you again, *Why Now?*"

Dan slumped against the wall. "Oh, I don't know ... !" he said fretfully.

Mordecai waited, but his pupil said nothing more for a long time. He tried again.

"Let us retread the journey. You were there when Johannes the Baptiser announced the Nazarene as Messiah. And it was the selfsame day, that Loukanos left you – without warning. Did you have any idea at the time, that he would not return?"

"Of course not! We thought he had walked off because he disbelieved, and couldn't share our excitement – or was annoyed with everyone's emotion, or had chanced on someone he knew in the crowd!" cried Dan. "Perhaps he was seeking the fishermen for our trip home ... anything! At first we dared not leave to search for him. We thought we should stay and be prepared to undertake whatever may be required of us by the Messiah. But the Nazarene also disappeared, and we waited in vain for either of them."

Mordecai knew the tale, having heard all the gossip of the day from Tanner Parosh as well as others. Parosh was a follower of the Baptist, and had confirmed it as truth ... that it was almost six weeks before the proclaimed man had emerged from the desert, all hollow eyes and skin-and-bone ... Had he become lost in that forbidding place, narrowly escaping a famished death? Was it a sign of madness – or a deliberate fast to chasten the flesh? Well-fed Parosh did not pretend to understand, but Mordecai, erstwhile beggar that he was, knew all about hunger, what it did to a man's body, what it did to his mind ... and he preferred the kind which was voluntary for the sake of holiness. Unfortunately there was no merit to simply starving in the street.

He replied, "At least the Nazarene reappeared – eventually."

"But Loukanos didn't," Dan said flatly. "He simply vanished, like Enoch, as Dinah said."

Mordecai well remembered how disappointed the family was when they had finally returned to Cana to find that Anna's brother was not already there, and how they had invented many plausible reasons for his absence. But they were all so stunned about what they had witnessed at the waters of Bethabara Decapolis, that the feverish matter of Messiah's revelation had overshadowed the mystery of Loukanos for some time.

Dan rushed on, almost falling over his words.

"Then everything was happening at once ... rebuilding our house ... moving back in again ... and I was back at school, or out in the field ... and learning so many new things ... and then the Nazarene came *here* and you know what happened at that wedding! ... and after that there were all those crowds chasing him everywhere – sweeping in and out of the hills and around the lake – with all those miracles and people running around telling everyone else, then he went to Jerusalem, so we were all waiting for something more to happen ... but it didn't ... and he just kept on wandering around the land ... doing the same things, and preaching about the Kingdom, only it still hasn't happened ..."

Mordecai thought he understood. "Yes, Dan, it was a tumultuous time. You had not long lost your father. Then your Uncle Bukki. Even your home. But everything following was such a powerful stimulant it dulled the pain, eh? Now that the excitement has faded, you have more time to reflect – and it hurts that Loukanos abandoned you."

"Us. He abandoned *us*. Leaving even his own sister without a word, too! Why, he was disgusted when Bukki did the same thing to Aunt Etta! I never thought he would be just as bad."

"You are still angry."

"Yes."

The scribe sighed. "He was a breath of fresh air, wasn't he, Dan? Quite a challenge for us – as we were, no doubt, to him. I miss him very much – he gave me a new life, and we worked well together. But he was free to go."

"You sound like Aunt Etta! Of course we knew he would leave, but to pretend for more than two years we do not exist? We have not hurt him! I can't see any sense in it."

"Not you, but something else has hurt him, perhaps," Mordecai murmured almost to himself. "I wonder ..."

"Yes, and so do I," Dan said rebelliously, picking flakes of whitewash from the sandstone wall. "We are all wondering, but I am the only one who still speaks of it, and I can only talk to Johanan – and only in letters. Uncle Asa and Aunt Mari are like my mother and aunt – they accept it as God's will, and say no more ... but they must feel it – he was their family too."

"Less so, Dan, surely?"

"Asa was his father – he brought him up!"

"Only a father by marriage, Dan ... and step-sons can be unforgiving that way ... Loukanos escaped from a father's control long ago. That childhood tie must have been loosened even more since kind Helen died, may she rest in peace."

Dan did not rejoin, "*May she rest in peace.*" He snorted. "Loukanos said she was standing in Elysian fields laughing to see how wrong she was all these years! The Greeks have very convenient ideas about death."

Mordecai lifted his scarred, almost hairless eyebrows in amusement at the boy's superior air.

"Well, we will discuss that another day."

A rivulet of sand trickled from under Dan's aggressive nails and whispered to the flagstone floor. Dan poked it about aimlessly with his finger. Once he had been fascinated by the differences in grains of sand, and had fashioned new and daring thoughts about the sand of the sea, the Promises and the seed of Abraham. Today, it was just grit on the floor.

"I wonder … I wonder," repeated the blind man. "Of course, he may have come to some harm, but it seems you do not think so." He scratched his moustache. "What does your mother think?"

"She believes that he is alive, and has his own reasons for staying out of reach," Dan answered, a little reluctantly. "But I know she is sad about his desertion."

"Not because he's absent in body, but because he's absent in spirit, eh?"

"Yes – as if he doesn't care any more! But he must, Mordecai. Even when he ran away as a boy, he still did care, you know. He asked Asa and Helen's forgiveness when he grew up, and later he came here for Anna's wedding, all the way from Philippi. It doesn't make sense."

"Well, Dan, I see why you were not pleased when I said *time, effort and patience* is how we understand things. It's still true, of course, but there are not always answers to every question."

Not always. Dan felt the nudge of an old memory. *Not for now, anyway.* He closed his eyes to hold the moment, but already it had slipped past, and Ammiel's voice had gone again. Dan thought impatiently that if 'later' was the time for answers, then surely they must be closer now than they had been.

"You also said patience needs hope, but I don't know how you're supposed to get hope when you don't already have it." He scuffed the fallen sand away with his leathery heel. "And you told me this morning that we will find answers sometime – if we have the right questions. You are my teacher – so help me to ask the right questions!"

48

Mordecai shifted restlessly, and then suddenly held up a hand.

"What words have we been using about Loukanos? *Disappeared, vanished, desertion, abandoned – escaped*," he said thoughtfully. "Yes … *absent in spirit* … and also, that he once *ran away*."

"Twice," corrected Dan. "First, when he was about my age, to his Uncle Joseph in Cyprus. Later, he ran away from him too, because he wanted to be like his Greek friends." He hugged his knees and stared out of the shaded room into the sunwashed white courtyard. "Johanan and I were sitting under that very tree when Anna told us the story," he said quietly. "It was a long time ago … when Johanan had run away himself."

"Yes, I heard … and why was *he* running away?" Mordecai already knew, but he wanted Dan to tell him.

"Oh! He was in lots of trouble! He'd been rude to his teacher in Jerusalem, arguing about the Baptiser – sure that he was the Messiah – the rabbi was furious – Heber at school was always leading the other boys to beat him up – and then he would be punished for fighting or missing classes … his mother was angry with him … he had plenty of reasons!" Dan's lips approached something like a smile for the first time. "I think Anna told us the story of Loukanos as a warning. She said, '*You see, boys, running away can become a habit.*'"

Mordecai smacked his hands together, startling Dan out of his retrospection.

"There is only one reason why anyone runs away – *fear* …"

"Loukanos wasn't afraid of anything," protested Dan. "He ran away because he didn't want to live like a Jew."

"He was afraid of not being able to do or be what he wanted," Mordecai said pointedly. "That's a strong fear in a young man.

49

Without fear, there is no need to run, or to hide. A man who is sure of himself can endure restrictions, and have patience, waiting for his time to come – but that is a courage belonging to long beards. Loukanos was barely out of boyhood – he ran away, therefore he was afraid."

Dan uncurled his legs and threw himself on his stomach.

"I don't understand ... even if it is true ... What's that got to do with now?"

Mordecai impatiently rubbed his forehead and rearranged the soft bandage which shielded his almost lidless eyes.

"It would mean a young Master Loukanos was afraid of being forced to do or become something he didn't like ..."

"Yes, that's just another way of saying the same thing, isn't it?"

"Perhaps. Every fear contains many anxieties."

Dan writhed in exasperation. "Very well! But that doesn't answer my question. What's that got to do with now?"

"I think it's becoming clearer. What did your mother say to you and Johanan? *Running away can become a habit!*"

"Johanan never did it again."

"I'm not talking about Johanan."

Dan gasped. "You mean, Loukanos disappeared *this* time because he was *also* afraid? So he *ran away*?"

Chapter Five

AGITATEDLY, Dan dug more vigorously at the whitewash until a small heap of flakes had floated to the floor, and more sand was trickling down the wall.

"But he's grown up! What would he be afraid of *now*?"

"The same thing."

"You mean – not being able to do or be what he wanted? But now he's a man – he *can* do anything he wants. And he *has* been doing exactly what he wants all this time."

"Will you leave that wall alone?" Mordecai knew Dan's frustration habit, and could feel the stonework in his favourite corner becoming more pitted with every visit. "I disagree with you. Loukanos did *not* want to stay in the land as long as he did … he was not interested in searching out the Messiah … he had not intended to stay and look after Anna, either. But he did stay. He still chose to do those things even though he didn't want to. Nobody forced him."

"Not forced, but you know it was because he promised his mother to stay with Anna till she found the Messiah. Nobody would break a deathbed promise!"

"Well, why not, if he fears no God? He didn't have to tell anyone about a promise nobody else heard him make. So what was to *stop* him leaving immediately after she died?"

"Oh! I suppose … well, nobody could stop him, but he would know he'd made the promise … he couldn't pretend he hadn't, could he? … not to himself, anyway. His conscience would remind him, even if nobody else did. But what's that got to do with him running away later?"

"Patience, I think we are getting somewhere, Dan. Remember we are trying to ask the right questions! Only then will we find the right answers. Loukanos made a promise which he honoured because he is an honest man. But, mark you, Dan, even though it was inconvenient, it did not require that he change anything about himself. Of course he wanted to return to Philippi, and no doubt many other places dear and familiar to him in Macedonia, Achaia and Greece, but he lost nothing by his time here, and he was under nobody's control. The only thing in his life which changed was where he lived, and he knew that would be temporary. Loukanos the healer ministered in Galilee instead of Philippi, and did much good."

"But doesn't that make even *less* sense, Mordecai? How or why would any of that prevent him from saying goodbye to his family and taking his leave in a proper way? If he stayed to be so honourable, why depart so dishonourably? What could be the fear you speak of?"

"Perhaps it was that same fear which drove him from his family the first time, and from his uncle the second … the fear that he would not be able to be or do what *he* wanted. And the other side of it of course, as I said before, would be the fear of being forced to be or do something he resented."

Mordecai paused and settled his bandage carefully. "Let us assume that he had stayed with you as promised while he could still be his own master. But no sooner was that promise discharged, than he ran. Something happened to make him afraid – afraid that he may no longer be able to be master of himself. Afraid that *he* may have to change. Now let us consider what else we know ..."

Dan traced tortured swirls in the fallen sand.

"But no grown up has to change anything he doesn't want to – does he? I mean, Johannes was always preaching that people had to change, and not everyone did."

Mordecai stretched and tapped his fingers together in concentration. "Dan, you may have hit upon the answer to that yourself, when you said that Loukanos could not pretend to himself. You have seen oxen pulling a heavy load?"

"Many times – but – "

"Patience! Have you seen them balk at an obstacle, or bellow and throw themselves around in the traces when they refuse a hill or become bogged? What happens then?"

Dan sighed impatiently but Mordecai held up his hand. "Humour me."

"Very well, then – the driver gives them a sharp pricking with a goad, and they give in."

"That can't be pleasant, eh, Dan? For the poor oxen?"

Dan shrugged. "They learn, though. If they kick against the goad it only hurts more, so it's no use, is it? They can't just stay there forever. They have to keep pulling, anyway. Maybe that's why they make such a fuss – because they know what's coming. Camels are worse. They complain for nothing. But Anna says a good driver won't hurt his team – just remind them who's in charge."

Dan thought of Rhoda's fear of camels and their irritable groaning. Funnily enough she wasn't afraid of oxen at all, despite their horns.

"And a good driver wouldn't ask his team to do the impossible, eh?"

"Of course not – what would be the use of that?"

"Well, some are cruel, of course, but a righteous man regards the life of his beast ..."

"Yes, I know – Father used to say the same thing – but why are we talking about oxen? My teacher, I am trying to be patient, but please can we get back to why you think Loukanos is running away!"

Mordecai got to his feet and felt for the window. He leaned on the wide sill and lifted his damaged face to the sun's warmth.

"Dan, your questions have always been good ones. They have always prompted me to beat new pathways in my well-trodden thoughts ...You said Loukanos would not be able to pretend to himself, and I agree with you. He is a man of integrity, but I think he is hiding from the truth for very fear that it is indeed true. He is an ox feeling the sting of the goad, something which he knows, deep down, is no use to struggle against."

The boy jumped to his feet impatiently. "What? What is he struggling against?! Or who?"

"Call it what you will! Against himself – or conscience – or God – but at heart it is a fight against the most important Truth of all – the truth of our faith and our Messiah! Loukanos was with you – he was there when you heard a voice from heaven, Dan! A voice which shook the rocks and said, *'Hear my beloved son!'* How could that be trickery?! It could only mean truth! But if so – it would mean changing all that Loukanos has fought to be, rejecting all he has clung to, embracing all he has denied for so long. Who would not be deeply afraid?"

The hairs stood up on Dan's thin brown arms.

"Oh, Mordecai – if only he had been there when Helen was talking to me – just before she died! She said she had to pass on to me all her wisdom in one package while she could – and do you know what she said? She said, *'Never hide from the truth, it's a waste of time and effort!'*"

"Ah, how true that is. Helen was indeed a wise woman, Dan, but even if Loukanos had heard, he would have merely agreed with her whilst thinking she should take her own advice."

"Oh – yes, I think I see what you mean … It's like what he said when she died … about the Elysian fields … that she would see how wrong she had been …"

"Of course! Because what man will hold as a truth, something which he *knows* is a lie? It is a contradiction! So it is that we tell ourselves that whatever we believe *must* be true … unless we are hypocrites, acting a part … covering our faces …"

Dan pulled a face of his own. "Anna told me about the Greek plays where the actors hide behind huge masks – but that's just for storytelling."

"It should be. But we all hide behind them at times. For the same reason as we run away from things. Fear." Mordecai paused, and Dan glanced at the ruined face with its wide bandage. That was a mask nobody would choose.

Suddenly he thought of Uncle Bukki, who indeed *had* chosen the mask of a blind man and begged hypocritically from the crowds at Judean Bethabara. Was that from fear? He shook himself restlessly. This discussion with Mordecai was becoming too complicated, and as so often seemed to happen, every answer created new questions.

Dan groaned with vexation, and slumped down to pick at his wall again, but Mordecai still had a point to make. He held up a hand for attention.

"See here, Dan – if we truly do believe a lie, the truth only confuses us more, no matter how plain the evidence … until we are almost mad with it. And it is not in the nature of man easily to accept that he is wrong." He rubbed his beard ruefully. "I was once lost for two days in Antioch because of this very stubbornness."

"You never get lost!" Dan said in amazement.

"No, not now. I have learned different ways to understand where I am. But I was lost then. Very lost indeed! My own confidence undid me. I was convinced that I was at the top end of Baker's Street, when I was actually in the lower part. It has a sharp elbow in it, which I did not know at the time, and so I believed the bend was the beginning of a different street. I retraced my steps again and again, baffled as to why I could not find the market which I knew must be there. All sorts of wild thoughts occurred to me – even that the whole thing had been spirited away, stalls, sellers, goods, crowds and all! West end or South end, the street is so similar along its length, you see, and I did not pick up the clues well in those days. It was midwinter – I had no sun to guide me."

Dan forgot his impatience about Loukanos as he listened with wide eyes. Mordecai had never spoken before of his blindness – and Dan had no idea he had ever been in Antioch. Why, it was a huge, sophisticated city, so Loukanos had told him. Surely anyone could get lost in such a place, let alone a blind man.

Mordecai laughed. "I knew there was a certain alley behind a bakery which would bring me to the right place. Of course, the street was full of bakeries – but as I kept choosing yet another wrong one, the alley I sought was never there. I ran up against walls again and again until I thought I was going out of my mind."

"But, Mordecai, did you not ask for help? For directions?"

"Ah, that's the most foolish part, Dan. I did not. Hard to believe, eh? But I was determined to find my own way. I had not yet accepted my fate, and I was full of false pride. I was not quite at the point of having to beg for my living. To myself I still was a whole, healthy, fine man who just happened to have a problem which might soon go away. I was not ready to admit helplessness. I was hungry and near demented before I gave in." His voice trailed off, and Dan waited quietly. He had never thought about blindness meaning anything else but the absence of sight.

Mordecai sighed, cleared his throat and said briskly, "You see, I understand about kicking against goads."

Dan picked up the flakes of whitewash on the floor and began building a pyramid with them on the deep window sill. There was a lot to think about.

"Mordecai, were you afraid?"

"Yes, I was deeply afraid – and deeply stubborn. But unlike Loukanos, I could not outrun my blindness."

"What happened?"

Mordecai shook his head. "That's a tale for another time." But he remained lost in thought until Dan crushed his little pile of white flakes and blew them out of the window with a single puff which was half a sigh.

Loukanos running away. It was too hard to think about. Could it be as Mordecai suggested?

"Is it really possible?" he wondered out loud. "I must ask what *Amma* thinks. I remember, it was strange, when we were at the Jordan – and she told him that he was free to go … he did not even smile. He just stood there …"

So similar was Anna's name to *Amma*, mother, that Dan often interchanged them, but as he did so now, Mordecai sat up, alert.

"There is something else," he said suddenly.

Chapter Six

"WHAT?" Dan cried. "What do you mean, something else?"

"Yes!" Mordecai said. "Dan, your father and Anna heard the Baptiser once, and were convinced! I heard him once and was convinced! And so it was with Old Caleb, and your Aunt Etta – and we were all baptised immediately, on the strength of that conviction. But how many times did Loukanos hear the Prophet?"

Dan blinked – he didn't see the point of the question.

"Well – twice. Firstly in Judea, at lower Bethabara near Bethany, when Father and Anna were baptised. Secondly, just before he disappeared, of course … at upper Bethabara in Decapolis. Aunt Etta and Caleb said they could never have stood in that deep rushing water without his help."

"H'mm … tell me, did Loukanos exchange any words with Prophet Johannes himself, Dan? Either of those times?"

Dan grinned. "The first time Loukanos was in a good mood, and took sides with him against the Pharisees – something about them not being the only seed of Abraham. The second time he and the Baptiser had something to say to each other, but I couldn't hear. He seemed to be rather cross about it. Aunt Etta or Caleb might remember."

Mordecai leaned forward and spoke intently.

"Dan, you have forgotten something … no doubt because it happened when your house burned down, and Anna adopted you, and many other things crowd your memory. But that was also the time when Loukanos asked what he could do for me, and I begged him to take me to the Baptiser. Again, he did not want to do it, but he honoured his promise. He patiently led me thirty miles south-east to Bethabara Decapolis to hear the Prophet speak, and then I too was baptised. So your uncle heard him more often than any of us!"

"Of course – of course! Did he talk to him then? Did he ask questions?" Dan asked eagerly.

"Ah!" Mordecai held up a finger and waved it significantly. "He did not! No, Dan, at that time Loukanos did *not* exchange words with him, neither would he do for me what he did for your Aunt and Caleb, and help me into the depths. For hours we sat in silence amidst the throng while the Baptiser preached from the river … and of course, unless he had stopped his ears, Loukanos heard every word as clearly as I did. By late afternoon I felt that understanding had flowed into my heart like oil and soothed the troubled waters of knowledge within. Truly this man was the messenger of the covenant! The words of scripture he spoke were so familiar to me! – but now they made such sense as they had never made before. The Nazirite was indeed warning of the coming of Messiah, and I knew I must be ready for him! At last I could bear it no longer and I urged Loukanos to take me down into the water, to the Prophet – at once. He had been very quiet, just drumming his fingers or sighing in exasperation from time to time. Now he sprang to his feet and hauled me after him without a word.

"He pushed and pulled me mercilessly through the crowd until water splashed over my feet – and then he stripped off my robe and said roughly, 'I have done my part, Jew! Now you must do yours. When you are wet enough, have someone take you to the tallest palm up by the ferryboat rope, and I will be waiting there.' Then he left me, in a thick press of people so restless that soon I had no idea whether I was facing the river or the bank."

Dan's mouth dropped open. Loukanos was sometimes rude, but this was …

"Unthinkable!" he blurted, disappointed.

Mordecai smiled a slow smile. "After all he had patiently done for me so far, I could not understand it myself, Dan. I think now I do."

"But how did you get out to the Baptiser without being drowned?" Dan remembered Aunt Etta's shuddering description of the whirling waters which had threatened to drag her away downstream. What must it have been like for a man who could not even see to keep his balance on the slippery rocks?

"Ah, Dan – I was afraid!" his teacher replied simply, "Gasping with the cold, jostled by the crowd – truly I was as helpless at that moment as I had been when lost in Antioch. But this time I had no pride at all. I lifted my face, my arms, and my voice and I shouted for help as loudly as I could."

Dan held his breath. He had long since forgotten to think of his beloved mentor as helpless.

"'Help me!' I cried. 'Baptist! Nazirite! Prophet! Hear me! I am blind – but not to my sins! Do for me what our holiest laws cannot do! Wash me today and make me clean! Help me, for I cannot help myself!'"

Mordecai paused in his passionate recital. He cleared his throat again. "Yes – I created as much stir as I could! And I continued to shout, for the people were noisy, and some laughed and some urged me to be silent, and others cried out as well … but I was like a man demented! Even when I felt someone grip my elbows, I shouted all the more. Here was my one chance, you see, and I was afraid of being hustled away, my mission unfulfilled. Then I heard a low voice in my ear.

'Fear not, friend,' it said, 'I hear you, and I have you safe. A few more steps and the water will be deep enough. Hold me – I won't let you slip.' And he turned me around, for by now I was indeed facing the wrong way … then put his arms about me, and drew me with him out into the river."

"Oh, Mordecai!" Dan breathed. "He came to you because you could not come to him! What a great man!"

"Aye, Dan, a great man." Mordecai was silent for a moment.

For a brief moment two displaced Levites, each so far removed from their ancestral calling, had been united, clasped together in the dark waters. The one who could not see the other's face, had heard no false notes in the melodious voice which had rung like a silver trumpet over the whole land … that stirring sound, now silenced. Mordecai did not tell Dan what the Prophet had said privately to him in his rich and cultured voice – the voice of a man born to serve among incense, gold and marble, to eat the best meats, to wear draped white linen and sanctify men with warm blood and fire … this same man who served instead among dirt, reeds and rocks, foraging for wild food, dressed in strips of leather and hair cloth, sanctifying the lowly of heart with cold, rushing water …

No, Mordecai would never forget that voice. Its sound had warmed his soul and its words had fired his heart. For the great Prophet Johannes had slid the bandage from his burned lids with their stony eyes and told him quietly, *Indeed you are not blind, Mordecai of Cana, for you see the real truth of the Law. Gladly do I baptise you now for the remission of your sins! Hold your breath, my brother, and trust me as the waters close over your head. I will bring you up safely before you know it. Now.*

The large, firm hands which pushed him under, had pulled him up just as swiftly. Mordecai felt his throat tighten as he remembered the surge of emotion which soared through him when he broke out of the water after his icy plunge. It would not have surprised him at that moment had he suddenly been able to see. But the Baptist retied the wet bandage as gently as a woman …

The blind man sighed, and blew his nose. "Then he returned me to the bank, and called on a stranger to guide me safely out of the crowd."

Mordecai laughed in a sudden change of mood as he recalled himself to the present.

"What a strange scene, eh, Dan? A blind Jew brought to a holy Seer. Dragged to the river's edge by an unrepentant Greek trained to heal, and kindly led back to him by a repentant Roman trained to kill!"

"What? How could you possibly know that?"

"My senses are very keen," Mordecai teased. "I could smell that he was a soldier, and just baptised, like me."

"No, really …?"

Mordecai relented, and laughed again. "Very well … It is true that I could sense a lot – I could smell the wet leather, hear the clinking metal on his uniform, feel the straps on his bare legs, and recognise his accent ... but the Prophet also cried out to him, 'Ho, centurion! As you have begun a good thing, so continue, and take care that this man has safe passage through the crowd, and finds dry clothes.' That touched me, Dan, that the great man of God would think of my physical needs as well as the spiritual. And the Roman obeyed – he a centurion with a hundred men under him – imagine that! He was just as cold and wet as I was, but he guided me a good distance away from the ford to the ferryboat crossing, and reassured me that he would not see me left half naked ... he had a spare tunic he would give me, if my own had been stolen. I confess this gave me a lesson – that his repentance was no less real than mine."

Mordecai smiled a little as he remembered the tanner Parosh awkwardly giving him the gift of a leather cloak long ago – admitting gruffly that the Baptiser had commanded his disciples to share their clothes. Yes, it did stink when it was wet, but Parosh had warned him of that, so it was an honest gift.

He continued, "Well, Loukanos had avoided facing the Baptiser, but he was waiting for me faithfully enough – I scarce had my hand on the ferry rope when he almost smothered me with blankets."

Dan screwed up his face. "I never thought before about *who* was baptised. What do you think about baptising Roman soldiers, Mordecai? They are not only Gentiles, but our enemies!"

Mordecai stood up and stretched. "Yet many such *were* baptised, Dan – and that centurion was even willing to clothe a shivering beggar, just as if I was a fatherless child protected by the Law. What do we make of that, then? If a man obeys the commandment of the Eternal, how can he be our enemy, eh? Those who are for our God cannot be against us, can they?"

Dan groaned. "Another question – always another question!"

Mordecai persisted, "And here's another – now that the great Johannes is dead, what happens to baptism for repentance of sins? What will others do? Especially unacceptables such as Gentiles and those like myself – who are barred from the synagogues? Prophet Johannes was truly a man of God – and the Land has undergone a great cleansing of heart because of him. He gave us a hope which was outside of the Law … but now what?"

Outside the Law! There was that niggling phrase which always caused Dan to feel a sense of confusion. How could anything Outside The Law be right? And yet Abraham didn't have the Law, as Aunt Etta had once reminded him! Dan wove his arms through his legs, squirming with a return of his impatience.

"The Messiah must have the answers! The Baptiser said he was the Lamb of God who takes away the sin of the world, so perhaps … well, the Dabab says his disciples are baptising people now, if you can believe anything she says … Anyway, Johannes said Messiah was even greater than he was, and would tell us all things! But what, and *when?*"

"*Ouf!* Yet another subject, Dan – and more questions! How far have we strayed from where we started? We were talking about Loukanos, fear, and running away, so let us return! Do you now see my point? Your uncle dutifully brought me from Galilee to Decapolis and down to the Bethabara ford, but then he abandoned me just when I needed him the most! Only now do I realise how his fear must have been growing. Once I was dry enough he almost dragged me away from the place, even though I wanted to stay longer … and he would not even suffer me to speak to him for a long time."

Old Dinah put her head around the door with a snort which made them jump. "Eh, and do I have sympathy with whoever you are speaking of!" she said peevishly, hastily smoothing a crumpled headcloth and knotting it behind her neck. "What chance do *I* have to stop you speaking for a long time, tell me that? Is a hard working woman to have no peace at all during the hour of rest?" She withdrew abruptly, grumbling all the way back to her kitchen.

The scribe and his pupil grinned. The sonorous rhythmic rumblings from Dinah's chamber had ceased only a few moments before she appeared. Dan unwound himself and took a deep breath as he stretched. It *must* be as Mordecai said. It made a lot of sense – where before there had been none at all.

"So you believe Loukanos was afraid even *then* that Johannes was a real prophet of God …!"

"Yes, now that we have properly considered all we know – I do believe so. Can you imagine therefore, how Loukanos felt later on when he *had* to face the man himself, with Etta and Caleb?"

"I must find out what they said to each other!" Dan cried.

"It would be interesting to know," Mordecai agreed, "but whatever it was, that was not the worst threat to his peace of mind, Dan. Less than an hour later, you all heard and saw and felt unearthly things! What I would have given to be there! Heaven itself declared that Jeshua the Nazarene was the beloved Son of promise – and it was *then* that Loukanos finally turned and ran in earnest."

"But, Mordecai, granted that he was afraid, *why* did he need to run?"

"Come, Dan, can't you see this was a habit with him from boyhood? It had set him free before, so he thought. Changing his whole life, his whole way of thinking, must have seemed impossible! What else could he do?"

"But couldn't he just say, 'I don't care, I won't change anyway'? And stay?"

"No, Dan. You said it yourself, remember. He couldn't pretend to himself, once he knew it was true. In the face of evidence of his own eyes and ears, he must trample his own conscience, or at the very least, try to discount what happened and forget it as fast as possible. Now how could he forget in the heart of a family and a country thrilling with excitement about their Messiah?"

"Oh, Mordecai – what does this mean, then?" Dan asked in dismay. "Surely he is not a wicked man?"

"No, Dan, a thousand times no!" Mordecai put an arm around his pupil and gave him a gentle shake. "Quite the opposite! It means he is an ox still kicking against the goads and bellowing with pain. Only time will tell whether he grows hardened enough to feel it no more, or whether he submits."

Dan stared through the deep window at the tree under which Loukanos had once sat painting a very bad picture of a pomegranate while admiring it approvingly, and simultaneously sneering at the foolishness of Jewish beliefs. Clever, educated, skilled, sarcastic Loukanos was blind, and wrong – and now he must know it! How would that feel?!

"He did not leave because of us, then, but because of himself!" Dan drew a sleeve across his eyes and heaved an immense sigh of relief. The anger was dissolving, the dark weight on his chest was lifting at last. He threw himself at Mordecai and hugged him fiercely.

"Thank you, Mordecai! Thank you! I should have talked to you long ago! You are right – you must be! I will write to Johanan at once! And the whole family will be grateful to you!"

Mordecai clutched vainly at his unravelling turban. "Have a care, Dan – you will knock me over and all the schoolwork I had planned to torment you with will be struck out of my skull! No doubt they have already thought all this out for themselves. Asa and Anna are clever people, Johanan is sharp, and your Aunt Etta is no fool."

Dan shook his head as he hastily straightened Mordecai's cap, apologetically wrapping and tying its linen band into a neatly edged turban once more. "No, my teacher – *none* of us had answers! I thank you for helping me ask the right questions – and I know Anna will thank you with her whole heart."

Mordecai waved him away. "Perhaps!" he answered offhandedly. "Now I know you still have young Rhoda and her mother on your mind, but that will wait – we must use the time we have left to review your studies, or we will both be in trouble with your mother! Off with you now and fetch your pen and parchments. Anna does not send you here to be another *Dabab*!"

"That old gossip!" rejoined Dan indignantly as he reached the door. "Her ideas about Loukanos have nearly made me choke! Do you know what she said to Aunt Etta the other day? And in front of *Amma*, too!"

"Aha, now you are being a *Dabab* yourself, you see? Go! Your women have enough sense not to allow such nonsense to hurt them." *At least, I hope so*, he thought.

As Dan obediently left the room, the sensitive fingers of the sightless man felt inside the bosom of his tunic, and touched a hidden talisman – a sky blue tassel, which had once kicked and swung at the hem of a woman's robe.

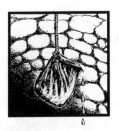

Chapter Seven

DAN had returned from Cana fairly fizzing with excitement and relief, and could not wait to tell Anna everything, as well as to question Aunt Etta (and Caleb, when he could find him) about what Loukanos and the Prophet had said to each other at the upper Jordan crossing. But he arrived home the next day to find the women fully occupied in putting down the olive harvest – a tedious business which was better shared. Miserly old Zaccheus the fig merchant having expanded his business to include olives, they were glad to buy the fresh fruit from him and save a long journey to the larger markets – but there was no way they would trust him to preserve it.

"He'll sell them to you cheap and save the work, all right. But mind, he'll pickle them in their own wash water and skimp on the salt," Etta had darkly warned the women at the well, "and if you think he'll trouble himself to sort them properly or pick out the rubbish you're either a saint or a fool."

Etta's warnings were heeded by most of the women, except for weary young Judith, still struggling as underpaid maid to grim Thaddeus, bullied by his motherless five year old, and oppressed by the innuendos of Rachel the *Dabab* – the Gossip. It was all very well for Etta to preach about Old Zack, but sometimes being underhanded was the only way to get by. She had enough to do without spending precious time preserving olives, which she personally disliked anyway. She thought to herself that perhaps if Thaddeus ate a few rotten ones from time to time, it might give him something else to be miserable about.

Of course it was a tragedy that his wife had died in childbirth, and that his devoted mother-in-law was afterwards smitten with a growth in the breast, which sucked the life out of her by painful degrees and deprived the boy of his only grandmother. *But!* It was just plain selfish to deny his son a proper father as well, and the boy needed a man's firm hand before he was totally spoiled, especially with no other relatives to share his upbringing. A wandering shepherd spent little enough time at home as it was, and of what use was his tenderness of heart towards a dead wife and unborn child if there was none left for the son who lived? The man's mourning had broken his spirit, and if nothing changed, it would break hers as well. She was sixteen already! – and who would ever marry her while she had another man's son at foot? But who would take little Thad if she left? It was not the child's fault he was virtually an orphan already. Judith sighed, took the boy's hand and marched off to where Zaccheus was stirring a large vat of olives in the sagging lean-to behind his dusty storehouse. She ordered two crocks of the finished product immediately, ignoring the spark of greed in his eyes, and turned tiredly back to the whining child.

Good-natured Marta had arrived at Anna's early that day, so laden with children that she had not been able to carry all her provisions. Now that they had been working all morning, and were running out of supplies, Anna had set off to Banayim with an old hand-cart to collect her friend's salt, olives and the rest of the new pots Ittai had thrown especially for the task. He had innovatively scratched the word 'Olives' on the sides before firing, for which Marta had thanked him politely while privately rolling her eyes. As she had muttered to Anna with a giggle, that would be *very* helpful later when the olives were used up and they wanted to put lentils or vinegar in the pots! – prompting a laughing Anna to slap her fingers for ingratitude. Now as she carefully packed the cart Anna smiled over her friend's wifely reaction. Marta knew full well how fortunate she was to have a man who was always thinking of new ideas to make his wife's life easier.

She hauled the heavy load into the clearing just as Dan's eager face appeared around the corner of the west track behind the house.

"Mother! Careful – you'll lose the lot!" He ran to help her with the wobbling heap of pots and sacks.

"Thank you, my Dan! I'm glad you're back! This is the most obstinate cart, sticking in every rut. It's fought me every step of the way."

Dan pulled a face. "Is it any wonder? Bukki made it."

"Ah!" Anna laughed. "It is a miracle it still holds together, then!"

Dan dismissed the detestable Bukki from his mind. "I have so much to tell you, *Amma!*"

"H'mm, so you have learned a lot on this trip, son?" she teased.

"Yes, but not Talmud, and not figuring … Mordecai and I have been putting together a very old puzzle!"

"Dear Dan, you must tell me all about it very soon, but right now we are so busy with the olives, and desperate for extra hands. Marta and the little ones are here, and having you home will be such a help to us all!"

"Oh, what would you do without me?" Dan sighed exaggeratedly as he steadied the cart along the last stretch of path to the house. Though he was itching to talk, he understood the difficulties of coherent conversation when the twins were around. He would wait until there was peace, and then they could take their time savouring the new theories which Mordecai and he had painstakingly pieced together.

Busily working in the mellow late summer light which streamed through the open door, Etta and Marta's fingertips and nails were stained purplish black after hours of picking through bushels of olives, plucking stems and leaves, washing and salting and filling the deep crocks Anna had wrested from Old Dinah last year. In one corner of the kitchen Isaac and Abigail, Marta's three year olds, squatted on the floor clattering Etta's wooden spoons, while their new baby brother kicked in an old market basket which hung from the rafters.

Etta had fussed mightily over the safety of this arrangement when Marta proposed it late that morning, but her friend had merely scoffed at her.

"My dear Etta, I know how to tie a decent knot, so don't cluck. Little Shuni will not be lifting his head for weeks yet, and if I leave him on the floor he is in far more danger of being choked by the twins, dropped into your meal-barrel or pushed into the fireplace. Look here, for example!" She bent down and turned back the covers to reveal a collection of half-squashed olives, leaves and twigs which Isaac and Abigail had lovingly pressed upon their baby brother while their mother's back was turned.

Etta's dark eyes crinkled in amusement and she glanced up at the children, who grinned at her happily.

"What's all this?" she asked them in mock surprise, pointing to their offerings.

Abigail and Isaac trotted up to look.

"Dinner," Abigail said proudly. "For baby Shuni."

Isaac nodded his dark head emphatically. "Share!" he agreed, snatching up an olive and trying to push it into Shuni's pouted mouth.

"No, no, *dodi,*" Marta said, rescuing the baby swiftly, as the infant spluttered his protest. "He's too little to eat olives. He's not a big boy like you. Hush, Shuni, hush …"

"A big boy!" Isaac boasted. "*I* eat them!" He bit down on the large purple olive and his chubby face froze in shock, then he spat shudderingly and began to wail, dribble pouring down his chin.

Marta stuffed the squalling baby into Etta's arms, picked up Isaac and buried his distressed face in her shoulder, shaking with suppressed laughter as she patted his back. "There, there, little one! These olives aren't ready yet! Not even for big boys. We have to put them to bed with salt first. Then they'll be very good later on."

As Isaac stopped sobbing she wiped his messy face and set him down with a comforting kiss.

"You see what I mean?" she hissed at Etta over his head, her eyes dancing. She relieved Etta of the indignant Shuni and tucked him in his basket, stroking his cheek soothingly with the smooth back of her work-rough hand. "Hush, little man, you're all right. Be a good boy, now …"

"Salt?" asked Abigail, clambering up and digging a grubby fist into the bowl of dim crystalline lumps on the table. "Salt!"

"Yes, Abi," Etta said, glancing up from her gourd sieve as she busily scooped the olives bobbing in a tub of water, "yes, that's salt, put it down, now."

"Put to bed with salt!" Abi crowed, and scattered her handful triumphantly into Shuni's basket, where the crying broke off in sheer astonishment.

As the women gasped, Abi asked cheerfully, "Baby Shuni good, now?"

Etta objected no more, and so the basket complete with baby was firmly tied up without further delay, just as Anna and Dan appeared in the doorway. The children jumped at them enthusiastically, and while Isaac clambered up Dan's legs demanding camel rides, Abigail wriggled out of Anna's hug to indulge her fascination with the knotted silk cap Auntie Anna wore under her veil.

"Have you been helping your *Amma*, Abi?" the tall woman smiled, as the small fingers toyed with her blue silk fringe. "Isaac? Oh – and where's little Shuni?"

Marta merely rolled her eyes at Etta, who chuckled, "They've been helping with the baby, or trying to. We've put him out of reach, anyway."

Being too wise a mother to talk about the children in front of them, Marta drew her friend outside to tell the tale, and soon Anna's characteristic gurgling laugh began bubbling through the window like giddy, hiccupping birdsong. In a while, she returned with a straight face and set the twins to sorting green olives from black, a task they took very seriously, and which kept them occupied until they finally drooped and fell asleep like puppies on their own sheepskin rug.

Marta gave a sigh of relief, but just then Shuni began to squeak like a rusty hinge. Marta groaned and Etta laughed. The child had been fed only an hour ago, just before Anna went to the village, so he was not hungry. After all the excitement of being showered with salt and olives and sticks, he was probably just wondering where everyone had gone. Dan hopped up obligingly to rock the basket. Rasping baby-cries set his teeth on edge … bleating lambs were more to his liking …

"Sh! Sh!" He blew gently on the sleepy face and the swaddled babe blinked, shutting his eyes with a little gasp of surprise which stopped the whimper before it became a lament.

"Sh! Shuni! Sh! Let your *Amma* rest now. Time to sleep!" Dan continued to blow softly on the infant's face, swinging the makeshift cradle, and soon the little one drowsily subsided into silence.

"Thank you, Dan!" smiled Marta. "You are a great help to a tired mother!" She tried to push the straggling white lock of hair back under her veil, which promptly slid down to her shoulders. "What is it about the men?" she asked enviously. "My Ittai was always the best at getting the twins to sleep, and now Dan has the touch with Shuni!" She swiftly raked the long dark hair back from her face with her fingers and pulled up the veil.

Anna leaned forward suddenly. "Marta, wait."

"Why, what is it?"

"Come to the light and let me look at your hair."

"Goodness, Anna – have I got lice without knowing it?" Obedient, but puzzled, Marta moved to the door while Anna carefully inspected her hair, parting it with her long fingers.

"Marta, did you know your hair is turning white? Not the silver streak you were born with, but at the side ... here ... Etta, can you see ...?"

Etta peered at her young friend's hair. "Eh, so it is! Look here, there's a finger-breadth of white at the roots – and another here, at the back of your neck."

The young mother laughed. "But I should be a grandmother first! Abi, did you marry that cross little Thad boy without telling me, you bad girl?" She looked at Anna's face and her smile faded. They were not joking.

"Are you sure?" she cried. "Perhaps it is the light ... Dan, you look! Your eyes are the sharpest ..."

Dan came over rather reluctantly as Marta parted her hair with her fingers and bent forward. It seemed to be discourteous to inspect the hair a married woman so often had covered, but she had asked, and Aunt Etta wasn't objecting, so it must be all right.

"It's true," he agreed at last. "Near your left ear, and at the back as well." He glanced shyly at Marta's smooth brown neck. "And see, Anna, there is another pale place ... here, and here ..." As he pointed them out, Anna looked closely, and compressed her lips suddenly.

Marta shook her hair back and looked at Anna anxiously as she rearranged her covering.

"Neither Ittai nor I have noticed, but that's not surprising. I can't see behind my own ears, and what man ever studies the back of a woman's neck?"

"Did your mother turn grey so young?" Etta asked hopefully. "It can run in families, you know."

"I don't think so," Marta faltered, "but I know so little about her."

As the Dabab sadly reminded them whenever Marta was expecting, the young woman's mother had died in childbirth. Her father later had taken a cheerful woman who bore him five sons but he never spoke of Marta's mother again. Now, he too had gone, and there was no-one left to ask.

However, Anna was shaking her head slowly. "I don't think this is the greying of age – early or not. It is pure white, in solid clumps – not a light salting like Widow Shana's, or iron streaks like Mari Jerusalem's … which would surely come first."

Marta looked alarmed, but Anna had not finished. She looked at Marta with a strange and compassionate expression.

"It's not just the hair, Marta dear," she said gently, putting an arm around her friend. "The whiteness is spreading into your skin. And look, here, even your hands have faded patches."

"Oh, no, Anna! No!" Marta went very pale and jumped up, shaking off Anna's arm. "Then stop! You had better not touch me!"

Anna's elbow knocked over Etta's sieve of washed olives, but no one seemed to notice.

"Now, Marta," she said faintly, as the fruit streamed unheeded off the table. "We must not jump to conclusions. There may be many explanations."

"What is wrong?" Dan demanded with dismay. "Tell me."

Etta put a trembling hand on his shoulder. "We cannot say for certain, Dan. And Anna is right, that we must not jump to conclusions. What we need is a priest …"

"What! Why?"

Marta looked at Dan with haunted eyes and shrank into the doorway, motioning him away.

"It may be nothing, Dan," she said through stiff lips, "but it is best we err on the safe side, and take precautions ...These are early signs of ... of leprosy ... so that is why I must be examined by a priest ..."

"Leprosy!" Dan sank on to the bench beside Aunt Etta, and numbly began collecting scattered olives without any real sense of what he was doing.

"What priest in Galilee has the training to discern disease as Moses commanded?" Anna said with rare vehemence. "What you need is a physician."

"Not one of those miserable leeches from the market place," Etta cried in alarm. "You know they do more witchcraft than doctoring!" She knew, from bitter experience.

"Of course not!" Anna answered shortly. "We must find a rare kind ... a man of true skill and wide experience ..."

Marta and Etta looked helplessly at each other. Was there such a man?

Dan looked from one woman to the other, and once again olives went flying, as he leapt to his feet.

"Yes!" he cried. "We must find Loukanos!"

Chapter Eight

"IT'S nonsense!" shouted Ittai, thumping the mound of clay on his table, rolling and folding and pounding it again. "Complete nonsense! Where or how is my wife supposed to have caught leprosy? There's never been a leper near Banayim as long as we've lived here."

Dan looked at the potter's haggard face. "I hope it *is* nonsense. But who knows who has breathed on her or touched her at the Magdala market? And you can't dismiss the last two years ... with thousands over-running the shores to chase the Nazarene around the Lake? And – late last spring – a leper was healed – only a few miles away."

Ittai stopped punching his clay and looked stricken.

"I didn't think of that," he said sickly. "How long had that man been mingling with the crowds? And there could have been others without us knowing ... There were hundreds with every disease under the sun, determined to beg a cure – and most of us gave a cup of water or shared a meal with some of the poor creatures ... but would a leper risk discovery?"

"Maybe I would," replied Dan, honestly. "If the signs were still hard to detect ... and if I thought I would be cured. What would I have to lose? A leper is already an outcast."

Ittai scraped the sticky clay from his hands and threw a wet sack over his table, breathing deeply.

"Where is my poor darling?" he demanded roughly. "She must be very frightened."

"At our house, for the moment. She would not come back into the village until you told her what to do."

"How should *I* know what is she supposed to do? What *are* we supposed to do? What of the children? The babe at her breast, eh? She's barely out of her days of purifying after the birth! Putting people outside the camp was all very well in Moses' day – or shutting them up for weeks on end! Pah! But were any of them *mothers*? Tell me that!" He was shouting again.

"Anna says we do not know if she has leprosy. We need to find out."

"And how are we going to do that – drag her all the way to find a decent priest in Jerusalem – children, baby and all? While keeping her away from everybody at the same time? It's impossible!"

"Please, Master Ittai, do not let the whole village know your distress." Crisply spoken words made them jump, as an old woman shuffled into the pottery. "Have some respect for your wife's feelings, and do not alarm any one without need!"

Dan turned with surprised relief. "Auntie! But I would have waited for you!"

"My own fault, Dan. Conscience smote us all after you left – it was not right to give you such a heavy message to bear on your own." Puffing a little, Aunt Etta sat down on Ittai's muddy stool and planted her stick firmly between her feet. "Anna wanted to come in my stead, but she is more use than I am with the children – so I made her stay."

"Blessings and peace, potter!" a shrill voice outside called eagerly. *Something must be going on … it was not like Ittai to shout and yell at his work!* And surely that was not Etta she had seen slipping through the door? Rachel advanced quickly upon the workshop, her ears straining, smile at the ready.

"*Shalom, Shalom!* I have just come to … oh! Well, this is a surprise! Young Dan! And Etta, it is rare to find you here at this hour!" Her piercing glance noted the strained faces around her with satisfaction. Yes, something was definitely going on.

"What do you want, Rachel?" Ittai asked ungraciously, "apart from news?"

"Dear me," Rachel answered, showing her teeth and wagging her finger playfully. "You are very cross today, young man, and here I was coming with a nice order for you … surely you have not been quarrelling with my dear friend Etta?"

Her dear friend Etta gave the Dabab a perfunctory greeting and rolled her eyes at Dan – this was a piece of bad luck!

Rachel looked enquiringly from one to the other. "Is anything wrong?" she asked innocently.

"Yes!" growled Ittai rudely. "There is a nosey woman in my pottery, sniffing around for gossip."

"Well! There's a fine way to treat your customers," huffed Rachel. "But I should have known not to expect manners – I could hear your temper a whole street away! I am only glad to see you were not shouting at your poor wife and innocent children!"

"What do you mean, my *poor wife*," blustered Ittai hastily, at which Rachel looked more suspicious than ever. Etta reached out and tapped him un-gently on the arm with her stick.

"Now, now, Ittai," she said quickly. "No use in pretending, my friend. He is a little upset, Rachel, as any fine young man would be on hearing his wife has been overtaken with a womanly infirmity, and cannot come home to his bed and his table."

"Oh!" said Rachel primly, looking pointedly at Dan.

"I'm not listening!" said Dan resignedly as Etta beckoned Rachel outside with a conspiratorial air. Nevertheless, he and Ittai ran to press their ears to the thin slat walls, where the women were whispering on the other side.

"Poor Marta has had an unfortunate set-back. She will have to undergo another period of cleansing," Etta told the gossip, truthfully enough. "She is in some distress, as you can imagine, since she has only recently finished her days of separation. But there's no doubt she needs to be set apart for a while. Anna and I will care for her, as there are no men in our household. I had not heard of such a thing before in such a healthy young mother …"

"Why, yes, Etta, it does happen!" Nodding wisely, Rachel whispered back, "Perhaps Ittai has been thoughtless in expecting her to resume all her wifely duties too soon … But is she in any danger?"

"I don't know, Rachel, but we will watch her very carefully. Neither Anna nor I have any experience of these things … not like yourself!" Etta replied very humbly. "Perhaps you would be the best person to give us assistance? A new baby is so demanding, and there are the twins, who are such lively, tiring creatures …

forever getting into things, and asking impossible questions, and of course, there will be so much extra washing …"

Rachel preened herself a little. "Well, of course, I do have a great deal of experience myself, as you say!"

There was a certain allurement in the possibilities of being closely involved in a feminine drama, especially that of someone whom Rachel always suspected of laughing in her sleeve. But those twins! And all that washing! Not to speak of …

"Any fever?" she asked sharply.

"H'mm, she was certainly feeling both hot and cold when I left her … but I'm sure there is no real danger of any infection, or of it spreading, if we are very careful …"

Infection! Rachael dusted her hands fastidiously and brushed imaginary specks of clay from her gown.

"I'm not sure, sometimes, that these things are not better-off left to time and rest," she said firmly, edging away from the older woman. "You had better keep her confined – and yourselves too, I would say – just in case. And of course, you must send Dan away at once. He is not quite a man but definitely past childhood, with that strange red moustache just beginning to show – if you look hard enough, that is. Still, it would not be proper for him to be loitering about the house with you until she is clean again."

Etta nearly hugged herself at the success of her ploy, but sighed instead.

"Time and rest! Yes, your advice is very sound, Rachel, and we must make the best of things, since the poor girl no longer has even her mother-in-law to rely on, may she rest in peace, for she was a kindly soul indeed. As for our Dan, he has not been near Marta, you know, since her – condition – was discovered, and she has been shut away in the long room since then. We will ensure that she remains there while Dan is with us tonight. Dear Anna is preparing a special meal for his homecoming, and he has much to tell us. But I will undertake to see that he leaves first thing in the morning, that there can be no offence to anyone. The lad can stop with Ittai for the moment, and run errands for us until he goes back to work, or until Marta comes right."

Rachel shook her head in an indulgence of simulated compassion so well done that she was quite moved by it herself.

"Poor Potter Ittai!" she said mournfully. "Birth is such a trying business on a man from beginning to end. No, I won't go back in," she said, patting Etta's arm understandingly. "I will order my new pot tomorrow. Just let him know I forgive his sharpness, and sympathise most sincerely. It is no comfort for a man to have a cold hearth and an empty bed to come home to after his hard day's work ..." (Or so her own husband had told her, pointedly, many times.)

And she trotted quickly away with her delicious new feast of news to dispense in tantalising morsels to the other women, leaving Etta to be whisked inside the workshop and congratulated heartily by the relieved eavesdroppers.

"Etta bath Amos – I never knew you had it in you, to lie like a Cretan!" said Ittai, admiringly.

Etta looked offended. "I never told one untruth, I'll thank you to remember, and Dan, don't you dare believe I did!"

"Auntie, you were wonderful!" Dan grinned. He was proud of her, but truth to tell, he was also proud that Rachel had noticed his budding moustache, even if she *was* so rude about it.

Aunt Etta sniffed. "Well, you men weren't doing much good on your own – and if the Dabab had one whiff of the real cause for our anxiety, she would scrape the village into the sea with her own hands, while calling heaven to witness that Marta had brought a judgement on herself. Now, let us go into your house, Ittai, and collect what we need for the family."

Ittai clutched her sleeve and looked down on the wrinkled dark face imploringly. "Now, Etta, what do you really think?"

Etta leaned on the smooth round curve of her walking stick and cast a compassionate eye on the agitated young potter. "I think it may well be a false cry of alarm," she said honestly. "But we cannot take chances until we know for sure."

"What of the Nazarene? Could he not help us?" Ittai muttered desperately. "He healed a leper in Capernaum only last year – he did, didn't he? Everyone says so, and they must believe it or there wouldn't be lepers secretly running around infecting innocent mothers ..."

Etta lifted her stick and waved him out of his own workshop.

"Now, stop that, young man, you don't know that any such thing happened here! And even the Nazarene cannot heal a woman who is not sick," she said impatiently. "Would you want to put Marta through the distress of chasing him around the countryside, dragging the baby with her, and struggling with the masses, just for nothing? No, Dan has the right idea. What we need is Loukanos – or someone like him."

Late that night, Dan, Anna and Etta sat talking in the lamplight and flickering shadows of the low fire. The long room had been turned over to Marta and the children. Exhausted, the young mother had finally fallen asleep with red eyes, baby tucked in the crook of her arm, and twins snuggled up beside her. They had all puzzled over the situation for half the evening. Should the twins be separated from their mother? What of the baby? Finally Anna declared that if Marta did have leprosy the children would all have been too exposed already for it to make any difference at this stage, and there was no point in separating them now.

"But what of you?" Marta asked nervously. "And Dan?"

"Dan's not going to be here after tonight," said Aunt Etta firmly, "and he's hardly seen you since he got here, nor even touched you. The Law, hygiene and commonsense – that's the best answer for most things."

"Yes, Etta," said Anna warmly. "How wise you are, my dear sister! Marta, until we know more, we will take care to keep you, your washing, your clothes, food and utensils separate. It should not be for too long, please God, and you must all stay in the long room together. It is pointless to separate the little ones from you now, and unnecessarily cruel. And while they show no signs, why should they be untouchable? It would be foolish."

Marta impulsively reached out to her friend, then stopped herself with a rueful laugh. "Thank you, Anna. Praise God for such friends as I have in this room! If the worst comes to the worst …" – her voice trailed off.

"If the worst comes to the worst," offered Dan suddenly, "Ittai and I will not stop till we find the Nazarene and make sure you are cured."

Marta smiled properly for the first time. "I will hold on to that, and pray for us all."

"That is the best you can do," nodded Etta approvingly, as Anna stood up with sudden resolve.

"Enough talking, then, and rest, my dear – or you will still be awake and exhausted at Shuni's next feed. The last thing you want is to lose your milk." Already Anna was pulling out blankets, unrolling mats and rearranging the long room.

"Think of this as a rare holiday," she encouraged with a smile, and Marta smiled back, though the fear was deep in her eyes.

Now that the immediate necessities were dealt with, and weary Marta and her children were asleep, the conversation went back to the question of what to do next. Anna sighed and pressed a hand to her forehead.

"I can't remember it all," she confessed quietly. "I know Marta has no itching or scaling, no inflammation … and I'm sure she doesn't have ringworm, either. I know what that looks like, and it's quite different. And there are so many different kinds of leprosy – but who memorises all the fine details of those laws except a scribe – or rabbi – or a priest?"

"A scribe!" Dan looked up quickly. "Mordecai!"

"Ah, yes, my Dan, but that does not really help us. His knowledge is no use without sight … and our sight is no use without knowledge … even if we had both, we do not have the trained discernment and authority to make a judgement – so what is left?"

She massaged her temples with her stained fingers, and the silk fringe of her cap shook to and fro. "Would you trust the hireling priests in Sepphoris? Or expect the Magdala rabbi to be calm or discreet? He recites from his books well enough, but he is not at ease with difficult questions."

Aunt Etta pursed up her lips. "You said a true word there, my dear. He's as nervous as a coney in the rocks, and deeply afraid of giving offence to his elders. He'd have poor Marta shut up tighter than a criminal awaiting justice, while he sent around the countryside for ten different opinions – and he'd never have the gumption to fix on any of them."

She shivered a little, and Anna wrapped her in another blanket.

"You really ought to go to bed, yourself, Etta," she said compassionately. "It has been such a long day, and there will be a lot of extra work tomorrow."

Etta put her feet out to toast at the fire, ignoring the suggestion.

"What I want to know is, what do we do with all those olives now? Are they unclean? I declare I am so confused I don't know which way is up."

Anna poked the coals. "That makes two of us," she admitted ruefully.

"Three," sleepily agreed Dan, swallowing a yawn. "Why not finish your salting? They can't be eaten for at least a month or so, anyway. By then we must know whether they should be eaten or destroyed."

"Sense in a man!" marvelled Aunt Etta. "That I should live to see the day! But of course, there are no whiskers yet, and they tend to push sense *out* of a man."

"You agreed there *were* some!" Dan cried, aggrieved. "Even the Dabab has noticed them!"

The women laughed at him.

"Well, she does notice everything, no matter how insignificant," chuckled Aunt Etta as Dan glared.

"Your Auntie is teasing you," Anna smiled, beginning to rub Etta's back. "Yours is a very good suggestion. We will do just as you say. Tomorrow we will finish the preserving and later on we can decide whether or not to keep them, when we know for sure about Marta."

Dan looked directly at Anna.

"When we find Loukanos," he corrected, as masterfully as if he had a beard already. "When I said we must find him, I was not just agreeing with you, or being a wishful thinker. I was serious."

"But, Dan, dear, what makes you think that we have a hope of finding your uncle after all this time, just because we want to?" Aunt Etta asked, her head nodding up and down as Anna's hands rhythmically circled up and down her spine. "Everyone has already tried to find him without success."

"We ought to pray for him more consistently," Anna put in abruptly, rubbing more briskly all of a sudden. "Dan, you remind me that we have not – no, *I* have not – been patient enough in continually holding up my hands to the Eternal for my brother."

Dan snorted. "Mordecai says patience needs a little hope to nurture it!"

Anna drew a sharp breath. Hope was painful; hope kept you from accepting the inevitable and making the best of it. Acceptance could be hard, but hope could be cruel. She looked up and spoke firmly.

"If only we knew *why* Loukanos left as he did, we might have some reason to hope. But Dan, it's late, and we are tired. Bank the fire, my son, and we will be off to bed."

Dan put his elbows squarely on the table. "Not yet, Mother. I have been waiting all day for a chance to speak in peace," he replied with equal firmness. "Remember, I told you Mordecai and I had been putting together an old puzzle. It was this – *why did Loukanos disappear?*"

Anna's hands stopped moving. "Oh, Dan!"

"So no matter how tired we are, you must hear me out. Because now, we really need him."

"Go on, my son," Anna said quietly. "Build up the fire. We are listening."

Chapter Nine

FOR another two hours, every moth in the clearing outside vainly courted the mellow rays escaping from the shuttered window of the Shepherd's House, before Anna and her family finally damped the fire, snuffed the wicks and crept gratefully into their beds, leaving the dazzled insects to blunder off into the night. Weak spectres of oily smoke from the pinched clay lamps had not long dissolved when a rasping squall began from the closed long room. It did not disturb Dan, sleeping in the lower level by the kitchen; he had already plunged into the river of sleep after his long day. Without the responsibility of a flock to keep, even his inner ear was blissfully deaf. Aunt Etta on her padded mat was equally oblivious in her corner of the small room she shared with Anna, having slept soundly from the instant her grizzled head sank into her favourite cushion stuffed with the Queen of Sheba's fleece.

On the low bed she had brought from Cana two years ago, her seven braids pillowed on a red-brown blanket, Anna herself was motionless, though nowhere near sleep. She opened her eyes and listened, stifling a murmur of envy faint as a bat squeak, while the squawking was overlaid with hushed maternal soothing, and lulled into an eager snuffle. The twins never stirred, and Marta suckled her babe peacefully in the darkness; through long practice still half-aboard her arrested boat of dreams; ready to drift off again as

91

soon as Shuni's shiny dark eyes had stopped bulging with the despair of imminent starvation, and were drooping with satiated relief.

It had been an intense night while they discussed the mystery of Loukanos – and Anna's mind was now relentlessly assessing all that Dan had told them. She felt in her heart that Mordecai must be right, that there was a deep fear in her brother which he would keep at bay as strenuously as he could. But why was this so hard a challenge when he had overcome so many others in his life? Was it just masculine pride? Was this enough to explain his fear of being wrong, fear of change, fear of being responsible to a God he disliked? *Even though he doesn't believe in Him, which is an interesting contradiction!* Was it fear of answering to a religious system he disapproved of, or to a God who would demand too much? *But surely all worshippers, of whichever gods, are in awe of divine powers, and feel the limitations of humanity!* she thought impatiently. *For my part, a capricious, amoral Zeus would frighten me far more than the unchangeable, longsuffering, Eternal Creator who carries us in His bosom!*

What else made Loukanos so stubborn? He had heard the supernatural Voice at the Jordan which had turned their knees to water. If it was not real, there was no need for fear, and if it was, there was no place for pride. *Loukanos! How can you be so adaptable in habit, so inflexible in mind ...*

What was the use of trying to sleep while her mind was so wide awake? She dragged the blanket around her shoulders and padded to the shuttered window, opening it a crack. *Ah, Louki!* A cold sliver of thin starlight poured in, and she breathed the air deeply, feeling it flowing through her like ice. *Where are you? What is it you fear?*

Somewhere out on the stark night hills a fox barked ... *What is Fear?* she thought wildly ... a distant, terrified squealing was cut off with a choke ... and the answer came ...

There is only one Fear, and it lies at the root of all others. Oh – this was indeed the heart of it. *The Fear of Suffering!* Slowly, she breathed out a prayer.

"Yes, truly, Thou Master of the Universe! Men may laugh at Death, the broken-hearted may court it – and a bold man may even dare to die a brave and speedy death ... but who does not recoil from Suffering? Who is not afraid of pain? It is only anguish which makes us long for death! And it is only those who tremble at suffering beyond the grave who fear death itself."

So, it is the suffering we fear most. And what we fear so deeply, is what we come to hate.

"Suffering – in all its forms – Oh, Eternal One, it is thy chastisement – and thy gift! Without it, how would we learn obedience? – and why would we try!"

At last I understand!

Yet how hard it was to embrace it – something which clawed at all you thought you were, and all you had, right down to your love and respect for God, for others, for yourself! Oh, how she knew what it was to feel such hidden fear like a smouldering ember suddenly raging into a reality which tore scorching through spirit, heart, body and mind! Suffering! Of every kind under the sun, it was all one in the end. She sighed. Did one only learn through pain? Surely love was a teacher too, though more easily forgotten in the heaviness of hurt. But suffering was so much more immediate, insistent, demanding of action! Well, was that not a neat description of Loukanos himself ...?

Louki, my brother – how could I have failed to see it!

Why, he became a *doctor* – a doctor who fought suffering with everything he could learn, invent, or trick his patients into believing – who laughed when they were cured, who swore when they were in agony, whose eyes blazed when they died, and who had no sympathy for malingerers.

Tears brimmed over her lashes and left cold streaks on her face.

"Ah, physician, heal thyself!" she whispered.

As she stared into the darkly shadowed, neatly swept clearing, a large owl swooped noiselessly down from the hill, and a tiny, struggling squeak was swiftly whisked into the sky. Anna shivered suddenly, latched the shutter, and returned to bed. She curled under her blankets, wondering where in the wide Empire Loukanos could be, on this cold autumn night when the bristling stars outshone the sickly new moon.

Half a mile away in Banayim, alone in his too-quiet house, there was one other who was struggling with his own fears. Ittai had stayed up as late as he wanted to for once, without anyone shushing him about the children; and he had enjoyed the all crunchy edges of the stewpot scrapings usually reserved for the twins' delectation, but it was a moping sort of pleasure without his family.

Eventually he gave up and went to bed, not even bothering to undress or wash like a civilised man, discarding only his belt, winding himself up in robe and blankets in a kind of miserable defiance. Marta was not there to complain that he was dirty, still smelled and would set the children a bad example. Oh, but he would do anything if she *was* there – if she came back and was not stricken with deadly disease! He would even dig a Roman bath, line it with glazed tiles and *sleep* in water every night if that would please her! That she should be an outcast, a leper was unbearable, unthinkable!

Marta had sent by Etta's hand, two *ostraca* written with tender lines to her husband, but it was not enough to reassure him, and although Ittai had eventually dropped off into a light doze, his eyes flew open out of habit at the hour Marta usually turned over to feed little Shuni, and he tossed and turned, his thoughts chasing themselves around anxiously in the black room.

Finally he could not bear to stay in bed with his agitation any longer. He would get up and calm his nerves by pacing the lake shore until he was tired out enough to sleep soundly. He sat up and sprang to his feet, but his attempt at another step brought him crashing down, clutching the air, bringing baskets, pots, and a dangling wine-skin with him in a blood-curdling howl of dismay. For a moment he lay there in a pool of gently flowing wine, stunned, trying to understand what had happened.

"I am bleeding!" he gasped, feeling the gush of sticky liquid. "Bleeding to death! Help! Help!"

He frantically felt himself for gaping wounds, inflicted he knew not how, and in so doing, leant a forearm on the wobbling skin, which promptly spurted out more wine. Ittai stopped thrashing and pulled himself together. He smiled weakly at his mistake, and as soon as his startled heart had stopped hammering, attempted to get up. Another shock!

"Oh, Eternal preserve me! Truly I *am* injured!"

For some reason, he seemed to be unable to walk.

"I am paralysed!" he gulped, flapping like a salamander on a sandbank.

In a panic, he pinched his legs – and felt nothing. Now panting in alarm, Ittai snatched at the draining wineskin and sucked up a medicinal mouthful to wet his dry lips. He crawled on his elbows towards the smouldering fireplace, groaning and half sobbing with fear. His terror for Marta had caused a sudden apoplexy! He dragged himself bravely on, feeling for a lamp, scrabbling for a taper beside the hearth. A sick feeling swept over him.

"Angelic keeper of my head, help me!" Everyone had their own guardian angel – but for what earthly use if he did not do any guarding?

"I will die here!" His voice broke. "They will find me stiff and cold – or bloated and flyblown – oh horrors! And my darling Marta will never know why!" But the accepted lore was that a guardian angel could take the form of the man he protected. Perhaps his angel would appear to Marta, and gently tell her what had happened, before vanishing to return to Heaven.

"Oh, Guardian of my days – tell her I died loving her and the children!" Ittai gasped, wild-eyed, to the darkness. "And Eternal God, I pray she may not have leprosy!"

With an effort, his trembling fingers had managed to light a lamp, and now cast about desperately for something to scrawl a last message to his beloved. Dizzily, he snatched a half-burnt stick from the coals and began to scratch 'Marta' on the floor. Oh! There was such a strange feeling in his feet, his legs! There it was again – oh, oh! It was surely the end! The tingling … the fizzing … the prickling … the … pins … and … needles …

Suddenly Ittai felt very foolish indeed.

He flopped on his back, added a few grateful tears to his purple-splashed sleeve – and abruptly began roaring with laughter, beating at his legs … his joyful paroxysms interspersed with yelps of discomfort as feeling slowly sizzled back to his limbs with every slap.

Finally he lay exhausted, still chortling a little with hysterical reaction – just as there came hurried steps, hissing voices – and a frantic rattling and bashing at his door.

"Potter! Potter! What ails you? What is happening? Are you ill?"

The door wrenched open to reveal an eager Dabab in a rug, all swivelling eyes and twitching nose, guttering lamp held high, pulling behind her the half-dressed, defensive little man who was her husband.

Ittai looked at their faces and tried to sound indignant, but his relief was too great, and their appearance so comical, that his deep laughter gurgled out again.

"You are too kind," he said as solemnly as he could, before breaking out afresh. "I'm afraid I am absolutely legless, but I expect a full recovery soon."

"He's drunk, Rachel," said the little man shortly, peering over her shoulder and sniffing the air suspiciously. "That's all. Now can we get back to bed?" He stamped off.

"Drunk!" Rachel stared in outrage at the wine-soaked clothes, the split skin still ebbing beside the tangled bedclothes, the chaotic jumble on the floor.

"I'm not drunk," chuckled Ittai. "I'm happy – well, not really happy, but …"

"Indeed you are!" answered Rachel sharply, tossing her head. "Drunk *and* happy! And you with your poor wife in separation, burdened by the woes of bearing your child, you selfish winebibber!" *Yes, she had been right to think there was something going on! Now she had the whole story! Young Master Superior Potter Ittai would be a little sorry he'd called her Nosey! Ittai, indeed! Fancy naming a son after a Philistine – it was no wonder he lived in mud and drank like a – like a – yes, like a turtle! He even looked like one, floundering helplessly on his back!*

She stepped out and slammed the door in disgust, though smugly pleased with her mental epithet ... it was quite clever, really, especially for the middle of the night ... she would make sure other people also relished her cunning description.

Ittai rolled over with a sigh, as he sobered quickly. *Hi-yi! that woman!* Well, his reputation would have an interesting new glaze overlaid by tomorrow noon, that was for sure and certain. With any luck it would entertain poor Marta and not worry her. He shook his legs, which were rapidly resurrecting themselves from the horrible deadness. What in the world had happened? He crawled uncomfortably around the floor for a while, cleaning up the mess, and by the time the unpleasant tingling had restored full feeling, he had it worked out.

It was his own fault. He had thrashed and wound himself around so much in bed that every turn had hitched and pulled and tightened thick rolls of his clay-stained tunic against his hips until he looked like a piece of washing wrung at both ends. He pulled up the offending garment and inspected the deep welts for confirmation. Yes, there was no doubt of it. While he slept, the ridges of cloth had dug hard into the bony bits, and the result was inevitable – two dead legs.

That would teach him not to be such a Philistine! So Marta would say, and she would giggle till she had hiccups, he was sure of it. It was their own private joke. They both knew he was proud to have been named after one of King David's faithful warriors, a man brave enough to leave his own people to fight for the Eternal's chosen one. And who cared about lineage – real or imagined – in Galilee of the Gentiles!

Oh, but why had he thought again of his wife and her lovely giggles – he could not imagine life without her! The fear and despair rose up all over again, and he reproached himself for finding *anything* funny at all in the circumstances. Surely she could not possibly have leprosy! That silver lock of hers had always been there – she was practically born with it, and nobody thought it was anything to worry about … but Anna had said the rest was different … uneven blocks of white hair which had drained the colour from the brown skin beneath as well … with a speckling and blotching of white patches on her neck … It was too strange – and worrying! And what of the children!

For the second time in a night, Ittai groaned and gave up on sleep. Cautiously ensuring that his legs were fully recovered, he wrapped himself in a warm cloak and threaded his way quietly through the sleeping houses, until he had wandered down to the lake which was so immense they called it a Sea. A gull untucked its head from a wing and eyed him with a sleepy croak like Shuni waking for a feed. The shush-shush of the waves reminded him of Marta's warning fingers on her smiling lips, and the gentle slap of water on rocks became the twins splashing in the water-barrel. He sighed heavily and lifted his eyes to pray for them all.

Suddenly even Marta was forgotten as the startled potter saw a light flickering in the upstairs window of the house closest to the shore – a house which just now was supposed to be vacant. The shore house, also known these days as the Travellers' House, belonged to Anna – it was the place which she and Etta and Dan had made their home after the fire, before the Shepherd's place was rebuilt. On this night nobody was meant to be occupying Anna's house, though it had sheltered many heads since the family moved back to the little hollow in the hills outside Banayim.

Wandering Marah All-Alone had stayed there often, as she criss-crossed the country trailing after the Nazarene, Old Caleb had slept there too, even Philip the Younger, the Cana fishmonger, who had once been delayed a whole night by a severe thunderstorm. Timid Judith with little Thad had found occasional refuge from hireling shepherd Thaddeus' harsh treatment, and Widow Shana had been able to house her entire visiting tribe of obnoxious grandchildren and odious daughters-in-law from Capernaum on several occasions. Last *Succoth*, Anna's father Asa had come all the way from Jerusalem with young Johanan to grace the humble house and build a fine family booth, even bringing his elegant sister Mari, who fascinated the village with her fine clothes and quick, precise speech.

Ittai's own dear mother had died in that same house – suddenly, last winter, after taking ill while visiting from Nain. Compassionate Anna had rescued her from the young couple's cramped, noisy little house and helped Marta nurse the quiet older woman until the inevitable end, and Ittai, swallowing a lump in his throat at the memory, knew he would never forget it.

Even the ben Zebedees had sheltered there one stormy midnight when their boat, with shredded sails, scudded crazily before the shrieking wind, smashing through wild waves until it struck a shifting sandbar and capsized on the very edge of the lake. They had salvaged it the very next morning with the help of fellow fishermen, but had not gone without leaving behind a token of thanks – a fine basket of their freshest catch. At least, presumably it was fresh when it was left in the kitchen. It was a pity they had given this gift so discreetly that the left hand did not know what the right was doing ... it was two weeks before anyone could use the house again. Despite this, even Anna was sorry that they rarely saw the brothers these days ... they had long since left their trade to follow the Nazarene, and the lakeside communities missed their raucous voices, the hearty jokes, the pranks, and the colour that Zebedee's boys had unpredictably splashed into their predictable days.

But it was not only friends and neighbours who had found hospitality – so also had many strangers. At the height of Nazarene fervour, Anna, Etta and Marta and some of the other women had ministered in that house to wave after wave of desperate seekers of healing, from all over the country – most of whom they never saw again.

Anna's generous uncle had intended that his gift be used for charitable purposes, or whatever Anna saw fit ... and she certainly had seen fit to share it just as he would have wanted ... but nobody, as Ittai told himself indignantly, *nobody* ever treated the place as if it were public property! It was not a playhouse for children, or a free inn for ne'er-do-wells! Everyone in the hamlet always knew who was at the Travellers' House, and why. Neither Anna, Etta, nor Dan had said a word about any new occupant, nor had Marta. Even the Dabab had been silent, and if she had known anything, without question the women at the well would have had heard some heavy hints by now. Who could be lurking inside at this hour? Nobody up to any good!

Ittai scrubbed his dusty head in momentary confusion. What to do? Interfere? Or not? The rest of the village was asleep, and there was clearly an illicit light in Anna's house. Did he want to risk Dan's family having to suffer another disastrous fire? Or was he going to do something about it? Oh, too much was happening tonight! But his duty was clear.

He squared his shoulders bravely and marched quickly across the shingle to the door, heaved up the clattering latch and strode purposefully into the dark room. It crossed his mind that he was now acting precisely as Rachel had, but there was no time to think about that.

Chapter Ten

ITTAI could just make out the shape of a traveller's bundle, dumped on the whitely-scrubbed wooden table – a table, had Ittai but known it, on which Old Caleb had once danced with whoops and yells of glee – but nobody was downstairs. As he stood uncertainly in the room, and defiantly shouted, "Who's that up there?" a light wavered down the narrow stairs, and an authoritative voice answered drily, "First you tell me who's that down there, calling *Who's that up there?*"

Ittai gulped, but stood his ground.

"I am Ittai the potter, of this village," he said firmly. "I am also a friend of Anna bath Netzir, and I demand to know what you are doing in her house at this time of night, without her leave."

A tall, plump man with a neatly trimmed beard and smart turban loomed out of the shadows, appearing to slide from the ceiling as his large Damascan slippers descended the last few stairs. He put his lamp on the table, and unexpectedly, smiled.

"It is true that the lady, as yet, has no idea I am here," he said politely. "Philip the fishmonger brought me from Cana only an hour ago, and I was not expected even there. As to what I am doing here, well, apparently I am being *questioned*, and very properly, too, I might say. Questioned, I have no doubt, by a very loyal and very good friend of my niece."

Suddenly Ittai was uncomfortably conscious of his dirty arms and legs, his scruffy hair, and the strong smell of wine which hung about his stained clothes. "You – " he croaked, wet his lips and tried again, "you – are Anna's Uncle Joseph?"

The well-dressed man put his thumbs in the braided armholes of his sleeveless coat, and waggled his fingers expansively. "The very same," he beamed. "Here, bring me that other lamp, there's a good man, excellent – there, I can see you properly and I like your face ... Now, let's take a cup of fellowship and talk about what is worrying you."

Ittai looked blank, as Anna's uncle calmly poured wine into thick glazed cups and waved him hospitably to the table.

"How do you know anything's worrying me?" he asked suspiciously, sipping cautiously at the wine. It was unlike any Ittai had tasted before – soft, smooth and sweet. Not like the astringent stuff usually drunk in Banayim. He took a proper mouthful and swallowed slowly.

"But of course something is worrying you," replied Anna's uncle, with just the curl of an accent to his mellow voice. "You are young, married with healthy children and a lovely wife – yes, I know all dear Anna's friends, she is a faithful correspondent to her lonely old uncle – and you ought to be at home in bed, sleeping soundly, or whispering delightfully together while the little ones sleep. Instead you are stamping around haggardly at the wrong end of the village in the middle of the night, still in your working clothes, reeking of cheap wine and shouting at other people's burglars. Now, my fellow night-owl, what is the burden of your sorrows?"

Astonished by this surprising insight and compassion from a virtual stranger, Ittai put down his cup. "I don't know – if I could – if I *should* – tell you ..." Shaking his head, he found his voice was choked with unexpected emotion.

Uncle Joseph topped up his cup encouragingly, helped himself to an inlaid box of toasted almonds, and waited, crunching patiently. Reluctantly at first, Ittai unburdened himself as invited. Having poured out his fears about Marta's baffling condition, he waited numbly for his host's response. Perhaps the man would be aghast now that he knew ... and Ittai would have to leave, more miserable than he had arrived.

"H'mmm," said Joseph, consideringly, at last. "H'mmmmmm. This is a difficult turn-up for you, my friend. Have some of these roasted almonds, why don't you, they're delicious. No point sorrowing on an empty stomach."

Ittai took a handful, disconsolately poking them about in his palm, chewing them obediently. Another time he would have relished the treat, but tonight it was mere dust and ashes.

"So you need a priest, or a physician," Joseph commented, pouring more wine and inhaling it pleasurably. "Well, I must see what I can do, starting tomorrow. I do have some contacts both here and at home who might be useful. We will deal with the problem of your wife's disorder one way or another, if I have to swim back to the Island myself and tow someone here to see her. Now, drink up, and finish those almonds – very soothing to a taxed mind, you know. I've often found them useful when settling disputes ... I've never been able to decide whether it is a medicinal property of the almonds, the roasting, or the action of the jaw – you know, as in the ruminating effect of chewing the cud. Perhaps it is all three. Unhappily it does not remedy the outcome of so much mental strain – the premature falling of one's hair."

"Settling – disputes – sir?" Trying to follow the thread, poor Ittai was by now totally bemused.

The other man shook his head, removed his embroidered turban regretfully, placed it gently on the table, and lovingly smoothed the dark wisps which still clung to his scalp. It was impossible to tell his age, with that near-bald head, and his unweathered indoor face. He smiled at his companion and shook his head again.

"Oh, no, no, no, my dear Ittai … nobody calls me 'Sir' – unless they are very conscious of wrong doing and want me to rule in their favour! Just call me Uncle Joseph, like Anna does – and everyone else too, young or old, it makes no difference. Otherwise I shall be constantly looking over my shoulder to see whom you mean."

The young potter sighed, started on his next cup, and gave up trying to understand anything. Uncle Joseph was the most unusual person he had ever come across, and seemed to be adept at discovering more information in others than he gave away about himself. Strange that the Dabab did the same, and yet the effect was so different! Perhaps it was because Rachel invariably made you feel worse and this man seemed to make you feel better.

Ittai tried to recall his manners. "Sir – Uncle Joseph – you give me some hope, and I thank you for your encouragement. Anna will be very glad to see you, I know, but you must not go to the Shepherd's House, in the circumstances. I will run to the well early in the morning and tell her you are here. Then she can visit you at once."

"It will be a long-awaited treat to me, my friend. But there is so much I have to discuss with my niece that I will not stop talking for a long time, and it would not do to keep the rest of the family waiting for their water."

A mournful smile flitted over the potter's face. "Oh, there is no fear of that. I will take it to them at once, and then I can talk to my darlings through the window."

Uncle Joseph looked at him good-humouredly. "A man doing women's work, for the love of his family, eh?"

Ittai shrugged. "There are women here doing men's work for the same reason. Banayim is a small place, and every house has empty places at its table. We do the best we can for each other."

"Good! Ah, yes, this is the spirit of the law, indeed! And I am reminded, that you too have an empty place in your heart. Anna wrote me that your mother was a kind and gentle woman, and you must feel her loss deeply. May the Eternal comfort you, friend, and may she rest in peace."

"Thank you. May she rest in peace," responded Ittai gruffly, and quaffed the last of his wine.

They sat in silence for a little longer. Uncle Joseph casually filled their cups again and Ittai sipped luxuriously, aware that this was probably the best wine he had ever tasted or ever would taste. As the fruity sweetness rolled around his palate, he felt the knots in his joints and muscles relaxing and his agitation replaced by a calm sense of well being. Idly he wondered what the man so urgently wanted to discuss with Anna. Her uncle had not visited the Land for many years, and here he was, suddenly popping up like a bubble in wet clay.

"May I ask," he began, "if it is not discourteous …"

"Ask by all means!"

"What can it be that brings you here, far from your home, without warning? I have been too full of my own troubles to enquire if all is well with you and yours."

"Ah! Not at all. Yes, thank you, all is quite well with me, and mine. Of course 'mine' is also a thin and fractured clan, much like those here at Banayim. I have only Asa and Mari's families to call my own, and as you know, they are not extensive. At home I am kept company only by my possessions, my servants, and my work. But I have many dear friends to love, and they are my family by choice, as it were."

He closed his eyes and sighed contentedly. "The Eternal has blessed me bountifully, and I rejoice that I can do much good to those closest to my heart. It is a comfort to a lonely man!"

Ittai felt rather confused by Uncle Joseph's combination of having dear friends close to his heart while being a lonely man. He still had not answered the question of why he had suddenly appeared in Galilee without telling the niece he had presumably come to visit.

"You have no thoughts of marriage, then, and a family of your own?" Ittai dared to ask, very surprised that a man with so much, had no one with whom to share it. Uncle Joseph sat up a little, straightening his shoulders.

"Oh, why, you know, I am still a young man," he said firmly, and looking as if he would like to believe it. "At least, in your tongue, a man may be called 'young' until he is forty, and I am not quite that, yet. The Patriarchs themselves had no children until they were much older. Abraham was nearly ninety, Isaac was sixty, Jacob was in his seventies and even my own father was quite ancient when I was born – at least sixty five, I believe – so I am in very good company. Perhaps I will settle down in a few years, find a sturdy young wife and beget a dynasty like the Pharaohs, eh? But not just yet, thank you."

He leaned back against the wall and laughed comfortably, though Ittai thought this plan was deplorable. Who would be an old man with young sons? Ittai could not wait for his sons to grow up so they could all be vigorous men together, sharing their work, their opinions and their families, their joys and sorrows. He was already impatient to be teaching them his trade, singing heartily with them, dancing arm in arm in the men's circle at festival times, swimming, splashing and shouting together in the Sea, like Zebedee and his boys – though as for little Abigail, it must be admitted that he was in no hurry at all where she was concerned – she would grow up *too* fast. He sighed again. Meanwhile they all rejoiced his soul with their trusting eyes and his heart turned over just to look at them.

Uncle Joseph poured another for himself, and reached for Ittai's cup with an enquiring air, but the potter shook his head regretfully.

"You are very kind, but I had better go home." He got to his feet and the room swayed slightly. Ittai decided that he must be more tired than he realised – why, he was quite dizzy with lack of sleep.

"Good night, sir – Uncle Joseph – and the Eternal bless you for your kindness."

"Bless you too, Potter Ittai," returned the bald man, suddenly looking weary, and pushing away his unfinished drink as he rose. "Your company has warmed me on this cold night."

Ittai walked back in rather a daze – strange, how his head was beginning to rock. He strode quickly down the narrow street, which seemed to have more bumps and dips in it than usual. Yes, he must be very tired indeed. He increased his pace and almost ran home, steadying himself occasionally against a wall with his hands, very anxious to reach his house before any pins and needles started in his head.

The Dabab heard rapidly striding feet and her eyes flicked open. She sprang up quickly from beside her longsuffering husband, whipped the shutter away and stuck her head out of the window at once.

"*H'mph!*" she said to herself in satisfaction, peering hard as Ittai loped past at a great rate.

"Will you get back to bed? There's a cold patch on my back!" her man grumbled.

Rachel banged the shutter and wriggled happily back under the covers.

"Well, Malachi, my dear, I'm very thankful to see that!" she commented piously to her husband's shoulder blades.

"What is it now, Rachel?" he sighed.

"Why, I'm a fair-minded woman," she replied proudly if untruthfully, turning over and planting her icy feet comfortably against his hairy calves. "Oh, do keep still, my dear ... you are such a fidget ... and I'm not one to hold grudges, as you well know ... so I'm very glad to see that young Master Ittai has been walking off his wine after that disgraceful drunken exhibition he made of himself tonight! I must have pricked his conscience, at least, and he has been taking some fresh air to clear his head. He was hurrying home, perfectly sober again."

Chapter Eleven

DAN was outside, ensuring that Isaac didn't fall into the privy hole, when Ittai marched into the clearing with Anna's heavy water-pot the next morning, and when they both emerged from the scrub the child crowed with delight at seeing his father.

"*Abba! Abba!* I didn't fall in! I'm a big boy!" He danced around happily and clutched his father's legs.

"Steady, my son, or we'll both get a wetting!" Ittai put down the pot with a thud. How the women did this so easily he would never know. The Master Potter must have shaped their skulls for it as he had shaped their hips for childbearing. He rubbed his head, which felt quite bruised, despite the pad of cloth which had supported the weight. He kissed Isaac on his scruffy little thatch of dark hair but did not scoop him into his arms as usual.

"Wash hands, like a good boy!" he admonished, "then tell *Amma* to open the window and look out. Won't she get a surprise to see me?"

The child nodded happily and held out his fists to Dan, who picked up the dipper from the barrel, and carefully trickled water over the wiggling fingers.

"Where is Anna, that you have brought the water?" Dan asked with some concern as Isaac scampered into the house.

Ittai's hurried explanation made Dan's eyes gleam – another precious relative had turned up to add to his small collection! He could not wait to meet Uncle Joseph, but until Ittai was ready to return he must be patient. Dan dived inside to make up his bundle, while the potter gloomily explained things to Aunt Etta, tipped his water into the kitchen pot and hurried outside, keeping the eager twins at arm's length as if to make up for allowing Isaac to come too close before he had permission.

"What am I to do now?" he asked the old woman unhappily. "Must I really stay away from my children as well?"

"None of us know what to do, my friend," she said apologetically, seating herself stiffly on the sunlit bench outside the door. "We have all been trying to decide what is best. Avoiding the children altogether would seem to be going too far. They show no signs of any disorder, but neither did Marta, so we think perhaps a little caution is in order, and some limits observed."

"What sense is any of this!" Ittai protested crossly. "Have I not been sharing the same bed with all of them until yesterday? Are you not still sharing the same house with them yourselves?"

"I know," Etta replied helplessly. "But short of shutting up the whole of Banayim in separate houses because we have all been in contact with each other, what can we do? Although I do not believe any of us are infectious, precautions are pointless unless they are consistent. We already have Marta totally separated from us in one room, the children are separate from other children, and Dan is not staying here either, he is going home with you."

"My love!" Marta's voice broke in, as she leaned anxiously from the window. Ittai ran towards her but she held up her hand. "No, my husband, don't come any closer … Etta is right … so play

112

with the babies all you want, but turn your face away … no kissing, no sharing food."

"No kissing," Ittai repeated glumly. "No sharing food." His manly heart went to butter when the twins planted enthusiastic kisses on his face, and one of their best games was to feed him with dinner scraps while he pretended to bite their fingers off. And he adored having his beard nuzzled by his children's snub noses!

Aunt Etta lowered her voice. "It seems hard, but we think it might be wise because Moses wrote that a leper must cover his upper lip. Perhaps it is spread through noxious qualities in the breath, or the mouth." She broke off and sighed, stabbing her stick impatiently at the ground. "It seems quite foolish to be so afraid. And yet how much more foolish to suffer the consequences of ignoring something which could be so dire."

"Anna's uncle has promised to help us, Etta. He is an interesting character. What do you think of him?"

"Oh, I have not seen Cypriot Joseph for many a long year! I think the last time was when Ammiel and Anna were about Dan's age, at his sister Mari's wedding. Like Dan's father, he was the surprise baby of the family, and is not a great deal older himself than Anna, you know."

"Was my father a surprise?" cried Dan, who had just emerged with his neatly tied bundle. "How could that be?"

Aunt Etta pulled a face at him. "Eh, Dan, you are not having an answer to that question today! That's a tale for when your beard is grown."

Dan pulled a face back at her. "That's exactly what father said when I asked him why he wasn't named Amos after his father and grandfather! And then he laughed. And I still don't know the answer."

Aunt Etta also began to laugh, making Dan wild with curiosity. "Oh, and you still don't have a beard, either!"

Dan felt his growing fuzz proudly and scowled. "It's coming as fast as it can. You'll have to tell me the tale before too much longer."

"Too much longer, yes, when the beard is much longer too ..." And Aunt Etta chuckled to herself while Dan snatched her stick and pretended to run off with it to punish her. After waving it all around the courtyard, he relented and handed it back, and her black eyes twinkled at him.

"I'll tell you before you're another year older, Dan. I promise."

Ittai, who had been murmuring lovingly to Marta through the window during this nonsense, impatiently dragged their attention back to the subject of Anna's uncle.

"You still haven't said what you think about him."

"Well now, he seemed to be very single-minded very young, you know – buying and selling was his passion. Trading was in his blood. If you stood still for too long, he'd have a label on you marked 'Special Price!' Neither he nor young Asa were interested in pursuing Levitical positions in the Land, which is hardly surprising, since they lived so long in Cyprus, but a pity for the Temple, with scarcely enough of the tribe left in these degenerate days. Ah, well, each to their own. Joseph was born on the Island, of course, and never cared for any other place. He was bright enough to spend a year at the Tarsus university and seemed to enjoy it, but he had barely returned home, when his mother died. Well, poor Asa the Elder packed up and moved them all back to Cana – and was dead himself within three months."

Ittai shook his head in sympathy. Such a sad time for any family! But why anyone ever wanted to wander around the world, he could not imagine. He wished Etta would get to the point and answer his question. Women might not get out of the house as much as men, but they made up for it by 'wandering around the world' themselves whenever they attempted to tell a man anything.

But Etta was enjoying herself. Cypriot Joseph's appearance in their tiny village was a rare chance to dust off her own old memories and embellish them with extra fragments collected from Anna, Asa and Mari over the last few years.

"Not surprisingly the boy was very unhappy – and homesick. Cana was a miserable little backwater compared to an important place like Salamis. I believe Master Joseph was very partial to its luxuries such as public baths, gymnasiums and theatres! Of course Cana was no fun at all to him, and now there were no parents left to indulge him. Well, Asa the Younger took over the import business of course, and put his little brother into the trade at once, even though Joseph was only about fourteen. Asa believed the boy needed to be useful, or he'd be in mischief in no time."

Dan, absently helping the twins build a pebble pyramid, paused in the act of balancing another stone on the top. This was exactly what Uncle Asa had said about Johanan at the same age – there was no secret about that either. Three years ago, kindly Asa had left beautiful Galilee for harsh Judea, and noisy Jerusalem – to give a solid fatherly presence to his sister's son. How strange life was! Here was a man with no sons of his own, forever taking under his wing those of other men. First his young brother Joseph, much later, his nephew Johanan … and of course, in between, there had also been his stepson Loukanos …

Isaac tried to put three pebbles on the pile at once and the whole thing collapsed. He burst out laughing and with flailing hands scattered the lot. Abigail giggled, scrambling to collect her share, and the game started again.

"Fourteen is quite old enough to begin," Ittai said firmly. "I was learning my trade long before that."

Aunt Etta patted his arm kindly. "Yes, my young friend. And you too lost your father at an early age."

Dan dropped a stone carelessly, and it slid down the growing heap, bringing several with it. He felt uneasy. Was the whole world full of fatherless men? But Aunt Etta was busily spinning her distaff and happily continuing to tell the tale to her audience.

"Asa was wise to train the lad, but it's my opinion that he would have made good, regardless. Imagine! It was only a year later that Master Joseph betook himself back to Cyprus and started in the wine market. He had a thriving business within a couple of years. Oh, he had the rare gift for making money, there's no doubt! But he worked hard for his fortune and his little kingdom, which he governs like a father, though he has no children to leave it all to. And the more he has, the harder he has to work, for Anna tells me he likes to oversee everything himself. I suppose that's why he rarely leaves Salamis – he has too much to do."

Ittai scratched his beard. "What you tell me doesn't seem to fit the man I met, Etta. A man whose whole life has been spent making money and ruling large estates, too busy to raise a family or visit the one he has … well, that makes him sound like a selfish Nabal, building ever bigger barns."

Etta looked indignant. "Did I say he was any such thing? It's not greed, but astuteness that built the wealth of Cypriot Joseph. Wise as a serpent, but harmless as a dove, that one. He had that house by the Sea built especially for his old nurse, and we didn't even know until a few years ago. Old Esther never gave out that it was anyone's but her own and said nothing of her life or connections, except that she wanted to spend her declining years by the Sea. Of course, she was already very forgetful and reclusive when she came here, but she lived comfortably, and that will have been Joseph's doing too. When she died, he could easily have sold the house, but that would not be his way. Anna tells me he has always been very involved in charitable works and in the synagogue, too, and that is a part of his all-round busy-ness, I'll be bound."

Dan chipped in. "He wasn't too busy to take in Loukanos, either." Uncle Joseph was now his uncle too, and must be defended! Dan refused to admit any more shady uncles – especially not after Bukki.

"Quite right," nodded Aunt Etta. "And I can tell you *I* would have thought twice about that! But there's no doubt he is a little eccentric, from what I have heard over the years. Well, a man with too much freedom and comfort often is, especially without a family to rub him smooth. The short time his nephew was with him would not have made much difference – not that I even knew there was such a person as Loukanos, back in those days."

Ittai was comforted. "I am glad to hear your good opinion of him, Etta. Joseph struck me as a generous and compassionate man, and he was most anxious to see his niece, who writes him often."

"It is not wise to quickly judge a man for either good or ill," Marta agreed, joining in from her window. "Whoever sees all of a man without living with him? The softest-spoken fellow may beat his wife, and the roughest may have a gentle heart." She smiled slyly at her husband. "Would a stranger who saw you slapping and punching and grunting at your clay imagine you were a tender husband and a doting father?"

Ittai turned red. "I am a very firm father, and a masterful husband. Get away from that window at once, woman."

"Yes, oh lordly one." Obediently Marta disappeared, and the young potter ran over at once.

"No, my darling Marta, please don't go! Bring the baby to the window for me and let me see you both again before I leave."

As Ittai thus busied himself being firm and masterful, Dan sat down next to Aunt Etta, rather staggered by all she had told them.

"Auntie, when Loukanos jumped ship at Cyprus and ran off to his uncle, do you think he realised how *young* Joseph was? From what you say, they must be very close in age!"

"Yes, Dan, I believe they are. But I doubt Loukanos knew the age of his uncle – after all, do you have any idea of how old your Uncle Bukki was?"

She corrected herself quickly. "*Is.* How old he *is.*"

Speaking of vanishing uncles! Etta's thoughts went off on a tangent. *Whether Bukki ben Bezaleel, Loukanos of Philippi or Cypriot Joseph!* What was it about these selfish men! Didn't they care about their family name? Why didn't they marry and give some poor woman a home! What were they thinking of – dropping in and out of people's lives – appearing and disappearing all over the place like Elijahs and Elishas! Did they ever think what distress and confusion they caused the people who loved them? *Though, to be perfectly truthful, could it be said that anyone ever really loved Bukki? Perhaps his poor sister did.* Etta thought of Dan's young mother Michal – oh, she was the pretty one and no mistake, but she had not learnt much patience in her short life. Brother Bukki also

118

came in for his share of her tongue, but he shrugged off her moods and irritations, and she shrugged off his. And they laughed together. Etta suddenly felt ashamed of herself. It had never before occurred to her that Bukki too had suffered when his sister died.

Etta sighed. *Yes, Ammiel and I did our duty by him, but it would be a lie to say my heart ever felt gladder in his presence.* He never had been loveable – perhaps because he loved no one but himself. But of course, surely Michal must have loved her older brother, and whatever he felt for her was probably the best there was in him to feel. Who was she to judge how others loved their families?

Still the fact remained that a sly, lazy, fretful child had become a sly, lazy, fretful man ... with neither enough love nor enough discomfort to inspire or provoke him to be anything else. She remembered Ammiel confessing that he was at fault in demanding too little of his brother-in-law, but now she doubted it would have made much of a difference to Bukki. With him it seemed to be just bred in the bone.

Yet miracles still happen! Etta reminded herself wryly, though she would challenge even the Nazarene to cure whatever it was that ailed Bukki. Meanwhile it was anyone's guess where he was these days, or how he had fared since he stamped away from the house in the hollow, shouting that he would visit many places, and do many things! *I suppose he is still alive.* Well, it didn't bear thinking about now.

It was strange, and a little pathetic, to realise that though Bukki had been a family fixture for many years, his disappearance had caused not a fraction of the heartburning produced by the vanishing of Loukanos, whom they had known for such a short time.

While these thoughts were winging through Etta's head Dan was scratching sums on the ground. He looked up.

119

"I don't suppose there would be as much as four years between them!" he said, astonished.

Aunt Etta quickly came back to the present. "I believe you are right," she answered thoughtfully. "Even if Loukanos had not known it, doubtless he felt sure to find a kindred spirit in an uncle who chose living with Greeks above settling in Cana. It must have been a shock to find that young Joseph of Cyprus had an unchangeably Jewish mind. No wonder he was not able to tame his own nephew, eh?"

Dan shook his head. No wonder, indeed! But what could he be doing here, now?

Chapter Twelve

JOSEPH of Salamis released his niece from a joyful embrace, looked her up and down, then retreated several steps up the stairs he had just descended. He beamed at her, pleased to be able to slip back into his own tongue instead of plodding along in Aramaic, though Anna warned him her Greek might be rusty. Since Loukanos had left, there was no-one around to keep her in practice, and unlike commercial towns such as Cana, Sepphorim, Tiberius, or Caesarea Philippi, and other trade-route centres, scrappy little Banayim had no use for it whatsoever.

"I think I shall talk to you from here, my dear, I feel so much more avuncular when I am taller than you."

Anna laughed at him. "Dear Uncle Joseph, you couldn't stop being avuncular if you tried. I believe you are the uncle of everyone you meet, from babes-in-arms to equally toothless Methuselahs. You'll never find a wife this way."

Joseph waved his hands dismissively. "Why does everyone want to marry me off?" he complained. "Is there no more to life than domesticity and begettal? I have far too many things still to do, and it would not be fair to tie any woman to a vagabond life."

Anna raised her straight eyebrows until they disappeared into the fringe of her cap.

"What is all this about a vagabond life? From the man who clings to his Salamis estate like an ancient barnacle to a galley?"

"Ah, you ignorant creature, how little you know, and how much I must tell you! How dare you liken my beautiful vineyards and olive groves to a slave driven galley! I say nothing of comparing your venerable uncle to a barnacle ... I shall put that down to Galilean bad taste. But I'll thank you not to call me ancient until you are a grandmother yourself ..."

Suddenly he stopped his teasing – she had sworn to remain a Nazirite until she saw Ammiel's face, a lifelong commitment which was serious enough by itself, but which for all he knew, may have held an unspoken determination never to marry either. Regardless, at her age, she was fast becoming unmarriageable. It was not likely she would ever be a mother, still less a grandmother ... *Such a waste.*

Just as quickly, Anna guessed the reason for his hesitation. She smiled reassuringly.

"Dear Uncle, when my son Dan has children, I will be just as much a grandmother as any other woman."

He smiled back, relieved. "Of course you will! And I will be a doubly-great-uncle – what an alarming responsibility! Come, my little niece – at least, you were little the last time we met, and it will take me time to shake the habit of thinking of you thus." Joseph came down the stairs and began piling up cushions. "Come, sit down, and let us talk sensibly together. You have made this a very cosy little hut, and I see we have all the comforts here."

Anna sank into the seat he made, feeling strange to be sitting down and taking her ease so early in the day. But Ittai was taking care of the water, and the explanations, and had promised to bring Dan when he returned. Neither Etta nor Marta really needed her right now, and something serious must be happening with Uncle Joseph, for him to leave his beloved Island and seek her out. She leaned back, waiting patiently. It was Uncle Joseph's way to hedge around a subject with irrelevant comments and nonsense, and he would not come to it until he was ready.

"Anna," her uncle said abruptly, leaning forward and looking at her hard. "Anna, have I changed much, do you think?"

Anna stared at him. "What a question to ask me, Uncle! When I have not seen you since I was a girl! It seems to me that you are much as I remembered you – only shorter." She sighed ruefully. "But that's only natural – back then I came up to your chest, and now I'm half a span taller than you. And you were quite lean, from my recollection. But your eyes, your face, your manner – these are unchanged, except more softened." She smiled and patted his hand. "Whether softened through an increase in wisdom, kindness or too much good living, I cannot say. Perhaps a little of all three."

Joseph removed his turban and looked at her mournfully. She clapped a hand over her mouth while her brown and hazel eyes twinkled at him. "Ah! Very well, I concede that you have lost most of your hair! You are now as bald as Marta's baby."

Joseph looked blank. "I thought they were twins – and long past babyhood by now. Is one of them still hairless, poor creature?"

"No, no, I am speaking of her new little son, Shuni! Perhaps you are losing your memory as well as your hair!" she said in mock horror. "I wrote you months ago that a new child was coming and Marta was bravely hoping it would be twins again to save time, if not trouble. But I suppose it's quite unreasonable of me to expect an old bachelor to remember trivial details about *domesticity and begettal*." Now she was definitely teasing him, and he looked

123

thoughtful. Anna wondered if she had unwittingly offended him and hastened to make amends.

"Never mind, dear Uncle! Having lost your hair so young, you do have the comfort of knowing it will never turn grey – you will probably look this age for ever."

His eyes brightened. "Anna! Do you think so? What a delightful thought! It had never occurred to me before. And of course, let us not forget the saving of time and money on haircuts."

Anna looked at him shrewdly. "Come now, Uncle Joseph, you did not travel all the way from Salamis and arrive so unexpectedly, just so you could ask my opinion of your looks."

"No," he replied. "But it was not an idle question, not as idle as it sounded. I will come to that presently. First let me correct you. I did not exactly *forget* that Marta and Ittai had a new child, because I did not even know it was on the way. I have not yet received your letter." He held up a hand as she raised her eyebrows in surprise. "No, no, it will not be lost. Anything you send with your father's consignments to the Island, reaches me faithfully – eventually."

"Then why – what do you mean?"

"Perhaps you had not noticed how tardy I have been in replying."

"I would never notice how late your replies, because you answer me so rarely! I believe you undertake them as a kind of Day of Atonement task, when you afflict your soul by laboriously scrawling half a hide's worth of parchment at once! You ask me many questions about myself and everyone and everything I know; you tell me all your liveliest stories – and if I am very lucky you may even answer *some* of my own questions. Then you dutifully sign your name, and trust that you have kept me satisfied and amused for another year. And indeed, so you have!" she conceded with a laugh. "I am always most humbly grateful to receive the smallest crumbs of news which fall from the rich man's overcrowded table. Their very unexpectedness gives them all the more relish. I know how busy you are, and your exports come first. Father has never complained about any tardiness *there*."

"Would it surprise you to know that for the past year, your own letters have taken almost three times as long to reach me?"

"Yes, it would! Why?"

Uncle Joseph pummelled his cushions into a more comfortable shape and settled back again.

"Because, my dear niece, I have not been at home to receive them. I have not been anywhere near Salamis. In fact, I have not even been on the Island at all."

Anna's mouth fell open. "But, you rarely leave it!

"Yet, I did leave it."

"What of your business?"

"My faithful steward Linus can be trusted in my absence."

Anna shook her head. She could not imagine Uncle Joseph ever leaving Cyprus for more than a few weeks, far less trusting anybody to manage his affairs, especially for so long!

"So, Uncle – where have you been?"

"First Seleucia then Antioch, where I had some trade to attend to. I was there several Sabbaths, and naturally I attended synagogue as usual, meeting some old friends, and making new ones, and this was all very pleasant, but nobody could talk of anything else but the Baptiser and the Nazarene. Of course, Salamis synagogues have been astir with it for a long time, and Asa, Mari and you have each written often enough, urging me to come and see these things for myself; but it never before seemed to be quite real to me, immersed as I was in my busy life and my pet charities on the Island."

True, Anna thought. *But even your charities are managed like a business, and as you go about dispensing comfort to all, who is comforting you?*

"Do you remember the old tales of the False Messiahs?" he asked her pensively. "Ill-fated Theudas, slain with his four hundred rebels! And a generation ago, Judah the Galilean, with his prophet Saddok, gathering many hundreds of followers, preaching that Jews must serve only Adonai their God and not the Romans?"

Anna did remember. "That was one of Louki's favourite bedtime stories."

Her uncle nodded. "And mine – all excitement and righteous indignation, and the blasphemer met a sticky end. Just what boys love. So, when I heard about all the excitement and righteous indignation here, on both sides – it seemed to be just another such story ... yet another Galilean and his prophet, you see, and more Messiah fever ... and which would probably end much the same way."

He sighed and rubbed his head wearily. "I admit, I did not take it as seriously as I ought. Living outside the Land, one develops a degree of detachment which unfortunately often passes for sophistication. Perhaps there is also a temptation to imagine that if we see a broader vista, we must be standing on higher ground – dangerous indeed. If I stood there, my pride deserved a fall."

Anna said nothing. She could not see much of it in her generous uncle, but she knew for herself how insidious Pride was, and what

126

fantastical shapes it could assume – even that of Humility. Joseph half-closed his eyes and drew his dark eyebrows together.

"For whatever reason I had treated the matter so casually before – once I was in Antioch, meeting the same reports in one synagogue after another, somehow it all seemed to be so much more substantial. I don't quite know how to explain why that was, Anna."

He got up and paced the room, picking things up and putting them down restlessly while Anna waited. Suddenly he turned and snapped his fingers.

"It was this way! Like any other Jew, in or out of the Land, I had my own ideas about the Messiah – what he should do, who he should be. Those ideas were a mere outline, an empty frame in my thoughts. Now, at home in Salamis, all the different things that I had heard about the Nazarene were just drifting around in my mind like a loose and shifting mixture of dry sand and lime and volcanic ash ... but in Antioch hearsay became fact. It was as if living water was slowly added to this untidy aggregate – and the whole was mightily stirred up and poured out into that waiting form in my head ... where gradually it solidified, and became a concrete object. You see, Anna? Finally I realised it was time for me to knock away my temporary frame and examine the reality before me."

Anna thought about his figure of speech and nodded slowly. Would the Messiah foundation hold true, and like Roman concrete, become even harder with time? Or would it crumble away when tested by the elements? Already the crowds were thinning, uncertainty was spreading, and the restoration of the Kingdom seemed to be no closer. The miracles were staggering, and God-given, and the Nazarene's words were as faultless as his life ... but

127

where was the preparation for Kingship, the expected revolt? Zealots who would have backed him with their own blood, were out of patience with the apparent absence of political leadership and planning in one who already had the national heart in his hand; and even the less warlike common people were bemused by exhortations to peacefulness and cooperation with their oppressors. She shifted uneasily on the cushions, berating herself for a faint fluttering of anxiety which might be a forerunner of doubt.

Joseph sat himself at the table, distractedly pushing empty cups around the scrubbed surface, as he continued, more quickly.

"I spoke to men who had themselves heard Johannes and been baptised by him, and men who had also been with the Nazarene. They told me with their own lips what they had seen, what they had heard, what they had experienced. And suddenly, I was appalled to see how narrow my life had become. What did it matter whether I found a new market for another hundred amphorae of oil, or another two hundred firkins of wine? If the Nazarene was truly the *Christos*, then life would change for every Jew, no matter where he might live. The Kingdom would be restored to us, and he would show us the way to inherit *everlasting* life, not just a long life in the Land."

"Yes." Anna's reply was troubled. "This is what we have all thought. And all his teachings have been about the Kingdom." *But what has actually happened to bring it about?*

The balding man stopped pacing, and replaced his turban firmly.

"Eternal life, Anna. That is all that really matters! Even more so, dare I say it, than the restoration of the Kingdom. For even if a kingdom is eternal, a man can only enjoy it for his allotted span of days. At the end of them he dies, and then what?"

"There is the Resurrection, and Judgement – then may come eternal life, if he is worthy."

"Vey well, Anna – but how does he become worthy? This is what I want to know. If I am not worthy, what difference does it make to me how long the Kingdom will continue? How does a man acquire the merit, eh? By the Law? I have striven for this since my youth, avoiding this, avoiding that, attempting the other…" He sighed.

He did not say to his niece, perhaps out of a sneaking sense of shame, that one of the things he had avoided was the wearisome complication of creating his own family. It was hard enough directing his own steps; and no matter how strict, a husband and father could not control his family forever, any more than his own father had managed with himself. He had seen the exhaustion and the pettiness and the temptations, the mundane struggles which cluttered the heavy responsibility of family life – and though it was a kind of cheating, he was thankful to have escaped it. Alone, it was far easier to applaud and appreciate the ideals while keeping his own way clear to bestow help wherever he chose. To be charitable and avuncular was to be loved and respected still – but free.

Anna shook her head slowly. "Call me a heretic, Uncle, but I cannot understand how anyone can ever acquire merit by the Law. It is surely impossible for any normal person to keep every law in every single respect. It is like walking through an ants' nest – if you avoid one it is only to tread on another! And not only that – the Law came after Abraham, so how will he, or those before him, be saved? But saved he will be, because the Eternal promised."

Joseph frowned. "Abraham will be saved because of his obedience – he did all that the Eternal commanded him, even taking up a knife to cut his own son's throat. Whatever is God's command is always His Law, even if not formalised by Moses. I do know what you mean about the impossibility of keeping all the rituals prescribed by the elders, but the spirit of the Law must still be kept. We must try our best. An honest heart and honest obedience to the Law – obeying the commandments as far as we are able – this is required of us, this is always possible, and this must count as merit."

"Oh, how *can* any merit of ours, outweigh our failures?" Anna spread her hands in appeal. "That is why we were so grateful for the ritual of baptism which Johannes gave us to wash away our past sins. But since the Prophet is dead, what do we do now? And even if he was alive, I am still not sure how that even baptism helps us with the problem of sins afterwards. Perhaps the Day of Atonement must suffice us, as it always has had to. But I don't really understand, Uncle. The preaching of Johannes, and the Nazarene, both declare that it is what we do as *individuals* which pleases God. That we cannot rely on simply being Jews to save us. But the Day of Atonement is a national Atonement, with a ritual performed by a single high priest for all of us ... so we *do* rely on simply being Jews to have our sins taken away."

She got to her feet and stretched. "I'm sorry, Uncle, we have strayed rather far from your story of the past year or so."

"We have not strayed as far as you think, my dear, because these are the same questions which assailed me in Antioch. I decided that in the end, it all comes back to Obedience," Uncle Joseph declared. "It has to, somehow. So, the Messiah *must* have some new thing for us to understand about that. It will be in his teaching, I am certain of it, but I have not yet fathomed exactly what it is. Now this is the point at which I will return to my story,

130

Anna. It was with this conviction that I sent instructions to Linus authorising him to assume full responsibility for the estate, and set out to find the answers for myself."

"Do you mean to tell me, Uncle, that you have been *in the Land* all this while?"

"Yes, I do mean. I have been following the Nazarene and his men."

Anna was so astounded that she sat down again. "And we never knew! Nobody told us! *You* didn't tell us! And you didn't visit!"

"No." Uncle Joseph looked rather ashamed. "Of course, it's not surprising nobody told you, Anna. It's been so many years since I was here, no-one would know me from Adam. I have, intentionally, not been very forthcoming to others about my personal details."

"I do not understand why! Or why you said nothing to your own brother and sister!" she replied indignantly. "You must have been all over the Land by this time, and often near Jerusalem! Father and Aunt Mari deserved your attention, surely? I am quite shocked, Uncle Joseph."

"And disappointed, too," he gave her a sympathetic glance, "though I had my reasons, my dear niece. I have not literally been following every footstep of the Nazarene and his twelve, though I have been studying them for many months. I have not yet been as far as Jerusalem, nor even in Judea, confining my travels largely to the north – Tyre, Sidon, Caesarea Philippi, Chorazin, Bethsaida, Gadara and so on, though not in that order. I have also been in Sepphoris and Nazareth. But I have based myself, as it were, firmly in one place – Samaria." He laughed at her astonishment. "You mean, it doesn't show? Oh, good!"

"Samaria!" Anna faintly wondered how many more shocks were in store. "But, oh! why not Galilee, Uncle? Why not Cana! With my father's house there for the asking, with Old Dinah to care for you and intelligent Mordecai as a whetstone to sharpen your thoughts? Close enough for us to visit you! Why this pretence and avoidance?" Her voice held reproach. "This is no better than Loukanos has done!"

Joseph rubbed his neatly clipped beard apologetically. "My dearest Anna, of course you are hurt, and I am sorry for it, but please try to understand. It was very important for me to make my investigations entirely without influence or reference to my family. I needed to be sure I was not prejudiced in any way; and much as I do love that family, you know as well as I that with relatives here and there, one gets very sidetracked. People must be visited, attentions must be given, respect paid, customs observed, celebrations and feasts attended ... and family opinions well pronounced, and discussed and argued and expected to be adopted ... No, perhaps selfishly, I needed to avoid the whole distraction!

"However, once I had come to a definite conclusion about where I stood on the matter, it *was* my intention to do exactly as you have just suggested – to come to Cana, and visit you, and be rejoiced over like any self-respecting long-lost uncle. But before then, I happened upon a man who had once appealed to me, and whom I am afraid, I did not – at the time – really help very much at all."

He sighed and rubbed his hands wearily over his well-fleshed face.

"It suddenly struck me that this single failure has driven me ever since, to attempt to help others." Joseph shrugged. "Of course we can never make up for starving one man, by feeding another

– but it seems to be the right thing to do, all the same." He paused, then continued quietly, "It is not often we have a second chance, especially one we have not sought of ourselves – and when this man needed me again after so many years, I determined not to fail him again."

"So you helped someone," Anna prompted, rather impatiently. "As you always do. No doubt you gave him food, money, clothing, perhaps you gave him work, and an ear to speak in, a shoulder to lean on – all good things. But how long did that take? More than a *year*? Was it more important than your own family?"

Uncle Joseph gave her a strange smile. "It was not to slight any of my beloved family that I chose not to announce myself, and remained out of sight as much as possible. In fact, quite the opposite."

A flurry of flying footsteps outside announced that Dan had outrun Ittai and was now hurrying impatiently towards the house.

"You see, it was not a matter of charity to a stranger," Uncle Joseph continued as he opened the door more widely. "I was also attempting to acquire merit in another way. I was trying to regain my brother."

Just as Dan stopped breathlessly in the doorway and grinned up at him, Joseph glanced at Anna over his shoulder and added, switching to Aramaic, "Or I should say, my nephew."

"Yes!" said Dan proudly. *Now, this uncle looked a bit more like the real thing.* "Yes, I am your nephew Dan. *Shalom!* Blessings and peace be to you, Uncle Joseph!"

"Blessings and peace be upon you, too, young man. My dear Dan, I have heard so much about you from your mother, and I am delighted to meet you at last."

Uncle Joseph formally embraced the lad, then smilingly held him at arm's length while they looked each other over with interest. Anna uncurled her tall frame from the cushions as swiftly as a cat, and darted towards them. She nodded fleetingly to Dan then laid her hand appealingly on Joseph's sleeve.

"Uncle, you have confused me! Please repeat what you said just before Dan spoke! You said you had been trying to regain your brother ... then ..."

"I said, '*I have been trying to regain my brother. Or I should say, my nephew*'."

"Oh," Dan broke in, disappointed. "I thought you meant me."

Anna suddenly paled. "No, Dan, I'm sorry. I think Uncle Joseph was talking about someone else ..." She clutched her uncle imploringly. "Tell me! Tell me at once! Is it possible ...? Oh, Uncle! Can you really mean ...?!"

Uncle Joseph took her hands, and looked at her frankly.

"Now, my dear, be calm. Yes, it's true – it's true – don't cry, dear Anna. Yes, I am speaking of my nephew, and your brother, Loukanos."

Dan stood frozen to the spot, as Uncle Joseph murmured, "Don't cry, my dear, he is safe and well. Safe and well. There, there, no need to cry ..."

But Anna had covered her face, and broken into a storm of weeping. As her body shook with sobs, the boy flung his arms around her, and Joseph gently held them both – until Anna had cried herself out. Dan leant his downy cheek against her shoulder, his thoughts whirling so fast that he didn't even notice his own tears.

134

Chapter Thirteen

DAN did not stay at Ittai's after all. With Uncle Joseph bringing such breathtaking news, it was decided that Dan would remain at the shore house and celebrate the Sabbath with him there, before returning to work on the First Day. Both Uncle Joseph and Dan wished to know each other better, and who knew when such a chance may come again for either of them? These days, as the Dabab enviously declared, people seemed to run to and fro upon the earth as they never had before, and nobody could be relied on to remain in the same place from one week to the next!

But there must always be work before leisure, especially on the Sixth Day, so Anna having dried her joyful tears and wrung as much information out of Joseph as she could, finally hurried back to the Hollow with her heart on wings, exulting in the good news she would tell Etta and Marta. Meanwhile, Dan took off eagerly to seek out Caleb, who was to share the Sabbath with them.

Samuel's Eli was always very affable about relieving the old shepherd on such days. He was most attentive in coming to Banayim (quite unnecessarily) to report to Caleb afterwards, before accompanying him back to the flock which he had temporarily left to one of his brothers. This peculiar and time-wasting habit was a puzzle to Dan for a long time, until he realised that Eli never came straight to the house, and never left by the most direct route either. It usually happened that some small business must take place at the hamlet itself. There would be a new bowl to buy from Ittai – perhaps a sack of sheep droppings to exchange for vegetables grown by Rachel's husband – goat curd to take to Marta – figs to buy from Old Zack – or fresh milk or cheese to deliver to Judith for little Thad. As a matter of fact, there was *always* something to deliver to Judith … Of course, the Dabab had noticed this before anyone, and Judith writhed under her insinuations.

"Thaddeus had better watch what is going on in his own house," she warned confidentially at the well. "A girl her age receiving young men while the master of the house is away … and very flushed and excited she looked, too."

Huldah's mother looked at her sideways. "Oh, do tell me, Rachel – I am so behind the times! Has custom changed so much lately that paying for cheese in a street doorway is considered to be 'receiving young men'?"

Rachel lifted her nose. "I saw him carry it into the house with my own eyes only last Sixth Day," she said primly, "and he did not come out again for a long time." She lowered her voice, "*And* there was a lot of bumping and giggling – even a little *screaming*! Then he came rushing out of the house and ran off!"

Widow Shana guffawed loudly. "Do you know what he was doing?"

"Well, I am not going to make baseless assumptions!" Rachel sounded horrified.

"Why change the habit of a lifetime?" muttered Huldah's mother as she hauled on the wet rope and dumped the leather bucket crossly into her pot.

136

"I know all about it," chortled the Widow. "He walked straight through the house from the front door to the back window, that's what. And if you ask me how I know, it's because I was outside it in the courtyard, making some of that noise myself. Thaddeus boarded it up from the inside in one of his tempers before he left. All because the poor girl complained about the shutters banging all night, and he refused to fix them."

Rachel looked at her disdainfully. "And who, pray, was giggling and screaming while you were thumping on shutters instead of knocking on doors like any civilised person?"

"If you will kindly let me finish, Rachel," Widow Shana said majestically, reverting to the ladylike manners she aspired to whenever she could remember, "you will also understand why Judith looked flustered, and why Eli went inside at all. That fat little menace of a Thad had climbed into the window sill from the outside, closed the shutters on himself and latched them fast. The child was completely locked in – boarded on one side, shuttered on the other – and he seemed to think it was all just a huge joke. Judith and I had been trying to coax him to undo the latch, but he just kicked and laughed and said some very unchildlike things."

Rachel narrowed her eyes. "And where did he pick those up, I wonder! You still have not explained the screaming."

Widow Shana elbowed her aside as she clutched for the bucket in her turn, and carelessly allowed some to spill in Rachel's direction. She dropped it into the well and as it hit the water with a muffled hollow splash she turned on the dampened Dabab.

"Let me tell you, Rachel, that if you had ever offered Judith some company, or minded that child while she had a moment's peace, you would not need to ask about the screaming! Young Eli prised open the boards enough for Judith to get her arm in and flick up the latch. ... and little Thad, whose temper matches his father's, *bit* her – hard! She screamed, he screamed back – I snatched the shutters open and pinned them – and Eli, bless him, ran outside and hauled the boy out of the window before he could try any more tricks."

"A plausible story," Rachel shrugged, "if oddly *complicated*."

Widow Shana snorted and dragged up another bucket, just as Judith herself came to the well. The girl preferred to be late in the hope of missing the Dabab, but sometimes she just had to take a deep breath and brave her anyway. If there was any gossip to be told, Rachel was capable of loitering there half the morning.

The other women stood aside for her sympathetically and Widow Shana winked at her. Judith smiled gratefully and lifted the jar from her head. Her sleeve fell back, and there on the smooth underside of her dark forearm, was an angry red bruise embedded with the purple imprint of two broken semi-circles.

Rachel eyed them narrowly, but even she could see these teeth marks were far too small to be Eli's, so she said nothing. Now, if it had been *Eli* who was bitten (especially by Judith!) it would have been *far* more interesting. She shook her head disapprovingly, out of habit, and marched off, thus missing the most exciting news of all – the arrival of a mysterious, wealthy-looking stranger to the Travellers' House. This information was in fact brought to the well by Judith herself, who being the last to arrive, had actually seen him open the door to Dan, and was now in the rare and delightful position of being the centre of rapt attention.

The poor Dabab would have been quite crushed had she realised all she was missing. Even while Rachel, with a doubtful air, was relaying the Widow's explanations about Eli and Judith to her husband, the news about Uncle Joseph – and Loukanos – was already outside the village. Fleet-footed Dan was only three hills away from the painfully neat and lonely house where Caleb lived with his daughter Extra Pressings, and his son-in-law. Dan remembered vaguely that Extra Pressings' real name was Keren, but nobody ever seemed to remember the name of her dull little husband, who was such a shadow of a man that he hardly seemed real. But the only name which was on Dan's mind right now was "Loukanos!" and joyfully he shouted it as he ran, varying his yells with a song he sang lustily, with breathless jerks as he hopped over rocks and swerved around trees.

God has turned my mourning into dancing for me

He has taken off my sackcloth!

He has turned my mourning into dancing!

It was a long time since he had felt so happy – and now, that letter he must write to Johanan would have to be extra long!

Anna, however, who had flown home to the clearing with a hope-lightened heart, met an unexpectedly quiet reception. She could hear Etta's voice off in the scrub, patiently supervising the twins at the privy, and smiled. It was their latest accomplishment, and despite the tediousness of forever hurrying them there, it must be encouraged! Inside the long room, Marta was sitting cross-legged with the baby in her lap, holding his tiny ankles in one hand, silently cleaning him with olive oil. Her deft, practised movements were as gentle as ever, but where were the giggles, babbling nonsense and tickles which were the usual conversation while he was being changed? As Anna opened the door, Marta's enquiring eyes were weary.

"Stop! Anna! Don't come in."

"Don't be silly, Marta, I've changed him myself before now! Oh! of course – how strange that once I'm home I keep forgetting about isolation. Well, I will stay here at the door, though right now I'm so happy I'm longing to hug anyone or anything!"

"Of course, it is a heart-warming thing for you to see your kind uncle after so many years," Marta acknowledged quietly, patting fine-sifted myrtle leaf powder gently onto the curd-soft skin.

"Oh, Marta, that is only the half of it! Just wait till I tell you!"

Anna stopped, realising that something was not right with Marta's flat response. She was enveloping Shuni's tiny hips in a precious square of fine cloth folded with loose lambswool, as expertly as ever. But there was no noisy bubble blowing, or rapturous toe kissing … not a single adoring smile or playful word.

"But – what is it, my dear friend? Why this sudden change in your spirits? This morning you rose from your prayers with a determination to be as cheerful as you could, until we found a physician. Are you more sad than yesterday? Is the baby sick? Are you missing Ittai? Are you in pain?"

Marta bit her lip and seemed reluctant to answer. She wrapped Shuni into a straight cocoon with swift, practised movements, tied the swaddling bands and tucked the ends carefully at his side where they could not press on his bulging little stomach. It was not until she had laid him in his basket that she turned to Anna and pulled up her sleeves.

"Look at my arms."

Anna came close, both of them forgetting her promise to stay by the door, looking carefully at the inside of Marta's forearms and elbows, where the fine brown flesh was not as sun-darkened as the rest. Deep red spots sprinkled the skin.

140

"And here …" She pulled open her gown to reveal a speckling of larger marks spreading from the base of her throat down to her breastbone. "And look … on my legs. No, not the bruises, I'm always getting those, they're nothing. You see the spots?"

Anna did – she returned her friend's look of dismay.

"Are they bites? Do they itch?"

"Not now, but this morning they did. I was lifting both the twins at once when I had a sudden tingle in my arms and legs and I itched for nearly an hour afterwards – that's why I looked in the first place. You can imagine my shock … but there's no irritation now, at all." She pressed the marks experimentally with her thumb. "They're not bites – I'm sure of it. I'd notice if that many fleas or ants or gnats bit me, don't you think? And the children are unmarked."

"A rash? Nettles? Something you ate? You haven't been using any of that awful soap Zaccheus was selling last Passover?"

"That soap? On my body?" Marta was shocked at the thought. "Certainly not! It took the skin off my hands when I used it for the washing, and that was bad enough. This is not an ordinary rash – the flesh is smooth, and see, the spots don't fade when pressed, any more than these bruises do." She looked at her friend imploringly, and the tears trembled in her eyes. "Oh, Anna! It doesn't look good for me, does it?"

Anna frowned. "I don't understand this. If it's a leprosy, would not the red spots be raised and in the white flesh? Lift your hair, Marta and let me look …"

Marta obliged, and Anna carefully inspected the back of her neck.

141

"Here, too, these white patches are unmarked and smooth – no roughness or inflammation – in fact, the skin really looks very healthy. All your skin does, Marta, apart from that collection of bruises ... you really must not let the children climb you like a tree. I could swear Abigail has a grip like a crocodile, and Isaac kicks like a mule." She shook her head. "You don't look sick, either, though your eyes are rather bloodshot – but it's probably just new-baby tiredness. As for the rest of it – well, I don't know. I just don't know *enough*. But, dearest Marta, let us not be too quickly downcast, because I have brought such very good news! I believe that soon we may have the very help we need to understand your condition."

She smiled encouragingly and Marta's eyes lifted hopefully.

"You have found a priest? A physician? Tell me at once, Anna!"

"What do you think?" Anna's own eyes suddenly filled, and her voice broke. "Oh, Marta – Loukanos is here in the land! And Uncle Joseph has been with him for more than a year!"

"What?" gasped Marta, forgetting her own troubles immediately in her surprise. "Where has he been? And why? And where is he now?"

"Ah! That's what we all want to know!" Anna admitted, blinking away her tears. "But even Uncle Joseph does not know everything."

Marta's questions were about to be repeated by an incredulous Old Caleb, who had been sent out by his daughter to weed her vegetable patch, only to be discovered there by an excited Dan. Extra Pressings was bent over her kneading but while she pushed and pulled her dough firmly, she was eyeing them sourly through the window, watching Dan jumping up and down around her father, who had stopped his work, and was chuckling happily. Really, the fuss that boy made of him, she would never understand.

142

She hoped he would not be expecting any lunch! The olives and figs were already counted out for the day, and if he stayed, he could just share the cold lentils put aside for the old man, that's what. Dan was Caleb's guest, not hers, after all.

Suddenly Dan bolted towards the house and rushed inside, nearly knocking her off her feet with a daring hug around her bony frame.

"Mercy on us!" she gasped in outrage, her hands still stuck in dough. "Is the sky falling? What do you mean by this, young man?"

Dan grinned and gave her gaunt cheeks a smacking kiss, once, twice, thrice.

"Rejoice with me, daughter of Caleb!" he laughed. "That which was lost has been found!"

"What in the world do you mean, Impudence?" she huffed, slapping the bread and refusing to smile. It had been many a long year since anyone had surprised her with such a spontaneous expression of warmth.

"It's my Uncle Loukanos!" Dan replied gleefully. "He has been lost to us for two years, and now we know he is in the Land – so we have some hope of finding him again! My mother and aunt are full of gladness! And so am I!"

"Well!" Extra Pressings sniffed. "I am rejoiced to hear it, I'm sure, for all your sakes. Though why you need to indulge in these extravagant gestures to a married woman is beyond me. You need to watch yourself, young man. You're not a child any more, and you may find yourself in trouble one of these days."

Dan sobered at once. "I ask your pardon," he said humbly, though his eyes still danced. "You are right. I have forgotten my manners – but you know," he added somewhat disingenuously,

"Old Caleb is so much a grandfather to me, that I forget you are not an aunt."

"H'mph!" retorted Extra Pressings, who saw straight through him, but nevertheless was not displeased with the compliment. "Funny I've not heard you call him *Sabba Caleb* yet, then. Well, since you're here, you may as well make yourself useful. I need more dried dung for the fire – it's around the back – and you can fetch me a fresh dipper of water while you're at it."

Dan dutifully obliged, and then escaped to share all he knew (and all his speculations concerning what he didn't) with Old Caleb, who was still happily shaking his grizzled head over the extraordinary news.

Had they but known it, the one person who could satisfy all the eager questions to which they had only half the answers, was a mere two days' journey to the north.

Chapter Fourteen

A CLUSTER of kneeling women was intently rubbing and slapping heavy wet garments on smooth rocks bordering a tiny stream which escaped slyly from the edge of a great spring. Water which was once snow on the mountain high above, surged up relentlessly from a gaping cave in the cliff, sliding heavily through the deep, deceptively calm pool for some distance before brimming over a ledge to thrash itself into roaring life on rocks below. The crash of this nearby cataract kept the women quieter than usual, and each was for a time involved with her own thoughts. With their bare heads, exposed arms, and skirts tucked up to their knees, it was not surprising that they jumped when an unexpectedly masculine shout of laughter echoed off the rocks. Bina gave a squeak and scowled.

"I do wish you wouldn't do that, Marah!" she complained. "You know I never get used to it – especially when nobody has even said anything funny."

She looked around nervously. Pagan shrines and niches studded the cliff face not far away, and their secluded stream might at any time be invaded by unwelcome visitors.

"I'm sorry!" Marah sniffed experimentally at the well-pummelled coat in her strong hands and her deep husky laugh bellowed out again. "I was just thinking of what Fisher Shimon's wife said to me the last time I saw her. She told me that I must still have a devil or two left in me if I was mad enough to wash his clothes – I'd *never* get the stink of fish out of them – and if I *did*, she would never forgive me, because it would make her look lazy!"

She grinned at the others. "I will have to avoid her next time we're in Capernaum – I really think the smell has gone at last, now that it's not being added to all the time."

The women giggled, even Bina, who was not sure that it was in the best of taste for Marah of all people to refer to devils and madness.

Jael sat back on her heels and stretched her neck and shoulders with a rueful grimace. "You need more than a cold stream to get stale rank sweat out of wool, though. I do wish men would realise they are *not* saving us work by hanging on to dirty clothes for weeks on end – they're only making it harder."

The others made sympathetic noises. It was a common complaint, but as such, nobody really expected it to change. They had all heard it from their mothers, and no doubt one day their daughters would be saying it too. Any woman who could educate her menfolk properly deserved fame in the age-old battle of the washing! Meanwhile, everyone knew you almost had to steal the clothes off a man's back before he would part with them.

Marah and Shoshana began wringing out together, twisting the opposite ends of each heavily sodden garment until it formed a bulky rope, and no more drops could be forced from the thick fabric. Briskly flapping and tugging and smoothing it into shape they draped their washing to dry over sunny rocks and bushes while Bina gave a final wet smacking to a thin tunic and wrung it expertly in her cold-reddened hands. The lightweight linen was fine enough not to need two of them for the job.

"At least this one is easy," she admitted, shaking it out approvingly to inspect its new cleanliness. "For one thing, I never get it too late – so there's one man in the world who *does* understand something about a woman's work – and for another, having no seams means it dries faster."

Marah reached out to finger the cloth. "Really nice workmanship, isn't it? I've never been good at the loom, myself – I've always had enough trouble weaving in the loose threads of my life!" She chuckled.

There she went again! Bina looked around for a place to spread her washing, trying not to glance at the long scars on Marah's forearms – some faded to white, some still red or purple. Bina saw miracles every day, but when a lame man walked, or a dumb child spoke, it was very obvious. She was still not completely easy around a woman like Marah, who, cured or not, remained unconventional and unpredictable.

"Here, Bina, I'll hang it out," Marah offered, adding mischievously, "Don't worry, I may still be mad enough to wash Shimon's fishy clothes, but I really don't see the dead walking any more, or – " She looked up, and paled. "I *don't* see the dead walking any more …!" she whispered fiercely.

The others, who had not caught her last words, followed her gaze, but by then Marah had relaxed, and the colour flooded back to her face, as she recognised the tall figure which had suddenly appeared high up on the hill path. She shook herself in annoyance. The stab of panic was a mere reflex, a hangover from the past. There was no need for fear – she knew she was well, entirely well.

"Ah! Your strange Greek friend!" the women teased, mistaking her breathless confusion for heart-flutterings, as the man above them raised a hand in greeting. "Go to him, and shoo him away. Do you think we want him to see us half naked?"

"Do you think he'd even notice?" Marah retorted, quickly recovered. "He's a doctor, isn't he?"

Jael snorted. "He's also a man. And even if he doesn't care, we do. So get rid of him."

They all burst out laughing.

"Go on, Marah," Shoshana said encouragingly. "It's you he wants to talk to – and we have nearly finished here. We will chaperone you from a distance, and if we hear any screams over the noise of the waterfall, we'll come running."

"Screams from him, that is," added Jael rudely, and they shrieked with laughter again.

Marah scrambled her clothes to modesty and shook her finger at them.

"You women have no finer feelings!"

She ran off lightly, sandals dangling from her hand, leaving her friends to exchange significant smiles.

The tall man looked at her disapprovingly as she approached. "Your shoes, Marah. Put them on – there are scorpions in these rocks."

"Greetings, my friend, and blessings and peace to you, too!" she answered with a touch of sarcasm. Nevertheless she leant down obediently to do his bidding, fumbling with her stiffly cold fingers.

"Here, let me," he said impatiently, bending to tie the laces. Marah raised her sharp black eyes and gave him a Look, and he stepped back.

"I beg your pardon. I am too hasty, as usual …" He passed his hands through his unruly dark hair and stared at the scene below, filling the silence with an uncharacteristically aimless remark. "Washing for the Twelve again?"

"Thirteen," she corrected. "But not all at once, thankfully."

"Thirteen, yes, but only half of them today, I see … apart from all your own things …"

He seemed to be avoiding the very conversation with her he had sought, murmuring inconsequential remarks almost to himself.

"I do believe I can tell for whom you women are nobly freezing your hands … the two striped robes are the ben Zebedees', short and bold like them … The big coat on the rocks will be Shimon's of course, Fisher Shimon, I mean … The embroidered sleeves on that tunic would be Levi's touch of luxury … and the plain linen belongs to Jude the Kerioth – ascetic as the man himself."

"Right except for the last," Marah commented, unsurprised at his discernment. She knew he had an artist's eye for detail. "Jude does have one very like it, except thicker, with seams. That one is woven in one piece. It's Jeshua's, the easiest to wash by far, and it dries quickly too."

Fisher Shimon and the ben Zebedees had gone on a private errand with the Teacher, and the women were hoping everything would be dry enough to wear by the time they returned and had to move on. At this time of year, the weather was unpredictable, and the mountain looming behind them produced its own unpredictable patterns of cloud and wind.

Her companion did not appear to be listening. He was staring at the white linen tunic splayed on the glistening black rock beside the sparkling stream, a striking contrast of light and shade, texture and hue, worthy of painting. Of course, people did not paint such objects, but it would be a challenging exercise, even if it was mistaken for the Greek letter *Tau* – or an artistically conceited way of writing the figure 300. From this height it reminded him of a cross-road marker. But was something less superficial was rising from submerged depths of memory … *Ah!*

"*Woven in one piece*," he muttered to himself, chewing his lip. "Yes, surely that's what it is – a linen ephod … *a priest's garment …*"

He did not realise he had spoken aloud until Marah stared at him.

"What nonsense are you talking, my Greek friend? Does a man's tunic change his tribe? Jeshua is our anointed King, not our priest – though what he is to you I have yet to understand. In any case, what is on your mind? Did you beckon me from my work just to discuss washing? If you have something to say, please do so at once."

Loukanos, for of course it was he, took a sharp breath. This woman was so different, he was never sure how to take her. She was not a girl, timid and giggling, or a woman who was shy and subservient – or modestly unassertive as a dutiful daughter in Israel was urged to be. Neither was she was bold, coarse, or self-seeking like many of the rich Roman matrons he dreaded treating. She was intelligent, direct, thoughtful – more like his sister Anna, but with a wild streak of something else he couldn't quite put his finger on. Perhaps that was why he constantly forgot to observe the normal conventionalities. He sighed, and held out a hand.

"Come, Marah All-Alone, walk with me. I have sought you simply for congenial company, because at the moment, I too am feeling All-Alone."

Marah declined his hand, and he felt her unspoken reproach for the contrived elegance and pathos of his invitation.

"Please remember *I* am not Grecian," she said firmly, deliberately fastening her veil over her face. "I will walk with you and welcome, but you will give nobody cause to talk, if you please. And take care what you call me. I have told you before, that since I was healed I will not answer to that name, because it is no longer true."

"It was habit – I meant no offence," Loukanos growled. "With so many Marahs and Mariahs and Maris and Miriams in this unimaginative country you still need a surname. If you reject the old, you must find a new."

Marah relented. "True," she agreed. "There must be at least three of us in our group already. Well, Magdala is where I lived most of my life, even though it is not where I was born. So surname me thus, if you need to distinguish me from the others."

He did not say to her, that to him she needed no distinguishing.

"Very well, Magdalan," he answered abruptly. "If *you* are not All-Alone any more, then *I* am even more so. Perhaps I have taken on some of your old demons."

Marah looked at him sideways, but his face was sober, and he was not seeking sympathy.

He strode ahead without looking at her, as she asked, "Why do you say that? And where are we going?"

151

"Downstream a little way … there's a track here bypassing the pool and saving a rougher walk. I set a fish trap yesterday, and it may hold our supper, if we're lucky."

She followed obediently. Etta had told her all she knew of Loukanos of Philippi, and there was no doubt he had learned a variety of such skills as a young runaway, let alone in his adult travels. Marah made her way down the narrow path behind him, ducking under branches, stepping over rocks, silently marvelling at this strange man, though it would not do to let him see her admiration.

Instead she repeated, "Why do you complain that you too are All Alone? How can you say so, while you frequent the company of those who follow the Son of the Most High?"

Loukanos stopped and turned around. "Yes, but *is* he? Even to ask the question in such company shows that I am indeed all alone among you, in the way I think, the way I doubt, and the confusion in what I feel."

"Then why seek my company in particular, since my own loneliness and doubts and confusion have gone?"

"Gone, but you remember the pain of it, and you are not ashamed to speak of those things. In this you are unusual – and valuable."

Marah shrugged. "If I forget what I was, how can I be grateful for what I am now? It would be foolish to pretend there was no chaos in my mind, and equally foolish to be ashamed of it. I am not sure why this makes me 'valuable', but in any case, I am in no danger of forgetting, and neither is anyone else. Especially not you," she added wryly.

No danger of forgetting, indeed.

As if it had not been enough to be in turmoil of spirit as he reluctantly retraced his steps back from his initial flight to Samaria … as if it had not been enough to be driven again to the Jordan by the goads of his intellect, first to lurk in the crowds around the Baptiser, then to mingle with the edges of the growing throng around the Nazarene … to daily feel more like a madman himself as he argued with his own reason, and fought to reconcile what he preferred to believe with what he really *saw* … with his craving for freedom wrestling the call to submit – a call as unbearable as it was undeniable …

As if that had not been enough … as if to mock his mental misery, he found his actions mirrored by a lone woman. He had seen her often in the crowd, he knew she had long since been immersed by the gaunt prophet – he had observed her slowly and obediently transfer attention from the fading Nazirite to the rising Nazarene … but she hung back, as he did, avoiding attention.

Loukanos believed that she was a seeker too, though with different doubts and fears. But there came a day when accidentally she met his glance, and suddenly her face changed and her deepset eyes lit with a fixed and piercing gleam. From that moment she became his shadow, lingering furtively wherever he turned, whispering frantically to herself with wild looks … creeping closer and closer until he could hear her constant babbling murmurs, "It is he! It is he! I knew it! Yes – he is alive! Oh, praise the Eternal – he lives! He lives!"

The reason for her earlier self-effacement now became clear – the poor woman had suffered a tragic bereavement, which had unhinged her mind, and left her living in constant fear of erratic visitations of madness. Loukanos watched her warily, but for some time she did not speak to him directly. Until one day, while he was still pondering whether to avoid or distract her, she staggered towards him through the press of people, with an odd, unbalanced gait, reached out – touched his clothes – fixed him with a burning look, clutched his hands, and suddenly threw clinging arms around his neck, kissing him repeatedly, crying incoherently.

"Yes, it is! Yes! My brother! My darling! Oh, God is good! Forgive me! Can you forgive me? Let me hold you! You are alive! My darling, forgive me! Oh, please forgive me! My brother! My little brother!"

Around them the apprehensive crowd thinned hastily. Half-crushed by her embrace, Loukanos, however, was not afraid, but still he thanked the stars that this madwoman's frenzy was of happiness and not rage. He drew her away to a quieter place, calming her, soothing with gentle words which echoed her own, remembering with chagrin a certain vial of *mandragora*, now uselessly gathering dust with other remedies in a house half a week away.

"Yes, yes, forgiven – you are forgiven!" he said quietly. "There is nothing to fear! Dear sister, all is well! God is good. Here I am, alive and safely with you … hush, now. Be still!"

So he had spoken kindly to her as she had clung to him deliriously, her eyes blazing with a weird joy.

"Ah! Praise the Eternal – he forgives me! Now I can rest! My darling – Oh, how glad I am I recognised you! I have seen you so often, tall and dark and slender as you are now – your curling hair – the ringlets of your beard – oh, yes, I knew you would look so when you grew! All the times and all the places I have seen you, followed you, longing to embrace you! But always you eluded me – or threw me off with harsh words, declaring you were not he! How that hurt me! But it was not your fault, I know – I had to atone, I had to be punished ... but now you remember! And you forgive me! Praise God! I did not mean to harm you, my precious little brother, only to save us both! But the soldiers have gone, and you are grown now, and just look at you! So fine and handsome a man, my darling! We must run and tell *Abba* and *Amma* at once! They must know everything! They must know you forgive me!"

"Yes, yes, of course ... come, we will tell them together ... yes, give me your hand. But tell me where we will find them, my sister ..."

And as he watched her intently, her eyes wavered, flickered – confusion gathered in her face – she stammered – flailed stiffly, and slid into an unconscious heap at his feet, lying awkwardly on sharp stubble and stones, her mouth slackly open and the whites of her eyes glaring blindly below twitching eyelids.

Loukanos acted with professional swiftness. He rolled her heavily limp body into a more natural position, scraped away the stones which were digging into her unresisting flesh, pillowed her head on his coat, draped her veil to protect her from flies, sun and curious eyes – and stood up, grimly.

Clever medicine! he sneered at himself. Once more the physician of Philippi was helpless before a malady he could not even touch, and suddenly he was angry – very angry. He stormed back through the crowd, searching grimly for any one of the twelve who were always present. At last he gripped the arm of a graceful young man in a simple tunic who turned to him with a flash of annoyed surprise, instantly suppressed.

"You!" Loukanos barked. "Come with me! The Kerioth, aren't you?"

"I am," he replied coolly, following without protest. "I recognise you too – the fringe-dwelling Greek with a conscience, who cannot stay and will not go."

"You can know nothing of me." Startled, Loukanos replied shortly.

The Kerioth smiled and nodded back towards the tightest part of the crowd.

"*He* knows what he sees in men's hearts. And *we* know what we see in their faces, day after day. And what I see now is that you are angry, and you want something which you will not beg of me, but demand."

"You are a perceptive man. Come with me."

He strode back to where he had left the unconscious Marah, and lifted the shielding cloth, impatiently brushing ants from her pale face. Small red welts showed she had already been bitten.

"You see this woman? Determined, dedicated, ready to serve your master – but plagued with phantoms which pounce on her from the shadows of her mind. She can neither go back nor forward. Do something for her if you have any compassion. A physician can do nothing – nothing."

Marah was stirring, returning to consciousness – she winced, rubbed the marks on her cheek, turned over, and saw the two men above her. Staring from one to the other with frightened eyes, she sprang to her feet.

Loukanos held her steadily, but she looked at him blankly now, no longer seeing a dead infant grown to manhood and walking out of a distant evil night of *gladius* blade and gore-slashed bodies. The bitter-sweet illusion had fled, and it was a strange tight-lipped Greek who stood before her. As she realised what had taken place, she dropped her eyes to hide the tears of resignation.

"Did I – have I – hurt – or offended – anyone?" she asked humbly.

Loukanos wanted to shake her. Why live like this if there was a better way?

"Woman, do you not believe in your *Christos?*" he demanded roughly. "Do you not believe he can release you as well as the hundreds of others? Or do you believe you are too hard for him to help?"

"Why, no, no!" she stammered, grasping for comprehension. "He is the One – the son of God most High - he has the power!"

"Then why have you not gone to him for healing?"

Marah bit her lip and gestured helplessly. "There is no end to the desperate people here … sick … agonised … crippled, blind, lepers, the truly lunatic! But I am strong, and healthy, and the great Johannes himself found me sane enough for baptism … How can I push in front of these others … when my body is sound, and my mind so often clear …"

"*Often* is not enough for a whole lifetime," Loukanos snapped. "Is it?"

"No!" she cried with sudden passion. "No, it is not! You are right!" She clasped her hands in supplication. "What use is baptism and remission of sins if I cannot leave my past with its demons behind me! If I cause fear to others?" Now there was hope flooding into her eyes! "The Teacher is *my* master too, and surely he will release me to serve him better – not with silent adoration or flattering speech but with my hands, my feet, my purse!"

The younger man gazed at her with waking interest.

"Acknowledge *your* need of him before you tell the Teacher what you will do for him," he warned her with an encouraging smile. "Only then can you give freely, with due humility."

Impatiently Loukanos released Marah to Jude the Kerioth, challenging him with a glance, and Jude nodded in understanding.

To Loukanos he said, "She will see him this very hour, Grecian." He turned to the dishevelled woman. "Come."

No, neither of them would forget.

Chapter Fifteen

THE rushing of the waterfall, punctuated by occasional peals of laughter from the women at their work, became muffled as Loukanos and Marah pushed through the overgrown track to a large pool which halted the busy offshoot of another crystal stream. Loukanos pulled up a strange contraption of netting and sticks which was his own invention. It looked peculiar, but inside were three good sized fish, at which Marah raised her eyebrows admiringly. He sank the trap back into the water.

"Aren't you going to take them out?" she asked in surprise.

"Soon. Let them live a little longer."

Of course – he wants to talk, Marah thought rather impatiently. Why did a man always believe a woman must be glad to drop everything and listen to him, no matter what else she had to do? But suddenly she caught herself – and was ashamed. Had she too not longed for someone – anyone! – to listen in her hours of bleak loneliness and turmoil? And how often was convention ever side-stepped to give an unmarried woman the chance of intelligent conversation with a truly disinterested man? *I should be grateful!* Neither the Baptiser nor the Teacher himself had enough hours in a day to hear the private stories which had brought all their

159

thousands of followers to them, and in any case their message urged attention not on people's past, but on their future.

Even more – had not Loukanos quietly listened to her many a time? Stony faced, it must be admitted, but still he had listened in the elated dizzy days after her healing, when the released memories which poured over her, whether sweet, sour, bitter, or salted with tears, demanded an audience. Often she felt that she was telling the tale of another person's life, and was hearing it for the first time herself. But he heard her patiently, and did not shun her. He was a Greek, an outsider – he was safe, he would not judge.

She had a sense deep down that even had she not been healed, he still would not have judged her. He did not recoil when she spoke of cutting her unfeeling flesh, both reliving and releasing the horrors of Herod's purge – when she had silently endured the blade which sliced into her hiding place, the night she had unwittingly smothered her infant brother into the silence of death, while her defiant parents met the swords of blood-frenzied men. He had only touched the ribbed scars lightly, compassionately, with warm fingers, and asked brief questions about how she treated the wounds.

His eyes betrayed no disbelief when she haltingly described how her slaughtered mother and father had come in and out of her visions to reproach, to condemn, to forgive, or to plead with her to save her newborn brother, to save all the little ones. This Greek needed no explanations for her behaviour towards him, and no apologies for the repentant kisses she had thought herself to be lavishing on a dead babe now grown and living. He listened. He nodded. He showed no surprise. Of course – he was a doctor.

160

More than two years ago, Old Etta – and Anna – had told him something of Marah All-Alone, and how her solitary life suddenly became chaotic after a severe fever – but he had never thought to meet her for himself. They had told him too of the strange sixth sense which once led her to birth chambers, begging mothers, midwives, even strangers, to let her safely hide the newborns ... of her fits of black despair ... the slashing of her arms ... her sudden fierce rages ... the trances ... the unpredictable coming and going of fractured memory ... and the eerie, transient conviction that the dead lived.

He had known of her as a curious case, a smitten woman with a searching heart, and a startling, uproarious laugh; but she had remained merely an intriguing collection of afflictions – until she stood before him, her misplaced humility aggravating him beyond bearing. Demons? She *had* all of them, and *was* none of them. She was a vibrant, passionate, courageous woman, whose qualities ought not to be wasted in living half a life; and since he could not help her she must be provoked to help herself.

As Loukanos sank his fish trap back into the pool, he wondered at how quickly the time had passed since that strange meeting. For over a year now she had been free and whole – and he had seen her flourish in the service and companionship of those who were closest to the Nazarene they called their Master, their Teacher, their own Rabbi.

Loukanos turned away from the wrinkled water, reflecting bitterly on the irony – Marah was now the one who was the clear-headed, the calm-eyed, the one with direction and purpose, while he who once believed he was all of those things, was anything but. He did not doubt that she was cured, but then many a disturbed woman had enough faith for the impossible – often that

161

was part of her problem – and he had seen faith healings before under the banners of every deity from Macedonia to Alexandria … and recently, even some in Samaria, performed by a sorcerer who hinted that he had the power of many spirits, while laying claim to no particular god at all.

Loukanos tossed his thick cloak over a boulder which still held the day's meagre warmth and sat down, leaning his back against it, trying to order his restless thoughts. Marah hoisted herself nimbly to the top and sat there. Her feet accidentally brushed his shoulder and she tucked them up, wrapping them inside her skirts. Loukanos glanced back up at her with a frown.

"Of course, we Gentile dogs may bite," he snapped. "Are you so afraid of me?"

Marah stared at him in astonishment. "My feet are cold!" she expostulated. "And I hope I do not affront your honour by telling you that right now I am far more afraid of leeches than I am of *you* – Doctor Zeus!"

Afraid of Loukanos! After working among raucous soldiers in Tiberius? She could hold her offended pose no longer, and burst out with her full-throated laughter.

Loukanos bridled. "What do you mean – *Doctor Zeus?*"

"Such ignorance!" she mocked him. "Do you not know your own gods? Is not Zeus the Thunder God? How well the title suits you! But I do not mean to offend you, so perhaps I shall call you Doctor Thundercloud whenever you are so full of dark rumblings and flashes of lightning. You and the ben Zebedees can be triplets – all Sons of Thunder together, eh?"

"Most amusing!" He tried to sound sardonic, but she could just hear the smile he was trying to suppress.

162

Encouraged, she coaxed, "Come, Master Loukanos, this is not gracious behaviour from an educated man. You are agitated and prickly – more so than usual. When you have never been shunned, to call yourself a Gentile dog – as if you are a snarling scavenger outside city walls! – is to speak as a child. Almost I believe you are pouting."

Loukanos grimaced and shook his head. "Now there's a flattering image," he said distastefully, swatting a mosquito which was exploring his ankles, "especially for a man who prides himself on maturity. Or used to."

Marah rolled her eyes but said nothing, glad that while she sat behind him, at least her face was free to express her feelings. *Uphill work, this man!* But he was the one who had pushed her towards healing, and while she breathed she would urge him likewise. She had once unhappily asked Jeshua the Master himself, what more she could do to make this stubborn man believe.

He looked at her consideringly, and smiled slowly. Marah flushed.

"Forgive me, Teacher, I am being very stupid! If the power of God which you constantly demonstrate under his superior Greek nose will not do it …" her voice trailed away, and she laughed a little, shaking her head. "I did not mean to be so presumptuous … I felt only that I must try …!"

Jeshua leaned closer and tapped her on the wrists she had penitentially scarred.

"No-one can give to the Eternal the price for another's soul, Marah, and nobody can grow faith in any but their own soil."

She sighed. "I think I see what you mean." There was a pause. "I knew a soldier in Tiberius," she resumed quietly, "a drunkard –

163

who took the horrors, convinced that monstrous deadly spiders were in his food and water. He refused to open his mouth and in days was near death. His friends begged and pleaded, eating and drinking from the same vessels to prove it was safe, but there was no reasoning with his terror. They could not give him their faith."

"The power of reason alone will not prevail over strong emotion. What we feel, drives us harder than what we *know*."

"His friends had strong feelings too ..." She shuddered. "To save him they forced water down his throat ..."

"But he died anyway?" interrupted Jude, who had heard Marah's voice and slipped over to join the conversation as she began her story.

"Yes," she answered shortly. "His friends had drowned him."

She stared at the ground, compressing her lips. How well she understood the bitter grief – when the attempt to save, actually killed! The Kerioth was quick enough to see her withdrawal.

"A distressing story, Marah," he said gently. "But if the man was already marked for death, his friends did not create that destiny. How could they stand by when he was bent on such a foolish course? They intended the best for him – some choking and pain and anger, no doubt – but they meant for him to recover and thank them later when he was in his right mind again."

"No doubt," she repeated evenly, raising her eyes at last. He gave her a warm smile and wandered off, casually biting his nails.

Jeshua looked after him thoughtfully, then turned back to Marah.

"Reason, feeling, faith," he prompted.

164

She continued gratefully. "Thank you, Teacher. I can see that my Greek friend has a battle with his pride, and with following a Jewish Saviour, but I was sure reason would convince a man of learning like him – and yet he still has no faith! I don't understand how anyone could deny you are the Chosen of God, when clearly His spirit is with you, and with the twelve. How many of the prophets had disciples who also could work miracles? Now, you said reason alone will not triumph over feelings. But does not the power of reason itself produce equally strong feelings?"

"Therefore?"

"Therefore you have two strong emotions ... well, warring against each other ..."

"And ..."

"Oh, I see what you mean ... and therefore you have an even greater struggle." She fell silent for a moment, then asked passionately, "Then how does Reason ever win when it is opposed to Feeling? I can see that faith must be a union of both ... but when you are in the grip of them, feelings are so natural that they appear to be entirely reasonable in themselves! How do you distinguish true reason from mere justification?"

After all, who knew better than herself?

He nodded understandingly. "Falsehood itself may be transformed into a messenger of enlightenment."

"So, Teacher, help me to understand – what turns the balance towards Faith? Is it love? Is it learning? Is it earning merit? What must come first?"

The Teacher indicated two knots of people milling around on opposite sides of the street, where families were busily making their farewells before the next journey.

"Watch. Listen. Remember."

Marah obeyed. One wife was sobbing, gasping and wailing as if her heart was broken, though her husband had left and returned many times before in perfect safety. All the trials of her temporary widowhood rolled off her tongue and were lamented to the heavens. The children, the chickens, the neighbours, the lack of money, the loneliness, the burden – all seemed to outweigh the fact that her husband had been honoured by the Master to work at his side.

Over the way, outside a tiny bakery, stood a tight circle of small children clinging to the legs of a short, plump man, who had his arms around a short, plump wife. The most uxorious of the Twelve, the baker stood with her in silent communion. He was leaving in her care three sons and two daughters, as well as a querulous grandmother, a soured aunt, and a bad tempered father. There were no cures for *their* kind of misery. Marah looked at the couple with affection. They weren't called Twin One and Twin Two for nothing. Theirs was an unusually felicitous union. Until the Teacher had called, they had been inseparable, toiling together in their crowded bakehouse, sharing every trial from ungrateful relatives and burnt bread (or burnt fingers) to Bakers' Wrist, with self-deprecating jokes, sing-songs with the children, and endless discussions about the prophecies of Daniel and Zecharias.

"What do you see?"

Marah opened her mouth to describe the scene, but before the details could pour out, she recalled that she was looking for the answer to her own particular questions, and time was short. She narrowed her eyes in concentration.

"I see two things – on the one hand, selfish anxiety. And on the other, I see loving acceptance."

Just then the Twins' youngest child, a mere toddler, spied Auntie Marah sitting under the tree. An association which had earlier that day formed in his mind, between her presence and the production of juicy raisins, loomed large. He broke free and tore gleefully towards her at a furious waddle. At the last minute he took his greedy little eyes off her long enough to see the flash of teeth in a dark beard and realised that someone else was sitting with her in the shadows – the child hesitated, overbalanced, and promptly tripped over Jeshua's feet, to land face downwards in his lap.

Marah clapped her hand over her mouth, realising just in time that her roar of laughter would startle the little one even more, and it would never do if he wet himself in fright. Jeshua scooped the baby up, turned him over and laughed at him reassuringly, clapping the pudgy brown feet together and tapping out a counting rhyme on the grubby toes. In a moment the child lay chattering contentedly in his lap, joyously joining in the only word he knew of *Five Little Beans*.

"Beans!" he crowed at each eagerly anticipated toe pinch. "Beans!"

The young man they called Teacher caught Marah's eye and smiled as he began to sway his knees up and down, giving the toddler a camel ride.

"Yes, you saw Anxiety and Acceptance. But which one fosters Faith?"

"Acceptance. The Twins surely show that," she replied.

"Acceptance is the start. You see this little one?" He nodded at the giggling child on his knees, who pitched and tossed and slid happily, totally relaxed despite the unfamiliar movement. "That's faith."

"And Loukanos, Teacher? I know he is in conflict."

"Then light is there, fighting darkness. But the battle can only be won if he surrenders."

All this went through Marah's mind as she gazed down on the dark head of the morose physician by the shaded pool. Had she herself not struggled with her private demons for years? And even after baptism, even after meeting the Teacher, had she not hesitated for a long while before surrendering totally? Even the prospect of a cure had half-frightened her – who would she be, what would she feel, what would be left, if the fears and terrors left her for ever? Oh, she needed far more patience! It was not for her to judge Loukanos any more than he had judged her.

You cannot give him your faith, Marah. You can only pray for him, and show him yours.

Chapter Sixteen

LOUKANOS and Marah remained immersed in their shared memories and unshared thoughts. The greenish, leaf-filtered light from the thicket over their heads, and the dark glinting of the pool at their feet, created a private grotto susurrating with the rush of the distant waterfall. Its muted sound swirled around them in the stillness, weaving a kind of half-world where time seemed to have been suspended. But back in Banayim, Dan's world was joyfully clear, bright, bustling, and bristling with possibilities.

He and Caleb had sung and shouted and stamped as if to demonstrate Marta's expression of "*legs, loudness, hair and horseplay*", all the way from Extra Pressings' roomy yet bare house to the tiny village of whitewashed huts. They had played toss-and-catch with a precious cheese, they had laughed themselves into coughing fits with ridiculous jokes, and concocted as many silly stories to explain why Loukanos was in the Land, as they had once made up serious ones to explain why he wasn't. They found Uncle Joseph in a similar good mood, having prevailed upon Ittai to join them later and share their rejoicing. Ittai at first was reluctant to accept, his own anxiety about Marta conflicting with any thought of celebrating, even for the sake of others. But Uncle Joseph was having none of it.

"You won't help your wife by wallowing in misery, young man," he told him kindly. "A cheerful countenance is the best ointment, and a husband must be strong enough for two – himself *and* the more delicate vessel, eh? – not to speak of the little half-pots in his care! So take heart."

His niece had already brought him word of Marta's puzzling spots, but Joseph had no intention of worrying poor Ittai even more today, when there was nothing he could do about it. Anna was with her, and old Etta, and in fact, whatever was or was not wrong with her, Marta would be benefitting from the rest and their company, even if she did have to talk through a window.

"There is every reason to hope," the large man continued, putting his arm around the young potter's back (the only clean place on his person) and giving him an encouraging shake. "Marta does not feel unwell at all, she has no pain, and she is certainly not dying. Loukanos is bound to know whether it is something simple, or something serious. If we do not find him within a week, or if he can not help her, we will seek the Nazarene at once. We may find even one of his men closer to home – of late, they too are preaching and have gifts of healing. So you see, we have not one, not seven, but *twice* seven men who can help your wife! This is a time to rejoice, not to mope! At what time in history has there ever been so much help for the poor and the sick? And just now, it is all here in Galilee! No need to cross oceans or deserts, eh?"

Ittai's eyes lit up gratefully. "Uncle Joseph, what a consolation you are! You are right! There *is* so much help close at hand, and as soon as Sabbath is over I will find it. Thank you, a thousand times."

"That's the way," Uncle Joseph beamed. "Now don't let me keep you from your work. I have already discussed this with Anna today, and she will have reassured Marta at once. Tonight your *dodi* will sing the prayers with her friends in good heart, trusting that answers will be found; and you will join our Sabbath table with gladness not guilt. Afterwards, my friend, don't go back to your empty house – stay the night! All of us will give praise and thanks, and pray together, then lay us down to sleep in peace with the angels of God around us, as the psalm says."

"Amen!" responded Ittai passionately. "Amen! And thank you!"

He watched as the elegant merchant turned and walked cheerfully up the narrow street, children pausing in their games to stare at his brilliant turban, the Dabab peering suspiciously from her doorway, and Judith snatching little Thad's hand just in time as he aimed a dusty clod at the colourful stranger. What an extraordinary person he was to find in such a humble little place! In his own way, he was as extraordinary as Loukanos. Yes, Anna bath Netzir had certainly brought some variety into the life of Banayim! And hope! After all, what was to stop Marta being cured as well as the next person? All over the land – and beyond! – thousands had been released from the misery and poverty which disease and deformity dragged in their grim wake.

The potter grinned triumphantly as he gave his doorstop (a badly warped pot) a more-enthusiastic-than-usual kick into place. He had kicked it many times before but unexpectedly the ugly thing shattered, revealing a heaped collection of enticing little treasures the children had obviously been secreting. The young father laughed as he squatted to lovingly gather up all the bright feathers, pretty stones and dried up, faded-crimson flowers from their broken pottery husk. Suddenly he paused as a striking thought illuminated him. Until now, he had never stopped to consider how many more thousands of other lives were *also* made free – husbands, wives, fathers, mothers, brothers, sisters! – all the crushing burdens of anxiety, grief and life-long care lifted from their own shoulders, as those they loved were made whole! Why, shouts of praise should be waking the very rocks all over the land!

He sprang to his feet, lifting his arms to heaven, his dirty fists raining tattered colour, his streaked face shining with a surge of gratitude.

"Praise the Eternal!" Ittai yelled loudly to the astonished street. "Praise Him all ye people! Praise Him for His Goodness!"

In the distance Uncle Joseph heard him and turned with a smile and a wave; and Ittai bounded back to stamp his clay with renewed vigour, not even feeling the piercing look the suspicious Dabab directed at his backbone. What had got into that man lately? *Sullen one minute, elated the next, and he on his own? And why is he waving all those feathers and things? Behaving like a savage!* Something was very peculiar there … well, she would just keep her eyes and ears open!

"So the potter will be here too, and it will be a Men's Sabbath tonight," Uncle Joseph told Dan and Caleb cheerfully. "But there's work to do before sundown, so let's get busy. I have a particularly tasty stew to prepare which needs time and loving attention."

"Oh, Uncle Joseph," Dan exclaimed with surprise, "but you have servants at home! Can you really make meals yourself, more than just bread and cheese?"

"Of course, Dan! Why, I taught my cook all she knows!" Uncle Joseph declared, rather less than truthfully. He turned and winked blatantly at Caleb, who chuckled. "But more importantly than that, my boy, a man who can't feed himself deserves to starve."

"Mother says that, too," Dan said wonderingly. "And *she* says it was a motto of Loukanos! But that's only half of it … the rest of it goes: *Servants come and servants go, but appetite lasts forever.*"

"Exactly right," replied Uncle Joseph, laughing, "and *he* learned it from *me*, in Cyprus! Well, it's good to know that something I taught him stuck, anyway. I can't count myself a total failure, then." He busied himself with opening various tiny bulging bags and little boxes, sniffing the spicy contents appreciatively. "And if you enjoy good food, why limit yourself to bread and cheese when you have a choice? Not I, when the good God has made everything to be received with thanksgiving."

"Amen," replied Caleb happily. He was going to enjoy this meal, and there would be enough of it to keep his stomach asleep all night, what's more. He was too loyal to say it aloud, but the days at home with his daughter left him fair pinched. It was her belief that the old did not need as much food as the middle-aged, though her hardy father did the work of men more than twenty years younger. "So, Master Joseph, how can I serve you? Shall I fetch water, or fuel, or have you some other task for me?"

"Bless you, old man, I tended to all that this morning, with enough for tomorrow as well, but I'll be glad of the extra hands in other ways. And speaking of cheese, Anna has told me you make something wonderful called *Festive Cheese* which I am eager to try. Just before we sit down, you must prepare some for us with that lovely one you brought me today, and we will have it nice and hot."

Caleb and Dan exchanged smiles. They had eaten many a rich chewy piece of *Festive Cheese* together since the cold morning it was invented by Dan's father when the three of them breakfasted at their campfire. As Ammiel had excitedly announced his decision to marry Anna, he had accidentally scattered bits of cheese on to the hot stones, where it sizzled temptingly. Dan had scraped it off to taste, and that one mouthful established it as a favourite treat from then on. Of course, they were not the first men ever to fry cheese, but the circumstances had made it special.

Before long the three of them were busy preparing the evening meal which could not be cooked after sundown. Joseph hunted out baskets from the storage corner, and packed them carefully with straw ready to keep the pots warm. Caleb – delighted to be in such merry company – insisted on grinding the barley, and a tedious job it was too, with enough bread needed to see them through until work could resume the next evening. Dan ran errands, scampering down the street for vegetables from the Dabab's husband, scrubbing and slicing under Uncle Joseph's direction, and thankful that Aunt Etta wasn't around to sing her usual doleful ditties about knives and fingers. It was an enjoyable novelty for Dan, whose home was exclusively female, and whose occupation was exclusively male. The two did not often overlap, and this was the first time he had found himself doing domestic things in purely masculine company.

Uncle Joseph turned rather officious as he cooked. He barged around the table briskly saying, "Excuse me! Excuse me!" with Dan and Caleb ducking his flying elbows; and he darted to and fro fetching this and that until his two minions, unable to read his mind and therefore constantly stepping into just the place he meant to go next, felt rather hounded. But fortunately they could all see the funny side, and good temper reigned as they worked.

Uncle Joseph finally took up his stand at the centre of the table, measuring large white beans, shredding dried fish, fussing with minute quantities of oil, salt, anise and sage, fastidiously compounding his stew. Caleb bravely volunteered to chop onions, and sniffled over them at one end of the table, while at the other

174

Dan whacked tops off leeks with gusto, peeled garlic, crushed coriander seeds and peppered his uncle with questions about Loukanos. Uncle Joseph obligingly repeated everything he had already told Anna, and undertook to tell all that he knew.

"I had made something of a pact with myself," he confessed, "that I would not allow family feeling – or anything else – to influence me, until I was absolutely certain about the Nazarene and his purpose. I took lodgings in Samaria where none would know me, and began my quest. For many months I was able to come and go, blending in with the mass of followers, whenever he was in the North, though avoiding Cana and this part of the Sea. I began to feel like a hunter in pursuit of prey … observing closely while trying not to be observed. I witnessed many of his miracles; but then, previously in Samaria I had also seen so-called miracles performed by another – a very popular sorcerer who claims God-like powers; though as something of a moveable feast he is not too specific about which deity has endowed him – conveniently leaving admirers to ascribe his gifts to their own gods, and thus equally enchanting everyone. As far as I know, this Simeon is still delighting his own devotees by conjuring tortoises out of turbans and healing hysterias. So, wonders on their own were not enough for me. I went further, pestering scribes for their scrolls, rabbis for their ideas, priests (when I could find any) for their opinions, and determined that I would not be swayed by emotional reaction. There have been false messiahs before now, and perhaps there will be false messiahs in future as well."

"True enough, Master Joseph!" Old Caleb burst out passionately, wiping away tears which may not have been from the onions, "but none ever was, and none other ever *will* be announced at birth by angels blazing in the night sky with a song of glory! I know – I was there!"

Joseph looked up and answered soberly, "Yes, Shepherd – so Anna wrote me over three years ago. This had much weight with me, I assure you, but not enough on its own. I was also keen to hear the Prophet Johannes."

Caleb nodded emphatically and swept his pile of onions into a bowl with a satisfied sniff. He rubbed his eyes with the back of his sleeve and looked around for another job, but his host waved a hand dismissively. "Just the bread now, but Dan can do that, can't you, Dan?"

"Yes – but you have no starter," the boy pointed out. "If you want it leavened, I will get some old dough from Marta. Oh, no, I can't," he remembered, even as he ran to the door. "I will ask Judith," he called over his shoulder, already half way down the street. "It won't take me a moment!"

To his surprise, Judith herself was walking towards him with a basket. Her rare smile appeared as she overheard his words.

"It won't take you even that long to ask me," she said cheerfully. "What do you need? Sour dough? Of course!" Young Thad was fast asleep after a busy day of tantrums and sulks, and though Judith knew he would wake refreshed enough to give her a tiring night, right now she was too relieved to care. She had slipped out, rejoicing in her brief freedom, with a handful of gifts for the visitors in a house where she always felt welcome.

"I will run straight back for some," she offered. "But first, Dan, do take this dried quince and pot of sesame paste to add to your Sabbath table. And look here – !" She showed him three sticky lumps wrapped in fig leaves.

"Honeycomb!" Dan's mouth watered. "But, isn't this what Caleb brought you for Thad – you know, from Eli?"

Judith lifted her chin rebelliously. "I am not going to reward that little monster with honeycomb. He is twice as naughty after eating it anyway, I've noticed. Neither am I saving it for his father, whenever he decides to come home – it will probably be full of ants by then." Tears of chagrin glinted in her tired eyes. "It's not often I have the chance to give anyone something worthwhile. I would much rather it went to your visitors."

"Silly Judith," Dan said with a grin, "do you really think Eli meant it for anyone but you? I don't."

Judith blushed hotly. "You are too young to know about such things," she said, attempting to flounce.

Dan laughed out loud. "I'm too old not to know," he retorted cheekily.

Judith giggled in spite of herself, but insisted, "No, Dan, you must take it. Please."

"I'll tell you what," Dan said consideringly. "There are three pieces here … give me one … that's right. Now, open your mouth – there!"

Taken completely off guard, Judith found the sweet morsel crammed between her teeth, oozing messily down her chin. Laughing, she snatched it into her mouth properly, licking her thin lips, wiping her chin with a finger and sucking it afterwards, her eyes rolling with surprise and delight – half outraged and totally enchanted with young Dan's daring. Oh, and the honey was so delicious! So sweet, so fragrant, and the wax so delightful to crush as it poured its richness onto her tongue! She closed her eyes and surrendered to the glory of it, luxuriating in every last, lingering swallow.

"Aunt Etta says you are far too skinny." Dan, watching her with satisfaction, became very paternal all of a sudden, as he accepted the remaining two packages obediently. "You need fattening up, and a lot more milk and honey."

Oh yes, Judith needed more milk and honey in her life, and in more ways than one, there was no doubt of that! But for now, the bit of nonsense Dan had just shared with her was as sweet and rare as the bliss of the honeycomb itself. Smiling she ran off to fetch Dan's sour dough with a skip in her step, so quickly that she almost beat him back to Joseph's door.

"Uncle Joseph," Dan called. "Here is some kindness from Judith your neighbour!"

The girl would have scurried away, but the large balding man was already in front of her.

"Greetings, young woman, blessings and peace on your house," he said genially. "Caleb and Dan and I thank you for these gifts!"

"Blessings and peace to you and yours, sir," she answered, ducking her still-sticky chin, of which she was suddenly painfully conscious. Oh, if only she had been in less of a hurry – it was too late now to lick it off properly or cover her face! Well, he was Anna's relative, probably Greek, so perhaps he wouldn't think the worst of her ... she edged away. "You are welcome among us."

There – now she could rush off again – and despite the humiliation of honey-smears she did so with a bubble of happiness lightening her bony body. Joseph watched after her thoughtfully. There was a tale to be told, somewhere there behind those shadowed eyes which lit up so gladly at the slightest courtesy. He might find it out some time, but not right now. Dan already had his hands in the barley flour and it was clear that he and Caleb were itching for the rest of Joseph's own story.

Chapter Seventeen

"NOW – the Baptiser, Master Joseph?" Caleb prompted eagerly. "What did you think of him?"

Uncle Joseph stirred the leathery white beans which had been soaking in salted water. Translucent membranes floated on the milky surface like the abandoned husks of mayflies which lived and died all in a long summer's day.

"I was too late. He was already imprisoned at Machaerus, and Herod's birthday came and went before I could even get close enough to the place."

"Herod's birth day. The Prophet's death day," Caleb shook his head. "What monster celebrates his own life with the death of a better man? Wickedness. Wickedness!"

"Yes, it was great wickedness," replied Joseph slowly, "but, you know, perhaps it would have been an even greater wickedness to have kept a man like that locked up for many years."

"Oh!" Dan's eyes widened at the horrible thought. He knew how he felt when he came in to his own house from several weeks in the pastures. There was something of a sense of being stifled – even in a familiar, welcoming room – which took a little wearing off every time. "Of course – he had lived all his life in the open – the fresh air, the sun, the wind! How terrible to be caged!"

Joseph nodded. "It was. It distressed him severely. The stale darkness, the mould, the stench, the stillness – the continual brief illusions of freedom as he was hauled out to preach for Herod's entertainment – imagine! Preaching to a man as flint-hearted as Pharaoh! – before being banished to chains and bars once more. It was no more than the life of a lion in a hideous Roman circus. It drained life and hope from him in the cruellest way, and tried his faith sorely."

He bent over the fire, dribbling more oil into the pungent onions, which were sizzling nicely with coriander and garlic, and stirring them vigorously. "You are wondering how I know all this? I have it from an eyewitness." He glanced over his shoulder, meeting Dan and Caleb's curious looks. "From Loukanos."

"What?" Dan breathed incredulously. "Our Loukanos?"

"Nobody else's," Joseph allowed himself a slight smile.

Caleb's mouth was hanging open in disbelief. "But how – where – when?" he stammered.

Dan's skin prickled. At last the mystery would be solved! "If he ran away, at least he ran back again!" he said, almost to himself.

"He did run away, Dan," Uncle Joseph replied. "When he left you at the Jordan, he was totally unnerved by what had happened there. It flew in the face of all he was certain of, and his reason was outraged by his eyes and ears. If it was a trick, he could not face his sister's shattered trust, and if it was not, he could not face his own. He took himself to Sychar and established a physician's circuit in the villages round about there – often following where the Sorcerer had effected a temporary cure in some poor soul with rheumatic joints, or painful cankers and the like. He even began to keep a journal, notes and sketches, of all he had seen and heard about the Baptiser and the Messiah since coming to the Land.

He hoped it might be a useful record to discredit their claims later. Useful to whom, I couldn't say – probably himself. Imagine his discomfort when the Nazarene and his men also turned up in Sychar for a while, and even Samaritans began accepting him as the Son of God!"

"So Master Loukanos had run away from the Messiah, and now he was being followed by him!" Caleb chuckled delightedly. "Truly God works in mysterious ways!"

"Verily! Well, my nephew was disturbed enough by this to take another tack," Joseph continued. "Eventually he bethought himself to go to the fortress of Machaerus, and if allowed to see the Baptiser in prison, he would question him closely, like a lawyer. He was indeed permitted to see Johannes. Having introduced himself to the authorities as a wandering physician he was almost dragged in to see him. The fact was, that Herod was rather worried by his captive's increasing sickliness, though he was not keen for many others to know of it, and he wanted to keep his pet as long as possible.

"True, the man of God had publicly accused him of corruption and adultery and warned of judgement! But by keeping the Prophet isolated and powerless, while Herod himself flourished in spite of everything, those words of doom would sound increasingly hollow, and lose their power. Meanwhile, the rope-haired, long-bearded Nazirite was a curiosity to entertain the court and tantalise the King's superstitious soul with hopes that he would perform some startling miracle. What a novelty, what a thrill for his guests, that would be – and of course it would enhance Herod's fame if the Prophet would dance to *his* tune. What kind of miracle he hoped for is not clear – loaves and fishes? Water into wine?"

"If I was Herod I would not have been so anxious for miracles!" muttered Caleb furiously. "Fire from heaven would be more like it!"

"Whatever happened, Herod still wanted approval from his subjects – while getting his own way. He had no intention of allowing the common people to say that their beloved Baptiser had starved or sickened to death in his care, and no doubt he thought Loukanos was just the man to prevent it. Unlike the ever-scheming Jews, a disinterested Greek physician might be relied on not to hatch plots! Naturally this suited Loukanos, even though it was clear Johannes was in no condition to be mercilessly grilled about his message, or Messiah, or anything else. So for a while Loukanos stayed in the barracks, attended the Prophet and did all he could for his physical comfort. As for mental comfort, well, they were two of a kind there, though for different reasons. Loukanos was fighting to resist belief and the Prophet was fighting to hold his faith as the prison bleakness crept into his mind and froze it into numbness."

"You don't mean to tell me that a great man like the Baptiser was doubting all that had happened?" cried Dan disgustedly. "All he knew? Even his own words? I don't believe it!"

"No, Dan, I don't think he doubted, but you must understand that there are demons which can bind a man against his will. It may be illness, it may be circumstance, it may be grief or anger, but sometimes all the prayers and knowledge in the world cannot remove an agony of spirit before which a mortal is helpless."

"Poor man, poor man," muttered Caleb. He understood about the blackness which could choke a man's faith and paralyse his reason. He knew what it was to feel the horror of great darkness.

182

He patted Dan's shoulder. "You are too young to comprehend this, my boy, and please God, you never will. But it is so, it is so."

Dan remembered Caleb's own dark story, and felt chastened.

"Was this what you felt after your family was killed … when you tried to drown your sadness in wine, Caleb?" he asked humbly.

"Something like that, my boy. But I have known of those whose melancholy has been far worse, and at times for no cause that can be found, and that is perhaps even harder to bear."

Uncle Joseph was silent for a moment, impressed by the old man's insight.

"I believe your uncle was of real help to the Prophet," he continued, consolingly. "Perhaps Louki's honest doubts were a refreshing antidote to Herod's deceitful interest – who knows? I do know that he attempted to keep him in health without violating the Nazirite vow, and that was worth something."

"He would have known a lot about it from Anna."

"No doubt, Dan, I hadn't thought of that! Perhaps he discussed the meaning of the vow with the Prophet as well, but probably not – Johannes was too deeply withdrawn, though I believe the Spirit moved him whenever he faced Herod. Truly that fox will be without excuse on the day of Judgement! Well, Loukanos heard enough from his patient to force him to juggle his cynicism with deep admiration – until even he could not deny that Johannes was a holy man of God. What that really meant to Loukanos of Philippi, he was still trying to work out. Of course, he also heard a great deal from Johannes' own disciples who brought news to the prison about his cousin's doings."

"Aye! I had forgotten!" Caleb pricked up his ears. "To be sure, they were kinsmen! They must have known each other well in days past."

"Perhaps – perhaps not. They were raised in different ends of the country, you know. They cannot have spent a great deal of time together, but when they did, I'm sure they spoke the same language, spiritually speaking."

Joseph shuffled his stewpot more firmly into the coals, and added the rest of his ingredients.

"Now, Dan, I am not telling any more until you stop mauling that dough and cover it. It will never rise if you don't leave it alone. There, put it near the hearth – not too close – that's right."

Uncle Joseph forbad any more conversation until he was satisfied that their preparations were complete. The stew was stirred, tasted, and an extra pinch or two of cumin tossed in, the fire was adjusted, the table cleared, dishes of nuts and olives set beside Judith's quince, and the honeycomb laid out with her pot of sesame paste. Wine and water were poured into tall jugs, lamps were filled, wicks and tapers trimmed, wash bowls and towels stood waiting. Even the upstairs room was made ready with blankets and sleeping mats laid out for its guests on the freshly swept floor. Finally Uncle Joseph gave a sigh of satisfaction. All was in order, and there was plenty of time until sunset. More than enough to bake the bread, and for Caleb to make Festive Cheese! He sat them down at the free end of the table and poured wine for them all – very well watered for Dan, not quite so watered for Caleb, and not watered at all for himself.

Old Caleb took a good mouthful, swished it around his crooked teeth, and gulped, smacking his lips appreciatively, bobbing his head and grinning his thanks to his host, who acknowledged him politely with raised cup.

"*Please* go on – what happened next?" Dan begged impatiently after two hasty sips. His uncle was a little taken aback at such lack of enthusiasm for what was one of his very best vintages, but then remembered the boy's wine was little more than coloured water. So Uncle Joseph put down his drink with a mental shrug, and obligingly took up the narrative again.

"The Baptist still languished," he told them. "The tales his own followers brought back about his cousin ceased to rouse him, even when they debated among themselves about the Nazarene's mission. If he was to be their King, they argued, why was he helping centurions, Samaritans, sinners and lunatics? What had happened to the baptising with the Holy Spirit, the gathering of the good wheat into barns, the winnowing of chaff and burning with fire that Johannes had boldly predicted? Where was the glorious revival of the Kingdom and the violent overthrow of the Gentiles?

"But Johannes' eyes had lost their fire, and his wasted body was sinking, and he seemed too exhausted to care.

'He must increase, and I must diminish,' was all he said, time and again.

"Herod scowled and ordered the doctor to prescribe tonics, but Loukanos knew that wasn't the answer. The man needed a miracle – or a like-minded soul – to uphold him, and the only one who could provide either was the Nazarene himself. For days Loukanos stamped around the dank corridors of the fortress, trying to think of a way to provoke a response from his patient. Finally he realised that even if Johannes had no care for his own life, he would care for his men and his God-given mission. So back he went, and his professional gentleness had vanished. In its place was the crisp voice of a man who was angered by unnecessary suffering.

'You were the voice crying in the wilderness, prophet, but your message is being drowned in confusion! If the trumpet gives an uncertain sound, who shall go forth to the battle?!'

There was silence for several heartbeats, then a faint sigh.

'I have done my part,' came a tired whisper from the gloom. 'I have shown them the Lamb of God.'

'You have shown them a Lamb while preaching to them of a Lion!' Loukanos retorted. 'Is it any wonder they are vacillating?'

Ah! The thin form was stirring on his straw! Loukanos motioned briskly to the guard, the iron key was turned, and he stepped inside the cramped cell. He met the prophet's confused gaze unflinchingly.

'Your men need clarity of vision!' he told him roughly. 'What use is their loyalty to you if it does not establish their faith in the one you came to preach? Diminish all you want, but do not leave your task unfinished! Send them to your cousin with a direct question demanding a direct answer to all these doubts. When they have that answer, you will have done all you can to set them unshakeably on their course. Will you do this?'

Johannes took a deep breath and closed his longing eyes.

'They will stretch their limbs in sweet morning air!' he murmured slowly. 'They will hear birds – feel clean cold waters – and they will see the sun …!'

Loukanos thought he was rambling, but he would not indulge him.

'*Where there is no vision, the people perish,*' he stated uncompromisingly.

The Baptist opened his eyes, looked directly at him, and spoke clearly at last, though his voice was still whisper quiet.

'Vision for the invisible … yes, you are right. There can be no lasting faith without it. They must see Jeshua the Nazarene, and plainly ask him *Are you really the One who was to come, or should we look for someone else?*'

Loukanos nodded firmly, hiding his relief. The man would have to rouse himself to instruct his men, go with them in his mind, imagine their journey, who and what they would see, count the days till their return, anticipate the message from a uniquely kindred soul, hope for and treasure any words of encouragement which they brought. The doctor within him was satisfied – the patient would hold on, would eat and drink – and would have a reason to distinguish the days.

'Good! – now drink this – I promise you nothing from the vine is in this cup.'

The potion revived him for a little while, as Loukanos had intended.

'Now, eat, prophet, to keep up your strength. I can't feed you locusts, but look – I have found some wild honey.'

'Thank you, physician!' The heavy eyes lifted gratefully. 'Yes – you are indeed the same man from the riverbank near Bethany so long ago – who could see that a seed of Abraham is not always a son of God … and do you yet see that a son of God is not always a seed of Abraham?'

'You remember that?' Loukanos was taken aback.

'I do, and more … I know you, Grecian – the man who brought a blind man to me at Bethabara Decapolis, yet left him to flounder while you rushed away …'

'That was not well done.' Loukanos was ashamed to admit it, and ashamed he had been so accurately observed.

'Ah, but you are also the man who afterwards did me a great service for which I thanked God. Later, you brought me an old shepherd who had heard the angels sing *Kabod!* at the birth of my Master, and – like Elijah – I realised then, that my witness had never been truly alone!'

Loukanos did not trust himself to speak.

The voice beside him in the greyness was no longer the huge rich sound which once rang out over bright waters and sunlit rocks. It was a still, small voice which echoed flatly from dim, bare dungeon stone, but it had lost none of its power to move.

Now it said softly, 'I asked you then, *Not you? Or not yet?* Do you still give the same answer?'

Loukanos stood up and took the empty cup, calling the gaoler to let him out.

'I have no answers,' he replied abruptly. 'Enjoy your honeycomb.' He turned back for a last word. 'Be sure your followers see their way clearly before you permit your own lamp to go out!' "

Uncle Joseph sighed, stretched and rose to check his cooking. Caleb sat immersed in his memories, half trembling at the honour of having cheered the Baptiser in his lonely hours. Dan reluctantly dragged himself from the table to knock down the bread for a second rising. He had no words for what he was feeling. Loukanos – and the Baptiser! Praise the Eternal! But whatever next?!

Chapter Eighteen

THE cups were refilled, and Uncle Joseph drank thoughtfully before resuming his tale.

"The very next day the Prophet sent two of his disciples as he had undertaken to do. The Nazarene seemed to see straight through them to his cousin, and maybe he even saw Loukanos too, who knows? Anyway, the answer he gave was not directed to the messengers, but to the imprisoned Baptiser and no-one else. *'Go and tell him everything you have seen and heard ...'* said he. But more than this, he gave them a specific instruction to tell Johannes that *good news was preached to those who had nothing,* and that *those who would not be disconcerted by their Messiah would be blessed.*"

"That last may have reassured the men," Dan said thoughtfully. "But did it help the Baptiser, Uncle?"

"Yes, Dan – it was a direct encouragement, you see! Who had nothing, if not imprisoned Johannes? And what did the miracles convey if not *Courage! I have the power to heal, to restore – even life from the dead, my dear cousin! This is the good news!* Don't you see how that would have uplifted the Prophet? His kinsman was telling him, *See the power of Emmanuel – the power of God with us! Take heart, you have nothing to fear, even from death itself ... don't be confused, you will be blessed!* Only those who would be offended by Messiah not doing what *they* wanted him to or expected him to, would be confused. That's what Loukanos believed he meant anyway ... *those who trust me, and not their own expectations will be blessed.* It cheered the prophet's disciples, and warned them at the same time.

"Strangely, as they excitedly discussed these things with Johannes, Loukanos found himself unwillingly recalling a scripture learned many years ago at his mother's knee. Of course, he did not necessarily believe it himself, but he thought to administer it as another useful medicine."

Caleb looked blank. "What kind of medicine do you mean?"

Uncle Joseph smiled. "The best medicine of all – the Elixir of Hope!" he replied. "When the man's disciples had left, Loukanos slipped into the cell with his satchel to do his duty by the patient.

'You have your answer now,' he said. 'Is it enough?'

The great man had lifted himself up – he was sitting, he was taking notice, and his eye was no longer dull.

'Yes, physician, truly Jeshua the Master is the One. My friends rejoice in their greater understanding. So plainly have they heard and seen and comprehended him that their doubts have cleared, and my own vision is also brightened in this dark place. None of us will presume any longer to know the exact steps he will walk. It will be according to God's will, so what does it matter how the work is accomplished? Sending them was wisdom, and I thank you for your counsel. Now I *have* truly done all I could. When I go, they will not be bereft, they have their path clearly set before them, just as you said.'

'And you? What is your path?'

'There is no more path for me, Grecian – no road out of this fortress, which is not called The Gallows for nothing. But I will no longer repine. Jeshua has always been the only man who understood my heart, and now, praise God, he has lightened my heaviness of spirit."

Loukanos knelt in the straw beside the prisoner, and snapped his fingers at the guard. Bribed beforehand with the promise of free treatment for his bad feet, the man fetched a burning twig from the courtyard brazier, and obediently lit the two pinch lamps which the physician passed through the bars. Apart from a muttered warning about the straw, the soldier then steadfastly looked the other way, thinking only of his aching arches, while Loukanos palmed the key which had been slipped to him with the lamps.

'I was raised a Jew,' Loukanos informed the lean, hollow-cheeked prisoner who was now, for the first time in weeks, watching him alertly. 'I know something of your scriptures. Your kinsman has sent you a message about his power of healing, while declaring to you, *Good news is preached to the poor* – a striking phrase. There is a place in your holy books where healing and preaching to the poor are written together. Perhaps he wished to remind you of it.'

He had aroused the prisoner's curiosity – a healthy sign. Loukanos dug in his satchel and brought out rolls of bandages, a pot of fine wood ash, a flask of sweet oil, and a large, clean woollen tunic. The prophet frowned thoughtfully. *Good, he is thinking.* Finally Loukanos produced the angular key, and unlocked the man's shackles, exposing raw flesh and crusted sores beneath the iron. He met the prophet's darkly glinting eyes with a slight smile, and nodded at the items beside them.

'These tools of my trade were also familiar to your prophet Isaias …' he began, but Johannes shot out a large hand and gripped him by the wrist with a swift intake of breath.

'Isaias? Praise God, Grecian!' he whispered fiercely, shaken from his stoicism at last. 'You are right! *The Spirit of the Eternal is upon me, because he has anointed me to preach good news to the poor!* Yes, it must be! He began his ministry with that scripture and wants me to think more deeply on it! And you, my strange and unlikely friend, you not only know the words – you and I *together* saw them come to pass, at the upper Jordan! Give me this further happiness, and say them with me now!"

Loukanos gritted his teeth – he had not expected to be asked to take his own medicine as well. But the patient must be humoured and so with only a few stumbles, he repeated the passage which Helen had taught him so very many years ago. They were indeed the same words with which the woodworker of Nazareth had opened his ministry in his home town, words for which his own neighbours had angrily attempted to hurl him over a cliff. But the Greek and the Nazirite in Herod's prison recited the whole passage freely with an indifferent audience – the gaoler Dex, who being mindful of his soothing bribes, did not interrupt.

The two men, so like and unalike, made an odd pair; both tall and lean and dark, so old in experience, yet still young in years, almost as young as the Nazarene himself. Both alone and independent from an early age, keen-minded, passionate, driven. One unshaven, uncut, unwell, living in darkness, walking in light. The other neat, clipped, healthy, living in sunlight, and walking in shadows.

The prophet spoke the words with joy and a strengthening voice, the Greek murmured quietly, reluctantly, and only for the wellbeing of his patient, trying to muffle an even quieter voice inside his head.

'The Spirit of the Eternal is upon me, because he has anointed me to preach good news to the poor …' Yes, they had both seen that anointing with their own eyes – the baptism, the dove!

I was there …

192

'He has sent me to bandage the broken hearted ...' Had not the heart of the great Johannes been breaking?

And tell me, physician, how whole is your heart?

'To shout LIBERTY! to the captives, and the opening of the gaol to them who are bound ...' Johannes would have liberty! Herod, bonds, gaol, had no power! Disease had no power! Death had no power!

I have no power.

'And to declare the year of His favour, and the day of His vengeance ...' Generous favour first – and brief vengeance to follow!

What of His vengeance for those who despise that favour?

'And to comfort all who are mourning in Zion ...' Yes, Johannes was comforted!

While I, carefree Loukanos, mourn for something without even knowing what it is. But come, Louki, my son, speak up! See what good this medicine is doing your patient, and be glad of that.

'Instead of ashes – to give them beauty. Instead of grief – to give them the oil of joy...'

Loukanos swabbed the sores with vinegar, mixed the ashes and oil, and anointed the raw, chafed flesh, bandaging it thickly.

'To exchange the spirit of heaviness for a garment of praise!'

He stripped the prophet of his filthy robe and replaced it with the clean one.

'Then they will be called a forest of upright ones! A magnificent forest planted by the Eternal – so that He may be glorified.'

They finished harmoniously together, Loukanos a little more firmly than he had begun. Johannes' voice wavered at the last, but his face was triumphant.

'Aye – so it shall be, all glory to Him! A forest of upright ones, freed from sin, from mortality. *Trees planted by rivers of waters which give forth fruit in their season, whose leaf shall not wither! But the ungodly are like chaff blown away by the wind …*'

'Yes, I know that one too,' Loukanos rejoined drily, 'and I have no doubt you can find a hundred more such stepping stones in your sacred river. Here's one which you laid yourself – *He will gather his wheat into his barn, but the chaff he will burn with relentless flame …*'

'Ah, you remember that?'

'I'm a doctor – it's my job to remember everything about my victims. Well, it seems to me that the flame is well and truly rekindled in your eyes, at least, and now I must withdraw before I set your parables into action with these very poor lamps, which are spitting badly. I see Dex is looking twitchy, and his shift will be changing soon.' He locked the irons back on the bony wrists and ankles, now well protected by their bandages. 'I'm sorry I can't leave you the key, but Dex will get very upset if I don't return it. I leave you to digest your mental store of scriptures, and speaking of digestion, you need to drink far more water. You're not standing in a river any more. I'll see to it you're not stinted.'

Leaving Johannes no chance to thank him, Loukanos left abruptly, to attend to Dex and his feet.

"Well, it may have been the words, or it may have been the Nazarene healing at a distance, as we know he can do … or perhaps both. Whichever it was, Loukanos was thankful that the entire exercise had rescued his patient from a dangerous malaise of spirit. On the other hand, which he was less thankful to find, it also had stirred up his own soul most uncomfortably. Soon afterwards, he told the Prophet that he must leave him.

194

'There is too much talk for it to be just talk,' he admitted reluctantly to the gaunt figure behind the bars. 'But I need to see with my own eyes if these cures are really cures, illusions, hysterias or more faith-healing ... and as for raising from the dead, that is something I cannot believe ... unless I see or smell the corruption first. I have seen apparent corpses revive before now.'

"Be sure you are sure, by all means," said Johannes warmly, his hollow eyes clear again. "But do not hide from the truth when you recognise it – it wastes too much time, and effort, and who knows how much a man has left?"

The physician stiffened slightly. *Never hide from the truth, it's a waste of time and effort!* They were words spoken by Loukanos' mother Helen the day she died, not to him, but to young Dan. Had she believed it was too late to warn her own son? But Johannes was still speaking.

'The good you have done to me, the servant of Adonai God, and His Son, you have done also to my Master. May you be blessed, and may you find peace.'

Then suddenly, unexpectedly, the man who was of the tribe of the priests, was holding out manacled hands, pronouncing upon the startled Greek, an ancient Levitical blessing – no, not pronouncing it! He was singing it! Singing, in his beautiful voice – singing in that stinking prison.

'The Eternal bless you and keep you. The Eternal make His face to shine upon you, and be gracious unto you. The Eternal lift up His countenance upon you and give you peace.'

Brave and unquenchable spirit! I salute thee! Loukanos set his teeth against an uninvited wave of emotion and gripped the thin arms extended to him through the bars. 'Thank you, prophet. Perhaps we will meet again in happier circumstances.'

Johannes' hip-length, prematurely greying beard flashed a glad smile not seen for many days. 'I believe we will.' He repeated the words he had spoken when they parted at the Jordan three years before. 'Thank *you*, Grecian. Do not forget this day!'

Loukanos turned abruptly and shouted angrily to the guard. 'Open this door, man!'

Startled, the soldier obeyed, but Loukanos took a quick step back into the cell – an impulsive embrace saluted his imprisoned patient for the first and last time – and then the physician was gone, the slow scrape of the lock overlaid by the sound of his pelting feet as he ran towards the light."

Dan and Caleb sat breathlessly. There must be more to come! There was, but Uncle Joseph was nearly at the end of what he could tell them.

"Loukanos went straight as an arrow, all the way from the Dead Sea to Galilee, to become something of a shadow in the crowds around the Nazarene, and like myself, careful to avoid anywhere he had previously frequented, especially Cana or Banayim ... getting to know a few of the Twelve, listening, observing, comparing, taking notes ... trying to determine what was fraudulent, what was faith healing, what was a rare gift for manipulating natural forces, and what was supernatural power. He had to rule out deceit and sleight of hand almost at once, though he still had not decided what else to credit. The cures were real enough – he had to admit. Once he even insisted that a disturbed woman should be healed when he could not help her himself! What the true purpose of it all was supposed to be, he would not accept. Like Johannes' men, in the Nazarene he did not see the politicking of a would-be King.

"But not long afterwards came the terrible news – that the great Baptist had been slaughtered by Herod, and for the worst possible reason – the drunken vanity of a weak man with more power than principle. The grief all over the Land was profound, as you know, and as you will have felt for yourselves. Everyone was shocked and lamenting his loss. Of course there was still the Nazarene, but Johannes had been so greatly admired, and respected. He had fired the whole nation, Jew and Gentiles alike. A beloved and holy man of God – the first the Land had seen for centuries – butchered like a sheep!"

They were all silent for a moment. It had indeed been unthinkable, and the mourning had been deeply personal for all who had known their Prophet. Uncle Joseph shook his head and continued.

"As I said, everyone was affected. But Loukanos was more upset than he could believe or understand, and *that* rattled him badly. He left the disciples, and fled back to Samaria again – and there, he and I practically fell over each other when we each took rooms in the same lodging house."

Dan and Caleb's mouths fell open, and Uncle Joseph smiled a little.

"You can imagine how much explaining we had to do to each other, after all those years! I don't think we stopped talking for days. I was all for telling Anna immediately that Loukanos had turned up – but the selfishness of our quests had made everything very complicated. I could not reveal him without revealing myself, and *vice versa*, as the Romans say."

He did not tell them what he had already related to Anna earlier in the day.

"Frankly, my dear, Louki was a mess. It was as if all the self-control he had ever pent up over the years had suddenly burst out, sweeping all before it. For weeks he was consumed with finding rational answers for everything. He wrote endless notes and scribbled over a whole Red Sea's worth of papyrus. He wept over the Prophet, and cursed himself because he wept. He slept either not at all or for days on end, and when he did, was plagued with nightmares in which the cursings of the law took bizarre shapes and fought with the gods of Olympus. He ate either nothing or everything in sight – and he was either silent for days or could not stop talking. He was continually angry, pleading with Helen for a sign from the Elysian Fields if she was truly there and demanding that the Baptist give him a sign from Abraham's bosom if she was not. His speech was disconnected – he walked himself to exhaustion – and at one point I truly feared for his reason.

"Now, now, don't weep, my dear! There is no need – the worst passed eventually, and I am not sure how much of that tempestuous time he may even remember now. I admit, he worried me to death for a while, but I kept very close, and tried to help him all I could, trusting that the storms would pass, and he would find himself again. I hired a grim fellow I called my manservant, but only he and I knew his real job was to watch over Loukanos when I could not do it myself.

Only once I had stopped foolishly bleating in my head, 'Oh, Physician, heal thyself!' and began praying for the Eternal to heal him in earnest, did I begin to feel easier myself. I prayed behind Louki's back, in front of him, and sometimes by his side. Slowly he began to emerge from the wreckage of his own pride and strength, and as he did, I resumed my own research as I had first begun."

Looking at Dan and Caleb's expectant faces, Uncle Joseph now continued without the slightest indication that he had left anything out.

"Loukanos and I shared our lodgings, but not our travels. After we had spent some time together, I set out on my own, leaving him to write down all his experiences with the holy men, both Nazirite and Nazarene, something he was still determined to document, if only to make sense of his own thoughts.

"As for myself, as I told Anna, although I did not literally track every footstep of the Nazarene, I did follow him in his home town, and Sepphoris, as well as observing him and the Twelve in Chorazin, Bethsaida, Gadara, Tyre, Sidon and lately, Caesarea Philippi. Meanwhile, having well rested, and set down events coherently enough for his own satisfaction, Loukanos finally left Samaria to rejoin the Nazarene's disciples, and again take up his search for the truth with his own eyes and ears. Our paths crossed occasionally, and I last saw him myself in an outlying village of Caesarea Philippi, where he may still be. He was much calmer, less agitated, more determined, but clearly still torn between the natural and the supernatural."

Caleb was shaking his head. "Ah, this bodes ill. How long can such a clever man halt between two opinions? He is taking dangerously too much time!"

"Right again, friend." Admiration gleamed from Joseph's eyes – this stringy old shepherd was no fool. "Cleverness itself can be paralysing. He must choose his path soon lest he forever remain tortured – or resolutely numb. Let us pray that the Eternal gives him a little push in the right direction. Now, my men – back to the present! Dan has bread to bake!"

"Wait, Uncle Joseph," persisted Dan. "I have two questions! You said you wouldn't reveal yourself to your family until you had made sure of your own opinion about Teacher Jeshua. Does this mean you have finally made up your mind?"

Uncle Joseph looked bemused. "Why, yes, of course it does, Dan. Did I not make that clear? I do believe that the Nazarene is indeed our Messiah, and that he has come to show us the way to eternal life. His teachings are elegant in principle, and no doubt preparatory to still greater revelations. Unlike some, I do not concern myself about whether it is the restoration of the Kingdom which will come first, or the revelation of what is required to secure immortality. Whichever it is, I am ready to obey!"

Caleb looked at his host with admiration, but Dan could hardly wait to ask the question which to him was the most important, though he spoke with trepidation.

"And Loukanos – does he still want to stay hidden from us?"

Uncle Joseph rubbed his chin thoughtfully. "I confess that I did not think to ask him that, specifically, but I did tell him I was now ready to find the family, and that once I did, I could not conceal my knowledge of him any longer. He said he understood."

Dan looked relieved, despite feeling rather let down that Loukanos had responded so neutrally. But once again Uncle Joseph had used his discretion.

"I understand," Loukanos had replied, and shrugged carelessly. "Well, tell them whatever you will – they will still be disappointed."

"You underestimate them – and yourself, Louki," his uncle responded quietly, as he left.

Loukanos turned ... to find himself face to face with Marah.

"More than that," she told him coldly, for her. "You underestimate the power of Emmanuel."

Chapter Nineteen

PERCHED on the rock above the restless Loukanos, Marah waited patiently for a while. If he wanted to talk, she would listen – but oh how much she wanted to drag the blindfold from his eyes! Was there anything as frustrating as an intelligent man who scorned his own emotions? Of course there must be balance in life, and the heart could not always rule the head ... but whoever travelled an unknown road without looking around to note the landmarks and the weather? *Still less acknowledging that he may even have a twisted ankle!*

She smiled to herself as she conjured up a comical picture of a determined lanky Loukanos grimly hobbling along in a desert, eyes glued to a map, sternly muttering to himself, "Fifty paces, turn right, forty paces, turn left," while all along scribing a gigantic, zig-zagging circle around the very oasis he was looking for. She looked down upon the thick black curls which were almost level with her feet, and an impish thought provoked the bizarre idea of raking them smooth with her toes. She sighed reluctantly – what a pity it was to be a middle-aged woman and not a giggling child. But she came down to earth with a bump when she realised Loukanos had finally come to speech, and presumably, the reason he had called her on this unorthodox excursion.

"Marah, I want to know something, and I want no mincing around, and manners can go hang. I'm so tired of chasing my thoughts, of weighing the scales so often I can no longer tell whether or not I am deliberately tipping the balance one way or another. What did you mean when you said the other day that I underestimated the power of Emmanuel? I was too rude to listen then ... too churned up. Now I'm listening. You were very angry ..."

Rather astonished, Marah wrapped her arms around her knees and frowned.

"I was, but I'm sorry for that now – it was presumptuous of me. *Emmanuel* – God With Us – is one of Messiah's titles, but of course you know that." She sighed. "I did not mean to be cryptic, I thought you had understood my meaning. Well, you have asked me to be honest, my friend, so please remember that, if I unwittingly stamp on your sandals. I must begin from your uncle's parting words, which you know I overheard. He said you underestimated yourself. There is something in that, you know – it is a petulant reaction in many a stubborn man who begins by *over*-estimating himself!"

Loukanos leant his head back and closed his eyes to hide their expression.

"Really!" he replied non-committally. "Why is that so, O wise woman?"

His voice was flat, and perhaps it was not meant to be a genuine question, but now he had piqued her a little, and he would get *that* answer whether he liked it or not. Did he think she had learned *nothing* in all her solitary, unprotected years?

"It is so, O wise man," she answered sardonically, "because under-confidence and over-confidence have the same root – a focus on self! They become entrenched through the usual twin forces of the masculine soul – pride and fear."

A little late, she remembered she had meant to make no personal judgements, so she softened her voice quickly.

"However, it is not for me to assume this of you, and I mean no offence. Only *you* can tell whether you have lost faith in your own powers of discernment. Perhaps you have – since your confusion has become a chronic state to which you seem almost resigned."

Loukanos twitched – at which she was perversely glad.

"Well done," he said ironically. "Have you any more bitter pills for the patient, Minerva? With my first question still unanswered, surely you must hold *some* in reserve."

Minerva! No doubt that was a return for her earlier teasing of 'Doctor Zeus'! But sarcastic reference to the Roman goddess of Wisdom and Medicine – and War! – was hardly justified when he had asked her for sober honesty. Marah's glowing resolve of compassion was as resilient, but ephemeral, as a soap bubble – it could rebound from a bump, but not from a barb, and now he had nettled her thoroughly. Pop! went her worthy intentions!

"Oh, I am still getting to your answer, never fear!" she replied warmly, gathering more heat as she went on. "What you think of yourself is your own affair, but when Joseph said you underestimated your family, I *knew* he was right … *You* may have forgotten – I haven't! – that a few years ago dear old Etta lodged me while you and all your family were off looking for our beloved Prophet – may he rest in peace! Do you think I don't *know* your family? How could I not when she shared her letters, her memories and her hopes with the madwoman to whom she had opened her arms and her home? How dare you give her and your sister, your father, your aunt, *and* your nephews, no credit for their love towards you? How dare you hide, and whine that they will only be disappointed in you – will they not rather weep for joy that you are alive and well, and looking for answers? Have you no respect for *their* integrity? Have you no bowels of compassion for *them*?"

Choking a little, she drew breath. God forgive her! To speak thus to a man! And she with no husband or father to cover her. Well – she was what she was, and thankfully, he was a not a Jew!

Loukanos had become very still, staring with narrowed eyes under his fine black brows. His ascetic lips were firmly compressed in that crisp glossy beard, but he opened them to say grimly,

"Go on. You will surely not stop now."

"Indeed – now that I have finally come to the heart of it, I will not. Underestimating yourself – as I said, that's your affair. Underestimating the love of your family – that is pure self-pity. But worse than that, Loukanos of Philippi – as I told you before, you underestimate the power of Emmanuel … the power of God to save, daily demonstrated among us! You see it do what man cannot, you shrug, you claim to be unsure of its origin … and you wonder why I am angry with you?"

She paused, picking at small pieces of crumbled rock on the slab beside her, flinging them one by one into the quiet waters beside them, where they splashed softly out of sight. Still he was silent. She threw the last stone too hard, and it overshot the pool altogether. Had she said too much? Enough?

"With so many struggling for life, who are you to turn your back on it? Like a stubborn patient refusing his cure from pride and fear! Yes, those words again! Only a fool claims he will not die, but is it not equally foolish to determine that you will not live? What, are you God, Louki?"

204

Every hair on his body prickled and suddenly a younger Loukanos was urgently shaking a phial onto Helen's panting tongue.

"*You will not die!*"

"*What, are you God, Louki? I am dying as we speak …*"

He rubbed his arms as if cold, and Marah thought he grew impatient. She sighed within herself but pressed on – there might never be another opportunity.

"Loukanos, you were brought up with the scriptures, and you know God has no pleasure in death – even of the wicked. Have you forgotten? '*The Eternal, the Eternal Power – merciful, gracious, longsuffering, full of goodness and verity, holding mercy for multitudes, forgiving*' – yes, forgiving everything, except flinty rebellion. You were there, you *heard* Him declare that the man Jeshua is His beloved son. And every day you can *see* the power, even while you still question its origin and his motives." She swallowed her frustration. "At least give Jeshua due credit for compassion, even if you deny it to your family! He is a healer – but what use is a cure to a healthy man? So, has he come only for lepers and madwomen – to put doctors like you out of business? Or is he demonstrating that the same power which renews bodies and minds, can transform sickened hearts and scarred souls? Emmanuel! *God With Us!* Discount that at your peril, my friend … You who can never fight death, disease and misery as he does – is your pride stronger than his power?"

He was now so still, she nearly lost heart. Was he even listening?

She burst out, "Ah, it is true what they say, that physicians make the worst patients!"

He waved a hand irritably, and Marah bit her tongue. She must take a lesson from the Teacher, who instructed with stories, with question and answer which were far more effective than nagging reproaches. With an effort, she continued more calmly.

"Let me express this in a way you may sympathise with more readily. Think of your work – the times you have healed people with your skill. If healing was not possible, you may have taken away their pain. If that was not possible you may have taken away their fear. Were you proud when you stopped their suffering?"

He took a deep breath and rubbed his temples wearily, before speaking reluctantly at last.

"Pride is always lurking somewhere in a man, as you say, but it was rarely my first sensation. Relief, perhaps. Sometimes triumph, which is somewhere between the two, I suppose."

"Did people thank you? Did they pay you?"

"The poor thanked me, the rich paid me, and sometimes either did both. What are you leading up to?"

"What if they gave their thanks to the coppersmith next door for his efficacious pots, or paid the tailor for his medicinal turban?"

"What childish nonsense are you inventing, woman?"

"Thank you! *Childish nonsense* is a very good description of the folly of ignoring the true source of any healing power! Especially a power which heals out of compassion, not pride. No, say nothing – I have not finished. Here is another hypothetical situation for you … What if you were unfailingly gentle with your patient, and tried to ease his pain, which you had full power to do, only to have him shriek loudly with terror, or flinch, duck and run every time you held out your healing hand? Would you be surprised, perhaps shocked … frustrated … angry?"

"All four, no doubt," he answered reluctantly. "And yes, I can see where you are leading me with this."

But she continued relentlessly, sliding down from her perch above him to crouch at his feet and stare into his face.

"How patient then is the Eternal with you, physician? When He has shown you His healing power by the hand of His Chosen, time and time again? When you have *seen* the spirit of God With Us? When you have *seen* Jeshua – and his Twelve! – cure with a touch, a word or the brush of his garment, conditions you could not remedy with a hundred years of medicine?

"Oh, I understand about the potency of faith healing – but since when have even the most hysterical of patients *believed* themselves out of dropsy, or *believed* missing limbs into existence? When has even the most *desperate* mother prised death's fingers from a son's corpse by faith, or a sheer effort of will?" She snatched his hands with an iron grip, searching his baffled eyes. "You may as well refuse to believe in the air you breathe! What is stopping you believing? *Who* is stopping you believing? Answer me, Louki!"

The world stood still. *Crossroad – linen ephod.*

He could feel his heart stop. *A king – a priest.*

It turned over. *Messianic psalm – Order of Melchizedek!*

Breathless now, white to the lips.

Nothing is stopping me.

Nothing.

"I am doing this to myself!" he whispered, mouth dry, staring at her incredulously.

His heart gave a great thump at last, and began hammering in his chest. His stomach churned. Sweat broke out on his pale face.

She released his hands and sat back on her heels with a gasp.

"Why?" she demanded.

He wiped his face and got stiffly to his feet, feeling utterly sick.

"Because I have been the biggest fool that ever lived."

He staggered suddenly ... the trees were beginning to whirl ...

"Sit down, quickly, and put your head between your knees," she cried, but it was too late – he swayed, lurched – and with a tremendous splash pitched headfirst into the icy pool.

Chapter Twenty

INSTANTLY Marah sprang after him, snatching a fistful of dark hair as it sank, yanking his head above the water, floundering as she clutched the limp body … but the danger passed just as suddenly as it had fallen. He came round almost at once – and they were only chest deep. Spluttering water and gulping air, Loukanos grunted painfully as she slumped him heavily against the muddy bank, both of them panting to regain the breath the cold had snatched away. His ribs heaved as he coughed and retched and spat blood. He clutched his head and groaned.

"Louki!" gasped Marah, wiping a red wash from his wet lips with her thumb. "Louki! Are you all right?" She patted the pallid face, examining it anxiously, stroking his bearded cheek. "You're bleeding! How can you be bleeding? Can you talk? Tell me!"

He groaned again, opened one eye, and said slowly, "I think I bit my tongue." He stuck it out for inspection.

Marah let him go at once, and pushed the long wet hair from her eyes with a sigh of relief.

"Yes you did. Well, that will make you think before you speak for a while."

Loukanos put his tongue away, flinched, and shook his head like a wet dog. He looked at her quizzically, his teeth chattering.

"Do you think this immersion will count for baptism? Or will I have to do it again? And if I do, will you please make sure nobody pulls my hair?" He rubbed his head tenderly. "I think I have a bald spot now ..."

Shaking with relief and cold as she was, Marah could not help herself – she sank back into the freezing pool and positively roared with laughter until Loukanos joined in. They laughed so much that their first gasping attempts to scramble out were doomed to failure, especially when Marah snagged herself hopelessly on the forgotten fish trap.

"The fish! Save our supper!" she cried, laughing harder than ever, but in fumbling at the sodden draperies of her dress, their numb fingers also jerked open the trap, and the fish flashed out before they realised it. Finally they calmed down enough to flounder back up the marshy bank where, mud-streaked and shivering, they wrung out as much of themselves as they could with decency. Anxious to bundle Marah quickly into his thick dry cloak, Loukanos snatched it up so hastily that several coins flew high out of a pocket and bounced off the rocks. Marah made a frantic snatch at one, nearly punching the startled Loukanos on the nose, but she succeeding only in knocking the bright coin straight towards the pool. There was a flickering splash, a gaping mouth and flip of a tail – and it was gone.

Marah turned to Loukanos with her jaw dropping. "Did you see that?"

He was still chuckling as he scratched up the other coins from the stones. "I've heard of Paying For Our Supper ... but perhaps you could call that, the Supper Paying Us Out ..."

"Or Us Paying the Supper ..." she laughed. "It was my fault, though. I'm sorry. Was it much?"

"Four drachmas," he shrugged, replacing the rest, and settling the cloak around her firmly, "but cheap at the price. You'd pay that much anywhere to see a fish do such a trick! Well, he'll be a nice surprise for someone when he's caught, if he doesn't choke on it first. Now let's get back quickly, or we'll be needing the rest to pay Charys the Ferryman," he said solemnly. Then he grinned at her. "That's a joke," he reassured. "But seriously, apart from the chance of freezing to death it's Sabbath this evening, and I know you women like to have things properly fussed over in plenty of time. Now, tighten your straps," he instructed, doing the same, "they'll be very slippery now, and you don't want to twist an ankle."

Oh, Loukanos and his sandals! Marta rolled her eyes. "Yes, *Abba!*" she said with mock humility as she obeyed, wishing there was a Greek god of Paternalism to tease him with.

She hugged his warm cloak closely around herself as they hustled along the path they had traversed in very different moods such a short time ago. Her heart was praising the Eternal, singing and shouting, and reproaching her, all at once. She rejoiced because her prayers had been answered, because Loukanos had surrendered at last, but her heart smote her for doing what she had not meant to do – she had judged him, and she had pushed him. She would talk to the Teacher about it – or if he was exhausted, Jude of Kerioth, who had showed such kindly interest in her from the beginning. Or perhaps the Twin – he must know the skill of balancing tension and harmony between man and wife if anyone did; he would understand her intentions had been good – or was she just trying to justify herself …?

Marah tossed her head with a guilty start … of *course* she didn't think of Loukanos in that way.

211

Loukanos was striding ahead of her, with a warm dizzy lightness in his head and chest, despite the sodden clothes which slapped his legs and kept his teeth chattering. There was a stiff breeze too, but the track was sheltered, and he was too elated to notice how strong it was becoming. He was still feeling somewhat incredulous, trying to grasp what had just happened to him.

There were old wounds in his soul, yes, that was it ... he had bandaged them over the years, hiding the festering sores with layers of dressings – wit, pride, self-sufficiency, education, prosperity, adulation – the usual coverings of men. But unwashed and unchanged, the bandages had become filthy rags, glued to his skin. He saw now that he had been trying to peel them off with excruciating slowness, a slowness which was self-defeating. The more it hurt, the slower he pulled, the more it hurt.

Praise the Eternal for Marah, who knew about agony, who knew about confusion, who knew about surrender! Was there ever such a woman! One who did not thrust her lamp under a basket, pleading custom to absolve her from involvement in helping another. It struck him that he would not have been able to hear the same words from another man, nor even from his own sister. Marah the Magdalan's very detachment had freed him to listen with honesty. Thank God again for this woman with the courage to challenge him, to push him forward when he wanted to retreat! She had put her finger right on the heart of it – and suddenly he had realised what he ought to have known all along – that the only way to release himself from the congealed, outworn bindings was one swift rip.

Cautiously he ventured to all the sore places in his mind, touching lightly the old wounds of pain, betrayal, anger, resentment and shame ... why, there was nothing now but faint tenderness, a little numbness … yes, healthy scar tissue! Why had he hugged his misery for so long? He began to understand what Marah meant when she admitted her strange reluctance to ask for the healing she needed. Pain and turmoil was part of who she was. It was dreadful, but she recognised herself. Who would she be if the old parts of her were gone? What would be left? *And it was I who forced her hand!* he remembered wryly.

All at once he realised how high the wind had risen, and how far he was striding ahead, while poor Marah was struggling along behind him in her wet clothes, hampered by his heavy cloak which although warm, would be whipped by the wind. He turned repentantly – *Even in the midst of thanking God for her, I'm too selfish to wait!* – and was just opening his mouth to call to her – she had just looked up and smiled – when the trees were blanched by a terrifying sheet of lightning and the world was suddenly blotted out in dark, smothering cloud.

By the stars! – old habits died hard – this made no sense! *Such a cloud with a fierce wind? And no rain? Are we on Sinai with Moses?! In a cleft of the rock with Elijah?* A different kind of chill swept over him.

Close by in the wild darkness was the crashing of the waterfall the others had long since left, but all Loukanos could hear was the frightened screaming of a brave woman. He dashed back down the blackened pathway, through the violent thrashing of invisibly flailing leaves and moaning, threatening branches – shouting to her.

"Marah! It's all right! I'm here – I'm here!"

Dazzled by the lightning's after-images he collided heavily with her and they fell to the ground. As she wailed in terror, he dragged her with him under a mercifully thick bush, pulling the cloak up over her head, wrapping her tightly, holding her like a child. She was sobbing now against his soaking wet chest – and he threw convention to the howling wind, rocking her in his arms.

"You're safe. I've got you. My darling, it's all right. It's only a storm."

Oh, the relief of saying it aloud, if only in a murmur she would not hear above the savage buffeting of the tempest! And had she not touched his face, his lips, looked searchingly into his eyes, called him Louki?

"My darling. My darling!"

He rested his cheek on her head, closing his eyes on sudden hot tears.

Ah, Great God of all creation! You have brought me here and turned me inside out! And if I die at this moment, I will die happy. Blessed be thou, Master of the Universe, who causes to come forth bread from the earth – and love from a selfish heart!

His arms tightened as her warmth stole through him, then tightened again as the ground shook with a long, rolling thunder and she shuddered uncontrollably. He was holding her as he never had thought to hold her, they were alone as they ought never to have been, but suddenly, at that moment all he could think of was the day the dusty carpenter from Nazareth passed him in a crowd, carelessly dropping a cloak over his Grecian sandals – the same pair Loukanos was wearing now – wading out to meet Johannes in the waters of the upper Jordan … waters which had their source right here at the foot of Hermon, in the very spring above them … the day when light had flashed, thunder darkled and rocks had trembled with a Divine voice proclaiming, *"This is my Son, the Beloved."* There was something in the air at this very moment, so eerily similar, that he half expected to hear that voice again – the Voice which he had for so long shut out.

Had it not been for *that* day, he would not be here right now, already wondering which of the Twelve would baptise him in his turn, and whether he could be baptised on the Sabbath. (How had he been so stubbornly blind for so long!) Had it not been for *that* day, he would not be here now, snatching an impossible moment with an impossible woman who was not, and never would be, his … a moment for which his heart swelled in gratitude, and which he would never forget. But at last the gale was dwindling … the cloud was thinning … the darkness fading … and conscious that it was the last time, he risked the luxury of words once more, this time in a mere whisper.

"Marah, my beloved Magdalan! … My darling! … thank you …!"

His lips brushed the top of the cloak, under which she had finally ceased to sob, ceased to tremble … the light was strengthening … the wind dropping further. He slowed his gentle rocking, released her to struggle free of the protective cloak, and readied a bright, brotherly smile.

She sat up, tugged at her twisted clothes, and looked at him uncertainly, her eyes swollen, wiping her face inelegantly on a wet sleeve.

"Well now, you're a sight for sore eyes," he commented.

"I'm sorry," she sniffled, trying to laugh at herself and almost succeeding. "Please – please! – do not ever tell anyone I was so foolish. My reputation will be quite lost, and it has been very hard won. I am completely ashamed of myself. I was a ridiculous baby just now – but there's something about thunder and lightning which completely unnerves me."

The wind, the blackness, the crashing, the flashing lights, the screams … and then the sword! It was no wonder, he thought.

She pleaded in a muffled voice, "And you have to admit, that was a very strange storm."

"It was. Very. In fact, everything about today has been very strange. Don't worry, I won't tell anyone you lost your nerve, if you won't tell anyone I lost my fish!"

They crawled out from under the sheltering bush, and scrambled stiffly to their feet, shaking off leaves and sticks which the ferocious wind had plastered onto their wet clothes – both suddenly becoming very matter-of-fact.

"Look, the sun at last!" he said briskly.

"But not for long, I think. Will we still get back to camp before it sets?"

"Easily, if we have no more frights. Are you very cold?"

"Not as much as I was, thanks to you. I was more chilled with fear, I think ... the blood was just pounding in my veins, and my legs are still trembling. Brrr! That was terrible – horrible! But you will be frozen stiff and must take the cloak yourself now ... my dress is wool and holds warmth even when wet. We will be even warmer if we run, so let's hurry."

And so they hurried, but Marah had not been entirely truthful. The experience of the freakish storm had indeed been horrible, but a stronger jolt to her self-control was the undeniable fact that deep inside her terror of the wind she had finally understood her own heart.

Sheltering in his arms had been more than comforting – it was tremulously precious, disturbingly sweet. Never before had a man so held her, never before had she received such enveloping warmth and protection, such tenderness and respect ... and for the first time in her life, she was flooded with an overwhelming feeling of relief at being where she belonged at last – at last!

For a brief, intoxicating moment, a wild flare of longing had thrown wistful dreams into stark relief – to be snuffed out the very instant she glimpsed shadows of the children she might yet bear him.

I begged to serve the Master with my hands, my feet, my purse! But how free would she be to do so, belatedly chasing ambitions which rightly belonged to young girls? Loukanos of Philippi was not a Jew, he was not hers, and he was not an ordinary man. He was a man who moved easily through natural barriers of caste, race, language and distance, a born traveller, with so many natural gifts … he was not meant for domesticity! The Teacher would find a greater work for him to do, and he must not be tied or smothered.

As she determinedly ran ahead up the path she knew her secret was safe. He had not heard her lamentation as her deepest desires died stillborn, muffled as the incoherent words were in the shriek of the wind … those pitiful sobs of, "Louki! Oh, Louki! This is impossible!" … nor had he felt her chilled lips pressed to the faint warmth of his wet clothes. And she knew full well it was only wishful thinking, to fancy that deep in his breast she had heard a husky answering murmur of *"Dodi! Dodi!"*

But she would not be so weak again. The restoration of the Kingdom was too close. Greeks might come and Greeks might go, but the Messiah, the Master, Jeshua the Nazarene, the Son of God Most High, would go on forever! Because of *him*, she was a whole woman again; because of *him*, she believed in the love of her Creator; because of *him*, there was already more joy in her life than she had ever known. She would not pine for more. Was Eternity real or not? She knew it was! Vaster than any private griefs – it would fill the voids. Had not Louki's own sister shown that joy could reign when bitterness was deposed? Very well, then! She would not seek for love, instead she would give it. There was no time for anything else, and nothing else mattered.

A deep, prayerful breath, a mental shake, and she went on. And though she never looked back, in one sense Louki never left her – in that she adopted the name he gave her, and was known as the Magdalan from that time forward.

Chapter Twenty-one

CALEB was munching in his sleep. Dan rolled over on his elbow and grinned at the familiar weatherbeaten face. It had been a good Sabbath dinner and Caleb seemed to be enjoying it all over again. Uncle Joseph and Ittai were already stirring downstairs; but luxuriating in the holiday, Dan hugged his bed a little longer. He rolled on his back, staring lazily at the mud and reed ceiling by the open window, where an industrious spider was mending a torn section of her gauzy labyrinth. She was also being watched by a bulge-eyed gecko which was sunning itself upside down in the roughly daubed frame. Intent on evading the lightning-fast tongue of the motionless little lizard, a large green and gold fly blundered carelessly into the web, protesting loudly as it thrashed itself into tighter bondage. The spider turned and rubbed her feet together, like Aunt Etta rubbing her hands as she surveyed her larder.

"The spider's the housekeeper," Dan amused himself idly. "The gecko is a thief ... he's waiting for her to turn her back ..."

The speckled gecko crept closer, tongue flickering.

"He's very impatient ..."

The spider stopped work and sat back, waving her legs warningly, and the gecko chirped.

"I'm only looking!" Dan squeaked in the gecko's voice. "Nice fly you have here."

The gecko cocked its head on one side and wailed sadly.

"I'm so hungry … and it's a big fly … can't you spare me a morsel?"

Suddenly with a black flick of feathers a raven swooped by the window and vanished, picking off the gecko as it went. Dan felt sorry.

"Goodbye, spider," he wailed. "I *told* you I was only look-k-k-kuk – kuk – kawk!"

He clutched his throat and rolled around, kicking and making desperate noises, immersed in his graphic imitation of the gecko's last moments.

A burst of laughter made him return to reality with a jump. Uncle Joseph and Ittai were applauding in the doorway, and Caleb, his deeply crinkled eyes wide awake, was chuckling and clapping from his blankets.

"Very good, Dan!" he chortled. "When you're too old for the fields, you can sit in the market and be a storyteller."

Dan blushed and grinned. "Sorry, I suppose I woke you."

"I suppose you would have woken the whole house," Uncle Joseph said affably, "except that we were already awake. Now, come down, wash, eat, and we will check on the women and babies before setting off to Magdala for synagogue. After the service we may hear something there which will help us find Loukanos, or the Nazarene, or both."

"And as soon as we do," Ittai said with feeling, "I shall be hot on their heels! After the Sabbath, that is," he added impatiently.

220

"*Oh that the Sabbath were over!*" Uncle Joseph quoted sympathetically.

Dan thought about the Sabbath in Jerusalem – long ago – when Johanan was reciting the very same words ... when they were longing to finish their journey to the region of Bethany, impatient to see the Prophet standing in the lower Jordan waters called Bethabara. How different would everything be today, had the great man already been preaching at the other Bethabara over in Decapolis, where they went so much later! The same name, for a similar 'place of passage' – but a different region – and a very different outcome! *If only Father and Anna had been baptised there instead – Bukki would have been a long way off. If only!*

If! Oh, what a weary word that was! *If* they had ... or *if* Bukki had been sober or *if* he had not stumbled onto the top of the stairs just at the wrong moment! Any of those *ifs* would do! Then today Ammiel would be living, happily married to his Anna; and Dan might be preening himself as an elder brother – no doubt treated with the same delightful combination of awe and reckless affection he received from Marta's little ones. Anna of course would never have taken the constricting Nazirite vow, constantly vigilant lest products of the vine came near her plate or cup. She would not need to bind the rough strands of her fever-damaged hair protectively into seven carefully undisturbed locks. Like other women, she would wash and comb it freely in the sun each month, and children would tug and play with it as they did Marta's. As it was, even the twins knew they must not touch Auntie Anna's hair in case they accidentally broke a single one, thus – so the rabbis held – breaking her vow.

He frowned as he splashed his face in the outdoor water barrel, dashing droplets everywhere – he had to admit there was another side. Had Ammiel still been alive, Uncle Loukanos would have escaped back to Philippi after the wedding, and never have met the Baptiser, seen the Messiah, or stayed in the land looking for truth. Lazy Bukki would still be living with them, grudging any service, quarrelling with poor Aunt Etta. Caleb would still be a hireling, not a Master of the Flock. Blind Mordecai might still be begging in the street and Old Dinah would not be ruling her own kitchen. Dan and many other boys in Cana would not have had Mordecai's wise tutoring in Asa's courtyard ... he was almost alarmed at how long the list was becoming! Dan sighed impatiently – did the blessings which had followed the tragedy justify it? Did thinking of them make him feel better – or worse? The idea that his father's death could have brought good things, was just too disturbing. He scrubbed his head with the towel and ran inside to rummage for breakfast. What was the use of wondering what might have been or might not have been, whether things were better or not? It only made your head spin, and changed nothing. Better just get on with it.

And right now there was plenty to get on with. Dan sent a wistful thought in the direction of Johanan up in Jerusalem, consoling himself that at least his cousin would be in Banayim very soon for *Succoth*, the Festival of Booths, and *then*, oh! wouldn't they just talk and talk!

Ittai and Marta exchanged endearments through her window, making a game of it for the children. The women had decided to say nothing to him of the red spots which had sprinkled Marta's body, nor admit that the excuse Etta had given the Dabab for Marta's renewed separation had overnight become ominously true.

"Please, Anna, there is no point," Marta begged. "He is worried sick already, and what can he do?"

Anna however, took Uncle Joseph aside and, entrusting him with a private letter for her brother, urged him to find Loukanos as soon as they could travel.

"I wish you could go in search of him this very day," she confessed, "but even Magdala itself is strictly too far away for a Sabbath journey; though we do stretch the law to get to the synagogue." She shook her head impatiently. "It strikes me that there is something not quite right about that."

Dan was under the shade tree rescuing a hapless little brown tortoise from the fascinated twins, and keeping an ear out for the conversation. *Do we break the law, then, by going to synagogue?* It was a strange paradox.

"No, Isaac! You can't ride him – you're too big." He put the docile creature safely into a crevice of the rocks around the herb garden, puzzling over the adults' comments as he shepherded the cheerfully capering little boy back towards the house and into Aunt Etta's welcoming kitchen.

"Mind Auntie's stick, now," Dan warned, knowing the children sometimes ran into it when excited, nearly toppling the deeply bent woman.

Isaac looked at it with great respect, dropped to all fours and announced, "Bad Donkey!" He kicked his back legs, and brayed noisily. "Auntie whack me!" he urged happily, pointing to the stick.

"Oh, what a good idea!" Aunt Etta chuckled, tapping him on the tail obligingly. Isaac giggled – his next trick would be a Good Donkey who needed an apple.

Dan laughed too as he ran outside, but inwardly he was wondering with a degree of exasperation, *If I have to walk a long* *way to a Sabbath service, and I **still** do it, isn't that **more** virtuous than if I only had to step across the street?"*

Joseph lightly drummed his manicured fingers on the packet Anna gave him, looking thoughtful.

"You know, my dear, I have kept all the commandments since I was a boy, and even read the whole of Moses for myself … but had it not been for the rabbis, I would never have dreamed that walking to worship my God or help my neighbour, counted as *servile work* which was not to be undertaken on a holy day. But if the learned men in the books of exposition have declared it must be thus, and have prescribed an appropriate distance to avoid inadvertent violations of law, do I risk thinking they are wrong? No – if obedience is the way to everlasting life, I do not risk any such thing. After all, who is more likely to be in error – those who study scripture all their lives, or a plain Cypriot merchant who ducks his Levitical privileges, to pursue commerce?"

Anna had been keeping an amused eye on Abi, who was towing patient Old Caleb around the clearing in search of another tortoise. Now she turned decidedly and looked her uncle full in the face.

"Do you know, Uncle Joseph, I believe if it was up to me, I would leave at once, regardless. I think – after all – that I must agree with what the Nazarene declared on his first tour here. He said it is *always* lawful to do good, *even* on the Sabbath, and the Law supports him. I respect your principles, Uncle, but since you are squeamish it may help if I remind you that both north and south of us, Magdala and Tiberius have expanded greatly since the time you had the shore house built. Banayim will be swallowed in the middle of them both before much longer! Therefore, you can easily count this place almost as an outer suburb of either town; in which case, as far as I am concerned, you are justified not only in travelling to synagogue, but also in taking your full two thousand cubits beyond the boundaries of either Tiberius *or* Magdala."

Uncle Joseph blinked, and Dan gaped.

"Anna! You are as good as the lawyers!" her uncle exclaimed – not sure whether or not she was joking.

"*Amma!* You are as bad as the Pharisees!" her boy declared, knowing she wasn't, on either count.

"Good for you, Anna bath Netzir!" said Ittai stoutly, having torn himself away from the baby and blown so many kisses to Marta that he felt quite lightheaded. "What you say makes sense to me!"

Anna nodded as decidedly if she was herself on the verge of setting out for Magdala and beyond.

"I must hear the Nazarene again, soon. He has a way of clearing the cobwebs from the scriptures. Surely they speak for themselves? Did every scribe who copied the records, roll himself up inside them to interpret? Remember the Prophet! *Practise the spirit of the Law*, he urged, and so does the Teacher." She sighed resignedly. "Marta needs help, and we are quibbling about how many steps are lawful before the sun sets. Let each obey his own conscience and not judge the other."

She hugged Dan. "God speed, my son. I know you and Caleb must leave early tomorrow, so make the most of your time today."

The men strode on to Magdala. Dan grinned to observe that Uncle Joseph was counting steps under his breath, but Ittai was sadly noticing how true was Anna's observation about Banayim. There were more and more dwellings crawling out towards them from Magdala these days and their little hamlet was no longer as isolated as it was. He loved the peace of village life and did not care for townships, but if it would help Marta he would live in a tree in Tiberius with all the fowls of the air twittering around his ears and a seething bazaar at his feet. Old Caleb stumped along jauntily, warbling to himself, out of tune as usual.

"How lovely thy dwellings, Eternal One, my soul longs for thy courts." He half-hummed, half sang, anticipating the pleasure of sitting in the stillness and calm of the cramped synagogue with its measured rise and fall of reverent voices.

"My heart, my body, seeks the Living God!" Dan's fresh young voice called back to him. Ittai and Joseph emerged from their own reveries to join in, until they were all singing heartily together – Caleb taking the exclamation and the rest of them chorusing the responses with as much harmony and feeling as they could muster while keeping up a good pace along the path.

"Homely sparrow, wandering swallow, each find houses for their young," croaked the old shepherd who had no home of his own.

"Thus do all find shelter in thine altars!" replied the others.

"Eternal King and Mighty God, Blest be the dwellers in Thy house," he chanted happily.

"They will sing and praise Thee evermore!" they answered, the last note rising to a triumphant height.

'But it's too short!" cried Dan. "Sing it again!"

So they did, several times. Oh, it felt good to be tramping along to synagogue, singing with the men! Dan swung his arms and lengthened his stride, filling his bony chest with the fresh morning air, feeling the breeze tickling his incipient moustache, singing out with all his might.

"How lovely thy dwellings, Eternal One, my soul longs for thy courts.

My heart, my being, seeks the Living God!

Homely sparrow, wandering swallow,

Each find houses for their young,

Thus do all find shelter in thine altars!

Eternal King and Mighty God,

Blest be the dwellers in Thy house,

They will sing and praise Thee evermore!"

There was a kind of choking sound from Dan as they sang the last word. Caleb looked at him, surprised that Dan would play his 'strangled gecko' trick at such a moment ... Dan coughed, cleared his throat, and sang again ... *"and praise Thee ever–m–*awk!"

The men looked at each other, they looked at Dan, and then they all roared with laughter, thumping his thin shoulders in congratulations.

"The Frog! The Frog! Dan's got the Frog!"

Dan beamed from ear to ear and jumped for joy. "Hah! Hah!" he yelled triumphantly. "Wait till I tell the women!"

"They'll probably cry," Ittai cautioned with a grin. "But they'll have plenty of time to get used to it before you sound very different."

Dan looked disappointed. "Oh! But Johanan's only hopped around for a little while and then dropped almost overnight!"

"No, no, this is better," Old Caleb encouraged him. "You're a slow but steady grower, Dan boy. It will be easier on you; and you know, your height will keep creeping up and your voice creeping down, for far longer than the fast sprouters like Johanan. You'll catch up in the end. Just you wait and see."

"Really? Is this true?"

Uncle Joseph scratched under his fine turban. "Possibly," he said cautiously. He'd never noticed. Babies were born, children grew, boys turned into men ... it was all rather a blur to him. Ittai, however, nodded emphatically.

"Yes," he agreed. Of course, there was no guarantee Dan would be any taller or have any deeper a voice at the end of it. But no need to say that. "Caleb is right – you won't outgrow your strength or have too much of the squeak and gargle when you talk – or sing. It's the sprouters who get the most pimples, too, so don't you envy them for a minute! See these pock marks on my face?"

Dan peered at them with respect. "Were you a sprouter, Ittai?"

Ittai groaned in mock despair. "Was I that! And moody! Oh, my poor mother! May she rest in peace, for I gave her none in those days! She used to say it was just as well I had the clay to punch when I was in a temper!" He guffawed suddenly. "I wonder she didn't bake me alive in one of my own ugly pots."

More laughter from his companions – it was the first time Ittai had spoken jovially of his mother since she had died, and it was good to hear. They arrived at the synagogue with cheerful faces; despite the inner questions which would demand a serious answer before long ...When, Where, and How would they find Loukanos?

Chapter Twenty-two

THE service was over, they had mingled afterwards and gleaned useful news. The Nazarene was in Iturea, possibly still as far north as Caesarea Philippi – but rumour was that he might soon be slowly working south for Festival of Booths in Jerusalem. Whether that was true or not, he was bound to pass through Galilee, and most likely, Capernaum. If Loukanos was still haunting the core group of followers, they might both be found in the same place.

That was enough for Ittai. He boldly went up to the Rabbi and asked where exactly in the Books of the Law did Moses declare a man might travel only two thousand cubits from his place on the Sabbath.

The Rabbi looked calculatingly down his long nose, took a deep breath, and waved his hands expressively. The *prescribed* Sabbath distance … ah, well, yes, h'rr'm! he could not say *exactly* where without consulting the holy books, and did Ittai seriously expect him to sit around unrolling scrolls and searching all afternoon? Why, that would be *work!* And today was the Sabbath!

"Is it still work if you search your memory and not your books?" Ittai asked bluntly.

The Rabbi looked taken aback.

"If it is so important," Ittai persisted, "and Moses himself wrote it down, wouldn't you know the passage by heart, or how many turns of which scroll would find the right place?"

"My dear Potter," the Rabbi answered with a kindness he did not feel, "let me also ask you a question. Would I expect you have by heart the precise recipes of all your glazes? Do I ask how you mingle your clays? Or do I trust you to know your trade, and accept your workmanship without question?"

Unimpressed, Ittai waited for more, but the Rabbi turned away, patting him on the shoulder. "Is a poor Rabbi not worthy of the same trust? Stick to your clay, my friend, and leave the finer points of the Law to those whose calling it is."

With a wide smile, the Rabbi hailed an invisible friend in the crowd, and excused himself quickly, leaving a frustrated Ittai resolved to take the same bold stand as Anna bath Netzir!

Two things he *did* know about working on the Sabbath – that a male of eight days was still to be circumcised, and a distressed animal was still to be rescued. For these, there must be no hesitation, no delay. The first he knew because any man took care to know everything there *was* to know about circumcision. The second he knew from Old Caleb himself, who on many a Sabbath over the years, had delivered lambs, tended wounds, fought predators, and dragged sheep out of dangers of all kinds.

"Quite lawful!" Caleb had nodded, proud of his knowledge. "Animals don't know the difference, you see? Not their fault!"

Ittai shook his head. *Save a lamb, or cut your son – both permitted on the Sabbath!* They didn't seem to be at all similar to him. He stamped over to Joseph and Dan and told them so.

230

"How *they* are allowed – when a bit of harmless walking is proscribed as rigidly as life and death – is beyond me," he complained heatedly.

Joseph tapped his fingers together. "Obedience is everything, of course … You could say that all obedience *is* ultimately about the choice between life and death … and I prefer to err on the safe side. Gathering sticks is harmless in itself, but the man who did so on the Sabbath died for his rebellion, not for the task." He looked at Ittai's darkened face, and hastened to add, "Understanding *why* a law is so, yes, I realise that is helpful, if not strictly necessary."

"Maybe it's not always necessary, but today it is, to me! So tell me if you know – why does Moses make exception for an animal and a baby?" Ittai expostulated. "What could they possibly have in common except noise, appetite, and a lack of house training?"

"Yes, why?" Dan asked curiously. It was a very good question.

Old Caleb shook his head at him fondly, his grizzled, Sabbath-combed beard wagging in sympathy.

"Why, Dan boy – it is clear! They are both ignorant and helpless!"

Joseph shot him another respectful look.

"Right, old man. It is the principle of the matter which connects them," he answered thoughtfully. "Neither can help itself, and both are in danger of death. The animal's danger is physical, the man child's is legal. He must be circumcised the eighth day, or remain outside the Covenant. Someone must save them, and that someone will be working on the Sabbath … but blamelessly. You see?"

"Yes, I see! The Sabbath law will not hinder the choice of Life over Death!" Dan's eyes widened at the revelation.

Uncle Joseph said seriously, "That is correct. But walking a certain distance has nothing to do with life and death, so obedience is still necessary."

Ittai squared his shoulders and set his jaw.

"In this case, I beg to differ," he said firmly. "In this case, it *may* be a matter of life over death, and my Marta is worth more than a sheep! I will not be waiting for sunset, Sabbath or no. I am not engaging in servile work, in fact, quite the reverse – I am *deserting* my work, to save my wife! If I am mistaken, God will forgive me."

"I understand your passion," Uncle Joseph replied cautiously, "and as my dear niece reminded us, we must not judge each other. I too, do not wish to lose any more time, and so will not retrace my steps to Banayim. However, I will wait out the day, according to my conscience. You will be only a half a day ahead of me. What say I take the west side of Jordan, and you the east? Good, it is agreed! But my friend, you will need more than your cloak and flask. No, no – repay me in kind later – there's hardly an uncracked dish left in the shore house. I plan to make *ostraca* of the lot!"

"Thank you, Uncle!" Accepting the generous purse which the foresighted Joseph had prudently stowed in his own capacious coat, Ittai embraced him warmly.

"God will reward you! You are truly a kind and neighbourly man. I will hunt out my finest bowls and cups for you when we return."

With good feeling, they went their various ways.

Ittai strode north, determined to beg a place on the first boat that appeared near the shore. If he could get most of the way to Bethsaida by water, it would save time, and he could then head up river towards Paneus.

Uncle Joseph went in search of lodgings, and a donkey, equally determined to hire both the moment the sun set. That arranged, he would sleep well, and begin at first light.

Old Caleb and young Dan waved them off, and started home. They were in a buoyant mood – singing snatches of song all the way back to Banayim; Dan testing his voice to see how high he could reach before the queer little catch would come in, and whether he would squeak and honk like Johanan had. He was relieved rather than otherwise to find that while he definitely had the Frog at last, he had only its husky croak, and not its unpredictable leap, unless he yelled. Yes, Caleb was right, as usual. A gradual change would save a lot of ribbing, no doubt.

"Well, what a day!" Caleb's contented voice broke in on Dan's thoughts. "Just as well we're back with the sheep tomorrow, eh? Nice and peaceful again! A man can't take too much hurry and scurry at my age, you know." He wheezed heavily to prove his point.

A teasing reply was on Dan's tongue – *The oldest chicken runs the fastest from the pot'* – which was one of Old Dinah's sayings – but just in time he remembered the severe chest cold which had prostrated Caleb only weeks ago. Anna had warned him that the old man would not have his full strength back for a long time, and he had completely forgotten. Guiltily the boy slowed his pace immediately but Caleb's creased eyes twinkled at him beneath their overhang of wiry grey eyebrow.

"It's all right, Dan, there's a bit of puff left in me yet! And we're nearly there."

As they approached the village, Dan rejoiced over how much exciting news they were bringing back. Where to start, that was the question! Should he begin with most important part first – the rumoured route of the Nazarene? Or should he do that irritating thing the women always did – start with all the *least* important bits, saving the best part like a special treat until last of all? He was opening his mouth to ask Caleb's opinion – when – *Wait!*

An unusual disturbance in the village! Swelling up and spilling out of the cluster of houses ahead – a clamour of voices – loud, indignant, angry – what was going on in Banayim?

Threaded through the commotion was an anguished, angry wailing, and the shuddering sobs of a child who has cried itself sick.

"Something's wrong!" Dan began to run.

"What is it?" Caleb cried, puffing along behind him, as the huddle of gesticulating villagers came into view. A tall woman in the centre of the crowd bent over, disappearing from their sight.

"Anna! Anna!" Dan shouted.

Forgetting all else, the two dashed down the hill towards the turbulent voices. To Dan's immense relief, Anna reappeared, standing up with young Thad in her arms, stroking his hair, murmuring to him. Over her shoulder was her medicine satchel, and beside her Aunt Etta was comforting a howling, crouching Judith, whose face was buried in her veil. Hovering around them was a very scared-looking Zaccheus.

"What has happened?" Puffing in earnest, Caleb stared at the street in bewilderment.

Rachel burst out of the press like froth from fermenting wine. "You may well ask!" she said crossly. "Oh, you may very well ask. Go home!" she added shrilly to Old Zack. "Now is not the time to throw a sop to your conscience!"

Caleb and Dan exchanged stunned glances.

234

Anna lifted her cheek from the child's head. "It's all right, Rachel, he means well. Etta and I will take care of them and Zaccheus will take care of the street." She looked at him pointedly. "Won't you." It was a statement, not a question.

There was a sharp intake of breath. It was still the Sabbath! Anna sighed impatiently, but the wizened fig-merchant spoke at once, his squinting eyes darting anxiously from one to another.

"On my mother's grave! I will begin as soon as the sun sets," he promised nervously, and escaped from the muttering faces.

"Go home for now, the rest of you," Anna's quiet, carrying voice stilled them. "But will you come to the Travellers' House after lamplight if you have anything more to tell? We will talk then."

Nodding and murmuring, the villagers melted away, and for the first time Dan noticed the mess – and a distinctive rotten smell. Smashed pottery littered the street, purple stains were splashed on walls, runnels of cloudy liquid splattered the dirt – and olives of all descriptions were everywhere. Black, green, purple – hard and round, withered, stalky, or squashed into paste – slimy stones stripped of their meat, and trodden like gravel in the stained dust.

"Is this some new plague of Egypt?" Caleb marvelled. "Has it been raining olives?"

Etta beckoned to him as they gently helped the gasping, limping girl – still drearily moaning, and doubled up in pain.

"Old friend – will you take two steps further to Ittai's? Bring us lamps, oil, vinegar and clean rags, if you can find any. And a couple of washing bowls. He will not grudge them, I know."

"Gladly," he replied, and ran immediately to load himself up from Marta's deserted kitchen, even though he was burning with curiosity. Every household had these things – why did they need to borrow Ittai's? Still, as Cypriot Joseph had implied, understanding was not necessary to obedience!

Meanwhile, at a sign from Anna, Dan followed the women to the hireling's house. He stepped into the gloom of the dwelling, with its boarded back window, and as his eyes adjusted to the dimness, he looked around in astonishment.

"What in the world happened here?" he muttered, aghast.

Not one stick of furniture was unbroken, and the heavy table was on its side in a jumble of rubbish. Every pot was smashed, every basket, box and bag overthrown, their contents flung around the room and dashed or smeared over the walls. Clothes, bedding and food – and more olives – were mingled together with shards of pottery, and the air was rank with the sharp smell of vomit, and the soiled clothes of a petrified child. Only a brass pot of water on the cold fire was undamaged, and it lay sideways in soggy ashes, half empty.

Aunt Etta took charge of the little boy, while Anna sat Judith down carefully just inside the door. Gently drawing aside the veil, she tilted the girl's exposed face to catch the light.

Dan gasped. With the tears, the blood, the purple swelling, the split lip and misshapen nose ... surely this could not be the same Judith of yesterday ... the young woman whose thin, careworn face had sparkled into glowing warmth and life simply because a mere boy had tricked her into treating herself with a gift she had meant for him.

"Make yourself useful, my son!" Anna almost snapped, unstrapping her satchel.

Dan shut his mouth and sprang to work. Underneath his shock and disbelief was running one dark certainty – whoever had done this ugly thing – Samuel's Eli would have his blood!

236

Chapter Twenty-three

IT was very black – wild – stormy – and somewhere there was a kind of whirlpool which sucked at the thoughts which spun crazily on the edge of the universe. There was a thud thud thud thud which might have been running feet, or his heart, but no matter which, because he could run like a gazelle and never tire, he could fly over the mountains, he could swim through the Harp, the sea, the sea which was a harp, Chinneroth, he could strum its strings with every stroke, and the kick of his feet would sound the beat. Ah, he was a chief musician, the chief musician upon Chinneroth! Yes, upon the harp, upon the sea – he could skim the sparkling waters in a lover's craft, where Naami sang with her harp and called him ... he could sing to her as deep answered deep, and walk on the water, as he ran to her side ... sweet Naami whose very name was Pleasant! And how pleasant she was, how sweetly she sang, billowing forth on the waves of Chinneroth, her gown billowing before her, swelling tightly, the waters breaking, singing louder, shrill, shriller – screaming! The harp moaning, a sweeping threnody of despair! Oh my Naami! Cry for the wise women! Shout for the midwife! Deliver her! Harp strings straining, snapping, one by one. Day and night and day and night and day breaking again. Breaking. Breaking my sweet Naami – so pale, so pained, so tired, too tired ... too quiet ...

Onwards he ran as the blackness swirled mercifully around, blotting out the sound of the rhythm of the words of the thoughts of the mind which could never rest unless it was sunk in the tortured pit. In the pit there were no words left, only pain. Over the pit lived another man who tended other men's sheep, who spoke and ate and moved almost like other men. Who came to the house which was once a home, and paid a cringing creature to keep a child who had Naami's eyes, which he could not bear to see. A man who sometimes lifted up the dweller in the pit, when they would become one, and feel strongly together in the safety of the anger. Today they had united in a violence he had not known before as he looked through the outside man, but somehow it had fractured their bond, and an evil had come of it he could taste but not see. There was a sick blankness where he ought to have been, with the pit opened to heaven. Perhaps the outer man was slipping away. Exhausted by the struggle. Like Naami. Exposed, frightened, he ran and ran and ran, and the lonely places heard his rending despair.

Chapter Twenty-four

DAN stretched himself stiffly. The sun had set, and Sabbath was over at last, but he and Caleb had already been working for some time without a break. He was glad they had earlier been discussing the matter of labouring on the Sabbath – it eased his conscience considerably. But, as Anna had firmly pointed out, how could they leave either Judith or Thad for hours in the state they were found, to satisfy a point of law? When Old Zack had run into the clearing shouting for her help, she and Etta had followed him back to find Banayim shocked and dithering, trying to console Judith, but doing nothing useful. Anna had solved the dilemma at once, ensuring that nobody else in the village felt obliged to break the Sabbath, by taking the responsibility on her own family. As for Old Caleb, he felt no conflict whatsoever. He was so outraged that he would have done far more than clear up a broken house on the day of rest – he would have built it from scratch, if it had made any difference to the poor young creature who had been so viciously assaulted.

Now the hireling's house was quiet, and if not totally clean yet, it was at least restored to some kind of order. The other women had promised to turn out in force and clean it properly in the morning, but for now, belongings were sorted, food salvaged, smashed items piled outside, and those which might be mended were set in one corner.

On the swept hearth, a low fire was glowing under a battered copper pot in which simmered barley water with honey. At the table, a stack of warm flat bread drizzled with oil had slowly been devoured in silence. Young Thad had been alternately distracted and soothed, washed, fed, and sung to sleep on Aunt Etta's generous lap, and now lay exhaustedly sleeping in the soft, warm bed which Anna had made up in the back room. Judith, one foot strapped, her ribs bound and her swollen face firmly swathed in bandages, lay beside him in an uneasy sleep, induced by an acrid extraction of lettuce and poppy, thanks to Anna's satchel.

In the street, Zaccheus had dutifully appeared as the sun sank, and was now sweeping and scraping busily. Soon everyone would be lighting lamps, and those who had more to tell, would meet at the end of the street. Dan caught his mother's eye and she smiled at him gratefully as he passed around the hot sweet barley water.

"You've done well, Dan, you and Caleb – and dear Etta, too."

The clearing up had been done with a burst of reactive energy after a nerve-jangling experience which Anna almost had not had the stomach to undertake. In preparation, Etta had whisked little Thad across the communal courtyard to Widow Shana's, for a noisy singing game about a lion hunt. As this involved much covering and uncovering of ears and eyes, with ferocious growls and a chorus of yells and claps, it had the desired effect of not only cheering the boy up, but making him deaf to all other sounds.

Inside the house, the others moved swiftly under Anna's direction. Braced against a wall, Old Caleb sat Judith between his knees, his strong, sinewy hands clamping her head back against his chest so she could neither move nor turn it. Dan knelt beside them, firmly imprisoning Judith's nervous hands in her lap, while the old shepherd murmured assurances as if to a trapped lamb. In a flash Anna was inelegantly straddling the frightened girl's thin body.

"Open your mouth and take a nice deep breath for me, *dodi!* Good girl. *(Eternal God! Help me!)* And breathe out hard – *now!*" Clenching her teeth Anna firmly realigned the broken bone and cartilage of Judith's nose.

Dan felt Judith's shriek rasp the flesh from his skeleton, but it was over in moments. Caleb gently released the swooning girl, tears coursing down his craggy face, as Anna slumped back, pale and clammy. Dan scrambled to his feet and staggered outside, where he was violently sick. But the ghastly job was done, and now that the poor girl was safely in her therapeutic sleep, Anna had only to hope it was done well enough. She had observed her brother performing this operation, but never had she attempted such a thing herself. Had she not, more than Judith's breathing may have been compromised.

How I wish Loukanos was here! If I have not righted it properly ... For a moment her thoughts trailed off into wordlessness as Blind Mordecai's crushed face came before her. Oh, how quickly a person's whole life could be changed, and how quickly could their whole character be judged differently because of a drastic change in appearance! Judith's crooked teeth and her thin cheeks gave a piquancy to her looks which was not unpleasant, but a thickened curled lip, and a grotesquely twisted nose suddenly would change that to an ugliness which would forever cast her in a different light to all who looked upon her. Anna prayed fervently that the lip would scar neatly, and that the nose would heal reasonably straight, even if a lump in it was inevitable.

Without beauty, without family, without skills, without money – who would marry such a girl? What would become of her? One who had been battered, a drudge whose eyes held fear and whose face showed her history – who else would take her to wife or to work, except another who felt justified in ill-treating someone so apparently worthless? Her old age did not bear thinking about, if she lived that long. Would the coming Kingdom of the Messiah make a difference to such as her? Surely it would – it must! But when – and how?

Anna shook herself. It was time she went up the street to meet the others. Etta would stay here. Dan could take a message back to Marta later on – the poor woman must be frantic with curiosity, if not anxiety by now, and … well, it would sort itself out. One thing at a time!

Old Caleb and Dan scuttled around in the Travellers' House, lighting lamps and piling cushions. Anna stood at the door as several people hurried in, eager to tell their story and ask about Judith and Thad. She held up her hand to stem the chatter.

"They are sleeping. Little Thad was not hurt, only badly shaken. Judith – well, you saw her face for yourself. I think she has some cracked or perhaps broken ribs, and certainly a broken nose … and black eyes. One foot is badly sprained, and she is covered in welts. Praise God, I don't think she is in any immediate danger. There is always the chance that a broken rib may pierce a lung, but I see no signs of that so far. Of course, I am not a doctor."

She sat at the table, gesturing for the others to sit as well. They crowded around, and those who could not fit on stools or benches took the straw mats and flat cushions on the stamped earth floor, and leaned comfortably against the plastered walls.

242

"Zaccheus, Rachel and Malachi, Widow Shana, Sabba Zimri – and little Huldah! You here too, and not in bed?"

Little Huldah looked up indignantly as she wriggled herself on to the bench beside sober, grey-haired Zimri.

"*Sabba!* Grandfather! I'm nine years old!" she blurted out to him, and Sabba Zimri patted her hand warningly.

"My granddaughter doesn't mean to be rude – and she is not here for curiosity. She does have something to tell us."

Anna reproached herself at once. *Oh, I must be growing old! Why should she be any less sharp than Dan was at that age, just because she's short and plump and only a little girl? And I have been musing about the cruelty of judging on appearances! Shame on you, Anna!*

"I'm sorry, Huldah, of course you are not a baby any more, are you? Thank you for coming here with your *Sabba* tonight. This is a sad business, and we must know more of what happened before we can decide what to do next."

"Exactly!" Rachel snapped. "What is the village coming to – that's what I'd like to know! And if it comes to that, what is the Land coming to? Nothing but tumult and upheaval for the last few years, and no Kingdom in sight, if you please."

Dan forgot his manners and interrupted.

"But you don't blame the holy prophets of God for this, surely? Our great Johannes, and Jeshua? Men who have preached nothing but peace and goodwill?"

Rachel narrowed her eyes. "Prophets of God? All I can say is, there's not so much extra peace and goodwill going around that you'd notice it, in my opinion."

"Neighbours – stop!"

It was Old Zack who held up his hand this time, his expression still haggard, his body stiff among the soft cushions. He was not in a mood for luxury tonight. He twisted his hands together remorsefully. "Let us not be distracted from our business here! I am seen as responsible, I know."

"Oh, we know!" Rachel retorted, but her husband put a rare restraining hand on her arm.

"Silence, Rachel!" he said sternly – and so shocked was she, that she obeyed at once, shutting her mouth with a breathless snap. "Let Zaccheus tell us all he knows."

"Please," Anna nodded.

Zaccheus took a steadying breath and plunged on. "She bought my olives, two big crocks of them. She was too tired to prepare her own, and I had been putting mine up for some weeks, so I had plenty ready for sale."

Rachel snorted. He had plenty because nobody in Banayim was fool enough to buy them – except Judith. Dried figs were one thing – you could see what you were getting, most of the time. But newly pickled olives swimming in a dark pot, still too fresh even to be tasted ... well, it was simply *asking* to be cheated.

"Oh, I know you all thought I would skimp on the salt!" Old Zack cried defensively, "and perhaps I am a little too saving at times ... but if people want cheap produce, they can't expect high quality, can they? Am I to pay for it out of my own pocket and make no profit? I am not a charity, I am a working man! And for those who buy ready-prepared, the convenience – or the quantity – is more important to them than a little lowering of the standards. *Cheap* olives or *no* olives may be the only choice for some. Well, many will take cheap, and nothing wrong with that, is there?"

Rachel was rolling her eyes and making barely suppressed huffing sounds under her breath. Sabba Zimri rapped impatiently on the table with his leathery knuckles.

"With respect, old man, you are not here to justify your trade. So Judith bought your olives. Now get on with the rest of it."

"I did not see what happened," Zaccheus gulped. "But I heard him roaring about the olives."

"I was in my vegetable garden," Malachi broke in. "Not weeding, of course, not working, just looking; when I saw him striding in from the far end of the street, straight out of the scrub."

Caleb and Dan exchanged glances – why was it that anyone who did not attend synagogue was at such pains to explain that they were not breaking the Sabbath!

Anna said crisply, "Whom did you see? Do you mean Zaccheus? Let us have clarity, please!"

"He means Thaddeus of course!" Widow Shana said excitedly. "I saw him myself! I was hanging out my – that is to say, I was hanging out *of* my window ..." She gave a mental shudder. Hanging out of a window was hardly ladylike, but better than admitting she had been hanging out her *dishcloth*, on the Sabbath! "... and there was Thaddeus simply marching like a legion up the street. He had nothing in his hands, so he wasn't bringing a gift for his little boy, and he didn't even look glad to be home for a Sabbath at last ... he looked stern and grim." She nodded. "Marching like a legion!" she repeated, proud of her description.

Dan privately doubted that one man could march like a whole legion of soldiers, but Widow Shana had not finished yet. "And there was something not right about his eyes," she added, less certainly.

245

Anna sat a little straighter. "Was there indeed!" she remarked thoughtfully. "Then what happened?"

Rachel leant forward. "Well, my dear, the Widow may say there was something wrong with his eyes, but he could see his own house clearly enough. I *happened* to be passing just then, and he flung open the door, and stamped on the doorstep roaring for Judith to give him food. She ran up, very flustered – of course, she had not expected him! She never had any idea from one week to the next when the wretched man might turn up, and more than once, my Malachi – such a soft heart – has had to give her vegetables on account just to get her through."

She glossed over the memories of all the times she had given her husband the rough edge of her tongue over this softness of heart, and continued.

"Well, you know, Judith was never very beforehand with her housekeeping, and she had only food for herself and the boy prepared, and it was clearly not enough for a hungry man who had not eaten for two days."

"Two days! How do you know he had not eaten for so long?" Anna asked.

"Why, my dear, half the village must have heard him bellowing the very words!" Rachel said, surprised. "But of course, I forget, in the Hollow, you would not have heard anything. What I can't understand is *why* he was so hungry. There is no need for *anyone* to starve at this time of year, with gleanings all around in fields and groves." She gave her head a little toss, reflecting that at times Judith could have taken the boy and done some gleaning herself, rather than accepting Malachi's vegetables before she had the money to pay. And if it came to that, everyone knew that grubby old Zaccheus was secretly the richest man standing in their synagogue (when he went, that is), and *he* could have been more charitable without feeling it half as much.

Anna frowned. What Rachel said was true – so it was disturbing that Thaddeus had not eaten, or believed he had not eaten, for so long. Widow Shana, however, had no patience for the Dabab's opinions which only slowed down the tale to be told.

"Regardless of his hunger, there was no excuse!" she said firmly. "The way he shouted at the poor girl! He wanted something more than pap for children! Was there nothing better than stale bread and herbs when a man came home after slaving for his ungrateful brat? He didn't expect a fatted calf, but he did expect a better welcome! Oh, the language! I had to cover my ears! He cursed and swore and threw things … I could hear the crashes clear across the courtyard, and hoped he wouldn't burst out of the back and start smashing up the cistern, or snapping my brooms! Poor Judith was frantically babbling away – trying to placate him. It must have been then that she dished out the olives … not quite matured, most likely, but they *should* have been perfectly edible."

They all looked at Zaccheus, who writhed uncomfortably.

"I swear to you I salted them properly," he protested miserably. "A few sticks, some leaves, no doubt, may have got past me, and perhaps I could have changed the waters more often, but I tell you I did use enough salt! Why would I risk spoiling my own merchandise and wasting all my efforts? How would I make money once word got around?"

Rachel gave him a flinty look. "You would have sold them in the markets at Tiberius and denied they were yours if anyone came looking for you," she accused.

"Fermented!" growled Sabba Zimri, jabbing a cracked forefinger at Old Zack. "They were rotten, stinking, and fermented. One

247

greedy mouthful of those and he turned sick as a dog, and angrier than ever. Of course, it was a plot! A plot to poison him! I heard him yelling it from half the street away."

"That's when we heard the worst of it – the beating – grunts and thuds, shrieks and smashing," Malachi's eyes were troubled. "The boy was screaming, Judith was screaming, Thaddeus was screaming – he was out of his mind – trying to destroy the girl, destroy the house … it sounded like all the bulls of Bashan were loose in there. That's when Zaccheus ran for you, Anna, fearing there'd be sad harm done."

Anna looked at him. She looked at Sabba Zimri – at Rachel, at the Widow. They fell over themselves to answer her unspoken reproach.

"We did!"

"We went at once!"

"That is, once we realised he had gone too far …"

"Every woman or child gets a beating occasionally – be they wife or servant or son – you know that!"

"No," Anna replied evenly. "No, I don't know that, and nor does Dan. And please God, neither does little Huldah here."

Rachel bridled. What would the Nazirite know? She had never been married, never been owned by any man, she was half Greek and did not comprehend true submission.

"It was not our business! He has treated her roughly before and no ill came of it …"

"How could we interfere in a man's domestic affairs? I tell you, we ran to her aid as soon as we understood this was more than the usual bit of temper."

Anna sighed. "You ran to her aid … so you stopped him?"

There was a brief pause.

"By then he had finished with the house and was smashing pots in the street," they admitted, "and Judith was cowering in the doorway, with the child clawing at her in terror. She was beside herself, too frightened to stay inside, too frightened to go into the street. She refused to move until she knew you were coming."

Thaddeus had long gone by the time Anna had flown to the village with an aghast Aunt Etta determinedly hobbling in her wake.

Anna massaged her temples with a weary sigh. "Well, then I arrived – and Etta, then Dan and Caleb. In all the confusion, I suppose nobody noticed what happened to Thaddeus, or where he went. So that's all the story we have."

"Not all," piped up Huldah, now squirming impatiently on her grandfather's lap. "That's why I'm here. I was playing funerals with Tirzah down on the shore – behind this very house. We heard all the noise and thought we'd better just keep out of the way. Anyhow, all the wailing and crying and shouting was perfect for our funeral, you see? We knelt by our bier – it was a nice flat rock actually, with a beautiful body we'd made with sticks for bones and sand for flesh, periwinkles for eyes and seaweed for hair – and of course we were doing some sobbing and wailing of our own …"

She paused. Yes, it had been a really good body! She had been very proud of it. They were going to bury it in pebbles as if many mourners had respectfully placed their tributes of the stone of life, and then they were going to pour water over it to have the body conveniently 'decompose' … and then collect the stick bones for

249

an ossuary ... she sighed ... then it was all spoiled ... She collected her thoughts and went on.

"Well, we were having a lot of fun when Thad's father just sprang out of nowhere and screamed at us ..."

"Did he hurt you?" Anna asked quickly, but Huldah shook her head.

"Oh no, I think *we* scared *him*!" she said, her eyes round with the wonder of it. "He jumped around as if he was bitten, and went all frantic – crying and clawing at his hair, shouting out something about being dead and needing to be buried. He leapt on our lovely body and kicked it all to pieces, and then ran like the wind towards Magdala, splashing along the beach and moaning about a harp, I think. He was really strange ... and his eyes ..."

"I *said* there was something wrong with his eyes!" Widow Shana insisted.

"What about his eyes, Huldah?" Anna prompted gently.

She shrugged. "I don't know. They looked like stars, only black. Sort of, shining ..." She shivered. "They gave me a crawly feel, they reminded me of something, someone ..."

Anna squeezed her pudgy hand. "Thank you, Huldah, what you have told us is very helpful."

"I know!" Huldah added suddenly. She looked around at the others, who were watching her expectantly. "Marah All-Alone! That's it. He reminded me of Marah All-Alone, that time when Marta's twins were born! I was only little then, but I remember her queer eyes, and how she clutched at her hair."

"Why, yes!" Widow Shana gasped. "I believe you are right, Huldah. I remember too – wild and storming, she was, tearing her hair and her eyes blazing, just the same! Then there is our answer! Thaddeus has a devil, just like she did!"

Anna stood up. "Thaddeus has been fighting some inner demon ever since his beloved Naami died, there is no doubt. I knew he was in trouble, but I had no idea it was this bad. He must be found before he hurts someone else – or himself. At least we know he is going north, but what we can do about it puzzles me for the moment. Nobody can follow him in the night, that is clear."

"Somebody can," spoke up a humble voice which had been silent till now. "Somebody who has followed many a lost sheep in the night. And tonight we are blessed – there is a moon."

"Caleb!" Anna's eyes filled with unexpected tears. "Dear old man! You have so recently been ill, too! How could we ask you to do such a thing!"

"You are not asking," he replied simply. "But it needs to be done, and I can do it. I know him, and he knows me – we have worked together. He may take some of our old grazing routes. He will trust me."

"Oh, Caleb, he is not himself, and may *not* trust you or even know you at all. And you have not been well! What if you were to fall – or if he should attack you – or –"

"Mother!" Dan spoke firmly. "If Thaddeus is not stopped, others may suffer. Why should he be afraid of an old man and a boy? I will go with Caleb."

"Dan!" she cried in unaccustomed dread, "As you say – you are a boy! Your arm is not as stout as your heart."

Caleb put his own wiry arm around Dan's shoulders and looked at Anna with dignity.

251

"Anna bath Netzir, do not underestimate your son. He is a fast and true shot with a sling – as good as Eli, if not better. He will be my David against any Goliath – and pray God it will not be needed."

"What of the flock?" she stammered. "Your work, your responsibility …"

Dan frowned. "I know, mother. I have not forgotten, but this is also a responsibility, and I think there is a way. What Eli can do for a few days, he may do for a few more, if Samuel is agreeable. It will also be much safer for Thaddeus, if Eli can be made to see reason and stay with the flock."

Caleb nodded, reaching for his coat. "There need be no delay, you see. The main flock is just outside of Magdala, and Huldah says Thaddeus is heading that way so we will be running straight past Samuel and the others. They may even have seen Thaddeus themselves."

Dan was already pushing his feet into sandals. He glanced up at Anna as he laced the straps.

"I promise to heed Samuel if he orders me to stay, but he will have to replace me if so. Caleb must go, but not alone."

Anna looked at the boy with an unfathomable expression, which held something of pain, trepidation, and pride. *Ah, Ammiel, your son is no longer a child!* She lifted her hands, palm upwards, in resignation.

"Take all you need. Go with God."

Chapter Twenty-five

BLACK-skinned Aida sat Parosh's fat son Manna on her bony little knees and took an exaggerated breath.

"Make my bricks! Make my bricks! Find your straw and make my bricks!" she sang in a gruff voice, scowling as sternly as she could.

Manna chanted back happily, "*How* many *bricks*, how *many*-do-I *make?*" and flung a flat stone from his sticky fist to the ground, where Auntie Aida had scratched random numbers in a circle.

"Oh!" she groaned, "Look, Manna – what number is that? Oh, dear, it's landed on a fifty! Fifty bricks! Poor Auntie Aida! Do I have to?"

"Yes, yes, yes, Auntie," he clapped excitedly. "Count lots!"

"Why did I start this game?" Aida pulled faces over her shoulder at her husband, who merely grinned at her as he totted up the figures on his wax tablets. She began obediently to jog the heavy child, a bounce for every brick. "One, two, three, four, five, six, seven, eight, nine ten – twenty – *fifty!*"

"No! No!" he protested with a triumphant chuckle. "Ten eleven *twelve!*"

Trust wily Tanner Parosh to teach a mere three-year-old to count so far – there was no hope of cheating! Philip the Younger wagged his stylus – and his eyebrows – admonishingly at his wife, and she laughed unrepentantly. Next time she would take a stick and write down nothing higher than a twenty, or maybe even a ten!

Fortunately for her knees, at that moment Parosh himself appeared in the courtyard, and Manna leapt off Auntie Aida's lap to fling himself happily at his rank-smelling father. The lingering stink was an inescapable fact of his trade, but Philip and Aida greeted him enthusiastically. A fishmonger's family was not bothered by such trivial things as strong odours, and if they waited for Parosh to smell like a lily of the field they'd never get to see him at all. Of course, not everyone was so broad-minded, so the tanner's circle of intimate friends was not extensive.

"How did you leave things in Sepphoris?" Aida demanded. "Is your daughter well?"

Parosh beamed. "Praise the Eternal, she is well, safely delivered of a little girl. Somewhat early, she declares, but what can you expect? – even the youngest females are impatient creatures, ha! ha! Still, the babe is strong, though bald as an egg. And the women are determined to call her Maya after her mother and grandmother – is that fair on a man? It was hard enough before, but now with a Maya for three generations in a row we will have a Little Maya, and a Young Maya; so of course my poor wife becomes Old Maya by default. I need only say 'Old Maya' once by mistake, and life won't be worth living. Well, I shall call the child Ya-ya and keep myself safe. My wife stays out the week with them, so meanwhile this young man and I will be two old bachelors together. Did you hear that, my son? You are an uncle again! Uncle Manna! Ha! Ha! Ha!"

Parosh never tired of the joke of having a son who was an uncle – in a manner of speaking – long before he was born.

"Praise the Eternal indeed!" Philip embraced his friend warmly, thumping his back in congratulations. "After three sons, a daughter will be a sweet thing for the mother, eh?"

Aida clucked and cooed and asked all the usual questions – that is, all that was decent to ask a man of his daughter's confinement. She would have to wait for all the *real* details until Parosh's wife returned home! Despite her child-like size, Aida herself had enough maternalism for a whole tribe, and even Philip did not escape her fussing over him just as much as she did over their own children. Although he complained loudly of this in public, he submitted to his tiny Egyptian wife's fondness with good humour and the sneaking suspicion that he was really a very lucky man.

"Oh, she has lots of help, even though they have not long been living there," Parosh assured Aida, with the casual air of an experienced *Sabba* of many. "His family is good to her, and they have many friends. And Sepphoris – well, you know – what a place! Can Rome itself offer more? Talk about convenience! No hauling buckets from a well for *my* daughter these days – with aqueducts on every hand. And a waste water system!" He shook his head at the wonders of modern life. Romans had a lot to answer for, but in some things, you had to hand it to them … they knew their engineering.

Philip picked up his sums and put them down again with a grimace. The answers weren't to his liking.

"I don't care two figs about the women's water," he said, rather unwisely, considering his hard-working wife was standing beside him with her little arms akimbo, "but that royal bank would be a handy thing to have close by, eh?" He clacked his abacus distractedly.

"Royal nonsense, you mean!" Aida stuck her hooked nose in the air and the sun winked off the jewelled hoop in her left nostril. "You would trust an *Argentarii* with your money?"

Philip scratched his head. "Perhaps not a private banker like that," he admitted, " but I have nothing against the public *Mensarii* in principle. They must keep reliable books, you know, my dear, to be answerable to the State. They are not all thieves simply because their trade is usury."

Aida sniffed disgustedly. "Romans! *P'tha!* Or men in Rome's pocket!"

Philip exchanged a knowing smile with Parosh and dropped the argument with a shrug. He slid the stylus neatly into its carved slot and folded up his tablets with a snap. *Women and money!* They weren't the ones who earned it … perhaps that's why they were always so anxious and suspicious unless it was somewhere they could keep an eye on it, such as on their faces and necks and wrists, if not stowed in some inconvenient hidey-hole. His Aida, for instance – forever finding cunning new places to secrete valuables, and forgetting where she'd put them! He coughed suddenly to smother a sudden snort of laughter – *they'd* better not end up with a late surprise like Parosh's little Manna one day. Aida would no doubt put the precious baby in a 'safe place' and lose it …

Still coughing, he gave Manna the abacus to play with, waving aside Aida's sudden concern for his chest.

"No, no, my dear, just a bit of dust, I'm sure. Now, some wine for the new grandfather, eh? And something gentler for the new uncle? Come, Parosh – I'll call the neighbours, and do you run off and fetch Mordecai and Old Dinah too, and no excuses from either of them! We must celebrate the happy news! I have time to spare before setting off to Magdala and with a glorious full moon tonight I don't care how late I am home again."

This last was said loudly to catch his wife's ears, but she knew his nonsense, and merely rolled her eyes before slipping off to her kitchen – where she did some swift calculations of her own regarding the state of her larder relative to the number of people who might cram the courtyard. Yes, there was plenty here, praise God, and there was always dried fish! Now, wine for Parosh, milk for Manna, by all means – but for her husband, there would be a sly lacing of his cup with precious brown cardamom and dried lemon peel. And perhaps she could stir in a little honey without him noticing … dust indeed! What if he was catching a cold? Not for the first time, she shook her head over men and their casual approach to their health, and then cheerfully set to work.

Parosh lifted his darkly tanned hand to joyfully rattle the wicket gate at Asa's old house opposite Blind Corner – and paused – so shocked that he narrowly escaped swearing. *Stinking skins! Is this an argument I hear? Mordecai and Old Dinah?*

"No, I won't!" Dinah's panicky tone rose angrily. "I can't even understand a word she says!"

"Where is your charity, woman?" Mordecai's normally mellow voice was rough with dismay. "I expected better of you – haven't you always been good to her?"

"Anyone can be good to a beggar!" she answered sharply. "Charity is nothing – it's easy, don't you know that, you of all people?" There was a hollow clang as a lid banged crossly on a copper pot. "Handing out food, clothes, words – even a bit of shelter … all that is simple … *Caring* for someone is quite another thing!"

"Nonsense. Why should it be any different?"

"Of course it's different! Especially now she's sick!" Now the pots were being slammed around in good earnest. "What am I supposed to do? How am I supposed to help? To know whether she's having a spasm which may choke her, or whether she's just trying to eat without swallowing her tongue? She can sleep in the courtyard, I'll go that far, but I'm not having her in the house – she stinks, and I'm not nursing her!"

"Of course she stinks! She sleeps with dirt and dogs – just as I did! And unlike me, she could barely clean herself even if she had water, poor wretch, and she a woman! You could wash her, Dinah – make her comfortable, tend her basic needs – and even if she *did* choke to death, she would die privately in a warm house with a human being close by ..." His voice broke. "She would not die alone in the cold and the rubbish, with jackals snuffing at her shame and ravens pecking at her eyes!"

An uneasy silence followed.

"It is not your house, Mordecai," the housekeeper said stiffly. "You have no right to order me to do this."

There was a pained sigh.

"I do not order you, Dinah. I am well aware it is not my house. But it is not yours either, and do you have the right to turn her away?"

Parosh, his hand still poised at the latch, stood frozen to the spot – what was he to do? Sneak away? Interrupt? No matter what – his proud news would be out of place right now. He turned to go, feeling very unhappy.

"Parosh! Wait! Quickly, Dinah – he stands outside – please!"

258

Old Dinah marched to the gate, whacked it open, and stamped back to her kitchen with a heated, mutinous face.

Mordecai came forward to greet his friend, rubbing agitatedly at his eye bandage. Parosh looked at him with concern, wishing now he had not hesitated at the gate. He ought to have known Mordecai's sharpened senses would detect a tanner even through the lattice.

"Blessings and peace, Mordecai!" he said, awkwardly in the face of neither blessings nor peace being obvious just at that moment. "Philip the Younger and Aida are filling their house with friends as we speak, to celebrate my daughter being safely delivered of a healthy child – my first granddaughter. They insist you and Old Dinah join us. But it seems I have chosen a bad time to bring good news!"

"There is never a bad time for good news," Mordecai rejoined wearily. "It is always refreshing, and the more so by contrast, like snow in the desert. Praise the Eternal for the new life, and I wish your family great joy. May she grow up to be a beautiful – and charitable – woman, a comfort to her parents, and a support in your old age."

Parosh shuffled his feet uncomfortably. The courteous blessing was welcome, but he could not ignore his friend's distress.

"What is it, Mordecai? I don't think I have ever seen you in such a mood. I will excuse you to Philip if you wish, but tell me quickly what can be so wrong here, that kind folk like you and Old Dinah speak to each other so harshly."

Blind Mordecai waved the tanner to the bench, and slumped beside him, leaning back against the tree.

"Disgraceful, is it not? I am very angry with her, but at the same time, I understand her feelings and ought to have more patience. I know at least she will not let my friend starve …" He sighed. "Sobek, you know Sobek – the Twisted. She is sick, very sick. Of course, she is often unwell … spoiled food, bad water, bites, worms, infected eyes, sores and scratches … only last week she cut her foot on a broken flask dropped by that slimy horse-trader who paws at her whenever he's drunk. She is never healthy, poor girl. But this is a different malady to the usual. Last night she was feverishly parched, but when I tried to give her water, she struggled and cried out so much that I was deathly afraid it might be hydrophobia."

Parosh sucked in his breath with sudden alarm, but Mordecai shook his head and waved a hand in hasty reassurance.

"No, no, it is *not* that, praise God! I questioned her very closely. She struggled because she could not swallow properly – her spasms were more rigid, more lasting – and she was desperately fearful of inhaling the water, of breaking her teeth on the cup, or perhaps even biting my fingers, poor creature. So I turned wet-nurse, pouring it on a cloth, and she sucked it up eagerly like a motherless babe. It was slow, but safer for her."

The tanner relaxed somewhat, and scratched his beard.

"Does she really need nursing for this, do you think?" he asked, consideringly. "Perhaps there are *Shedim* in her throat … which might exorcised by magic?"

Mordecai turned his blindfolded face fiercely towards his hearty, robust friend and spoke with stern deliberation.

"Parosh, you should not listen to the filth which has come from Babylon with the traditions of Pharisees. Having countenanced such blasphemies, they have had also to embrace magicians and sorcerers – which the Law condemns. You will not find evil spirits in Moses, only the encouragement of cleanliness in body and mind to avoid the diseases of Egypt."

Parosh looked shamefaced. "It is hard for an unlearned tanner to know what is sound doctrine, Mordecai," he apologised humbly, and the blind man checked himself with a sigh.

"*Hi-yi!* That is the fault of those who obscure the scriptures, not you, my friend, and I ask your pardon, I meant no reproach. Sobek is very ill. It is more than the new convulsions, or difficulty in swallowing ... her whole body is strangely tense ... she has severe pain, fever, sweating ... Even with nursing, I believe she may die ... just as beggars do, alone ... just as I might also have died on the streets years ago, had God not been merciful to me."

"Ah," Parosh replied lamely. Of course, beggars died. Those like Sobek usually sooner than others. "But you were no ordinary beggar! You were – you *are* – a man of unusual intelligence and learning ... and you have come along way since those days."

"Does that make me more worthy of life than Sobek? Who can never be more than she is, no matter who takes pity on her? I was blessed – I was born normal! I was a whole creature, I had a fulfilling life, I was able for nearly thirty years to run and feel and laugh and love and learn like other men. Even now, my blindness does not disgust or frighten people, despite the ugliness of my scarred face. I can speak my mind, and I have usefulness, and I am a man who could fight back if attacked – even if I was worth attacking." Mordecai spoke with increasing bitterness. "What of Sobek? Who knows or cares about *her* thoughts, *her* intelligence, *her* loneliness, *her* grief? She cannot communicate, she is grotesque, she is filthy, she annoys people, she has nothing to give, she cannot work, she is a temptation to the depraved, and she cannot defend herself … she is worthless! So, should she be allowed to die and reduce the surplus population of beggars?" His voice was savage.

Parosh stood up and laid a hand gently on the blind scribe's shoulder.

"I do not know how to answer you, my friend," he said helplessly. "But this afternoon Philip takes his buying trip to Magdala … shall I write you a letter for him to give Anna the Nazirite? This is her father's house, and she has authority to command whom it shelters. She is a good woman, and respects you as a valued teacher of her boy. I believe she would want Sobek to be cared for here – if only for your sake."

Mordecai's knuckles whitened as he gripped the stone seat beneath him. *If only for my sake!* He took a breath, wiped the dust from his hands, and raised them thankfully.

"The Eternal bless you indeed, tanner! This is excellent advice, and I accept it gratefully. Write the letter – and by tomorrow morning there will be an answer. As iron sharpens iron, so you have sharpened my dull countenance this day – and saved me from the sin of an evil temper tonight. Yes! I will wash my face, make amends with Dinah, and we will celebrate with you in cheerfulness of spirit."

He strode over to the kitchen door and called.

"Dinah! Good Dinah! I, Blind Mordecai of Cana, repent of my angry words, and forgive you for yours. Come – bring out the spice cakes you made this morning! And the quinces you pickled last New Moon! Our days are too short to hold grudges, and there is a new life to rejoice over."

So they joined the impromptu festivities hosted by Philip the Younger in a lighter mood than they might have thought possible only an hour before. Parosh was proud that he had come up with such an excellent suggestion as writing to Anna and he slipped away to scribble it as quickly as he could on some reject leather which served nicely for parchment, before rejoining the gaiety. Philip told some of his best (and worst) grandfather jokes to roars of male laughter, while Aida was in her element, pressing titbits on her neighbours as they whispered secret women's business relevant to the occasion. As for Old Dinah – she was delighted with the little holiday and the happier mood of her lodger. She swirled her ample skirts in the dance and sang lustily with the women in their song of rejoicing. A son was a fine thing, but ah! a daughter was balm to the feminine heart, a kindred soul with whom to share the amazement, the pride, and the sheer exasperation caused by all the men in their world! So they sang as a sisterhood.

"The Eternal be praised, a child is born today

A little one, a daughter fair.

God grant she will grow to bring her parents joy

With Leah's eyes and Samson's hair!

Yes, soft, kind eyes, and flowing hair!"

(Clap-clap! Slap-slap! Stamp-stamp! And twirl!)

Only Mordecai was not feeling as joyful as he appeared. He ate the food, drank the wine, obligingly piped the songs for them with fleet, nimble fingers, and clapped out the dances, but inwardly he was feeling the same frustration which Dan had expressed to him not so long ago, and about which, he now decided remorsefully, he must have been irritatingly calm.

Loukanos! Wherever you are, my friend – don't you know you are needed here?

263

When the celebrations were over, Philip assured Mordecai that he had Parosh's letter to Anna safely in his coat, and promised he would have an answer by next morning. Mordecai thanked him and felt his way swiftly through the streets to the market place, where he ministered to Sobek as best he could, rebandaging the gash on her contorted foot, helping her drink as before. He fed her slowly with Aida's lentil paste, frustratingly aware of the folly of a man who could not see, feeding a woman who could not control her head. Afterwards he cleaned her face as best as he could with a wet rag, and despite the sinking sensation he felt within, left her, with all the reassurances he could muster. But a cruel realisation was dawning upon him, and by the time he had flitted back to the house at Blind Corner, he had already made up his mind that Parosh's letter to Anna was not enough.

Late that afternoon Philip the fishmonger set out from Cana towards Magdala. With him went five kisses (one each from his wife and children), four donkeys, three packages of food, two extra vests (because of his cough) and one unexpected passenger; a blind man who clung grimly to his shambling donkey. The letter would still go to the gentle Nazirite in the hope that she would instruct that Sobek be succoured, and though Mordecai's heart beat a little faster, knowing he might for the first time in many months hear Anna's voice, feel her presence, perhaps even touch her hand – this was not his sole motive for the journey. Blind or not, he knew he must look further than Banayim to find lasting help for his poor, drooling, twisted friend.

There was one who could help her – if he could only be found in time. But it was not Loukanos. Because not even Loukanos could cure lockjaw.

Chapter Twenty-six

MORDECAI clung to the coarse mane to steady himself, and stretched his legs carefully to ease his sore muscles. His knees had been tightly gripping for so long that he wondered if he'd ever walk straight again. Without sight to aid a man's balance, riding was an uneasy business, and he had nearly come off more than once. He felt the warm flanks shift under his aching thighs, the solid bodies of the other pack animals nudging his legs as the donkeys patiently nibbled at the scrub around them. It was evening, and the air in the Hollow was chilled and damp.

Now he listened, almost motionless, as if sitting very still would slow the pounding in his chest, while Philip tramped across the clearing and knocked at the Shepherd's House. A woman's voice answering tentatively from within, an exclamation from Philip, more murmuring, and – what was that? A baby's cry? Anna, ever hospitable, must have visitors.

Philip returned to Mordecai's side and took up the head rope.

"Anna is not home," he reported, pushing the donkeys into line and walking them out of the clearing. "She is in the village caring for the son of Thaddeus, and his servant girl, Judith. There's been some trouble there."

"Then who is it in the house? That was not old Etta's voice I heard."

"No, it was Marta, the potter's wife. She and her children are staying while Ittai is on a journey. Etta is with Anna, she says. Well, I'm sorry to say that young Marta seems to have changed her manner somewhat since I last saw her. Considering that we are old acquaintances, it was rather unfriendly to answer me through a closed window. Perhaps I committed the unforgiveable sin of waking the baby when I banged on the door. I still remember what *that* does to a woman!"

"She may already have had the children in bed with her and not been able to get up to you," Mordecai shrugged, but his mind was not on Marta. The lurch of disappointment when he realised Anna was not home had been replaced with another painful thud of anticipation, and he was angry with himself for both reactions. Resolutely he concentrated only on keeping his seat as the donkeys picked their way along the track. By the time they were in the village street, he was his usual cool self once more.

The arrival of two men and four donkeys at such a late hour of the day did not go unnoticed. It was rare that anyone broke a journey at Banayim and of course, when they did, it was a matter of great interest and speculation. Doors opened and heads popped out of windows, one of which belonged to the Dabab.

"Would you believe!" she exclaimed to her husband. "There's a positive caravan of creatures at the Travellers' House, and two strangers with it!"

She scuttled out of her house, calling sweetly to the men in greeting.

"*Shalom!* Blessings and peace, friends, on this chilly eve! Whom do you seek?"

266

The stocky fishmonger looked up as he hitched the leading donkey, and assisted Mordecai to dismount.

"Oh, it's you, Philip the Younger!" Her face fell until she realised who his companion was, when she perked up at once. Well, something interesting must be going on, that the blind man from Cana was with the fishmonger! The last time she'd seen him was when the Shepherd's House burnt down. She narrowed her eyes thoughtfully. All sorts of things were happening around the village lately – there was a sort of secretive undercurrent which she must discover and bring to light!

"Pray tell me, friends, what brings you here to Banayim tonight?"

"Greetings to you and yours, Rachel," Philip answered perfunctorily. "I have a letter for the Nazirite. I am told she is with young Judith."

"A letter? Well, it must be urgent that you come so late – is all well in Cana?"

"This is my regular trip," he replied shortly, ignoring her question. "Which is the right house?"

Rachel hastened to bring them to Thaddeus' door, and hovered as they knocked.

"Thank you," Philip said rather pointedly.

"Oh, it's no trouble at all," she assured him kindly. He wouldn't get rid of her that easily, and see, here was Anna opening the door, surprised all over her face – yes, and even more than surprised, almost shocked to see who was Philip's companion. And no wonder! The last time Rachel and Malachi had been in Cana, the man who had given Blind Corner its name had been a common beggar, who sat in the dirt on the street, exchanging his wit for alms from passers by. What was the world coming to, that he now put himself on the same level as decent, clean-living householders, she'd like to know? Why, this was the second time he had come to Banayim as if he was a regular type of house guest. But Anna was greeting them warmly – *Both of them!* – thanking Rachel absently, and – shutting the door politely in her face. The Dabab stalked home, feeling quite put out.

Anna's charges were already tucked up in bed, asleep in the back room. A pain-wracked Judith had barely left hers since the Sabbath, and Thad was worn out after yet another day of pitting his will against a deceptively gentle Auntie Anna. As for Aunt Etta, she had already been asleep for some hours, knowing Anna would wake her later when she went to bed herself. It was less tiring for Etta to watch during the midnight hours than to run around after Thad during the day. Tomorrow she would return to the Hollow, with kindly Shana taking her place. Even Rachel had piously offered to "Share the burden," for an hour each evening (during the tedium of Malachi's after-dinner nap.) A few more days, Anna thought, and the girl should be well enough for less vigilance. Meanwhile, she rejoiced in her unexpected visitors – a fresh breath from the world outside the sickroom and, though it seemed disloyal to say it, beyond the confines of Banayim.

"Sit down, my friends, there is soup in the pot. I have not eaten myself yet, and will be glad of your company. Yes, Philip, I know Aida will have sent you away with enough provisions for an army, but this is hot food, and the night is cold. You have the time?"

Philip sniffed the tantalising aroma and rubbed his hands, knowing they would only have to wait on the beach if they left too soon. A warm kitchen was better than a cold shore any time.

"A full moon and fair weather – the boats will be out late tonight, I'll be bound. Besides, I knew you would be full of questions, and did not expect to hurry. We accept with pleasure."

"With great pleasure," Mordecai added quietly, despite his feeling of urgency. If the fishermen who would be his most useful informants at that hour were still on the water, there was no point in reaching Magdala until their night's work was over.

As they ate, Anna explained what had happened at the hireling's house, and that Dan and Caleb were even now searching for Thaddeus. What they would do with him once they found him would depend on his state of mind at the time, and therefore that was anyone's guess. Anna could only trust to Caleb's commonsense and Dan's resourcefulness.

"A sorry tale," Philip shook his head sadly. "And awkward for you too, having to come here, even while a friend was visiting in your own home."

Anna said nothing, but Mordecai, alive to every nuance of her presence, felt her stiffen slightly with caution. Her reserve was out of place for the commonplace politeness of Philip's remark, and he felt that something was not quite right.

"Your friend Marta," he ventured casually, "is she a fearful woman?"

She looked at him with surprise. "Why, no!" she replied, baffled by the question. "Why ever do you ask?"

Mordecai shrugged. "Forgive me if I appear to be inquisitive, but it seems strange to me that she would go to the inconvenience of conveying herself and three little ones down to your house, so far from the well, unless she was nervous of being alone while her husband was away. And even that is odd, because here in the village she has far more neighbours closer at hand. And if that was still not enough, surely it would have been simpler to ask you to stay with *her* in Ittai's absence?"

Anna was taken off guard. Quickly she rifled mentally through several answers which she might give, but each seemed lamer than the last. She was saved by Philip's guffaw.

"Now, now! Has it occurred to you, my good scribe, that her husband might be a jealous man, and wanted her safely tucked away out of sight?"

He laughed again. Anna smiled limply – well, perhaps if they thought so, they would not press her further. Was failing to correct Philip, fostering a lie and a slur on her friends? She was pondering this when Mordecai fluttered his fingers like eyelashes, and nodded with a knowing smile.

"Ah, so young Marta is a great beauty, then!"

"H'mm!" Philip considered this seriously. "You know, a good potter has an eye for form and symmetry, so it's no surprise he chose Marta. I think you could say she is attractive – but not really what you might call beautiful, not with that white hair."

Anna had the feeling that the conversation was getting out of control. She rapped on the table smartly.

"Enough! She is hardly snow-capped like an old woman! After all, it is only one white lock, and although *you* have no business commenting on it, *I* think it is rather pretty by sheer contrast."

"Yes, I believe she's been lucky with that *leucoderma*," Mordecai commented, scraping up the last of his soup with a flat fold of bread. "Loukanos thought her silver streak was charming, though he said it might not be so pretty if it spread to her face. People do not like unusual faces," he added without thinking, and then kicked himself for sounding self-pitying.

Anna stared at him. Her bread dropped into her soup and sank, and she leaned forward so far that one of her braids slid off her shoulder and splashed into the bowl like a well rope. She gripped Mordecai's arm so hard he jumped.

"What did you say? What did you say?" she stammered.

"I said, people do not like unusual faces." Mordecai repeated reluctantly, squirming inwardly at having to repeat his clumsy remark. Worse than self-pitying, it sounded as if he was judging a woman – her friend! – whom he could not even see. *Hi-yi!* The first time he was near Anna for many long months, he was making an utter fool of himself, stepping out of a cow-pat into a bog!

"No, no, before that … Loukanos …"

"Oh, that!" Mordecai was relieved. "When Loukanos was discussing one of his cases with me, as he often did, he mentioned the potter's wife at Banayim, and he said he thought her streak of silver hair was luckily placed, and quite charming …"

Philip the Younger was mystified by this conversation. Why was Anna so stirred up about her brother's opinion of her married friend? Surely she realised that men had eyes!

"That was good soup," he remarked in the hope of distracting her attention to something less intense. Anna automatically helped him to more, almost grinding her teeth in frustration as Mordecai missed her point once again. But without knowing her private fears, how could he understand what she wanted to know?

"Please, Mordecai," she said as calmly as she could manage. "I have reasons for asking you very particular questions about this. Why did Loukanos mention Marta? What case was he discussing with you?"

"As I said, Anna, *leucoderma*. A maid in Nain had it, and her parents came privately to see him, very worried about leprosy, poor souls. Well, Loukanos had seen plenty of this problem in Egypt, though not so much here, and told me how disfiguring it was on black skin. He said his young patient had a streak in her hair, too, only it was at the back, as if she'd leant on a whitewashed wall before it was dry, and it was nowhere near as charming as the silvery stripe that the Banayim potter's wife had. So that's why he mentioned Marta."

"What else did he say about her? Anything at all!"

"He said he could see she had the condition, but it seemed to be very stable, and she may not even realise what it was. He had noticed the hair first of all, of course, and his trained eye could tell that she already had the beginnings of it in her hands, her wrists, her neck – where the skin appeared slightly translucent."

"But this must have been more than two *years* ago!"

"Yes, it was. But Anna, forgive me, you seem to be very agitated about this. Why does it matter?"

"Tell me all you know about this white skin disease!"

Mordecai considered. "I don't know if it's a disease, exactly. The skin simply fades in patches until it is completely white, and will not tan any more. I suppose you could call it the opposite of moles or freckles ... but are *they* a disease? It is not contagious, and it does not produce any inflammation unless sunburned, or even affect anything except a person's vanity, as far as I know. Loukanos said its cause is unknown but it can run in families."

"Marta has five half-brothers in Hazor, but I don't think they have it – she would have said so. Could this really be what she has?"

"Woman, you are asking a blind man!" Philip protested. "And remember he is not a doctor himself."

Anna sat back, absently noting that one braid was dripping soup. She squeezed it dry gently with a dishcloth, but ploughed right on with her questions.

"I'm sorry, Mordecai, I do not mean to be rude. Is there anything else Loukanos told you about this … condition? What provokes it, how does it progress?"

"I don't know much else, Anna, I'm afraid. A few have it from childhood, though Loukanos believed that deep changes in a person's life could hasten the onset, such as either bearing a child, or losing the ability to do so. His little patient became more affected as she became a woman, and he had seen it worsen in men who lost their livelihood or suffered terrible grief."

"Did he say any more about Marta?"

"Only the comment that if it began on her face it would not be so pretty."

Anna put her face in her hands and tried to breathe steadily. She looked up to see Philip's consternation.

"Please, Anna!" he insisted. "What is all this about! All these questions, and Marta?"

So she dried her eyes and told them of all their fears, and why Marta and the children were isolated at the Shepherd's House.

"Everything you have said, fits, Mordecai," she said finally, touching his shoulder briefly. "I am so thankful! The greatest wonder is that we do not have to guess – that Loukanos himself recognised it, and now all that you have said confirms his diagnosis even more. Marta *has* always had it, and with no ill effect, as you say. Clearly Shuni's birth has aggravated the condition – but oh! to know that it is harmless! Such a relief!"

Mordecai nodded. "So you see, there is no need to worry. There is no cure, but for the girl whose parents insisted on treatment, Loukanos prescribed yellow *kharkoum* spice. Not that he had much faith in it, but it made the parents feel they were doing something. I don't know whether she was supposed to eat it, or rub it on, or both. Perhaps staining her skin made it less obvious, but he didn't believe it would do much more than that."

"There is one more thing, though," Anna added despondently. "Marta has also developed a rash of fine red pin-prick spots everywhere."

Mordecai shook his head. "As Philip says, I am not a doctor, but as Loukanos was quite sure about the *leucoderma*, all I can suggest is that a rash is likely to be totally unrelated."

Anna hoped he was right. She was not going to confess in this company that Marta was again 'unclean' … that would be going too far.

"Oh!" Her hand flew to her forehead. "How could I forget the most important thing! I told you Ittai was on a journey – and the truth is that he is seeking help for Marta! Poor Ittai and Uncle Joseph – their search will be for nothing!"

"Uncle Joseph?" the men were astonished. "Your uncle from Cyprus?"

"Yes, yes! They have both headed north, looking for the Nazarene, or Loukanos, determined to find either one of them within the week."

"What?! Loukanos?!" This time both men raised their voices.

274

Chapter Twenty-seven

ANNA waved her hands hurriedly. "Hush, please! You will wake poor Judith and Etta, not to speak of young Thad! Yes, Loukanos is in the Land! Uncle Joseph stumbled across him some time ago and came here especially to inform us. Oh, there is simply too much to relate, and you must soon be off, I know! Suffice it to say that Louki has been through great turmoil of spirit since he left us, and is now frequenting the company of the Teacher's closest followers. That is why Uncle Joseph and Ittai have every hope of finding him soon. But whatever happens, praise the Eternal, my friends, that Loukanos is finally searching for truth!"

"Praise the Eternal indeed!" responded Philip the Younger, almost stupefied, "and may He prosper his quest! *And* that of Ittai and your uncle! Well, it seems half your family and friends are chasing each other around the countryside – including Mordecai here!"

"You, Mordecai?"

"Yes, Anna, I too am on a quest for the sake of one who is suffering. But first I must tell you how joyful to my ears is this news of Loukanos," the blind man replied. "How thankful I am for his sake, and how glad for you and Dan that your distress is being eased at last! I pray my prayers will be equally blessed with a good answer, but quickly. There is little time left – the window of hope may shut at any moment."

"Mordecai, old friend!" Anna reached out repentantly and took his hands full in hers this time. "Can you forgive me for my selfishness? Here you are, turning up on the doorstep, such a rare occasion! and happy as I am to see you, I have been so full of my own troubles and fears, that I did not even stop to ask why you are here. I am ashamed! Tell me now what is wrong, and who is suffering, and how I can help!"

Mordecai felt as if his hands were burning. He pulled them away and straightened his eye bandage.

"No, no – there is no need to be ashamed … I need a miracle, that's all. A miracle for my friend Sobek. Read this letter, if you will."

"Why, yes, I remember Sobek, poor woman." Anna pulled open the letter and read it swiftly.

She looked up at Philip in confusion.

"I don't understand. Tanner Parosh has expressed things very clearly in this letter, but he writes on behalf of you, Mordecai. Why this letter, if you have come here yourself? Or why come yourself, when there is the letter?"

Watch your tongue, Anna! What have you just said? Do you think that the journey was easy for him?

"Of course," she hastily added, "I am delighted – and honoured – that you have come yourself!"

Her scattered wits decently scraped back together again, she abandoned her questions and returned to the substance of the letter, speaking firmly.

"Of course poor Sobek must find shelter in my father's house, and you must find a caring woman to nurse her. I will be answerable for the cost. Father would want that, I know, and there is no time to waste. And when I say 'in my father's house' I don't mean in the courtyard – the wind won't be any warmer there. Anyway that is your public schoolroom most days, until the rains. No, she can have my old room. It has a door which opens to the fresh air and will be less confining for her, as well as more convenient in other ways. She had better have the clothes I left behind, too, as hers must be burned. They will be full of lice and vermin. Don't let anyone shave her hair off, though. Make the nurse scour it properly instead. Poor creature, it's the only femininity she has."

"And what of Dinah's objections?" Philip asked. "You would not dismiss her? She is a faithful steward."

"There is no question of dismissing her, of course. As you say, she is a faithful steward. She may fear the responsibility of nursing someone like Sobek, and it is probably too much to ask of her abilities. It will not be an easy task. I think Mordecai is the only person who can really understand Sobek, at the best of times." Anna frowned. "If Dinah is unwilling to stay, she can take herself off to visit her children, but with Mordecai, Sobek and a nurse all in the house, someone must be hired to take her place for the time being."

"Aida will find a trustworthy woman," Philip offered. "She has a good eye for reliable servants."

Anna thanked him, and tapped her teeth thoughtfully.

"Of course, the ideal person would be little Rhoda! Aunt Mari would gladly spare her, I know. If Dinah leaves, Rhoda could take over the housekeeping from the hired help. She is quite capable and has that uncommon quality so poorly named commonsense. And should Dinah have a change of heart and decide to stay after all, I know the girl would still make herself useful in a thousand ways. I think it would be very helpful to have her there, no matter what happens. Philip, if you can wait a little longer – I will write to Aunt Mari this moment. Will you be kind enough to take it back to Cana for me and give it to Shalal's post at once? His camel relays carry news to Jerusalem in only a day, and he will have it delivered to her immediately for a small surcharge."

By way of answer, Philip reached into his capacious coat, and handed her a slender, carved travel-case of pens and ink-block, which he used to keep his meticulous financial records. Without delay, Anna wet the ink, and scratched out a hasty note to Mari Jerusalem at the foot of Parosh's letter. She waved it dry, tied it up, and handed it over with several silver coins.

"There, that will do. Parosh's letter saves long explanations, and will inform my father as well as Aunt Mari. He will be glad the house is being used for good works. Father does not plan to visit this side of the Festival of Booths, so he won't accompany Rhoda himself. But they have only to entrust her to Shalal – he's a God-fearing man and will treat her with respect, I know. She'll be in Galilee in no time, even if she has to endure twelve hours of misery getting there, poor girl. With her mother about to remarry, it is in any case a convenient time for Rhoda to return to Cana – later there will various family matters for them to arrange, I am sure. Then, after *Succoth* with us, Father and Johanan will be going to Cana themselves, so they can take Rhoda back to Jerusalem with them, if necessary."

She smiled at them with relief.

"There, that was not difficult – surely you did not need a miracle, or a letter *and* a visit, to persuade me?"

"I am grateful to you, Anna bath Netzir," Mordecai responded seriously. "I had every confidence in your compassion, and your generosity. Unfortunately, I still need a miracle."

Philip interrupted. "Tonight Parosh is watching Sobek, Anna, but at first light tomorrow, Aida and I will be glad to undertake all the arrangements you suggest. Meanwhile Mordecai won't be needing his courtyard schoolroom anyway – he will be on the road. He did not come all this way simply to hand you a letter – which was written some hours before he decided to accompany it. He is seeking none other but the Nazarene – because as he says, he still needs a miracle."

"Literally," the blind scribe told her frankly. "What Philip says is true. Parosh wrote the letter for me, which I intended to send with Philip. But afterwards I visited Sobek again, and was even more deeply disturbed by her symptoms. She is desperately ill. When I said there is not much time, and I need a miracle, it was no figure of speech. I am convinced she has lockjaw."

"Oh, Mordecai, how frightful!" Anna shuddered. "Even Loukanos –"

"Precisely."

"But my friend, what more can you do? Her case is so urgent … it is night … you are blind … the Nazarene may still be as far away as Iturea, and Philip goes no further than Magdala!"

"The night makes no difference to me," he pointed out wryly. "Magdala is still a step closer to my goal than Cana, and the Teacher can not be more than a couple of days away. The road is well trodden, I am told, and perhaps I may even come across Dan and Caleb – or Ittai, or Joseph, who knows? If so, I will be sure to tell them Marta is not ill, and they may help me to find the Nazarene for Sobek instead. One thing is certain – if I do nothing,

Sobek has no hope at all. But if I make a start, then I give the angels something to work with."

Anna gestured helplessly. "Oh, if only I could go with you and be useful!"

Of course, it was unthinkable that she would travel alone with any man who was unrelated to her, blind or not, and they all knew it.

"Mercy on us, woman!" Philip grumbled. "This is becoming like the children's game of Five Little Foxes! Each one running down the hole to find the last until they have all vanished ... *Somebody* has to stay behind with the stuff!"

Mordecai and Anna laughed and the tension was broken.

"And it's always Mother Fox who stays behind until the very last, I know," she responded with a tired smile. "Mother Fox must not delay you longer, then. Mordecai, forgive me asking, but do you have money?"

"Enough. I had some very difficult pupils this last year. Fortunately for me, they had fathers who took seriously the injunction that the labourer is worthy of his hire, and their donations were generous."

*They **must** have been difficult boys!* Anna thought with respect. Mordecai taught without charge any who cared to come to the courtyard. It occurred to her that in her quiet, busy life, she had no idea what trials her son's mentor laboured over every day; and her heart smote her. She quietly untied her purse from her girdle and noisily packed up the beautifully carved writing case.

"Philip, your pens ..."

Her eyes appealed to the fishmonger and he nodded, tapping his nose wisely, tucking the slim box together with the purse she slipped him, inside his coat. He would find the right moment later on. Mordecai might accept such from him, but never from Anna herself.

"The Eternal bless you, my friends," she said soberly as they rose to leave. "You have relieved a painful anxiety about dearest Marta, bringing me peace and great thankfulness of heart. How she and Etta will rejoice and thank you and praise God when I run to them with the good news at daybreak! How glad I am Loukanos observed Marta so closely! How glad I am you spoke about her looks so freely, or the subject never would have arisen! That has taught me a lesson, I think. Dear Mordecai, praise God for your long memory, for your keen interest in people, and your acute mind! It has never been put to such happy use."

Her relief was great – it was not like Anna to express herself so extravagantly, but her full heart demanded an overflow.

"It has been so good to see you again, and I wish you could have stayed longer! I confess there are times when I hanker for discourse with a disciplined and educated mind such as yours – to sharpen my own thinking, which easily dulls. Perhaps at a less difficult time you will return and visit here – maybe during the Festival, depending on how things are in Cana? It will be so good for Dan and Johanan, and my father will also relish your company. You could take the Travellers' House with the boys, or –"

"Stop making women's plans," Philip warned her with a grin. "He will come, or he won't come, and the details will work themselves out either way."

"Do send word, if you can, Mordecai. Philip, my friend! How can I thank you? See you bring me every new thing you hear of Mordecai, or Sobek … or my son … or …" Her voice failed her.

Once more, the men were leaving and everyone had gone … Dan, Caleb, Uncle Joseph, Ittai, Mordecai. Brave, selfless Mordecai! Once more she would be alone, left with people to comfort, people to succour, people who relied on her – and a guilty longing to lay her head on a stronger shoulder and be comforted herself.

"Not *Blind* Mordecai? And Philip? What? You here?" A barrage of astonished questions was hissed from the inner doorway, and a rumpled-looking Aunt Etta poked her dishevelled white-frosted head around the curtain.

"Oh, Etta – I'm so sorry we woke you!" Anna said guiltily, "I completely forgot to be quiet!"

"It wasn't you, my dear," Etta said with a sniff. "It was those rumbling male voices shaking my very bed … don't you dare wake the poor children, now …"

"Etta, old friend!" The men laughed (quietly, or at least, so they thought) and exchanged greetings and hurried explanations. Etta's eyes sobered as she heard of Mordecai's plan.

"*Hi-yi!* my fine scribe!" she said emotionally. "And how will you fare without eyes, pray?"

"I have done so for many years, Etta," he answered. "Philip – you say it's bright moonlight – will you look out for a strong thin branch on our way to Magdala? On unknown paths it will steady me … I used a rod for many years, a faithful servant it was too, serving admirably for eyes once I knew how to use it."

Etta shook her head. "A raw stick will leave sap and splinters in your hand – it will be untested, and bend or break when you need it most … No, my friend, I have a much better idea."

She disappeared behind the curtain for an instant and reappeared almost at once.

"My friend, my courageous friend, take this. It was crafted by the skilful hands of very man you seek."

"Jeshua – the Nazarene – he made this?"

"So my brother Ammiel told me, and Dan and Anna could bear witness. They were with him the day it was bought at the workshop *Ben Netser*."

"Yes, Mordecai," Anna said softly, remembering that happy day full of nonsense and fun. "I was there."

He did not protest politely or ask how Etta would get on without her precious walking stick; he knew she would manage with another. An empty formality would dishonour her sincerity, and her gift of trust was worth far more than the loan itself. Mordecai was deeply touched. He bowed respectfully.

"I will treasure this all the more, and my choicest words cannot thank you."

He held up his hand. "Goodbye. God bless you and keep you, Etta bath Amos. God bless you and keep you, Anna bath Netzir."

The men stepped into the starry street.

"I will pray for you!" she called after them.

Mordecai was silent on the remainder of the journey to Magdala. She would pray for him. Yes, she had said that before. His hand strayed to the cord around his neck, and he fingered the sky blue tassel which hung there.

"A talisman for a good friend. Pray for me every time you laugh at finding it in your purse – and I will pray for you every time I see the gap in my hem."

In the three years since, the heavy silken ornament had never seen the inside of his purse, and never been laughed at, but many a prayer had been offered for her, with no need to ask. But did she really pray for him? His mouth twisted in disgust at his foolishness. How often would a woman wear a garment with a gap where a decoration had been torn away? And how often would a woman look down at such a hem, without thinking only of mending it?

Well, she had said tonight that she would pray for him, and tonight, he believed she would. Let that be enough!

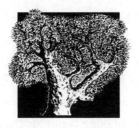

Chapter Twenty-eight

LOUKANOS was striding at the pace of his thoughts; his legs carrying him without effort as his mind flew from one thing to another. At some level, no doubt, his senses took in the earthy tang of the fallow fields, the clinging damp air, the soft clear light, the lowing complaints of grumbling oxen set to plough too early for easy tillage of the hard soil, the barked shouts of a farmer guiding the wavering furrow of his apprentice boy, the dull clunk of rocks being picked and tossed on a growing pile by a diligent wife, the snickering of a herd of restive goats being counted for tithing.

The olives had long since been shaken, and groves of shining deep green leaves sighed gently, freed of their black-polished, clustering burden. Nearby stood a village, houses stacked together like cubes of white cheese, the rooftops darkly speckled with swathes of dates and late summer figs spread out to dry until the last moment before the early rains set in – and from them wafted a rich sweet spiciness. The terrain was fresh to Loukanos' eyes, but the scenery was oh, so familiar. Somewhere deep within his heart, a nostalgic Grecian string was being plucked, its slow vibration adding to his sense of melancholy.

But Loukanos of Macedonian Philippi was lately come from the regions of Caesarea Philippi, and if he recognised the irony he would not admit it. Though his body went about its business of observing the surroundings, smelling the air, treading the road, he was elsewhere in spirit. He was thinking only of a late conversation with the Magdalan and the Kerioth. They had all been walking quite quickly for most of the day, and finally the group of disciples were making camp for the evening. The women were starting their fires, the men were clearing places to sleep, one for men, one for women, while families made shift for themselves a little apart. Loukanos had questions for Marah, but he had barely begun when Jude walked over, showing him an infected finger. The physician bathed and bandaged the angry flesh with a poultice, casting an observant eye over the long-fingered hands.

"Man, how long have you been chewing your nails to your knuckles and tearing at the quicks? There is blood on every finger! What is eating your heart, that you eat your own flesh?"

The Kerioth pulled his hands away with a dismissive gesture.

"Oh, it's nothing," he laughed. "Merely a childhood habit I have never grown out of. You have my permission to slap the backs of my hands if you catch me at it!"

"As your mother did, eh? No, thank you. Clearly it was no deterrent, and I will not waste my energy. But take care, my friend. Even a poisoned finger can kill a man if it is neglected."

He turned readily to Marah the Magdalan who was quietly waiting beside him, to resume their conversation, but Jude made no move to return to the others.

"Please, continue your discourse," he said courteously. "Shall I call another woman to join you? However, if the Magdalan has questions, be assured I am glad to give what answers I can."

286

"She is not the one with the questions," Loukanos said, hoping he would go away. They were already sitting in broad view of the whole company! What *was* this Jewish insistence on so closely chaperoning a mature woman whose life was already above reproach? He had not expected such from the Teacher's men – especially Jude, with his gloss of sophistication – yet still he ran up against it. The women, as he had already experienced at the waterfall several days before, had more faith in each other.

"Well, in that case, of course I will stay for your sake instead," Jude responded cheerfully, settling himself more comfortably, and carelessly nibbling at his nails. "It is no trouble."

The man was one of the Twelve – and willing to help – there was no point in reluctance, and plain weakness in false pride. With an effort, Loukanos successfully swallowed an instinct to resist, and so it was to both of them that he found himself attempting to define his conflict.

"I simply have no idea what I am supposed to do next," he shrugged. "The Day of Atonement is fast approaching, but I do not understand what this means to me as a Greek. I have been baptised for the remission of my sins, I have a new life now. Where does the Atonement of the Law come in to this – especially for a Gentile?"

Jude smiled at him. "Gentile or not, your sins were washed away, just as ours were – but of course you must fully convert now. What will you do if you are *not* made a Jew? We are so blessed in having the Day of Atonement! Of course there are the sin offerings, but one sin forgiven is followed by a hundred committed, and we would forever be in the Temple! Praise the Eternal for *Yom Kippur*! Whatever sin we commit, no matter how terrible, it is wiped out when the High Priest sprinkles blood on the Mercy Seat every year. No matter how many we have not sacrificed for, how many unwitting trespasses, or how many private sins – the whole nation is covered! Do you not see how liberating this is? Of course we fast and afflict our souls in recognition of our failings, and our grief for our own actions; but then we can go forward with joy again. Good may come even out of evil. As Jews, whether by birth or by conversion, nothing can change our surety before God! What advantage could there possibly be in remaining a Gentile?"

The Magdalan frowned. "I see what you are saying, but there are two things which disturb me … the first is that since the days of the Babylonian captivity there has been *no* Mercy Seat, no Ark of the Covenant. So when the High Priest sprinkles the stone which has been put in its place, does he still fulfil the Law? And, it may be the way you have expressed it … or perhaps I have misunderstood you … but I feel that there seems to be a confusion between individual forgiveness and national atonement. Surely, when you think of the personal significance of the rite of baptism, there is something which is not quite –"

"Woman," he interrupted gently, "my words were for the Greek to answer. This is men's talk."

She looked at him, nonplussed. "I beg your pardon. Do women not need to understand forgiveness?"

The Kerioth leaned over to lay a kindly arm around her shoulders.

"You have suffered a great deal, I know, and for many years you had no control over your mind, or your actions. Thanks to Loukanos here, and myself, you were brought to the Teacher and healed, and we all rejoice in that, truly. But now you must be aware that your illness accustomed you to an unfeminine freedom and equality. This cannot continue unmoderated, without leaving you open to unfortunate interpretations. Meanwhile don't be disheartened – you may still find a good man under whose wings you may shelter. Eventually, I am sure you will develop enough sound womanly maturity, and trust, to leave the deep spiritual matters to the men."

"I don't believe that the Teacher shares your opinions," Loukanos said with irritation, clenching his fists restlessly as Jude gave the Magdalan's shoulders several paternal little pats.

The calm young man looked at him with surprise tinged with regret.

"I am one of his Chosen out of the thousands of Israel," he answered humbly with a disarming shrug. "How could he and I fail to agree? We share an uncommon compassion and tolerance towards women as I think everyone knows; but the fact remains that a woman has her God-given place – she has come from man, and nothing can change that."

"And man does not come from woman?" the Magdalan responded with a flash of her old temper, and a little toss which suddenly dislodged his arm. She wriggled her shoulders away from him and her smouldering eyes spoke volumes to Loukanos, who suddenly wanted to give her a 'thumbs-up' signal, but remembered just in time it would be rather out of place, and probably misunderstood.

Jude coolly smoothed his clean linen tunic with the hand she had shrugged off.

"Yes, of course he does!" he replied reassuringly. "Who better to nurture and understand children than the lovely creatures who still have so much of the child about themselves? But when boys become men, they are launched like great ships into a deeper sea – to defend the borders, engage the enemy, carry the trade, explore the world, fly with the wind! But who would ask a humble boat-builder to captain a ship just because he had carved its timbers, eh?"

He laughed at the thought, and pointed up the hill.

"Now, look – surely that is Bina beckoning you to the cooking pots? A woman's work is never done, I know, but never let it be said that the Teacher's disciples do not know how to appreciate their loving service."

The Magdalan gave Loukanos a helpless look. The Kerioth was, after all, one of the Chosen, just as he said. She stood up and walked away.

Loukanos flexed his fingers impatiently. Like the Magdalan he felt instinctively that there was a fly in the ointment somewhere, but it would have to be fished out later. Jude's attitude to her was an irritant less easily dismissed. He realised afresh how differently his own family looked at these things – but of course, they were half Greek, and bound to be more balanced! *These Jews!* His instinctive reaction only increased his irritability. '*These Jews*' were the Chosen Ones of the Chosen One, but despite everything he could not feel part of them.

As if there had been no diversion, Jude turned back to the original question.

"Now, the Day of Atonement … Perhaps I can explain more about it to you."

Loukanos felt a fresh stab of annoyance.

"There is no need. I have no difficulty understanding its purpose. I was brought up with the Law from a child, and my adoptive father was a faithful man who taught me as thoroughly as any rabbi could require. What I don't understand is where I stand today, as a Gentile. Yes, I am now baptised, and Yes, I am finally convinced that Jeshua of Nazareth is the Messiah and has the power of God at his command. But does this make me a Jew?"

The Kerioth picked thoughtfully at his bandage, but said nothing as Loukanos continued to unburden himself.

"Do I now undertake the prescribed steps? Am I supposed to present myself to three scribes from the school of Shammai, as a prospective proselyte? Of course, to be on the safe side," he added ironically, "I discount Hillel's followers, who may not be not strict enough to satisfy every Jew to whom I may present myself in future!"

"A difficult question," Jude conceded reluctantly, either not noticing his tone, or refusing to acknowledge it.

"Will they give me instruction? Too late, I have had it, being raised in a Jewish house. Will they demand literal circumcision as proof of my circumcision of heart? Too late, it was done when I was an ignorant three-year-old!"

Jude raised his bandaged finger and nodded wisely. "You see why we could not have had a woman in this conversation!"

Loukanos ignored this remark.

"Will they ask for immersion? Too late, I have just been immersed! Must I be so again? Will they ask me to sacrifice, and change my name? Why not? Perhaps if I call myself Uri and sacrifice a goat, they will sacrifice their disapproval, presuming they can sort everything else out to their legal satisfaction …" He snorted. "Ah, but, no! I have left out the very first step … they must also test my motives!"

He paused for breath, while Jude raised his eyebrows.

"Ah, yes, motives are slippery things … but surely this is the one thing you could be sure of?"

"What?" Loukanos demanded testily. "How do you think your Pharisees and lawyers would respond if I told them my motives were inextricable from the fact that I am a follower of the Nazarene? That I believe in the man whom they count as a blasphemer?"

He raked his fingers frustratedly through his unruly hair.

"I am not even a simple Hellenist either – admiring your moral values, adopting your God and your customs, attending synagogue, lighting Sabbath lamps and so on. Oh, no! I have bypassed all this, I have accepted the *heart* of your religion – the Messiah himself! And yet now I feel more confused than ever about how I should worship; how I should serve him, and how I should honour the Creator. Why is this so? What do you say to others in my situation? Surely I am not the only one with these questions!"

"These are profound matters, friend," Jude answered seriously. "But what is one man's fleeting distress amongst so much that is everlastingly good? You must have faith that your way will be made clear. Life is full of conflict and confusion, even for the best of us."

He squeezed his arm sympathetically and left.

Loukanos idly scratched up stones from the dirt and began flicking them, hard, at a nearby rock, listening for the satisfying crack as they hit. He wondered how he could be feeling so dismayed and almost angry, so quickly after the glory he had felt sweeping through him only days before. The Twelve were also distracted of late. Since the day of that sudden strange storm, Fisher Shimon and the ben Zebedees had been behaving as if they knew something they could not tell. A fresh awe seemed to tinge their words when they spoke to the Teacher, and a new sense of importance seemed to be settling around them.

292

As for Marah the Magdalan, Loukanos saw her attend to Jeshua and his men with a steadfast dedication which seemed to exclude all else, especially himself, and her eyes held something back, though what it was, he could not tell. For her to swallow the rebuke of the Kerioth as she just had, though, was a testament to her strength and resolve to do what she believed was right … and she should not find him less resolved. Right now, he was not fit company for her, or anyone else.

Wearily, he got to his feet and wandered away in an attempt to rediscover his lost temper. The Twelve were busy near the fire and the food; the crowds which normally thronged them had thinned to a handful. Nobody had known the route they would take as they travelled back to Galilee, and the resulting peace was restorative.

Loukanos slipped away through a dark grove of bay trees, past a stunted clump of wild pomegranates, and around an outcrop of creamy sandstone hollowed with burrows and littered with rabbit droppings. With a feeling of thankfulness, he found himself in a silent dell of dappled shade and sun warmed grasses.

But wait – someone else had found it first – and was sitting as if asleep, his back against a rough-barked fir sapling, arms resting loosely on his bent knees. His intense face was tilted to a deep periwinkle sky which was fading to pink where it touched the trees and already adorned with the evening star, hanging like a bright jewel below the huge golden moon.

Startled, Loukanos was about to dart away at once – when, without opening his eyes, the man spoke.

"Sit with me."

"But I interrupt your meditations, and you have precious little time alone. I will go."

"The work is great, and my time is short. But you are part of that work, so there will be time. Stay."

Loukanos obeyed, thinking guiltily, *Oh, if you knew the questions I could ask you!*

The tired, travel-stained man opened his deepset, keenly-discerning eyes, looked into the flushed face of his unwilling companion, and smiled slowly.

"Oh, if you knew the answers I could give you!" he said.

Chapter Twenty-nine

"MUST you leave?"

"Yes."

"Why?" She lifted her eyes to his, willing them to be steady.

"Because I am not one of you." He met her gaze coolly, telling himself he was glad to find no silent searching or pleading in her face.

"Not one in spirit?"

"How can you ask? Of course I am one of you in spirit! But not in race, and not in custom. The very way you worship is rooted in a history of anticipating Messiah – but now he is here! Have you considered how this must affect your traditions? Since the Captivity your rabbis have been so concerned with hair-splitting applications of the Law that in parts they have legalised it into sheer folly. Pardon my bluntness. But all those deputies who have crowded so greedily into Moses seat, must be displaced now that the greater than Moses is here! Do you think *he* cares whether the egg he eats was laid on the Sabbath? You know he doesn't, and the conflict between them is deepening by the day. To turn proselyte under these conditions would be a false step."

"I confess that I have thought only of the Kingdom being restored ... but of course, that too will change many things. Yes,

I think I see what you mean! There must be adjustments – and that may be quite difficult."

"Monumentally difficult, I would say, for such an inflexible people! And in the meantime, what of those like myself? You see, Magdalan, I am a very new vintage, am I not? Too raw, too sharp, still fermenting! – and I cannot be contained in stiff old bottles without cracking such long-cured leather. To return to your question, yes I must go, but I *am* with you in spirit. I must work elsewhere, that is all. There are many, many synagogues abroad where there are devout Jews and proselytes, all waiting for Messiah, and living on rumours of the last few years. They need to hear the facts from an eyewitness – especially a non-Jew and former sceptic such as myself."

She dropped her eyes at last.

"So you will leave the Land, Loukanos of Philippi."

"I think I must," he replied quietly. "But not yet. Three years ago I deserted family and friends in the most cowardly fashion, and I am no true disciple of my Teacher, if I do not seek them out and make amends. I will stay with them at least until Passover, and if they are willing, bring them all with me to Jerusalem to celebrate it there – for the first time as a united family – and I'm determined that poor old Etta will not be left behind this time."

"Ah! I rejoice to hear it! That is a lovely plan! And will it be your Passover too – Jew or not?"

"Moses declared the same law for both Gentile sojourner *and* Jew, when it came to Passover, so I am safe there," he answered with a wink. "You know, as a child it was my duty to ask each year, 'Father, what mean ye by this ritual?' and the answer telling of 'when we were slaves in Egypt' seemed nonsense to a Greek boy. But I see now that I *was* enslaved – only in a different kind of

296

Egypt. *This* Passover, though! ... it will have such meaning as never before, and how my longsuffering father and sister in particular will feel, I can barely imagine. Yes, I think I will like this Passover very much! Afterwards, I must bring Anna and her family safely home again ... and not till then I will leave." He paused, then added, "I have missed them. More than I ever thought I would."

The Magdalan brushed his hand with her cold fingertips.

"Loukanos, you are a good man. Shall we meet again?"

He took her hand gently.

"Yes, come the Kingdom. Perhaps even before then, especially if you are going up for Passover yourself."

"Then there is no need to say goodbye. Go with God."

"Go with God, Magdalan."

"I am a grown man!" Loukanos told himself fiercely, blinking the mist from his eyes and swallowing hard to ease the painful tightness of his throat. He pounded the road beneath his feet as if he could stamp out the burning in his chest. "This is mere emotional reaction! This too will pass."

And striding alone through the countryside, so he kept telling himself, over and over. He knew he was not far ahead of the ben Zebedees whose turn it was to walk to the next town to prepare lodgings for the next day, but having made his decision to leave the group, Loukanos could not bear to delay any longer. Neither did he want company, even of these genial fishermen, who had once taken him and his family on board their boat, and laughed with them all the way across the lake and down the river to find the Baptist. None of the former fishermen, Shimon included, had been themselves lately and he felt a growing coolness which puzzled him. But even had they been the best company in the world, he wanted no-one with him just now.

There was only one road, and if he was to retain his isolation he must keep up the pace, but he had not reckoned on the draining effect of the grief which welled up within him. He had often reminded others that 'sorrow saps the body', but now it was no longer a physician's observation; it was something he felt for himself as he never had before, not even when his mother died. As the fields ebbed into a thicket of plane trees, he plunged off the road, suddenly desperate to rest. He dropped his satchel and flung himself down against a mottled trunk, intending only to doze briefly, enough to refresh him for the next stage of his journey.

But as his chest began to heave uncontrollably, he put his head down in his arms, finally surrendering to the painful, wrenching sobs of a man who rarely wept.

For a while there seemed to be two of him, one who cried like a heartbroken mourner, and one who watched in dismay, remembering the dark place into which he had plunged following the death of the prophet. But as the worst of it passed, and he came back to himself, he knew his misery was mere heart-ache – the same as any normal man's. Still, the quieter, low keening, had not yet all escaped from his body, when the last of it was shocked clean out of him by a sudden stricken cry! – a sudden pounce! – and he found himself gripped, smothered and tossed by a pair of powerful arms.

Loukanos gasped and struggled and cried out – but his attacker had a crazed strength – and amid the outrage and confusion and uproar, for the first time in his life the physician was truly afraid of another man. He fought mightily to free himself, but the frenetic,

298

thickset assailant gave him no quarter – flinging him around, shaking him violently, dragging him, crushing him, clutching him, weeping and babbling and shouting in a kind of agonised ecstacy.

"Oh, woe! Grief! Calamity! Do you weep for a death? Do you weep for a woman? Only these can wrench a man to his entrails! Cry! Howl! Scream for your loss! Roar to the winds! She will not return! Demand it of Sheol and shriek to the tomb! There is no comfort, no pity, no life from the dead! Shake your fist at the heavens and yell your rage to the angels in vain! Misery and corruption and silence! The grave claims the victory and the dark power of death! All is blackness and there is no light – no light! Eternal One, I defy You! I defy You! Kill me! Kill me now! Kill this man with me and let us be at peace together! Where is Your salvation? Where is Your power? Where are You? Is there no God with us?"

God with us! Emmanuel!

Amidst the screaming storm of the mad man's raving, there it was – a still, small voice – and Loukanos heard it.

Irresistibly a white flame seemed to flare up within him – he rose tall and strong, he plucked the locked, clutching arms from his neck and held them down without force – and looked deep into the wild, tortured eyes.

"In the name of Emmanuel! In the name of Jeshua who is the Son of the Living God, I command this spirit of torment to leave you! *Be at peace.*"

The eyes rolled up, the lids fluttered, and the hireling Thaddeus crumpled to the ground. Instantly Loukanos dropped beside him, feeling for a heartbeat, lifting the eyelids with his thumb, touching the pale clammy skin.

"Stop! Stop this! Stop!" Two men were running from the roadside towards them, shouting and gesticulating angrily. The ben Zebedees! They had caught him up, and now how thankful he was to see them! But there was no need for them to worry.

"No – all is well!" Loukanos cried out reassuringly. "See, he has not hurt me! And look, he breathes normally! His heart does not pound – his colour is returning! Praise the Eternal!"

A sob arose in his throat at the wonder of it all. He looked up at them, his eyes shining.

"Praise the Eternal! Praise the power of Jeshua's name, brethren!"

The brothers looked at him coldly.

"Brethren? You are not one of us, Grecian! It is only the chosen ones who share the power to heal! How dare you take the Teacher's name in vain!"

Loukanos got to his feet, his knees shaking, looking from one to the other in pained astonishment. He gestured to the man on the ground, who opened his eyes – bewildered, but clear and calm.

"Did I indeed take his name in vain?" Loukanos asked, quietly.

Thaddeus sat up and held his head. He looked around vaguely and squinted at Loukanos.

"What's happened? What am I doing here? Where are the sheep?"

Loukanos squatted beside him and put an arm around his shoulders.

"You're safe, my friend, and someone else is caring for the sheep. Tell me – does anything hurt?"

"No – ow – yes, I think – why, how is this? I am covered in cuts and bruises! Have I been drunk?"

"In a way, but not with wine. Can you tell me your name?"

"Thaddeus of Banayim, of course, everyone knows me – but I don't know you, do I?'

"We have met, but it was a long time ago, during the Festival of Booths at Banayim."

The man snapped his fingers. "Yes, I remember – you are the Nazirite's brother, the physician." He looked puzzled. "Am I sick? I feel strange sensations …"

Loukanos helped him to his feet. "You *were* sick, my friend, but no longer, praise God. What do you feel that is strange?"

"My head and my chest feel so queerly still – and free – and light – like thistledown which might float away in a breeze."

"That's a good feeling, friend, you will learn to enjoy it. You have been carrying a crushing burden in your heart for a long time, and now it has gone. So you will have to get used to being well. But first, how long is it since you have eaten, or drunk?"

Suddenly he realised that the Zebedee brothers had gone. There they went, hurrying down the road. He watched them disappear and had a brief struggle with himself. Should he be angry with them? Disappointed? Baffled, he certainly was.

"Ah, physician, I can't remember when I last ate or drank, but now you've mentioned it, I am hungry as a wolf."

Loukanos turned his full attention back to the man for whom a wonder had been wrought. That was what mattered! How Jeshua's men felt about it was not anyone's business but theirs and their Master's. He untied his flask, dug food from his satchel and laid it before the famished man, who fell on it thankfully.

Loukanos knew full well he could have done nothing of himself – the power was the spirit of the *Christos* alone – and how it had happened was beyond the science of any physician. He felt as if he had stepped through an invisible door which had forever closed behind him. Almost he marvelled that he could have wept so miserably such a short time ago. After all, what had he lost? Surely he could not lose what had never been his in the first place.

He and Marah had each chosen to serve according to their different talents. That bond would unite them no matter where they went or what happened. And that this choice was sanctioned, he now had assurance – assurance that he was no longer a mere spectator, that he too was one of the Teacher's workers, and chosen to spread his Truth. What greater gift could he have been given, than the power to heal where a physician was helpless!

Would such a moment ever come again? Loukanos did not know, but he did not care. It had been granted this once, and confirmed his path, and nothing would ever be able to shake him from that certainty thereafter. The same spirit which moved the Messiah, had suddenly moved a Greek disciple and worked through him. Never before had he felt so strongly, that even the best doctor of medicine was only an instrument of healing, and not the healer himself. The heaviness in his own heart seemed to have flown away with all that ailed Thaddeus. Now they were both free – praise Adonai God!

Thaddeus made short work of the barley loaves and dried fish Loukanos had given him. He drank most of the water, stoppered up the flask with a thump of his hard hand on the leather-bound bung and looked curiously at Loukanos.

"What now? I have no idea where we are, or how I got here. All I remember is hearing the name of the Nazarene – with a strange feeling that I was somehow rushing towards him from the depths of a deep cave – but he is not here, so perhaps I was delirious. I don't think I have seen my son for weeks. I must get back to him. He has no mother, you know, and though young Judith is a good servant and does her best for him, the boy is fretful. He will be off to school next year, so I must take the chance to have him with me more often – it's time I gave him a taste of his father's life, I think."

"Ah, Thaddeus, this is good to hear!" Loukanos answered, knowing nothing of the devastation the man had left behind in Banayim. "They will both be glad to see you, I am sure! And the whole village no doubt has been concerned about you. Come, we will journey home together. I too am heading for Banayim, and on the way I will explain as much as I can."

Thaddeus grinned. "Thank you, Loukanos! You see, now I can even remember your name! Let us be off then – I am impatient to hear you, but first, tell me, will we be there before dark?"

Loukanos laughed and shook his head. "If only! We are more than a day's journey away, my friend! There will be plenty of time for talking."

The two began walking together, and though Loukanos wondered what he should do or say if they overtook the haughty ben Zebedees, they did not see them. As the miles went by, he unfolded to Thaddeus what had happened – as much as he knew. Thaddeus grew very sober as he spoke.

"I have been in a bad way since poor Naami died. I did not realise how bad, though, until now – nothing is very clear to me since Passover last. I hope I have not done anything to disgrace my son but no doubt the Dabab will be glad to let me know if I have. I am indebted to you, Loukanos – and indebted to Nazarene

303

Jeshua, your Teacher. I had heard something of his wonderful miracles before my days became nightmares – but I did not know he also delegated his powers to others."

"You owe me nothing," Loukanos replied briefly, "and I owe the Teacher more than I can tell you."

Chapter Thirty

IT seemed that miracles were abroad that crisp autumn afternoon. As they drew near to the next town, two figures were seen striding resolutely towards them – one a half grown boy. Loukanos narrowed his eyes and shook his head. No, it couldn't possibly be – not here! But the boy gave a shout, clutching his friend by the arm, hurrying him forward – and the heart of Loukanos beat faster. He hung back, pulling his headcloth further around his face, almost dreading to be recognised, waiting for the painful reproaches which surely would follow.

"What is it?" Thaddeus asked half jokingly. "You're not afraid of robbers? These two are no threat to us!"

Loukanos did not answer – but it was not his name the boy called out as he slowed his pace a mere stone's throw away.

"Thaddeus? Is it you? It is!"

"Thaddeus, my brother! Have no fear – here is your old friend, Caleb!"

"Don't worry, Thaddeus! You are safe with us! We have come to help you!"

"Softly, Dan, do not startle him. Stranger, have a care, this man is not himself. Move away from your companion, Thaddeus, and come quietly to us. We are your friends, we mean you no harm."

"Caleb! You, here?! But why talk to me this way? What is this about?" Thaddeus replied, astonished. "And young Dan! Is this some New Moon prank?"

"I think he's all right at the moment," Dan whispered in surprise, and Caleb nodded cautiously.

"No prank, Thaddeus, my friend," he answered kindly. "You are a long way from home, and we have been searching for you as for a lost lamb. Your village is very worried about you."

"Ah!" Thaddeus replied, grimly. He murmured to Loukanos, "You were right. I must have been in a very deep hole."

He looked at Dan and Caleb with something very like gratitude, and stepping forward, grasped their outstretched hands warmly. "You are good friends, my brother shepherds, to have such a care for my welfare, and I thank you for it! But don't concern yourselves, I have come to no harm at all. In fact, thanks to my companion here … why, of course, you know *him* already."

Dan looked properly for the first time – his face drained – he could not move.

"It is! Oh, praise the Eternal, it is he!" Old Caleb quavered, but nobody heard him. Loukanos had taken a swift step forward and snatched the boy into a bone-crushing embrace which had him gasping for breath.

"Dan! I left you – you and Anna – and everyone – without warning … it was selfish, and cowardly … and I am truly sorry!"

"So you should be!" Dan gritted, struggling free. "So you should be!" He shook his head angrily and tried to swallow the pain in his throat. "Leaving was bad enough – but no word to *anyone* afterwards?" It was impossible to convey in this moment either

306

their grief or their anxiety for him during the last two years. "That was the *worst*, Loukanos of Philippi!"

Loukanos held him at arms' length and looked soberly into the scowling young face which was already losing its boyish softness.

"Hear me, Dan," he said seriously. "I was wrong. I was very wrong – and very blind! But the Eternal has opened my eyes – and now I too am a follower of the Nazarene. I have lately been baptised, and God has forgiven me, but can you forgive me too? Enough to call me Uncle again?"

Tears welled in his eyes as he spoke – tears from unsentimental Loukanos! Dan needed no greater proof of sincerity. He hugged his uncle ferociously as he nodded, too choked to speak. He forgot he was nurturing a budding moustache and a husky voice, and sobbed like the child he still was. Old Caleb stood with unashamed drops coursing through his wrinkles to form tributaries in his beard, until Loukanos scruffed him affectionately as well, and suddenly all the tears dried up into a noisy masculine chaos. The antics of the three were something to behold; as they shouted and leapt and slapped each other, and generally behaved like schoolboys let out of class for an unexpected holiday, until even Thaddeus actually laughed out loud to see them. This joyful sound from a man who had not been known to smile for years was so startling to Caleb and Dan that they stopped their prancings to draw breath and stare. Loukanos held up a hand as Dan opened his mouth.

"You will have many, many questions, both of you – and they all deserve full and sincere answers. But first, I applaud you both for seeking out Thaddeus – he has been bedevilled for a long time, has he not? From the way he met me, I know that you must have needed great courage to attempt to regain your brother. Rest assured that he is once again in his right mind, and let him tell you what has befallen him this very day."

So Caleb and Dan listened intently – first to Thaddeus, then to Loukanos – and were overwhelmed by the shock of all they heard. Loukanos! More than a baptised penitent, or curious follower – a true disciple of the Nazarene?

"*You* cured him?"

"Not I, Dan, the power of Emmanuel. It is a long story, and I will tell it presently."

"You might be surprised to hear how much we already know," Dan told him proudly, but Caleb lifted his hand for attention.

"Master Loukanos, I rejoice and praise the Eternal for what you have told us already," he said earnestly, "but we must talk to Thaddeus before we go any further. There are things which he needs to know."

"Yes!" the hireling agreed eagerly. "For a start, how is my boy? And how long have I been away from home? Long enough to cause him and the girl hardship? If so, I beat my breast!"

Dan felt shaken – how to reply to this man who was so crazed, so recently?! It was clear he remembered nothing.

"Judith and Thad have often been close to hardship," he said boldly. "But nobody in Banayim would ever see them hungry."

"Good people," Thaddeus acknowledged with humility. "I will thank them, every one, on my knees!"

"It is not to the villagers you must bend your knees, my friend," Caleb said regretfully. "It is to your God, and to your own household."

The shepherd paled. "What have I done? Tell me everything!"

Old Caleb raised an eyebrow at Loukanos, who nodded, dreading the answer almost as much as Thaddeus. But whatever it was, the man would have to know. So Caleb told him, while the poor hireling's face changed miserably.

"Everyone was afraid of what you might do next," Dan added, "so we came looking for you."

"Was – where was – little Thad?"

"Watching."

Thaddeus clutched his head in anguish. "God forgive me! For him to see his father destroy his own home and beat a defenceless girl! Poor little creatures, both! How could I do such a thing?"

Overcome, he began to weep despairingly. Loukanos put an arm around his shoulder.

"You were not in your right mind, then, my friend," he said firmly, "nor for a very long time before it, but you are now, and can make whatever amends are possible."

"Young Judith – is she in any danger?"

"A lot of pain – but no danger so far." Dan winced as he remembered the sickening business of pinning her down to be hurt even more. "Not unless her broken bones cause more mischief – so Anna says. But her face … she will never look the same again."

"God forgive me! "Thaddeus cried again. "Oh, how will He forgive me?"

"Stop, now," Loukanos commanded. "I say again, you were not yourself! And don't you realise that God *has* forgiven you already?"

"What? How? *How?* Tell me, lest I am totally crushed on this day which so lately was triumphant!"

Loukanos spoke slowly.

"He is the Eternal, from everlasting to everlasting … therefore He knows everything, doesn't He? He knows the end from the beginning. Very well! Did He know you were desperately deranged? Of course He did. Did He know you would be remorseful and anxious to seek forgiveness? Yes to that also. But how *could* you be, while you were so demented, with no comprehension of your sin?"

As Thaddeus hung on every word, light began to dawn in his eyes.

"How to break that impossible circle?" Loukanos continued. "To be forgiven, you must repent. To repent, you must be aware of your sin. Well, to be aware of your sin, you had to be healed. As they say in the theatre, *Enter Physician, wearing mask of Woe* … a woe I was whisked out of very smartly when the Spirit moved me on your behalf. *Two* people were healed today, I think. Would the Eternal heal a man so that he could repent, but then *not* forgive him when he did?"

"Of course not!" interrupted Dan excitedly. "That would be pointless!"

Caleb was only just managing to keep up, and Thaddeus seemed to have forgotten to breathe but Loukanos swept on triumphantly. "Exactly! Thaddeus, my friend, you have just prayed *God forgive me!* Now ask yourself this – does forgiveness take any longer than healing? Does the God of all Eternity need *time?*"

"There!" Dan cried delightedly, as the stricken shepherd gave a gasp of relief. "That is your answer!"

"Thank you, my friend! You are right – praise the Eternal, you are right!"

310

Thaddeus dropped to his knees on the spot, and lifted his hands and his face to the heavens, where a crimson sun was spreading purple and gold glory over the fading sky.

"Great God of Abraham, Master of the Universe – I praise and thank Thee for the wonderful things done this day! For the stranger Loukanos whom Thou has brought to the dwellings of Thy people; for the power of Jeshua Thine anointed, granted through Loukanos for my healing; for Caleb and Dan's care for me even while I was worthless; and for the comfort of wise counsel. My God, I thank Thee for forgiving me the great evil I have done to the fatherless Judith, to my motherless son, and my neglected friends. Show me swiftly how I may right the wrongs I have created! I exalt Thee, O God, and the power of Thy Salvation. Amen! Friends, bear me witness that I praise and thank Him!

"Amen!" they replied gladly. "Amen!"

"Well said, Thaddeus," Loukanos said quietly. He had not expected such eloquence from an uneducated hireling shepherd. When would he ever learn, he reminded himself impatiently, that the most exalted sentiments may come from the humblest of men, and the most eloquence from those whose meditations outnumbered their speeches.

There was no stopping them after that. The next town was reached, a meal procured, lodgings taken – the night passed in thankful oblivion, the grey morning greeted with eagerness, and they set out again.

So anxious was Dan to reveal both Loukanos and Thaddeus triumphantly to Banayim that he felt he gladly could have marched on without sleep, but Loukanos had other ideas. Having heard about Caleb's recent illness, he would not countenance them camping in the open, and insisted on the warmth of proper lodgings, regardless of how stuffy it was, or that yet another night's halt nearly drove Dan frantic with impatience.

But apart from the inconvenience of sleep, they kept up a brisk pace. Mile after mile was rapidly eaten up under their stride; words pouring forth from each of them in turn, filling in the years which had passed, until roads by day and walls by night echoed with their explanations and discussion, laughter and wonder.

Loukanos spoke of his conversion – though not of Marah – and was amazed to hear that Uncle Joseph and Ittai were even now searching for *him* because of Marta's condition. Dan told him all he knew of it, and was astonished in his turn to see his uncle shrug smilingly.

"*Leucoderma*, Dan," he nodded offhandedly. "I noticed it years ago ... and it's just spreading now, that's all, as it often does with age. Quite harmless!"

Dan, who did not know about Marta's rash, grinned from ear to ear. What a relief! Well, there was nothing they could do to recall Joseph and Ittai, except leave word wherever they could.

"Have you noticed anything about *me*?" he asked casually, fingering his upper lip. Loukanos grinned back.

"You mean, the glow of the sunset on your face?" He punched Dan playfully on the shoulder. "Should be interesting when it grows, boy! Almost as interesting as your voice ... yes, I noticed ... you've got the Frog all right. Congratulations. But please – when you sing, do it softly to spare my musical sensitivities."

On they went ... Bethsaida, and the glittering expanse of the Sea ... Capernaum ... a boat ... Magdala ... and finally, the road to Banayim!

As they crested the last hill, Thaddeus' feet lagged. Caleb took his arm reassuringly.

"I will walk with you as slowly as you wish, my friend," he told him. "But we will let the others go ahead, eh? Let them enjoy their reunion for a little while, first of all."

He planted his dirty, gnarled feet firmly and put his hands to his mouth like a trumpet. Taking a great breath, he bawled with surprising force to the huddle of dwellings below them.

"ANNA! Fetch Anna the Nazirite! ANNA!"

He grinned happily, giving Dan and Loukanos a hefty push.

"Run, then! Are you graven images? Run!"

They needed no second bidding. Loukanos took off like an athlete, leaving Dan to scramble after him, but the boy overtook him by the simple expedient of leaping clean off the brow of the hill and landing ahead of him like a cat.

"Mother!" Dan yelled at the top of his lungs, not even caring that his voice skipped like a stone on water. "We found him! We found him!"

Faces appeared at windows, eager bodies ran into the street, there was pointing and pushing, and a tall woman anxiously waving, surging through the little crowd which parted like the Red Sea.

"*Amma!*" Dan waved back madly as he ran towards her. "He's here! We found him!"

"Dan! Praise the Eternal you're safe! You found Thaddeus?"

"No! I mean yes! But No!" Dan panted, stopping with a sudden stitch in his side.

Tearing off his head cloth to expose his face, Loukanos swept past him. The trembling woman gasped, and flew into his open arms with a cry which came from the depths of her astonished heart.

"Louki! Louki! Oh, *Louki!* Praise God! Louki!"

"Yes, Anna! Praise God indeed! My sister! Forgive me!"

Both were half-laughing, half-weeping with incoherent explanations and reassurances only part of which they could hear or understand, but it made no difference. More than two years of agonised emotion would take a long time to spill out, but all that mattered for now was that a splintered family had been put back together again.

Thronged by the whole village, the brother and sister were hugged and kissed and congratulated so persistently that Dan had to fight his way to their side. Never had there been so many incredulous voices, so many sympathetic tears of gladness. Soon it seemed that everyone was sobbing freely and luxuriously – even the Dabab wailing her happiness at the sight of the long lost physician who gave free advice. Widow Shana enthusiastically embraced every unsuspecting person within arms' reach, and began a joyful ululation which the other women took up, until even Marta and Etta, still sequestered with the children, heard it a quarter-mile away.

The two friends had been vastly relieved at hearing what Mordecai had said about Marta's skin, but as there were other things about her condition which he did not know, it was decided that she should remain at the Hollow until they had further advice, or until she was no longer unclean. Now, the shrill notes from the village wafted thinly to their ears, driving them wild with curiosity. Marta begged Etta to find out what was happening. Laughingly, she brandished a broom at her, pretending to sweep her out of the door.

"Don't you dare come back without news!" she threatened.

Etta chuckled and agreed. She did not mind the walk when she had nothing to carry, though dear Marta really had no idea of how much effort it took these days. Still, despite the aching bones, it would be an outing, and a little peace from the persistent twins would not go amiss. She went to fetch her cloak.

At Banayim, a glowing Anna finally managed to extricate herself from the chattering throng, as impromptu celebrations began. Already several voices were singing, hands were clapping and feet were itching to dance in the street. Anna hugged Dan gratefully, trying to think of six different things at once.

"Dan, my precious son! My young hero! Whoever would have thought you would find Loukanos! What wonderful tales you and Caleb will have to tell us later! I suppose the old man went straight home to Extra Pressings – I do wish he had not, he deserves more than she will greet him with. But Dan, you must run quickly to the Hollow and tell Marta and Etta the glad news – Etta can join us, I am sure. Oh, and of course, I should ask Louki properly to examine Marta soon! but that can wait now till tomorrow's light … and now I must slip back to Thaddeus' place and let poor Judith know what is happening here, and that I want Louki to see her for himself."

"Thaddeus!" Dan cried guiltily. "Oh, but, Anna, we did find him too! He is –"

But there was no need to say more – the hubbub around them ground into stunned silence, as Thaddeus himself, escorted by Old Caleb, finally walked into the hamlet. There was an uneasy murmur, children were hustled behind skirts, or pushed inside doors, people were shrinking away.

"Friends, please hear me," Caleb held up a bony hand. "Yes, here is Thaddeus, your neighbour. He will not hurt you, and he is quite well again. Loukanos can vouch for him."

"Yes, this is the truth," Loukanos said boldly. "Thaddeus is healed of his affliction, by the power of the Nazarene. Let him speak for himself."

The murmuring swelled to a muttering, and the little crowd closed in again, but Thaddeus was determined to speak, nervous as he was.

"My brethren, they have told me what I did here last Sabbath. And also what kind of man I have been during the last couple of years. It is to me a bad dream from which I have been awoken, by the mercy and goodness of Almighty God." As he had promised, he dropped to his knees and looked bravely at them all.

"Before the Eternal, I ask your pardon for the wrongs I have inflicted on you, and in particular, I will now go to ask it of my servant girl, Judith – even before I take my son in my arms and kiss him. And I thank all of you for your care of them both."

Old Caleb helped him to his feet, amid whispers of approval. On his knees to the whole village! How could you doubt the man! But even as the first hands were outstretched towards him, someone voiced the thoughts no one else would admit to.

"You seem very sensible now, I'll agree," the Dabab admitted grudgingly, "and praise the Eternal indeed, that you are healed and can again take up the proper management of your household. But all the forgiveness in the world will not mend young Judith's face."

"Yes, indeed!" Widow Shana added hotly. "A fatherless, defenceless girl with no dowry – and what is to become of her, I'd like to know! What decent man will marry her now?"

Thaddeus felt the prickle of hostility around him. He had prayed for the Eternal to show him the way to make amends. Well, here it was. He took a deep, unsteady breath.

"I will," he said humbly. "I will marry her myself."

There was an audible gasp all round. Thaddeus lifted his eyes and spoke to Anna.

"Please, Anna – and everyone else – please continue your celebrations for Loukanos! I must go to my house … perhaps Widow Shana will chaperone …"

"Gladly!" shouted Widow Shana, forgetting her ladylike manners as she did in moments of excitement. "What a man, hey? What a man! Come, everyone! Celebrate *two* men who have in a figure, returned from the dead! Rejoice over them, friends! Rejoice over long lost Loukanos, rejoice over long lost Thaddeus, sisters – here is a man whose repentance is genuine! How rare is that? Clear the street, start the dancing! Bring out the food – Rachel, I know you baked honey cakes yesterday … and Zaccheus, forget you're an old skinflint for once and be generous to your neighbours … Come on, Thaddeus, before you change your mind …!"

Whooping joyfully, she dragged him down the street to his house, then shook herself straight, laid a finger primly on her lips, and took him inside.

Instantly the frozen village thawed back to life and began to bustle. Food began emerging from houses – in napkins, baskets, pots and bowls – and Old Zack dived into his house, to stagger out with his biggest wineskin which he had been saving for the Festival of Booths.

Anna turned to Loukanos with shining eyes.

"Well!" she marvelled. "Well! What a solution! Praise the Eternal, whose ways are wonderful and past finding out! Thad will have a mother, Judith will have security, and Thaddeus will have atoned, and be all the better for it."

Dan goggled. "Do you think he means it?"

Loukanos laughed. "I think he does. What do you think, Caleb?"

Caleb scratched his grizzled beard.

"Very noble," he said glumly. "But ..."

"Oh, Caleb, you're right!" Dan interrupted, looking stricken. "What about Eli?"

Chapter Thirty-one

WITH that question burning in his mind, Dan obediently ran to the Hollow – which Aunt Etta had not yet left. She was still attempting to extricate herself from the clinging arms of the twins who, with woebegone looks and careful tears, were reminding her earnestly of bedtime story promises she had rashly made.

Dan's triumphant arrival saved her from further effort, and in the joy of the moment the twins forgot to pull sad faces, and happily jumped around and all over him instead. Aunt Etta loudly praised the Eternal again and again that her beloved boy was safely home, and privately was not sorry to be spared the walk to the hamlet at an hour when her wretched back most craved relief. Dan gabbled out as much of the essential parts of his story as he could in a hurry, and once more there were tears of rejoicing, and a most satisfactory stupefaction all round. Marta sighed at not being able to share the news with Ittai, then excused herself, whisking the children off to her room. Much as she longed to join in the merry-making she would stay apart until Loukanos knew the whole of her condition. Dan had assured her that his uncle held to his opinion concerning her whitened skin, and intended to tell her so himself the next morning. She would be able to ask him about other matters then. She may even confess to the headaches she had not mentioned to anyone, being rather ashamed of her anxiety. Willow-bark brews had eased them, until Mordecai's opinion had banished them altogether. What a relief! Oh, God was good, and things were getting better all the time.

"Now, you mustn't stay here any longer. Go back to the celebrations, Dan," Aunt Etta insisted, "Marta and I will be happier tonight than we have been for a long time, and everything else will keep till morning."

"Oh, no, Etta," Marta called out in protest from the long room. "Why don't you go with Dan and join in – and stay the night with Anna? You were going anyway, before Dan arrived."

"Thank you, my dear, but truth to tell, I would much rather be resting my back within the next hour anyway. You settle the baby, and I'll come and tell the children about Noah's Ark as I promised – and I'll warrant they'll be asleep before we get to the raven, let alone the rainbow. Then we can talk everything over as much as we like by the fire. We have a lot of people to pray for."

With all Dan had told them, they may need the whole night, she thought. Thaddeus ... Judith ... Loukanos ... Sobek ... Mordecai, wandering somewhere on the northern roads ...

"Yes, with Uncle Joseph and my darling Ittai still out searching on my account," Marta added wistfully, her mind following the same track.

"We left word for them everywhere we went," Dan assured her, "but you know, Loukanos said the Nazarene was right behind him, heading for Capernaum, and so they may already have found him. And some of the followers knew Uncle Louki was heading here, and could tell them so if they asked."

Marta cheered up at once. "Help from all directions – praise the Eternal! Let's hope Blind Mordecai is equally blessed with success, for Sobek's sake!"

Aunt Etta beckoned Dan to lean down, kissed him on the forehead, and lovingly ruffled his curls. "Thank you for all this wonderful news, Dan! Now off you run, until tomorrow!"

"It will be only a quick visit," Dan warned, rubbing his head vigorously. Women and hair! Did they never stop interfering with it? "Caleb and I must get back to relieve Samuel's Eli."

He felt a cold qualm at the thought of telling Eli about Thaddeus' offer to marry Judith, but there was no point borrowing trouble from tomorrow. He gave Aunt Etta a fierce hug, waved to Marta through the doorway and disappeared into the fast-falling dusk, leaving the women exchanging watery smiles.

By moonrise the street of Banayim was good and noisy – there was laughter and gossip, and children were begging to stay up. Malachi had lit fires in several rusty braziers dragged out of Old Zack's storehouse; Rachel's honey cakes were laid on a cloth, along with many other morsels which had been freely supplied by the women, and the only food conspicuously absent was olives. There seemed to be an unspoken feeling that it would not be tactful to produce these tonight. Old Zack, who had been tasting his wine just in *case* something had gone wrong with it too, was a little unsteady on his legs by now but holding forth on the subject of the olives to Dan; swearing yet again that he *had* put in *plenty* of salt, and that the brine was good and strong, and the olives were fresh, sound fruit when he preserved them, and he'd even eaten a few himself and found no fault with them.

Dan frowned thoughtfully. "Then it makes no sense, does it, that Judith's should have been so bad? And you say nobody believes you?"

"Nobody," he replied mournfully. "Not that it makes any difference now. At the time, I suppose Thaddeus was in such a state that anything could have set him off, even a bit of grit in his bread." He groaned bitterly. "Folk will think evil of me every time they see that poor girl's face, no doubt, and I will never live it down. The more I protest, the more they will wag their fingers and say, *Aha!* And yet I measured out nearly all the salt I had for those wretched berries."

"Do you have any left?" Dan asked suddenly, as an idea struck him.

Zaccheus shrugged. "A little – a *mina* or two, maybe three. I had more, but I sold some to Rachel. I didn't buy a lot – pickling olives was a new idea for me, see? I wanted to see how successful it was first, and you know salt is expensive. But I didn't stint on it!" he added stubbornly. "I got it for a bargain price on my last trip down to Jericho, so I didn't need to cut any corners. And it's good stuff, too. Here – taste this – I brought a bit of it ready crushed to share around tonight, just for a treat ... it's delicious with this fresh bread, with some of this creamy curd, see, then a little sprinkle of salt ... like so ... Good? Eh? Eh? See, I told you ...!"

Dan took a cautious mouthful and swallowed with a shudder. Suddenly he reached over, took the small pouch from Old Zack and dug out a fistful of brownish crystals.

"Here – be careful with that, boy!" Zaccheus protested anxiously, but to his astonishment Dan suddenly threw the whole lot into his mouth and began to crunch – then spat it out, and wiped his lips. He grinned at the dumbfounded old merchant.

"Tell me – how long ago did you lose your sense of taste?"

"What? *What?* You don't mean ...?"

"Sorry, Zaccheus, but I do mean. This stuff is useless. You've been tricked."

Zaccheus put his head in his hands and howled. "But they said it was good quality – and I tasted it for myself!"

"But you can't taste properly any more, can you? That curd is really on the turn, and you didn't even notice. Old Caleb is the same … but if you tell him something is delicious, or sweet or spicy he really believes it. He says he goes on memory and that does him very well."

Zaccheus was fuming. "Taking advantage of a poor old man! Laughing in their sleeves! The scrapings, that's all I got! Cheap rubbish chipped from weathered rock and left in the blazing sun! Me! Fooled! I'll never hear the last of it! And I have only sold two other pots! Oh, such a waste of money – the salt, the fruit – and all that work …!"

"Cheer up!" Dan consoled him, "It proves the bad olives were not your fault, doesn't it? And maybe you can find your other customers and explain what happened … it's better than losing your good name, and they will respect you more for it. Perhaps you can offer them some of your figs in exchange?"

"And earn myself merit, perhaps," Zaccheus looked mollified. Dried figs were a lot less work, and last year's leftovers were probably still good enough. No sense in giving away the very freshest. After all, he *had* sold the olives very cheaply. "Well, you may be right." And with that he snatched back his bag of salt and ran to spread the word, anxiously pressing his neighbours to taste and see how he had been duped – growing happier by the moment at their commiserating responses – until the Dabab came marching out with a small sack which she dumped at his feet.

"Well, I'll have the money back for this lot, then," she said briskly, making him rue the day he had sold it to her. "Luckily for you I hadn't opened it yet, or you might be another one with a broken nose!"

"Stick to your dried figs!" Caleb advised him in a low whisper. "Nothing goes wrong with figs, give or take a few weevils – and even a Pharisee can't tell them from seeds when it comes to the crunch between the teeth."

"Well done, Dan!" Anna and Loukanos congratulated him as they were dragged out of their separate conversations to hear the story. "Very well done! You have saved face for Zaccheus and he will be more careful in future."

Saved face! Not for Judith, though …

"Judith!" Loukanos exclaimed guiltily. "Shame on me, Anna – I should see her at once – but Thaddeus and Shana are still with her."

"Not any longer." Anna pointed. Thaddeus was marching back up the street towards them with little Thad clinging to him as happily as a lizard curled around a warm rock, Widow Shana trailing fussily behind. One look at all the expectant faces, though, and the widow gave a gesture of impatience, and overtook him in a flash. What she had to say could not wait for convention, and even a plump woman could run faster than a man carrying a heavy lump of a child.

The setting out of the food halted while Widow Shana was duly besieged with questions about the forthcoming betrothal, to which she waved a hand imperiously, or as imperiously as she could manage while panting heavily.

She paused for effect (or breath) and hissed dramatically, "No betrothal! She turned him down!"

Sensation all round! Thaddeus was appealed to.

"It's true," he admitted uncomfortably. "The Widow and I did our best to persuade her, but she only wept, and refused."

"You won't be leaving it at that!" the Dabab demanded. "Why, the girl has no future!"

"I think she is too shocked to take it in – and not surprisingly, she is very unsure of me. I think she should be left in peace to think it over. I promise I will ask her again, when she is better recovered." He looked humbly at Loukanos. "Physician, will you see to her now?"

"Come, Anna, you had better hold her hand – she barely knows me." Loukanos strode off towards the house, and Anna hurried behind him.

"Oh! But, wait, Louki!" she cried, tugging his sleeve in sudden anguish. "How could I forget! I know you have barely eaten yet, but Judith is not the only patient who needs you! I meant to tell you about Marta –"

"Yes, it's all right, I know about her, Dan told me, and I've said I'll see her tomorrow. *Leucoderma*, that's all, nothing fatal."

"So Mordecai said, my dear brother, but she has other symptoms which Dan does not know."

Loukanos turned and stared at her even as he stretched out his hand for the door latch.

"Mordecai? Blind Mordecai? He was here? Or were you there?"

"He came here, with Philip – but they left, or at least, Philip went back to Cana and Mordecai didn't, he – oh! Where should I start!"

"Anna, Anna, Anna! It is not like you to be so flustered. Where is the calm cool sister I left behind me?"

Anna bit her lip. "I have become rather old womanish, haven't I, my brother? Well, it is no surprise. My life has been full of unexpected changes in the last few years, as you know, and though it sounds disloyal to say so – living with only the young or the old, I have missed the strength of a vigorous male mind against which to sharpen my thoughts." She clapped a hand to her head. "Mordecai!" She was unconscious of the association which instantly sprang to Loukanos' mind.

"Mordecai – brave Mordecai! Oh, Louki – that is another thing! His friend Sobek is in desperate need – so desperate that despite his affliction he has actually set out alone to find the Nazarene!"

"A brave man indeed!" Loukanos whistled. "I remember Sobek. But at least, now I am here, perhaps I can be of use. What ails her? I can leave this very night if need be!"

Anna shook her head regretfully. "I don't think you can help her, Loukanos."

She quickly related all Mordecai had said of Sobek, and her brother frowned.

"I'm much afraid his diagnosis is right," he said reluctantly. "It does not look good for her, but in God's grace she may survive despite everything. Not every lockjaw patient dies … though, it would be a miracle if she didn't, especially given her palsied condition. You say Philip is finding a woman to attend her?"

"Yes, and I wrote Aunt Mari to send Judith to help with the house, because – oh, I had better not begin any more tales just now, or you'll never get through this door! Come – but you will visit Marta in the morning?"

"First thing, I promise. Now – one patient at a time."

As Loukanos attended to a nervous, flinching Judith he felt growing unease, not about her, but about all Anna had told him of Sobek. He had not had time to tell his sister anything other than the fact of his baptism and his new conviction about the Nazarene. In all the commotion of the reunion he had not yet revealed to Anna that it was by his unwitting instrumentality that Thaddeus had been healed. This was something which already he had strictly enjoined Thaddeus, Dan and Caleb to keep to themselves. Now it troubled him deeply to think of the terrible symptoms poor Sobek would be suffering, which could only have one end, and he was unsure what to do.

In the uplift of healing Thaddeus, he had not concerned himself about whether he would ever experience such a moment again … it had not been of his choosing, after all. But now, what? Was it only a gift for one occasion? Should he seek to exercise it again – or go about his business as usual, and trust that the Spirit would move again if the Eternal so willed? It was agitating, not to know what the right answer was! What was his responsibility here, his calling? *Was* it even a calling? Should he rush to Sobek's side and hope or pray for another miracle? What if there was none? He would have left the oasis of his family – again – for another anxiety-born mirage of his own making. Anxiety and wishful thinking – yes, he could see that now, *they* were the source of his compulsions to act, to run … to make something happen … anything, rather than submit to an inevitability which was not to his liking.

Ugh! – he had been through such dizzying cycles of thought before, so many times, as he had struggled for surrender to Truth. It was a maze, in which he second-guessed himself until he was totally confused. Was it a faithful act, to rush to Sobek and pray for her healing? Or was that in itself, a selfconscious act of pride?

327

Were these conflicting thoughts themselves another test, another trial?

Judith cried out as the arm supporting her twitched involuntarily.

"*Ach!* I'm sorry! Poor girl! That was very clumsy of me – I'm so sorry, little maid … I didn't mean to hurt you more than I have done already. Hush, now, drink this – it will make you sleep quickly. You may wake in fright if you try to breathe through those bandages but don't worry, someone will be looking after you all night, and give you sips of water if your mouth gets too dry. You've been a very brave girl. Anna, she mustn't lie flat … will you make her comfortable, please … that ankle needs another cushion to steady it, and here, too, under the knees, and a bit more support for her back … mind those ribs … I've finished here."

He stretched wearily, cleaned his instruments, threw the blood-soaked wads of cloth into a bowl, and began to pack his satchel. Soon Anna slid an arm through his.

"She's sleeping already – what's wrong, Loukanos?"

He looked sideways at her in the wavering lamplight.

"You know me too well, don't you, my sister? I was a fool to imagine that discipleship would mean a glowing light cast over life's path to illuminate every step. At times I feel as much in the dark as ever."

"Come, no more introspection!" she rebuked him. "Not tonight! Save it for tomorrow if you must, my brother. Just tell me one thing – how is her nose? I went cold all over when you released that trapped blood – it was horrible!"

"Horrible, but necessary or the bone would die, and her nose collapse later on, like Mordecai's, which would be a lot more horrible, I can assure you. Compared to that, a lump or a twist is nothing. You did very well, Anna, and I'm proud of you, but I'm glad I was here so soon after the injury. I don't know whether she'll ever be able to breathe freely through it or not – noses are unpredictable in their healing – but no more can be done. I'm concerned about her front teeth, they're still quite loose, but let's hope they tighten up. Soft food, and caution, is all I can advise. As long as they don't start to discolour, they should be all right."

"Well, that is hopeful, and good to hear – thank you! Now, Judith is asleep, here's Rachel coming to watch her already, and the party in the street is waiting. So, hearken to your sister! You are to forget your patients for this evening, and begin one last cure ..."

"A contradiction! How like a woman."

She wagged her finger at him. "No, no, Not-So-Clever Loukanos! You can't help anyone else tonight – except yourself, and your family. *That's* the last cure – and it begins now! Come on, the night is young. Everyone has given of their best to honour two returned vagabonds – each of you, madmen who have been delivered from your own demons and darkness by the grace of Almighty God – and so you and I and Dan are going to eat, and drink, and talk, and laugh, and dance and sing!"

Loukanos winced. "Sing? Oh, please – with your flat voice and Dan's frog? Can't you both just hum or whistle?"

Anna burst into the bubbling, hiccuping laugh which not even Loukanos could imitate, but which made him grin just to hear it. He had missed that ridiculous sound!

So shaking himself free of clinging doubts he took her hand and ran with her back to the top of the street where food was sizzling, chatter was loud, and the mood was happy. The laden dishes were passed around to much appreciation, Old Zack's wine sipped (a little suspiciously at first) by all except Anna, and pronounced surprisingly drinkable. Loukanos and Thaddeus were blessed and embraced and joked over. Instruments rejoiced, feet stamped and skipped on the beaten earth, fingers clicked, hands clapped, and voices rose in triumphant song. The Eternal was praised in music, in dance, and in eating and drinking, and in the incense of thankfulness which rose from every gladdened heart.

One by one the children were packed off to bed, and voices became lower, and slower, until the reality of sleep had to be faced. Night clouds trailing grey wisps across its pearly face, the moon was sailing high and cold by the time Malachi had lifted up his hands in a final prayer of thanks … a long prayer which began with Loukanos and Thaddeus, digressed to Moses – and Judith – and wandered around the scriptures for a while, before ending up where it began. Loud *Amens* were affirmed hastily lest Malachi had forgotten how to stop. It was quite likely, since Rachel, long since gone to sit with Judith, was not present to dig him with her sharp elbow.

The street emptied at once, the last goodnights were called and Dan, Caleb, Anna and Loukanos took themselves to sleep at the Travellers' House. As they rolled into their blankets, the minds of each became directed towards those distant individuals at whose welfare they could only guess. The physician thought of suffering Sobek; the old shepherd thought of Ittai and Joseph on their quest; the young shepherd thought of his friends Judith and Eli, each in a different kind of misery. As for the Nazirite, alone in the small upstairs chamber, her gratitude concerning Loukanos was overwhelming – but while her shadowed brown and hazel eyes stared unseeingly into the night, she was thinking about a blind man who was looking for a miracle.

Chapter Thirty-two

"PITY for the blind!" he called, hands outstretched, tapping his way as he had not done for many years. "Pity for the blind! Will someone with charity in his heart lead a blind man?"

How long it had been since he had needed to cry the beggar's plaint! The streets of Cana were engraved in his senses, the voices of its inhabitants, their occupations, their lives – he knew that place, and it knew him – the rare journeys he had made outside it were in the company of faithful friends who saw who he was, not what he was. Now all this was stripped away.

He pushed down a distaste which he was out of the habit of suppressing, reminding himself of how far he had come, and how blessed he had been. Whether walking wide Roman roads or narrow travellers' tracks, he had met with sound footing, and few spills – none interfering with his business, and some even encouraging him, such as the various folk who were following rumours of the Nazarene's return to Galilee, and had borne him along willingly with them for hours at a time. If only there had been some certainty of the whereabouts of the unschooled rabbi perhaps he could have reached his goal by now, but some said one thing and some another; and as groups split up to pursue the man who worked miracles, the blind man had at times been left by the wayside, or following a false trail. He would not be deterred, though, walking on doggedly with Etta's curved stick searching the path before him. Only one accident had him still laughing ruefully.

Having passed through a grove of poplar, which blazed unseen around him in a glory of rustling gold and crimson, Mordecai heard the shuffling crunch of footsteps through the fallen leaves. Encouraged by the lively sound of a deep voice humming happily to itself, he turned and called out.

"Greetings, friend, blessings and peace to you!"

"*Shalom*, fellow traveller! We meet on a good day, with fair weather for walking! And where may you be heading?"

"Thank you, it is a good day indeed. I am on my way to Capernaum but as yet I do not know my final destination. I seek the Nazarene and his men – do you know where they may be found?"

"Why, I too would rejoice to come across them!" was the cheerful reply. "There is talk of him going up for the Feast of Booths, you know, though he has not been seen in public for a little while. I must also pass through Capernaum, where some of his men have families. Someone there is bound to know more. We are not far from it now, and I would be glad of some company for the last few miles. Take my arm, brother, walk with me and we will help each other."

Though rather suspicious of the man's easy joviality which exuded the breath of the grape, Mordecai, with some fumbling, grasped his arm gratefully, glad of some relief from the concentration of using the stick, which he now hooked into his narrow girdle and tied securely. It would never do to lose Ammiel's last gift to his sister, and even apart from sentimental value, it was a beautiful thing to use, smooth on the palm, and easy to grip, with its lovely curved head.

The two men set off together, but before long the staggering gait of his newfound companion made Mordecai wonder whether he would be better off without him after all. Meanwhile, it puzzled him that the fellow's speech was nowhere as drunk as his feet. Just as he was beginning to feel decidedly off-balance himself, there was a stumble, a curse, and a yell – Mordecai was dragged sideways, and the two of them tumbled down together.

"Well! A poor guide you are!" the stranger hiccupped crossly, as they sat, stunned, in a soggy roadside rut caused the day before by two impatient carters refusing to give way to each other.

"I? A poor guide? What did you expect from a blind man?" Mordecai asked in astonishment, rubbing a bruised hip. How thankful he was that he had not landed on the other one, when he must surely have broken Etta's stick in the fall! "Here, help me up, won't you?"

The stranger did not move.

"Did you say, a *blind man*?" he asked, in a hollow voice.

"Yes – though it seems to me, you have no more eyes than I have!" He scrambled awkwardly to his feet, and was astonished to hear the other begin to chuckle, quietly at first, and then louder, until he was roaring with laughter.

"Pray tell me your name, friend, that I may know who it is that finds the misfortunes of the afflicted so amusing?" Mordecai asked coldly.

His companion only laughed all the more, finally managing to chortle a reply.

"I – I am Jabel of Chorazin. They call me Jabel the Blind. It is not quite true, for though darkness is before me, some sight is left to me still, right at the edges, as it were. I get by, but it is rather a strain. I thought *your* arm would help *me*, so I just rested my poor eyes for a while. To tell you the truth, I was beginning to wonder if you were drunk."

Mordecai grinned again over the incident. It had taught them both something, that was for sure. Jabel had proved to be a good companion once they had things straightened out. Delighted to find his clay flask unbroken, he insisted Mordecai refresh himself from it, and assured him that the town where so many friends and relatives of the Twelve lived, would surely provide them with news.

And so now Mordecai was in Capernaum, feeling his way with a crook-headed rod carved and polished by the hands of the man he so desperately sought. He was alone. Having drunk his flask dry, Jabel had stopped to replenish it at the first tavern they came to – an untidy establishment a stone's throw from the edge of town, where most of the customers were rowdy off-duty soldiers, disinclined to discuss the miracle worker of Galilee. Jabel refused to refill his flask without sampling what was to go inside it … and when Mordecai realised his companion was intent on turning himself into a walking wineskin, he reluctantly left him there. Sobek could not wait, and therefore neither could he. He went on, searching out the hazards of the town with his hands, his stick, and his voice.

"Charity for the blind!" he called, careful to keep bitterness from his tone. Yes, he had earned his keep, he had earned respect, he once more had a place – if not in the synagogue – in society, but only in Cana, and in the tiny hamlet of Banayim; and only among those who knew him. Here, he was just another beggar – but for Sobek's sake he must beg, and beg he would. What was his ridiculous pride compared to a woman's life?

He found himself jostled, and by the smells and sounds knew he was approaching a market place, and this being the Fifth Day, it would be crowded. Good! The more people heard him, the better.

"Men and brethren – I seek the Nazarene rabbi! Does anyone know where he may be found?"

But lakeside Capernaum – well-watered, business-like, bustling Capernaum – was weary of charity, tired of importunate sufferers clogging its streets, and too small-minded to be large-hearted. Like many minor towns in Galilee it was busy, but unremarkable; a place where Romans and Jews and Gentiles of all races lived bearded cheek by shaven jowl. They were an uneasy assortment of temperaments, customs, and status, such as was found all over the Empire, but they rubbed along together in pragmatic and superficial harmony most of the time, despite the conflicts rankling deep in the hearts of those who were the most rigid in either politics or religion.

Comfortable merchants and Sadducees walked among hardbitten soldiers and fishermen; bored, overfed matrons sauntered through the streets fingering the produce of their lean, overworked sisters. Sulky servants bargained ferociously with tired tradesmen, while unveiled women with glittering, heavily kohled eyes watched noisy young families from their curtained doorways.

And then there were others who frequented the crossroads – in more senses than one. Alert for easy pickings from tired, harassed, footsore travellers and wayworn merchants, vagabonds on the wrong side of the law loitered there. Doing much the same, (supposedly on the right side of it) were the customs officers at their posts. These were men with easy-living homes and easier-living consciences, and there was many an official among them whose right hand squarely out for Caesar never knew what the left hand was privately putting in its pocket. But those who were taxed had a fair grasp of the matter, whether they were local traders of dried fish and fruit from the fertile countryside, or those bringing rich silk and spices along the Via Maris from Damascus. The tax gatherers shrugged off their unpopularity – a cheap price for such a good position. Only one tribute did they receive without asking, and it came unstintingly, ungrudgingly, and even generously from rich and poor alike – and that was an equal measure of the contempt reserved for Jews, honest or dishonest, who worked for the detested Emperor.

Overseeing this mixed multitude were the rulers of garrison and synagogue, two men linked by bonds of service, each of whom commanded, conversely, an equal and unusual respect.

Blind Mordecai had held hopes of Capernaum. Straggling back from its cramped shoreline, Capernaum was down-to-earth, and workaday, with few pretensions – like the five men the Nazarene had chosen from within it – a place where one might expect the works of a prophet to be readily accepted at face value, where there might be enthusiasm for his works, and a willingness to help those who sought him. Yet Mordecai's appeals met a lukewarm response. The town had seen so much of Jeshua and his men – so many signs and miracles! Were the people immune to wonders now? he asked himself incredulously.

The blind man's investigating hand met a smooth, cool surface, and from the familiar sound of a chanting, singsong voice, muffled by the thickness of the wall, he realised that he had chanced upon Capernaum's one oddity – and perhaps an explanation of the town's concord – a neat black basalt synagogue which local Jews had not been able to afford for themselves. The building was the gift of an unlikely benefactor – the Roman who was Head of the Garrison, no less – a centurion who not only respected the Faith, but loved the Jewish nation. This in itself was practically a contradiction in terms, but the place of worship seemed to be honoured all the more because of that unusual fact. Today, being market day, was one of congregation, and three appointed men were reading from the Law in turn, to educate the faithful who might then go to the bazaar and do their business with a clear conscience, having dutifully served God before appeasing Mammon.

Mordecai felt a surge of renewed hope. Surely the synagogue might hold a person who could help him. The service was nearly over, and some were already leaving – he would wait no longer. He raised his voice and appealed to the approaching footsteps.

"Brethren, men of Israel, you have heard his words, you have seen his works! Can you tell me where is Jeshua the Teacher? Where is the man who has brought peace and healing to this place? Will someone help a blind man to find him?"

A waft of scented oil accosted him, mingled with the unmistakeable freshness of newly washed garments, and as it passed by, a sharp voice spoke with clipped accents.

"Beggar, you are blind in more ways than one. The Nazarene is a deceiver of the people."

Mordecai turned almost angrily. "I may be blind, sir, but I see clearly enough – and I am not deaf. I have heard of the mighty works with which he has blessed this very town – not to speak of this building behind me. All Galilee has heard the miracles he has done *inside* this synagogue, and for the *builder* of this synagogue, and the greatest was even for the very *Ruler* of this synagogue where you have been worshipping today!"

He sensed that the man was already striding off – and raised his voice. "Was his dead daughter deceived into believing she lived? Answer me that!" he shouted after him defiantly, but the Sadducee had gone.

A hasty step from behind – a timid hand touched his arm, and a young voice whispered earnestly.

"No, sir, the dead hear nothing! She was *not* deceived. She *was* truly dead, and then, truly alive again."

"Ah! Out of the mouths of babes and sucklings! You knew her, child?"

There was a pause, a little sigh, and then a reluctant confession.

"I am she." Rapidly she added, "But I am not a child any more, I am past fourteen, and should not talk with you alone … my mother will be out of the synagogue at any moment and she is quick to imagine lapses of modesty. It was forward of me to speak first, but I was so glad to hear you defend the one who saved me – and you could not see me smile to thank you. Otherwise I would have said nothing – my parents do not like me to talk about what happened."

Mordecai sucked in a ragged breath as her words sank in. He was in the presence of one who had tasted death! Who been through the Valley of the Shadow, and who had returned! Who *knew!* He gripped the stick so hard his darkly tanned knuckles whitened.

"I think I understand," he said with dry lips. "You have become a curiosity, questioned endlessly –"

"I don't mind the questions," she responded so petulantly, that Mordecai could swear she tossed her head as she spoke, "but I scorn those who reject my answers! Even some of my own friends

338

have said I was mistaken, I was only deeply asleep, or unconscious. The Pharisees demand a description of heaven or hell, or Abraham's bosom, and shake their heads because I saw neither angels nor demons ... the mystics refuse to believe I was not floating like a cloud, tethered by a silver cord, watching my own body on the bed ... and as for the Sadducee who just spoke to you, he is the worst. He demands I tell the truth – but when I do, he will not believe me."

"Naturally, you are a desperate inconvenience to one who denies resurrection. But, maid, you give me great encouragement, and I will not torment you with my own questions. All I ask is where your saviour may be now."

"Daughter!" called an anxious voice. "Come here at once! Come away from that beggar!"

"Goodbye, blind man. I'm sorry I have no money to give you." The girl threw him the words as she ran obediently to her mother, leaving Mordecai ready to weep with frustration.

"I do not ask for money!" he cried despairingly, as the synagogue emptied, men and women and more children flowing around him on their way past. "I ask for the Nazarene! Jeshua the Nazarene! The Healer! The Teacher! The Anointed! The Son of God – the Messiah of Israel! He has slept in your town, taught in your streets, healed on your beaches, sailed in your boats, fed you on your hillsides! Some of his men have homes and families here! Does no-one know where he is? Will no-one show me or tell me where I may find him? My need is desperate!"

He stood waiting for the crowd to disperse, ears strained for any response to his pleas. Was poor tortured Sobek even still alive? He must not give up now!

"Where is the Teacher Jeshua? Where is he? Or any of his men? Please help me! I implore someone to guide me!"

"Keep away, dear, it's just another blind beggar, looking for some eyes," he heard an old woman mutter. "Everyone expects a miracle, these days ..."

"It is not for myself that I need him," Mordecai said heavily, knowing he was talking to himself. He leant his sweating forehead against the synagogue wall, willing his mind to see beyond, picturing the ark of scrolls within, the reading desk, the holy lamp, the seats of honour. In such a place his voice had once led congregations in prayer – but none of the age-old benedictions or eulogies once intoned by a young Mordecai the Scribe would do here – not now – not for a greying, deformed, sightless man who was excluded from its sanctuary and left to beg in the streets.

Oblivious to the people hurrying to and fro around him, he turned from the silent dark stones to face the sunlight, lifting his hands – still grasping the polished stick – as Moses had held his rod in the day of battle; like Moses, praying for a victory which was out of his power to influence in any other way. In this manner did Mordecai the Blind, with stark simplicity and humbly bowed head, pray as earnestly as if he was in the temple at Jerusalem itself ... and as he did so, the clamour of the market congregation faded into the unseen distance.

"Master of the Universe, I beseech Thee! Show me the way!"

A hand gently drew the smoothly carved guiding rod from his grip.

"I am the way."

He looked up.

Chapter Thirty-three

DAN was annoyed with himself. Samuel had set him the task of counting the combined flocks that afternoon – and he had arrived at a different number several times running. The pasture was a rocky one, and the animals seemed to melt into the landscape. He was puzzled by one disobedient ram which would not come at his call. He was even forced to go chasing after it. It was most unlike Golan to ignore his shepherd, and Dan wondered if the sheep was sickening for something – perhaps had been bitten by a snake. The thought made him look twice as he trod the scrubby pasture, but he knew it was an insensible dread and he was in no danger at this time of year – snakes were gorging for winter hibernation, and would not be irritably quick to strike, as they might in early spring.

Dan lost sight of Golan several times, but spying fresh droppings gleaming like olives in the sun, he persevered, being mindful of the temper of the watchman who presided over the vineyard on the next hill, where gnarled vines sprawled invitingly, their large clusters of grapes sagging from the forked props which held them off the ground. So close to harvest, vigilance was essential. Dan's sheep were well trained and obedient, but Golan had let him down badly today, and if he took it into his newly rebellious head to leap the low wall there would be trouble. Chasing a heavy, skittish ram through a fine crop of grapes did not bear thinking about! The young shepherd employed all his cunning, and finally managed to creep up on the animal as it busily cropped at a tall broom bush, strangely uninterested in the tasty tufts of fresh green at its hooves. He threw a noose over the curving horns, and gave a triumphant tug.

Ach! Dan abruptly felt his body sag. What a fool he was! He flopped to the ground and groaned, whereupon Samuel's tamest buck looked over his shoulder, blinked, and snickered at him before returning to his bush, unconcerned.

"Come on, Nimrod," Dan sighed, dragging him away. "Time to go home. How did you take me in, you old rogue, you? I should have known by your smell."

Samuel grinned sympathetically when Dan told his tale of woe.

"You're not the first, Dan, and you won't be the last. Nimrod is very like Golan, in more ways than his coat, except for that black bib under his chin, and that broken tail of his fools everyone. He has a decided liking for your flock, too – he doesn't understand why you won't have a smart old goat like him to lead it, especially as your girls don't mind him around. Even with good eyes, it's easy to mistake them. Now, tell me what you missed."

"Just about everything! He was ahead of me, so I missed the bib, but I should have taken more note of his gait – and how he kept trotting to the high points – and he went for bushes not grass – and I didn't even think about his horns. Nimrod's left one curls more, but I was so sure it was Golan, I didn't look for any differences. I didn't even notice how he smelled!"

Samuel nodded. "And the other end?"

"I didn't look closely at his droppings either, but now I think of it, they were too big, and not round enough. And of course, even apart from his dropped tail, his rump is nowhere near as fat." He kicked a pebble disgustedly. "I'm ashamed I didn't trust my own ram – Golan is one of the best behaved, too! But he always comes when I call – so where is he?"

"Don't worry, Dan, look at it this way – you found and brought back my errant Nimrod, and saved one of us the job. As for Golan – if I'd heard you calling him earlier I could have told you – Caleb found him lame three hours ago and shut him in the fold, with a nice dollop of that magic grease on his hock. He will be all right." But Dan was off already, with a relieved grin.

"Mind you get the rest of those sheep watered and folded by sunset!" Samuel shouted after him. "And send Eli to me as soon as you're able!"

Dan waved cheerfully by way of reply, and Samuel whistled one of his dogs out of a burrow where it was exploring some tantalising scents.

"Come out of there, Barley Boy, you wastrel! We've got goats to round up – not rabbits!"

Dan had just finished leading the flock into the fold to join poor hobbling Golan, with Caleb patiently shepherding the late-comers, when Eli returned from his father. Together they pinned the gate and made up the fire, rubbing their hands over the flames, shuffling their stew pot into a secure place at the edge, unpacking their bread and carefully setting cloves of garlic to roast deliciously on the hot stones. Dan pushed Moses' greedy muzzle off his lap.

"Behave, or you'll be in there with the rest of them tonight!" He looked at Eli enquiringly.

343

"Didn't Samuel want you for anything after all?"

"Only to talk."

"Is all well, young man?" Caleb asked kindly, of the frowning face.

Eli's heavy brows did not clear. "Yes – with everyone but myself! My father thinks – but I don't agree ..." He stopped, and gave his head an annoyed shake.

"Don't agree about what?" Dan asked, surprised by this disjointed response.

"Look, it's like this." Eli seemed to make up his mind to talk after all. "You know he forbad me to see poor Judith."

"Perhaps that was wise, you know," Caleb put in, remembering the sad state of her face. "Do you think she would have wanted you to see her all bruised and battered? And it would not help you in forgiving poor Thaddeus, who hurt her so unknowingly."

Eli clenched his fists convulsively. "Yes, yes, I know, very wise, no doubt," he said impatiently, "but it has been tearing my vitals ever since. There's no sense in pretending – you must know I wanted to make her my wife! And then *this* happened – and while I am still trying to stop myself marching off to Banayim to beat the stuffing out of Thaddeus, I find he has offered reparation by asking her to marry him!"

"Well, what else could he do? She's not a slave, so he can't set her free for the damage he did ... not that it would help anyway," Dan pointed out. "And *an eye for an eye* is no use either. Breaking *his* bones wouldn't fix anything."

He fondled Moses' woolly head idly. He'd never been able to make that part of the Law fit with *'Vengeance is mine, I will repay, declares the Eternal.'* He would talk it over with Johanan when he visited for the Festival, which seemed to be very slow in coming this year. It seemed like an age since he had spoken to him, or even had a letter from anyone in Jerusalem. Everyone was so busy these days. With some dismay, Dan realised that his careless childhood had already been replaced by the bustle of youth, a grasping for experience and learning. Eventually he too would pass into that adult realm, from which was no escape. He was not sure whether this prospect was daunting or exciting. Perhaps it was both.

"True," Caleb agreed. "Exacting the law here would help no-one. Not Thaddeus – not his boy – nor Judith either. The man's only scraping by as it is, and wouldn't have the money to recompense her with a dowry or a living. With her prospects spoiled, offering her security was the right thing for him to do."

Eli screwed up his face and his courage. "But I love her!" he blurted out furiously. "Her prospects aren't spoiled for *me*! I don't care if she's not the prettiest girl in Galilee!"

Caleb looked at him shrewdly. "No, of course you don't care, not at the moment. Not in your hotheaded passion, young man, when you would be a great and gracious fellow and rescue her from her misery. But when the bruises go and if her face is still askew, and her teeth missing, as she ages and her face lines – if by thirty she already looks like a crone with henna'd hair – what then, eh? Will you still rejoice to see such a face smile at you in your bed? Or will you turn from her with resentment, or close your eyes and take refuge in unholy imaginings?"

"Caleb!" Dan gasped but the old shepherd was unrepentant. Nobody could expect a young man to think like a greybeard, and Eli did not understand the pitfalls in a union where there was buried disappointment and regret.

"This is strong language, old man," muttered Eli, taken aback. "Am I not capable of selfless behaviour?"

"Strong language suits strong feelings, and mine are as strong as yours, despite my age, and your youth," Caleb said stoutly. "Marriage is not to be entered on a youthful whim. Nor as a grand gesture to earn merit." He raised a warning finger. "Don't you see, young man? Even to talk of it as *selfless* behaviour is to see yourself doing something noble! But take heed to an old man, and an old friend, when I tell you this — *no woman wants to be married out of pity*. It wears thin very quickly and is poor warmth even while it lasts."

Dan and Eli exchanged uncomfortable glances.

"I did not mean to be noble," Eli said sulkily. "And this is no whim. I told you I love her. Why should she have to marry a man who beat her, whether he meant to or not?"

"But she's *not* marrying him," Dan pointed out. "She refused." He gave Moses a date and pushed him away from the garlic.

"I know she did — and no wonder, she would still fear him! — but he's going to keep asking her," Eli blew on the fire crossly, and flinched as a spark singed his cheek, "and I know he'll wear her down till she says yes. He has as much to gain as she does."

"Then she will have a home at least, and a husband whose motive is not pity, but atonement, and even some gratitude," Caleb asserted.

Dan was more direct. "But not if she says Yes to you first, Eli! She has no family, the choice will be hers alone."

Eli shook his head.

346

"My father gave me the same lecture you just did," he growled, "about pity, and what happens if I change my mind too late, and all the rest."

Fathers! Caleb mused. *Their words may as well be mime to a young man!* Well, he must speak as boldly as he could from the vantage ground of old age – and know he had done his duty by God and men.

"Anyone would think *I* am the villain here!" Eli added with a scowl.

The night was growing damp. Eli was too heated to care, but Dan pulled on the felted wool cap Aunt Etta had made for his last birthday, while Caleb flipped his mantle over his balding head and scratched his chin thoughtfully. Was the young man simply impatient for a wife, or was his tenderness for the girl more than calf-love – something which would not wither quickly, but survive, grow and flourish with the years? Well, a little more sharp prodding would not go amiss.

"No, Eli, you are not at all a villain." The old man patted his shoulder kindly. "Still, you must think clearly – could you face a long life together? Forgive my plain speech, but Thaddeus already knows the fret and tear in wedlock, and he will not expect more than a maid such as Judith can give. Strong emotions disturb peace in a marriage, you know. Without passion on either side, she may be quietly content and bear him many more children for his old age."

Agitated, Eli sprang to his feet, knocking over the stewpot, which Dan quickly rescued, while Moses braved a burnt tongue in helpfully cleaning up the spillage slopped on the dirt.

"How dare you talk this way!" the young shepherd gritted, his teeth gleaming savagely in his thick black beard. "This is my sweet, long-suffering Judith, whose gentle eyes light up when she laughs! How much will those eyes light up, how often will that laugh be heard, if she marries that miserable old Thaddeus – cured or not – and is stuck with his headstrong son who will probably beat her himself one day? Is she to pay for peace with her happiness? Has *she* no soul? Has *she* no feelings, that her love for *me* should be ignored?"

"Does she really love you back, Eli?" Dan asked eagerly. "How can you tell?"

"Ah, sit down, my young friend, sit down," Caleb gave a relieved chuckle. Yes, the boy was sincere all right. "I have been pushing you hard – with reason. What else does your father say?"

"He says she can bring nothing to a marriage except herself; no dowry, no family, and no support. He does not object in principle, but reminded me that if I ever regretted the union she would be more destitute than if I had left her a virgin, so I must be doubly certain for her sake if not my own. Once she is out of bandages, I may see her, but I must make neither promise nor offer until the first lamp of the Festival of Lights – if I still want to. My mother is at one with him. She says changing my mind is no shame, but she will be disgusted if I hold to my first decision out of false pride." He poked the fire glumly.

Caleb raised his hands. "Well, then! Why are you so miserable? You have wise parents, Eli. Wise and loving, in their advice for both you and the girl. You are young – you have plenty of time!"

Eli sat down with an exclamation of impatience.

"But don't you see? I know I won't change my mind, but what if Thaddeus changes *her* mind *before* then! I can't very well say, 'Oh, please don't accept him till I've had several months to decide whether *I* still want you or not'!"

348

"Aha!" cried Dan, watering the diminished stew and stirring vigorously. "So that's why you are so twitchy! Why, it sounds like you need a go-between, that's all."

"Not you!" Eli said ungratefully. "You're just a puppy!"

"I am not!" Dan responded indignantly, with an unconvincing squeak. He cleared his throat. "I'm growing whiskers as fast as I can, aren't I? No, I didn't mean me – but shall I talk to Anna about it? She can explain things privately, and then at least Judith will know Thaddeus may not be her *only* choice. That would be worth waiting for, wouldn't it?"

Caleb nodded his approval, and Eli's face cleared at last. He reached out and smacked Dan's woollen cap off his head in a brotherly fashion.

"Good for you, Dan. I like that idea. If she loves me –"

"And if she *trusts* you!" put in Caleb warningly. Eli pointedly ignored him.

"If she loves me – then she'll wait."

"If she doesn't?" Dan dared, retrieving his cap before Moses chewed it to a pulp.

"Then she won't – but of course she does! Aren't I the best looking man she knows?" Eli preened himself, with the glint back in his keen dark eyes at last.

Dan grinned, and began to warble his favourite song, Moses bleating a few notes by way of a chorus.

"My love loves me because I am handsome!
My love loves me because I am wise
My love loves me because I am hairy!
And bearded clear up to my eyes!"

Eli and Caleb laughed, and joined in, and although the old man couldn't resist hissing "*Red*-bearded" at his apprentice in between verses, Dan just pulled a face at him and sang all the louder.

"Bearded clear up to your eyes! Oh yes!

Bearded clear up to your eyes!

Oh! I'm handsome and wise and hairy,

And bearded clear up to my eyes!" they howled to the moon.

From Moses in his privileged position by the fire, to sore-legged Golan in the fold, together with his comfortable ewes, the sheep were accustomed to the sound of singing shepherds. Raucous, sad, merry or soulful, the sound of their masters' voices was the sound of safety. They tucked their noses between their bony knees and slept while the moon sailed bumpily through the starlit clouds, and the fire crackled, and the voices laughed, and sang, and murmured on.

Chapter Thirty-four

"YOU should have been here two days ago," the portly taverner said reprovingly, snatching dirty cups and pots from the deserted, rough wooden tables, and dumping them on his tray with clashing abandon. "They've all gone, now, thank the stars – not that it's not good for business, of course, but stampedes exhaust a man. Are you after a drink? A bed? Otherwise, if you don't mind, some of us have work to do." He picked up the tray, hunched up one shoulder, wiped his sizeable nose on it with a hearty sniff, and wove his way to the back of the shambolic room as gracefully as the pale, voluptuous dancer who performed on market nights.

Ittai dropped onto a narrow bench, sick with dismay. He had already searched up to Paneus, and over to Hazor, where he had visited Marta's five half-brothers under pretext of business. It had not been easy – they had been so eager to oblige him that he had been forced to accept five separate commissions for work which he knew would be uneconomical to transport. It had been even harder to play the happy brother-in-law, telling them all about his family and their new nephew, and it filled him with chagrin to hear their rough cynicism about the Nazarene he had come to find.

"Do you know where they were headed?" The thought of having to retrace his steps back to Hazor, and perhaps bump into Marta's brothers again, was depressing.

"Not me. Somewhere in Galilee, that's all – probably off to the Festival eventually. So they say. He's been keeping pretty quiet around here of late. Bewilders people, but there you are. Prophets are entitled to their eccentricities, I reckon."

He bawled an order to his harassed pot boy, who appeared in the low doorway, looking as grey and damp as his own dishrag, to whisk the tray away to some evil cubbyhole where the vessels were – supposedly – washed. "You drinking, or not?"

"Yes, yes, a drink, then – no, not that barley beer," Ittai added hastily as the man sloshed dark amber liquid from a jug. He remembered all too well the last time he'd been unwise enough to accept some.

The taverner leered at him, and gave a snuffling chuckle, "H'nff! h'nff! h'nff! Keeping a steady head, eh?" and with a quick twist of his thick wrist tossed the drink down his own capacious throat. "Aaahhh! A bit of fizz does a man good! Blows you up, belches out all the bad humours!"

He demonstrated with satisfaction, and wiped his lips with the back of a hairy fist. "No? What'll it be, then? Rough-and-ready Roman, Good-for-a-gargle Greek, General-purpose Judean? Or shall it be a Smooth-and-spicy Cypriot – like me, h'nff! h'nff! Specially imported from my old friend in Salamis? Very sophisticated!"

"Sophisticated?" Ittai sat up hopefully, thinking of Uncle Joseph. "Do you mean the wine or the friend?" *Certainly not you*, he thought to himself.

"Both, of course! Come on, live dangerously! Try a drop – it's worth the extra. Eh? Not that I'm biased. H'nff! h'nff! h'nff!"

"Are you from Salamis yourself, then? Who is your friend?" Ittai almost fell over his words in his eagerness.

352

"Salamis? Not me – I'm from copper country, near Phorades. But I'd rather have a red nose than green hair in my old age, so it was off to the land of opportunity, first chance I got. Knew someone who knew someone in the trade, and so it went, and here I am, and there you go … Pluto, my absent friend, your health!" He downed his beer and grinned at Ittai's disappointed face.

"You wouldn't know the vintner and wine merchant Joseph of Salamis, I suppose?" he asked rather despondently.

"I might. I know a lot of people. And then again, I might not. You'd be surprised how many I'm *supposed* to know if they think they'll get a free drink out of me. What do you want him for?"

"We're both looking for the Nazarene, and took separate paths. We agreed to leave word for each other whenever we could."

"As I said before, *crowds* through here earlier this week. He could have pickled himself in one of my own vats and I'd never have noticed. You read? Well, have a look at the privy door out back. Chalked all over with graffiti, it is. That's the message board here. Never know your luck."

"Thank you!" Ittai sprang up and dashed outside.

"Hey! What about that drink?" the man shouted indignantly as he disappeared.

Before long, Ittai burst back through the doorway, laughing like a madman.

"Charcoal, my good host! Thank you!"

He disappeared again – and came back more sedately, grinning all over his face.

"He may have been invisible to you, but he was here all right! Now, yes, I will have that drink, and it will be the smooth Cypriot too – but half cut with water, mind."

The innkeeper snorted. "Waste of the good stuff! But the same price!" he warned.

Ittai bristled. "Very well, I'll have the full cup of wine, *and* a full cup of water, and a third cup to mix them in!"

The stout man tapped his nose approvingly and nodded. "Not as green as you look! Here, drink up, then. So you found a message – well, Felicitas and Fortuna both smile on you, that's what I say. Hope it wasn't meant for someone else."

"*To Potter Ittai of Banayim*, it said. That's me all right."

It was almost too good to believe. Among the many smudged chalk and charcoal messages scrawled on both sides of the weathered wood – some boldly formed, some barely literate – amongst lewd nonsense, and crude sketches, there it was, freshly written plain and large in thick black characters. *To Potter Ittai of Banayim. Go home. All is well with Marta.* Everyone knew by now that the Nazarene could heal at a distance and Ittai had no doubt that Joseph had found him first. Now the crushing weight fell from his shoulders. Either she was cured, or the Prophet had said she had no dread disease after all – either way, the news was joyful! Joyful! Joyful!

"Go home, all is well with Marta!" Oh, praise and thanks to the King of the Universe above, and His Power at work in the land! Ittai had rubbed a clean space and scribbled a hurried postscript just in case Joseph was now looking for *him*, and might pass this way again before returning to Banayim. *To Joseph of Salamis. A thousand thanks. Returning at once. Ittai.* He added the insignia he used to mark his pots, that there be no mistaking the writer.

Now he could drink his wine without the ashen taste of anxiety, and tonight he could sleep!

"The wine is good," he called happily.

The innkeeper grunted as he tied the strings of his stained sacking apron with an effort.

"Told you. Want more?"

"No, but you can fill my water flask, with *water*, that is, and I need a bed for tonight. I haven't slept properly for days. A cheap one, mind – I'll be gone at sunrise."

"H'm. Half the Garrison's off duty tonight, and the house is taken. Any objections to camels?"

"Yes!" Ittai answered coldly.

"Ah. Sheep?"

"Sheep, I can live with. Camels, nobody can live with."

"You said a true thing there. Well, back of the courtyard, then, in the stable. Up the ladder. Sheep under, you over. Camels in the next stall, but don't open the second trapdoor and you'll be all right. Probably a bit of a riot here tonight. Not a patch on Saturnalia, thank the stars. But better stay put if you don't like Romans behaving badly. I tell you what – no charge if you help clean up in the morning."

"Thank you," Ittai said with dignity, "but I'll pay in advance."

The sun was already sinking, and down the road came the scuffling of approaching feet and jeering of raucous horseplay, as a high-spirited party of legionaries abused some hapless, weary road-menders by way of getting their night off to a rollicking start. Ittai settled his account, and strode through the filthy courtyard behind the ramshackle tavern. He looked gloomily at the row of narrow doorways which announced the cramped rooms built against the walls – soon to be filled with racketing men escaping military discipline for twelve hours of licence. He wondered whether it was worth a night of shelter from the cold and rain. Still, he had a good handful of fleece to stuff in his ears, and if it could keep out a baby's wails it should work for soldiers just as well.

He passed the well in the centre of the courtyard, and read the sign burned into the thick plank cover – *Those who Let Down the Landlord here will be Let Down here by the Landlord. Pay Your Slate or Else!* He had to read it twice before he got the sense of it. No doubt it was meant to be a joke, but from the look of the establishment, perhaps it wasn't. He climbed the shaky ladder in the sheep pen through a trapdoor to the cramped storeroom above the divided stable, and piled himself a bed with old sacks. A gurgling snort came from under his feet, and a second trapdoor in the corner slowly lifted with a wobble. A large, damp, hairy nostril quivered in the gap, and a baleful, long-lashed eye glared up from beneath it. The potter quickly shoved several solid sheaves of dusty hay over the spot, and sat on it until the bumping stopped, and he thought it was safe to get up. The things a man had to do to keep camels out of his bed! He watched warily but although it jerked occasionally, the hay was heavy enough on its own, and the inquisitive nostril was successfully suppressed. Ittai even felt slightly sorry for the camel, it had no more headroom than he did. But about the rest of his accommodation he had few complaints.

Through the rough slats of the wall poured enough cold rain-washed air to dilute the pungent odour of damp sheep and camel rising through the many gaps in the stained floorboards, and on the whole, he was thankful not to be sleeping in one of rank smelling, flea-ridden kennels huddled against the walls below. He crammed his ears with wool, poured out his thanks to the Eternal, then threw down his cloak and gratefully rolled into it, soon sleeping far too soundly to be disturbed by the noisiest laughter, or even the occasional bump from the camel underneath. Even when Legionary Lexus accidentally set his tunic on fire in the middle of the night and was dropped into the well by helpful colleagues, (to be rescued half drowned and coughing his lungs out), he heard nothing; not the yells, the heavy scraping of the well-cover, the splash, the echoing roar of rage from the depths as the bucket hit Lexus on the head, nor the hilarity and commotion as they hauled him out. The potter's conscience was clear, his heart was light, and his sleep was sweet. Fresh and rested, Ittai rose before the sun and hurried on his way, his heart singing to think of his dear, *healthy* wife and family waiting for him only a day or so away in Banayim.

Six hours later, Cypriot Joseph, fastidiously lifting his mud-splashed blue hem, stepped into the tavern where a few soldiers still slumped among the pots. The taverner held up a broad hairy hand to stop his flow of questions.

"Seems to me I've heard all this already. You the wine merchant, are you? From Salamis?"

"Why, yes, I am, Joseph's my name ..."

"Ah! Yes, that's it. Your young friend, the potter from somewhere-or-other, was here asking about you only yesterday. Very pleased when he got your message, he was. Left you one too, in case you came back this way."

"Message?"

"Usual place – privy door. Right under yours. Should still be there if some fool hasn't scuffed it off already."

"Mine? Are you sure?" Joseph ran outside to look, and returned with a thoughtful frown. "But I don't understand it!" he said, raising his richly-trimmed turban and smoothing the strands of hair on his scalp to aid his powers of thought.

"What? Can't even read your own writing? Or his? So much for learning! H'nff! h'nff!"

Joseph gave him a pained look. "That note for Ittai is not my writing. I've never been here before in my life."

The innkeeper winked. "That's what they all say when the wives come looking for them ... H'nff! h'nff! h'nff! No use asking me either, specially after a busy night. You're lucky any of it's still readable. So now you'll be off, too, eh?"

"Yes. Whoever wrote it left good news."

"Not leaving already? What about a drink? Cypriot wine – may even be yours! Fine stuff."

Joseph sniffed at the proffered cup suspiciously, sipped it cautiously, and handed it back with grimace. "Someone's fooling you, my friend."

"Really?" The man looked crestfallen. "They all like it, you know, for special occasions. I'm a beer man myself."

"H'm. No wonder, then. Well, if they like it, they like it. But don't you pay top price next time you buy it in."

"Well, won't I just have a little word to my friend Pluto, that's all. I tell you what, I'll fill your flask for the road – half price!"

"No, thank you. But I'm much obliged to you for the potter's message. Now I can return to Banayim myself. I'm sure I'll hear the whole story once I'm there."

The innkeeper deftly caught the coin Joseph flicked him, snatching it out of the air and thrusting it into his apron in one easy movement.

"Can't understand these Jews," he muttered to his pot-washer, as Joseph carefully enveloped himself, turban and all, in his thick cloak, and set out into the drizzle. "That's two of them I've offered favours to in one day, and they turned me down! They're a strange people ..."

Chapter Thirty-five

JUDITH, her nose still swollen, her eyes puffily blooming in decaying shades of purple and yellow, was now able to sit up, propped on cushions. Loukanos had strapped her ribs till she was swaddled as firmly as a newborn, and though she was still in considerable pain, she could move carefully and was out of any danger. Greatly relieved to hear it, Thaddeus, who had been staying in the Travellers' House meanwhile, was all for renewing his offer of marriage at once. Widow Shana, however, being in Anna's confidence concerning Eli, took the shepherd aside and advised him not to press the matter.

"She needs time to finish healing, Thaddeus, my friend," she warned. "You have hurt her trust, not just her body. You must go away – find work quickly before you are greater in debt – and give the poor child till Passover, at least!"

"That's six months away!" Thaddeus objected. "She may think I have dishonoured my offer, and I will lose face." He bit his lip with chagrin, realising what he had just said, but the Widow replied kindly.

"Nonsense, didn't she refuse you? But, since you are so impatient, what about *Purim* time? Still too long? Festival of Lights then, yes, *Chanukah* – that's only half as long! The moment the eighth lamp is lit, I promise to bring her in to my house so you can ask her with all due respect for the decencies. Stay away till then, and your patience will be rewarded. She and little Thad will not be alone, with me playing *Amma* to both of them only three steps across the courtyard. Why, we are almost in the same house as it is. Now, assure her of your sincerity, and that she has plenty of time to recover and reconsider before you will ask again. Go! Go!"

So Thaddeus took the Widow's advice, and the Widow took both Judith and little Thad under her wing, nursing private plots in her deep bosom the while; and a general feeling prevailed that the right thing was being done by all. With the tension over, a relieved Anna went home again, while Thaddeus immediately went in search of work once more, knowing his old master would not have him back – and that was only to be expected. His bizarre behaviour in the past had hardly inspired ease in his presence or confidence in his work, and neither sheep nor goats could make allowances for unreliable shepherds.

Thus it was that, with a hank of wool pinned to his coat, crook and rod in hand, Thaddeus stood patiently in the Magdala market for a whole day, while flock masters in need of extra hands skirted around him without meeting his eyes, hiring men less experienced, but (in their eyes at least) more trustworthy. With a resigned shrug, Thaddeus took himself off to the relative anonymity of Tiberius. There he was seized gratefully by a head shepherd whose animals were in dire need of milking, and whose three Sidonian hirelings had succumbed to the hideous perils of a cheap wedding banquet – a mixture of tainted wine, the wrong mushrooms, and a single suspect oyster in a pot of fish-head soup.

Back at the Hollow, Loukanos had lost no time in examining Marta and the result was all good news. He pronounced that there was nothing whatever the matter with her except the *leucoderma* he had long known about, and concurred with Marta's own opinion that the headaches she no longer had must simply have been due to her anxiety. Surprisingly, the red lesions dotting her skin were also quickly fading, and although he felt an itch of curiosity about them, he agreed with Mordecai's suggestion to Anna that they were an insignificant, if unusual rash, and a mere coincidence. As for her other issue, Loukanos told her that it was just a very early return to the manner of women, and promised to have a word to Ittai about taking extra care of her when he returned. So having thanked the doctor with many grateful words and a few tears, Marta collected her babies and her baggage, smothered Anna and Etta with hugs, and they all burst out of the Hollow, flying along the track as lightly as freed birds, to ready Ittai's house for his homecoming, which surely must be soon.

"All settled?" Loukanos asked as Anna returned from helping the little family in this pleasant task. She dropped onto the bench outside the door, enjoying the caressing warmth of the mellow sunlight on her tired eyelids, and sighed thankfully.

"Yes, all happily settled and the twins rediscovering the fun of chasing Hanoch's chickens … Oh, this sun is beautiful … I wish I could just sit here for a hundred years!"

"A pretty sight you'd be by then, indeed," her brother agreed sarcastically, and she sat up with a laugh.

"Always you bring me down to earth, Louki! But surely I need that much time to hear all you have to tell me about the missing years …"

"And what of *your* missing years, my sister? Being mother *and* father to a boy growing to manhood – on your own?"

"Yes, Etta and I both have felt the want of a man in the house for that, I confess. But I have not been entirely without menfolk to assist with my boy. Dear Caleb is such a good, steady fellow for Dan, Samuel too – and father has also done his best, with letters and visits – even young Eli and Johanan have helped in their own way. He has had wise, strong and sound men both young and old, all around him, and it has sufficed. After all, nobody could have replaced his own father, not even you." She smiled at him.

Loukanos looked at her shrewdly. "Why did you leave out Mordecai?"

Anna started. "Oh, how ungrateful of me," she answered quickly. "Of course, he has been wonderful for Dan – such an intelligent and learned mind, full of the scriptures!"

"A warm, compassionate heart with it, too," Loukanos agreed, but try as he would he could learn nothing from her dropped eyes, "not to speak of a lot of commonsense for an educated man. What happened to him in Antioch was a tragedy – all that potential, wasted."

Anna replied calmly, "You should not say he has wasted his potential. In recent years he has made more use of his talents than many a sighted man. But you are right about his heart – what he is doing for poor Sobek shows selfless compassion."

Loukanos thought he had said enough about Mordecai for the moment.

"Sobek," he repeated, frowning. "I have been praying about her, uncertain what I should do. But when I think of a blind man searching for the Teacher despite knowing the woman is surely dying, if not already dead … surely I can do no less than exert myself to do all I can! So I have decided, now that I have attended to Judith and Marta, to set off for Cana at once. Who is caring for the poor creature except a hired woman she does not know? Even if Rhoda *and* Dinah are helping, none of them can do more than

362

feed and clean her. Lockjaw is an agonising, dreadful thing, and few survive, even those who are healthy to begin with. What of her fear and pain? Pray that the Spirit of God may cure her, or that I may ease her suffering with medicine, but either way, I must go to her. I cannot wash my hands because Mordecai is already doing something. We have no idea how he is faring."

"You are right," Anna replied immediately, jumping up from her seat. "I admit that I have felt very unhappy about it myself, wondering if there was anything more I could or should do, other than praying for her. Yet who knows, but that the Eternal will be merciful? When we do what we can, God will do what we can't. Well, let us leave this instant. If we are too late, which Heaven forbid, we can at least ensure her a decent burial."

"Ah, you will come with me? I'm glad of it. But what about Etta?"

"What about her?" the old woman replied briskly, sticking her white head out of the window suddenly, and revealing that she had heard every word. "Don't you think I need a rest cure after this week's commotion and clamour? I will have a nice little holiday here, all on my own, with some blessed peace and quiet! You just send to Marta now, and she will see that I am visited each day, and have my water brought, and all my needs taken care of, and there will be no need to hurry back on my account, whatever happens. Come inside, you must not even wait to eat before you leave, but take food with you, and not lose another moment. Loukanos, fill that water bottle, take this fresh bread, and lift that string of figs down from the ceiling for me … Anna, don't just stand there, fetch your cloak at once!"

"Etta, my dear sister! Was ever such a woman as you?" Anna kissed her hastily and hurried to obey.

Oh, how fast their corner of the world was changing! Had they ever run to and fro across the countryside as much as they had in the last few years? Life had sprawled out until it was crowded as a Greek stage, and she was beginning to feel like the Chorus, present in every scene, but powerless, an onlooker, no longer with a part all her own. It may have been why she was determined to go with Loukanos to Cana. Or perhaps it was her interest in her former little maid Rhoda and the news she would bring from Jerusalem, which was the spur – or even the genuine concern she had for twisted Sobek, not to speak of the hours on the journey when she could hear more of the lost years from her brother, who was now more precious to her than ever. As she crammed a few necessities into a soft reed basket and threw on her heavy cloak, she kept her mind busily innocent of any other motive.

Instead she reminded herself that if Sobek was to die in her presence, she would not be able to give the woman the comfort of touch, of holding her in her arms as the spark of life faded away; nor would she be able to prepare the wasted body for burial. Such would violate the Nazirite vow; and in the fear and the violence and the despair of her grief three years ago, she had put no earthly time limit on that vow. She shook her head suddenly, to dislodge a disquieting thought – how would it glorify God, how would it help anyone else, to deprive someone of loving hands at the solemn hour of death? Was her vow then a selfish thing? Yet she had undertaken it to guard herself from selfishness.

As she and Loukanos tramped their way across the windblown, rain splattered ridges of the serene autumnal hills that afternoon, she was unusually subdued. She listened avidly to all he had to tell her of the time they had been apart, of his conversion, his baptism, and his extraordinary experience with Thaddeus. She heard far more than he confessed in words, particularly in regard to the woman now known as the Magdalan, but to him she said little, professing breathlessness from their haste. With Sobek's desperate state in their minds, they hurried on without rest, for which Anna was thankful – silence may have required that she speak of herself. As for her own story – well, what was there to tell? A string of anecdotes about Dan, Etta, and their necessarily limited observations of the Nazarene fever – a fever which had swept over Galilee, spiked, and was now waning, leaving a sense of confusion and a growing, wretched restlessness within her soul. That was all there was to tell, surely. It could wait ... there was a mission to fulfil which left no room for anything else ... and now they were here, in Cana, picking their way down the chalky path, the familiar streets swallowing them up, and their feet hurrying with a renewed sense of urgency, and her heart beating faster as Blind Corner came in sight, and opposite it, the house she had not seen for many months ... the gate ... Anna suddenly outrunning her brother and calling out, knocking agitatedly on the wicket ... little Rhoda – no, not so little any more – rushing to the gate and running back into the house in confusion ...

"Oh, I am dreaming! Am I dreaming? It's *Mistress Anna!* Oh! Oh! this is a day of miracles! Dinah! Old Dinah! Come quickly! It's my dear Mistress Anna at the gate!"

Old Dinah's voice exasperatedly shouting from the depths of her kitchen, "Well, is she a phantom who can walk through walls? Open it, you silly girl! I'm in the middle of a chicken!"

Rhoda running again, fumbling with the latch, weeping with excited joy, flinging herself into Anna's arms and apologising – gasping – her pretty eyes widening in astonishment – *Loukanos!* – shrinking slightly as he passed, flustered by his warm greeting. Anna, kissing her quickly, rushing inside, feeling the sense of haste more strongly now they were here, than when they had left

Banayim. Loukanos too, striding through the vestibule so carelessly he tripped over a walking stick propped against the wall, biting off the curse which from habit still flew to his lips. Rhoda still apologising, snatching it up quickly behind them, hastily scooping up dropped belongings, hurrying after them … and they halted in the large central room, looking around eagerly in the fading light of the late afternoon.

From a shadowy seat in the deep window, a plainly dressed, gaunt little woman with large eyes rose to greet them, bowing humbly.

"Greetings, blessings and peace to you and all yours," she said timidly. "You will be Anna bath Netzir, and Loukanos of Philippi, I believe?"

She spoke with a strange, hesitating accent but even Loukanos could not place it. Well, it didn't matter where she came from, or even how she knew who he was, the question was, why was she not attending Sobek, as she had been hired to do? His heart sank, as he and Anna exchanged an unhappy look.

"Is Sobek asleep?" Anna cried anxiously, for once in her life abandoning formalities. It was the only hope … "Why are you not with her?"

"No, Lady, she is not asleep." The answer came in an unsteady voice. "There is no longer any need to watch."

Anna turned and clutched her brother's arms. "Oh! Louki! Poor Sobek! Poor Mordecai! I am so sorry!"

Loukanos turned on the woman. "When did she die?" he asked harshly. "If you are still here, we must be only just too late."

Weary tears spilled down Anna's dusty face – to have missed comforting Mordecai's friend by so little! And now, she knew, there was nothing else she could do herself, except follow the bier at a distance, and ensure the outcast had a good number of mourners. Pipes too, she told herself fiercely. She turned almost sharply to Rhoda.

"Lamps, Rhoda! Light the lamps! And be sure there are plenty around Sobek! She was a brave woman, and in death at least deserves the respect she never had in her miserable life."

But poor Rhoda seemed to have turned hysterical – gasping and crying and flapping her hands anxiously in the background – gesticulating helplessly towards a tall, greying man who suddenly emerged from the kitchen, wiping his hands on a towel, with Old Dinah – now free of her chicken – bustling importantly behind him. He looked piercingly at the group and cleared his throat.

"Please do not distress yourselves," he said in a tight voice. "Sobek is still alive, and free of pain."

"Oh, Dinah! Rhoda! You found an apothecary willing to help her! In Cana?" Anna's eyes shone with relief. "Oh, sir! How can we thank you!"

Loukanos strode forward and held out his hands impulsively.

"The Eternal bless you, my fellow physician, for giving her relief in her last hours! Definitely lockjaw, would you say?"

"Yes, I believe so."

"I feared as much! How long before the end? Where is she? Quickly – we would comfort her with our presence, and our prayers before it is too late, if she is not too drugged to know we are there."

"She is not drugged, sir," the man replied stiffly, "but she knows you are here, and will be glad of your prayers."

With faltering steps, the small thin woman came forward, and sank to her knees.

"Yes, praise the Eternal! Indeed she always has been!" She held out her trembling hands to them in an indescribable gesture. "Friends! Almighty God and the angels in Heaven reward your compassion! You were always my benefactors ... even when I was despised and rejected ..."

"No!" Anna gasped. Her quivering lips could barely frame the word. "No! Are you – not – Sobek's nurse ...?"

"No!" whispered the young woman, huge eyes swimming in her angular dark face. "No, Mistress Anna! I am Sobek!"

Loukanos rubbed the gooseflesh which prickled his arms. "Praise the Eternal!" he muttered under his breath. "Praise Emmanuel! Thanks be to Lord Jeshua, the Son of the most High God! He who can reach across distance and heal with a word!"

Tall Anna dropped to her knees beside Sobek and incredulously gathered the shaking little woman in her arms. Rhoda and Old Dinah flung themselves down beside them, huddling together in a sympathetic outpouring of emotion.

"Dear Mordecai!" Anna wept helplessly as the women sobbed together. "He did it! He found him! Blessed, brave, noble Mordecai!"

It was a while before the women were ready to be sensible again. When finally they had cried themselves out, they rose and did all the things women do at such times – laughed, mopped their eyes, shed a few more tears, blew their noses, fanned themselves, went off to wash their faces, ran back, laughed again, shook their heads and hugged, exclaimed and sighed, and so finally soothed themselves back to normality.

Loukanos and the apothecary had watched in deeply moved silence, which was none the less heartfelt, or prayerful, for that. Now, they too stirred themselves; the apothecary counselling

Sobek to wrap up more warmly, Loukanos ordering Old Dinah back to her kitchen to prepare the best feast she could scare up at such short notice. Rhoda, delirious with happiness at seeing her beloved mistress Anna again and dizzy with awe over the day's happenings, refused to move until she had washed the travellers' feet. Then she obediently danced off to gather friends and neighbours to share the rejoicing, beginning with Philip the Younger and Aida, not forgetting the Tanner's family at the edge of the town, and everyone she could find in between. Among them were the broom makers once called the Hushed Lamechs. Not so hushed these days, though. Since determinedly following the Nazarene half way around Galilee the year before, they were now known as the Chattering Lamechs, and the sour-tongued held that their brooms had never recovered from the shock.

"Mordecai told me he would search out a miracle," Sobek was telling Anna quietly. She snuggled gratefully into the striped blanket. "I thought I should die happy, knowing such a man would do so much for me! But my heart almost broke to see him go and I prayed to stay alive at least until he returned – and how I fought to do so! Just one more breath, just one more! And you see! God had mercy on me. On *me!*"

"Oh, poor girl," Anna shuddered. "What a terrible, terrible time!"

Sobek's eyes were still full of wonder.

"It was almost more than I dared pray for, to be freed from the agonising spasms in every part of my body, my back arching till I thought it would snap, and my jaws so tight I nearly choked! But, oh, Mistress Anna! *Never* did I even dream I might also be freed from the palsy I was born with! And yet, in the midst of the most cruel convulsions suddenly my chest filled, my spine softened, my teeth unclamped – and it was as if my whole body was being poured full of warmth and light … it was such bliss that I had to be dreaming … or dying … but Rhoda's screams soon assured me I was awake and alive! … and then … I *knew!* Not only could I breathe freely, with all the dreadful pain quite gone, but I was *still.* The relentless movement, the twisting, the feebleness, was banished. I thought to lift my hand and it obeyed me gracefully. That seemed almost more unbelievable than anything. I wished to sit up and lo, I found myself sitting! Poor Rhoda was trembling as if she'd seen a phantom. I wished to comfort her – and I held out my arms! I stood upright! Even my wounded foot was healed! I walked! Oh, Mistress Anna, I walked right over to her and I could speak freely as well! I thought the girl would die from the shock of it."

"My poor little lamb!" Anna half laughed, half sobbed.

"No, Mistress, she is not a little one any more," Sobek assured her. "She is grown up now, and stronger than she looks. She was so tired and stiff when she arrived, but she did not rest for an instant. Did you not wonder where your hired woman had gone? She was kind enough, but Rhoda sent her away, and nursed me herself, patiently trickling milk and soup and wine through my teeth, rubbing my aching limbs with oil, wrapping me with hot towels! Dear Rhoda! I have not forgotten how years ago she used to scamper up to me nervously with food from Dinah, and try to help me eat. She would cry when I bit myself, and stand and flap away the torturing flies, then run away again. I think I frightened her badly, but she still came."

Camels frightened Rhoda too, but she had lurched and swayed on one for many hours, grimly clutching the back of Shalal's girdle, for the sake of a beggar, and love of her mistress. Anna thought of this with humility; sitting in the window seat holding Sobek's long-fingered hand, caressing it, marvelling at its straightness, and at the calmness of the finely boned, sun-etched face with its wide eyes, narrow lips and radiant expression.

She shook her head, incredulously. "I have seen miracles before, but having known you for so long it seems all the more extraordinary, and of course your name is now all wrong now you are no longer 'Twisted'."

Sobek looked joyfully down at her own bony ankles, flexing and stretching her feet pleasurably, exulting in the sensation of pain-free limbs which were relaxed and strong and did her bidding.

"I don't care!" she said happily. "My name will ever witness to my blessed cure by the word of Lord Jeshua and the power of the Eternal!"

Anna could hardly believe the difference in her appearance, now that the alert face was not constantly moving and jerking with a chewing and gaping jaw; now that the tongue was under control, no longer roaming drooling lips. And more, her body was changed – the painfully twisted, useless body with its ulcers and sores, its rope-taut tendons and turned, clawed hands – all the ugliness of deformity was gone. It came to Anna then that the woman had only been deformed by the disobedience of an otherwise perfect body, which continually moved or locked all the wrong muscles. She remembered now, that once she had come across Sobek asleep, when her emaciated limbs were relaxed as a baby's. It was only when she awoke that the contortions gripped her. For this, there was no explanation, but it seemed to Anna to be a dark parable of human nature – that it was mankind's own consciousness which distorted and made ugly what God had first created lovely, and innocent.

371

For a moment she was wrapped in these thoughts, then said contritely, "My dear, please forgive me if I stare. I think I am still stunned."

Sobek's oddly inflected voice hastened to answer. "Mistress Anna, do not apologise – stare all you want – I am still staring at myself! It has been barely a day since this happened and I woke this morning in a cold sweat lest it was a dream. I wonder if I shall ever get used to it … I hope I don't, in a way. But I have so much to learn. Things even children can do are new to me. I am nearly twenty, I think, but I have never in my life been able even to comb my hair. Now I shall learn to braid, to wash, to cook, even to sew! I will be able to *work* – at something, anything! Oh! I am so happy!"

"Only yesterday?" No wonder Banayim had not yet heard news of this wonderful miracle. "Then of course it is too early for our good Mordecai to have found his way home again. I pray he meets with no harm. I wonder how far he had to go – he will have some tales to tell us, I'm sure! I will talk to my brother and insist that we stay a few days in the hope of seeing him before we return. Loukanos will be as eager as I am to hear every detail of how he found the Nazarene, and what words he spoke!"

Sobek looked at her and smiled curiously.

Meanwhile Loukanos had excused himself, and gone to wash. He looked nostalgically at the bench under the tree in the courtyard, where he had spent many hours painting. Painting! He could not remember now when he had last picked up a brush, though he had scrawled many hasty sketches to aid his memory over the last few years. He wandered into the schoolroom – once the place where he had consulted with his patients, and where Blind Mordecai had patiently assisted him so long ago. He stepped out again and apologised to the quiet apothecary, whom he had insisted must stay to share their celebrations.

"I beg your pardon, sir, I have been impolite," he said courteously. "As a man of medicine yourself, you may like to compare notes – it must have been a shock to see your patient suddenly revive, cured of far more than the lockjaw! Do you follow the Nazarene? Have you seen such happen before, as I have? I have been travelling widely, and would be glad to discuss with you some new remedies I have discovered – that is apart from the miraculous cures I have witnessed!" He laughed briefly as he realised how oddly the two types of 'remedies' went together. "Please to sit in here with me and we will let the women talk in private for a while. Forgive me, I know I am babbling … this house holds many memories for me … and I have been away a long time."

He waved the silent man to the pile of cushions where Dan liked to throw himself when he had finished his lessons. The stranger sat there obligingly, looking thoughtfully at the many little holes picked in the whitewash. Loukanos ran his hands through his hair until it stood up rampantly, and sighed. His mind seemed to be quite scrambled, and he had not even noticed that he had omitted all the normal customs such as enquiring after the apothecary's name and family.

"Sir, I thank you with all my heart for coming to aid Sobek – I really did not believe even Aida could find a man to do so – no doubt it was she who found you? And of course you will be well paid."

"Thank you," the man answered quietly. "I came of my own accord, and there is no need to pay me. Sobek had recovered before I set foot in the door, and never was a man so glad to find himself superfluous. I understand you used to treat the unfortunate free of charge, yourself, in this very room – so you set a good example to this town."

To Loukanos' surprise the apothecary reached under the worn bench, and slid out the box of wax tablets which had been gathering dust there since Dan's last visit.

"These are interesting records," he commented, flipping through them one by one. He caught Loukanos' eye and smiled, running his hands lightly over the wax surfaces as he did so. "Do you remember the time you had to treat that griping old gorgon of a matriarch who was convinced she had a growth, but had only been over-eating? Now, what did you treat her with? Ah, yes, here it is."

Still holding Loukanos' astonished gaze he pulled out a tablet and fingered it swiftly. "Peppermint and chamomile infusion, which you called by some extravagant name you made up on the spot, and which cured her in three days. Very grateful, she was."

The stranger had not once glanced at the records under his hand. Loukanos sank on to the bench and gripped the edge. Was he going mad? That voice! Just then, there was a loud shriek from the other room. There was a clattering crash as a stool was knocked recklessly to the floor by flying skirts – running feet – and Anna burst panting through the doorway, her face white.

"Louki!" she cried wildly, totally unnerved, pointing with a shaking hand. "Louki! Look! Are we blind!?"

"Yes, my dear Anna," the stranger answered gently, rising to his feet and meeting the brown and hazel eyes which were staring wide in disbelief. He held out his hands and grasped her icy fingers, struggling for composure, his fine, sparkling eyes welling up, his melodious voice breaking at last. "You are both blind! But, praise the Lord Jeshua, and praise the Eternal my God – I, Mordecai of Cana, am not!"

Chapter Thirty-six

WHAT was in the air that week, that so many extraordinary things took place in, around, and for the quiet folk of Banayim? Until now, they had been relatively removed from the years of frantic activity since the Baptiser Johannes of Jordan had lifted his voice and thundered across the waters that he who was the Anointed of God had come, that the Messiah stood in their presence. But for every one who wanted something from the Nazarene, and could go after it, there were scores who could not, or did not – though they too believed in him, just as surely as they believed in Caesar, or Herod, or the High Priest. He was a fact of life.

Banayim was not slow to believe all they heard, and saw. They had succoured those who tramped through their village hunting for a man with a miracle to spare, they had marvelled as the cripples danced back along the shore, as the dumb shouted themselves hoarse, as the maimed clapped pain-free hands, and the haunted sang joyfully with eyes full of glory. They had watched shadow-thin women slipping along fearfully in the wake of the mobs, returning unashamedly with pink-cheeked vigour. They had seen ancient men painfully staggering past with swollen dropsied legs, coughing vainly to clear their half-drowned lungs, panting anxiously with blue-tinged mouths – and they had seen these same men striding back past the village as hale old fellows who breathed deeply through lips of a healthy colour, rejoicing heartily in their stick-thin shanks, and overcome with awe that the dread Shadow had retreated to await another day.

Not one of them in Banayim had disorders to compare with these. And so while they talked eagerly of what the Nazarene did, and to whom, what he had to say, what it meant, or what may happen next, they had never asked or expected anything for themselves. When blind men braved the dangers of the highway to beg for sight, who would ask for a dose of pink-eye to be healed, or that the sundial of time turn back to restore the sharp, flexible vision of youth? When a paralytic was cured of intolerable twisted agony, who would ask a cure for backache? When bald lepers begged with outstretched gecko fingers, and stumped to the Teacher on blunted limbs, who would ask the Nazarene to rethatch a grandfather's hairless head, to treat a woman's kitchen scald, a child's worms, or a sore toe? Life went on as usual, and it was not until now, when tension was waxing and fervour was waning in the Land around them, that they were finding themselves more involved than ever they had anticipated.

That the fervour *was* waning, there was no doubt. Too much time had passed to sustain it. Nearly three years of miracles and excitement and anticipation of the restoration of the Kingdom of Israel had not changed the reality of Roman rule, had not softened the hearts of the stern Sanhedrin, had not done anything except create irritation, suspicion, and growing disgust with the harshness of those who sat in Moses' seat. Whose were all those obfuscations of words, and the hair-splitting definitions to constrain the unstoppable changes in modern society? Not the Eternal's, that was for certain, and now the common people were realising it for themselves.

The young carpenter from Nazareth cut out the dead wood from the sickly ancient tree of the Law – tottering under the weight of a thousand parasitic growths – and pruned it clear down to the roots. How *could* the Law ever stand as it once did? And why did they ever think it would when for so long there had been no Shekinah glory, no Ark of the Covenant, no purely Aaronic high priesthood, no Davidic King, no Cities of Refuge, no political or legal autonomy. How was the Law to function with so little of the national structure to implement it, so much of the theoretical, and only a faint breath of the spiritual strength left? Overshadowing the lives of people struggling to live and move and have their being, the Law, drained of its unwritten spirit of love and joyful service, had been smothered under the groaning tomes of fretful, book-bound men who over hundreds of years, had laboriously pieced back together scraps of a religious and social system corrupted from the Babylonian Exile.

Without apology Jeshua turned his back on the monstrous hybrid. He had the effrontery to imply that people needed only to love God and neighbour, and intelligently embrace the inspired scriptures – trusting all else to faith, prayer, and commonsense. In short, he implied, they did not need a hierarchy of men – of various contradictory beliefs – with esoteric and rusty keys of knowledge to locks they had themselves fashioned to bind God's word. For those men, whose stranglehold on religion was harsher than Rome's, such an implication from such a man was an unforgiveable sin.

How many hundreds – thousands – of eager people from all the provinces and coasts of Israel had flocked to hear the plain-speaking man who taught without ceremony? Yet how many such people ever pushed and shoved and pleaded to hear the rabbis of the synagogue, and doctors of law, and scribes, priests, elders, rulers,

Sadducees and Pharisees who frequented the temple? How many hearts or minds or lives had *those* learned men transformed by a voice, a message, a pair of hands, and heavenly power?

Never man spoke like this man! No laborious *line upon line, precept upon precept* from the ancients did he quote to support his words – no authority but *'it is written'* and *'what saith the scripture?'* His mandate was tangible in signs and wonders, and in the scintillating truth and clarity of his words. Just as the Eternal had done in the beginning of all things – he spoke, and It Was So. Masterfully, he distilled from scripture the essence of what it meant to embrace the spirit of the Word, what it was to aspire to God-likeness in the heart and mind – and it was so far removed from the painstaking legalism of acquiring merit, that the icy burdens of guilty hopelessness melted from chilled souls like snow in summer. And in every word, every step, every look and gesture, did the lean, prematurely lined tradesman from Nazareth demonstrate that he was the son of his Father in Heaven. The Divine in abstract became intensely physical in his person.

Did the Eternal love His children? Jeshua touched the untouchables, took children on his knee, reached out to women and shared salt with all men regardless of standing. Did the Eternal countenance evil? Jeshua also denounced it even when it was buried too deep for human eyes to see. Did the Eternal provide for His people? Jeshua fed them by the thousands – Jew and Gentile alike. Did the Eternal give life? Every day Jeshua saved lives – from misery, from disease, from confusion, from fear – and even gave it back to the dead. Why, his very name meant *'He Who Saves'* and who dared gainsay it? In only two matters would the intense dark-browed man decline to exercise his Father's powers – the same two powers which men had ever been eager to usurp since the world began ... he would not judge, and he would not avenge.

Even his detractors could never call him anything but extraordinary, a man who was like other men and yet nothing like them.

Aunt Etta, now alone with the silence in the Shepherd's House in the Hollow, was brooding on all these things as she hobbled through her tasks. The floors were swept, the herbs watered, the table scrubbed, and now she was slowly grinding her barley for the evening's bread. She sat astraddle on the sturdy wooden bench outside, rhythmically rubbing her cylindrical stone over the kernels – forward and back, forward and back – and it was greatly conducive to meditative thought. Scandalous as it may have looked with her skirts pulled up to expose her fat, darkly chapped old knees, nobody was there to see, and she knew from bitter experience that if she knelt on the ground in the usual fashion, she would not be able to get up without help. She now slept on a raised bed like an Egyptian, and many simple tasks were a strain. But Marta would visit each day and there was nothing vital to be done.

What *was* important was Loukanos and Anna rushing off to a tortured woman – praying and hoping against hope that Blind Mordecai might against all expectations, somehow find the Prophet of Nazareth and entreat a miracle for her, even as Ittai and Joseph were attempting to do for Marta. She hoped the two of them would soon be safely home again, especially now that Marta had turned out not to need any miracle after all.

Etta shook her head at herself. Talking of miracles as if they were something to buy in the market place for the asking! Yes, they were taking miracles for granted these days – and to think she had once wondered how Israel in the wilderness could possibly have stopped seeing the marvel in the manna, and the pillars of smoke and fire, and everlasting clothes and shoe leather, astonishments which they had apparently shrugged off as unconcernedly as the miracles of sunrise and sunset. She was

379

disturbed to realise how quickly awe could dissolve into acceptance, even complacency. Uneasily she wondered why the great Healer was often challenged or accused of evil, when the Baptiser had been revered by all, even though he had wrought no miracles. *Except to change hearts – and surely that was a mighty miracle for some!* Etta thought wryly, and sighed.

They were bereft of the beloved Prophet who had been tied to the riverbank, but now they had a still mightier prophet – Johannes' own kinsman, who could not be tied anywhere, but roamed over hills and fields, from hamlets to the capital, even to places where Gentiles outnumbered Jews. He tramped Roman roads, climbed mountains, and sailed the deep in all weathers, riding wet boards or a heap of damp stinking nets in craft which bucked crazily over the unpredictable lake they called the Sea. He spoke in synagogues and houses both rich and poor, but it was out of doors that his preaching stirred the masses. He would sit in a boat and give lessons from the farm, the sheepcote, the vineyard. He would sit on a bare hill and speak plain uncompromising words about the dark side of crowded neighbourhood life – lust, greed, hatred and envy. He taught Gentiles, warned Jews, savaged religious hypocrisy, avoided politics and answered all questions with breathtaking wisdom and few words. Well, no wonder the whole world had gone after him!

But of course, the whole world did not go after him all at once, not literally, and just as well for that. It was madness enough when the crowds were so thick they trod on each other, and were swinging down sick men by ropes from rooftops above the press of people, as if they were so much cargo. *Once one person did it, the others followed, and a mercy it is that nobody has been hanged by now.*

What did it really mean, though – where would it end? Like so many others, Etta herself was confused about the very things which had thrilled her. Perhaps it would only be once the Land was free of all sickness in people's bodies and minds, that the next wave of cleansing could begin … surely that would be the removal of corruption in high places … *and if that doesn't mean those precious Sadducees I don't know who it does mean – 'No Resurrection', indeed! when everyone knows about that girl in Capernaum, and the young man in Nain … well, Sadducees have surely become a laughing stock among reasonable people, and very grateful they must be to him for that, I don't think!*

The old woman gave a final heavy scrape to her grindstone and looked with pleased surprise at the ground meal. She had been musing and grinding for longer than she'd realised, and the flour was fine enough for a wedding. *Speaking of weddings …* She wondered what would happen with Judith. From her observations, just privately, she didn't think Judith's face was going to turn out anywhere near as badly as they had all feared at first. Anna's courage in setting the bone was going to pay off, not to speak of Loukanos' attentions, and Widow Shana had promised to keep feeding the girl nothing but pap until the loose teeth were safe. But, of course, the women had an unspoken pact that Judith's chances for marriage were to be bewailed heavily. Thaddeus must be spurred on to provide Eli with lashings of jealousy, and may the best man win! If she turned out to be less marred than expected, well, so much the better, and nobody lost anything – least of all Judith.

Chuckling to herself, Etta tapped her grindstone and dusted it off with her wrinkled fingers. Much as she loved Marta and the children, much as she loved Dan and Anna, it was quite a luxury to be alone. So it had been years ago, when Dan had been away with his father, and Bukki off on one of his jaunts, but in those days it was a different kind of 'alone', with hard work unshared, and anxiety a constant companion. Now, it was a pleasant thing, for a short while, anyway. Etta closed her eyes and took a deep, appreciative breath, thinking gratefully of all the things she did *not* have to do today, and feeling the rare pleasure of the sun's warmth on her bare knees, the cold breeze tickling her hairy ankles.

Suddenly, alarmingly, there was a stumbling shake of nearby bushes – a sharp masculine exclamation of pain and annoyance – crashing and thrashing in the scrub! With a squawk poor Etta, mindful of her naked legs, lurched to her feet, forgetting that she was astride the bench. Grindstone and tray thudded to the ground, beautifully ground barley was flung to the wind in a flurry of skirts – Etta trying to pull them down even as the broad planks held them up – her balance gone, solid legs scrambling ineffectually on opposite sides of the wide seat – with a truly distressing cry, the old woman fell sideways, landing heavily on the hard dirt with the thick bench still pinned between her knees.

A storm of self-reproach burst from the slender young man who tore out of the scrub. He ran to her side, dropping a dirty clay flask from his hand, dragging the bench clear of Etta's bruised, scraped and bleeding legs, quickly tugging her dishevelled clothes into decency, lifting her shoulders and cradling her grizzled old head in his muscular arms.

"Oh – my dear lady! I am sorry! I am so sorry! It was my fault, I startled you, dear lady!"

Etta was winded, dazed, and too astonished at first even to cry from the savagely sharp pains shooting like flame-barbed arrows through her hip and back.

Hi-yi! Have I died and gone to Abraham's bosom? A young, handsome Abraham at that?! Ah, the faithful ones shall indeed renew their youth like eagles as the Psalmist said! I think I shall stay dead for a while longer, thank you.

She shut her eyes quickly and moaned a little.

Chapter Thirty-seven

DAN and Eli had fought a minor battle with Samuel late that morning and come off second best. Caleb had used the last of his precious ointment on Golan's leg, and although he had more at home, it was no use to man or beast three miles away. Samuel would not hear of the old man returning to his daughter's to fetch it, and Eli had begged for the errand. His father was adamant – Eli was not to go, and Eli was furious.

"He doesn't trust me, that's what it is," the young man said angrily. "He thinks I'll go running off to see Judith on the way."

"Well, would you?"

Eli flushed and flung Dan a sheepish look. "No ... probably ... not ... but I didn't promise not to go to Banayim at *all*, and if I saw her by accident it wouldn't be my fault, would it?"

"Ah!" Dan laughed, and ran off to beg Samuel to let him go with Eli and keep him honest. But Samuel didn't see the funny side.

"If he has to be *kept* honest, he is *not* honest, Dan. I appreciate your intent, but nobody can pass off their trustworthiness to another like that. If he has to excuse himself in advance with a bit of legalism, that's tells you something! He stays. But we need that unguent and since you're so keen to use your legs, you can fetch it yourself, on your own. Make it a round trip – go to Ada afterwards, I have a list for her – and you may as well visit your family, since you have to go right past Banayim. You can even see Judith if they'll let you in, and then report back to my moon-calf of a son. I want you back first thing in the morning, mind."

At first Dan was almost as disappointed as Eli – a hurried trip with the two of them could have been fun, but on his own the distance would seem longer. Still, he could look on it as an unexpected holiday. Extra Pressings would have very little time for him, not even a cup of cold water unless he asked for it; but Ada always met him with a welcoming smile and titbits from her larder, and if she didn't load him up too much with things to take back to her men, it would still be worth it. So it proved to be. Samuel's instructions merely concerned things for her to do, and not one package did he have to take back, if you didn't count the dried fruit tied up in a cloth which was 'just for growing boys' as Ada confided, with a finger to her lips and a knowing smile. Dan had no intention of passing on that comment – Eli would be offended, and Caleb would miss out – but he appreciated the gesture, and gratefully tucked the bundle into his bosom beside the jar of ointment which Extra Pressings had handed him with scarcely a word.

He trotted into the streets of Banayim in the late afternoon, finding it largely deserted. At the scrub end, Sabba Zimri was squatting with Hanoch and Malachi – chickens scratching around them – and from the fretful voices and passionate gesticulations, Dan guessed he was the daysman in a heated debate over the impossibility of vegetable-growing and chicken-raising as companionable activities. The women were inside with children or preparing meals, and even the Dabab was not peering from her favourite window, or lurking in her doorway. Dan spied her deep in Malachi's garden, taking advantage of her husband's absence to kick disapprovingly at his favourite melon vine which had trespassed into *her* favourite patch of onions. He grinned and slipped down the alley to Widow Shana's.

The Widow had insinuated herself across the shared courtyard to make herself quite at home in the house with Judith and little Thad, and a fine job she seemed to be doing of caring for them all. The room was clean and tidy, the evening meal was simmering nicely on the neatly swept hearth. Judith was sitting up looking much brighter in spirits, as well as in her face, which in the parts peeking out of her bandages was as colourful as a stormy sunset, and painted an interesting mixture of black, purple, yellow and crimson, with a delicate touch of green and blue. Even young Thad was losing his sulky look. The Widow was rolling and patting her bread to cook on the clay oven, and under her supervision, the boy was playing with scraps of dough, pretending to be a potter, and chortling at his floppy plates and squishy bowls.

Dan garnered all the latest news – glad to hear about Thaddeus finding work and Marta returning home again with the children. He then stuck his head into Marta's to congratulate her on her health and agree that Ittai must surely be back soon. Marta told him of Anna and Loukanos' mission of mercy to Cana, and, assuring him she would look after Etta in their absence, gave him a handful of honey cracknels as a treat for them both. Dan carefully poked them into his scrip and thanked her.

"Give me a spare water-pot, Marta," he said masterfully, unconsciously smoothing the reddish hairs on his upper lip. "I'll run to the well and take Auntie's water with me right now. That'll save you extra work in the morning. But you'd better stand guard and warn me if the Dabab looks my way. She'll make a meal out of a man doing women's work, and I'll be hounded with questions just when I want to get away."

Marta smiled at him in her sleeve, remembering her five brothers at the 'hair and horseplay' stage. A year ago Dan wouldn't have cared what the Dabab thought, but he was at an age when no boy wanted to look ridiculous, not even to a suspicious old busybody. She promised solemnly, and played a noisy game of ball-and-stick with the twins outside the door while she kept watch. Dan slunk away safely, nodding conspiratorially to her as he left, while the Dabab at the other end of the street pursed up her mouth and tutted over the slackness of young mothers who romped with their children just when they should have been getting their husbands' dinners. The fact that Marta's husband was not even at home had no significance whatsoever! Routine was routine!

Despite the weight of the heavy jar on his narrow shoulder, Dan walked briskly along the track to the Hollow, congratulating himself that his muscles must be growing stronger at last. Why, such a small pot was a lot lighter than an armful of newborn lambs, and a lot less trouble, too! Nevertheless, he was glad he was almost there. What a surprise Aunt Etta would have to see him! He hoped she had not already spied him from a window, it would be fun to see her astonished face when she came to the door.

While carefully swinging the water down from his shoulder Dan noticed that someone had moved the bench, now standing carelessly at an angle in the clearing instead of in its time-honoured place beside the door. At first he felt faintly put out by the change, but then he shrugged with a grin. It was probably Loukanos, who was always restless, always fiddling with things. Who cared *how* many things he changed now – the main thing was, he was back! And more than that, at last, he was one of the family in spirit, in faith, and in hope – and had even been confirmed as chosen, by the conferring of a miraculous power – no matter how temporary.

Aunt Etta was very quiet; surely she had heard him set the pot down with a gentle thud by the door – but perhaps she was taking a nap. He could hear a kind of snuffling from inside which was probably her snoring. The rest hour often stretched out for her on a bad day, and with nobody around to disturb her, she might sleep till bedtime! Dan laughed to himself at the thought, and stepped through the open door.

"Aunt Etta!" he called gaily into the gloom, his eyes still dazzled by the late afternoon sun. "Wake up! It's me, Dan! I've brought your water."

"Dan! My darling boy! What a wonderful surprise to see you! And how thoughtful, to bring the water."

Aunt Etta was sitting on her favourite stool, by a table strewn with half finished tasks, busily spinning her distaff, and yes, she was sniffling quietly to herself, hurriedly wiping her curved nose before holding out her hands to him, thread and all.

"Why, Auntie, what's all this? Have you got a cold?" Dan asked anxiously.

He knelt down and gave her a sympathetic hug, forgetful of Caleb's tub of ointment which was stuffed down his tunic beside Ada's package, and which sank into Aunt Etta's generous bosom, but dug into his own bony ribs.

"Ouch!"

"Mercy on us, Dan, dear! What have you got there?" She extricated herself hastily.

"Oh, it's only Caleb's healing magic in a pot! I'm sorry, I forgot about it." He stood up and rubbed his chest tenderly. "Maybe I should use some on myself!" he laughed.

Aunt Etta held him at arm's length and her eyes lit up with an odd expression. She put down her work.

"Is it good stuff, Dan?"

"Yes – the best. Father used it too, you know, and he said there was nothing to touch Caleb's secret recipe. It's worked wonders on poor Golan's lame leg already, but that took the last bit we had with us. Samuel was worried about not having any handy, and sent me off to fetch more, which is why I'm here! That's how good it is."

"Ah! You are truly good shepherds, with a loving care for your flock! But why should the sheep have all the best medicine? All these years, Dan, I have suffered with my back, and tried many remedies in vain – yet neither your father nor Caleb ever thought to suggest *this* one … Oh, Dan! Do you think it just might work on *me*?"

Her face was struggling, and Dan was astonished, realising that she did not have a cold – she must have been crying when he came in.

"Why, Aunt Etta, are you in very bad pain tonight? Don't cry! It's a good idea – I never thought of it either! But why not? But how – I mean – Anna's not here to help …"

"Oh, I see – well, I will just do the best I can by myself. See here, rub some on my palm, and on the back of my hand too, yes, that's the way. Now, stand up and turn your back, and I will see what I can manage one way or another. You may be amazed at how determined a woman can be when she thinks a new potion will do something wonderful for her …"

She reached up to pat him lovingly on the cheek with her free hand and then turned him around firmly. Dan obediently stared out of the door at the gathering pinks and softly smudged purples of the sunset, as behind him came noises which seemed to indicate some struggling and effort on his aunt's part. Dear Aunt Etta! Perhaps Caleb's cure-all would at least take away some of the pain at best, and ease the stiffness if nothing else.

"You will have to stay nice and warm and rested all tomorrow for it to be effective," he advised optimistically.

Suddenly a pair of stout arms wrapped themselves around him from behind – and snatched him clean off his legs in a swift swinging arc which had his flying feet sweeping every last thing off the table. He gasped and yelled, and truth to tell, very nearly forgot himself with terror. Panicking, he twisted himself around to see his captor – and found himself staring, bulge-eyed, into the face of a near-hysterical Aunt Etta, silver-haired, wrinkled – and a full head taller than himself.

"Why, Dan! It works!" she giggled, yes, she actually giggled – and dropped him.

Dan was utterly speechless. Aunt Etta's face changed, she darted outside and back, to hastily hold to his white lips a dipper of water snatched from the full jar he had just delivered.

"Dan, my darling boy! That was unforgiveable – to play a childish trick like that! My boy, my boy, how sorry I am!" She hugged him remorsefully. "Somehow it was almost irresistible! All of a sudden I felt ten years old again and full of mischief."

Dan was still shaking. He looked at her with every nerve jangling.

"I nearly wet myself!" he said reproachfully, then began to cry from sheer shock. "What – how – surely not the ointment!"

"No, no, not the ointment!" Aunt Etta held him tightly, resting her wrinkled chin on his untidy black head, which now only came up to her shoulder. "That was a very foolish inspiration of the moment – oh, but Dan, what a great temptation to surprise you in such a happy, silly way – totally selfish, and I repent in dust and ashes!"

She sat him down gently, and reached up effortlessly for the wineskin hanging from the ceiling. "Here, half a cup will settle your nerves." Dan's hand trembled badly as he slurped from the cup and rattled it down on the table. He took a deep breath, and looked a thousand questions. Aunt Etta took his hands, and now the tears she had swallowed when Dan arrived, were allowed to fall freely.

"You see, this only happened two hours ago – I think I am still quite unhinged myself! I have been sitting here trying to steady myself sensible with some soothing hand-work, and stop this silly crying, though my heart is shouting praises I can hardly utter. I long to run out and tell Marta and the whole village but I am so overwhelmed and giddy I have not dared to stir. And such a double blessing for me, Dan, dear – that you have come – the first to know! – and can rejoice with me, and calm me down again!"

"Tell me! Oh, Aunt Etta – tell me! I am to stay overnight so there is plenty of time. I promise we will run and tell the village at first light, but for now – oh, start at the very beginning and don't leave anything out!"

So she told him how the Teacher of Nazareth was departing Galilee, and moving on towards Jerusalem for the Festival; and as he often did, was sending his men ahead to prepare lodgings in various places. Setting out west for Samaria, one of the Twelve had broken off from his friends to make a short detour from Magdala through Banayim.

"What business would one of the Teacher's Chosen have here?" Dan was amazed.

"Believe it or not, Dan he was looking for me!"

"What?!"

Aunt Etta nodded. "Not really for myself, as such – he actually came to ask about Marah All-Alone, who's been with them a long time – the Magdalan, he said they call her now."

Dan opened his mouth to ask more questions, but Aunt Etta flapped a hand at him as she darted around happily picking up from the beaten earth floor the scattered wooden plates, copper pot, peeled onions, yarn-tied bunch of herbs, distaff and wool he had kicked off the table. She replaced everything tidily.

"Hush, and listen."

The Teacher's companion was very interested in Marah, said Etta, and it was her opinion it was more than kindness or curiosity. Since her healing, Marah had spoken openly of her time in Banayim, of how her friend Etta had taken her in at a time when she was badly troubled, and of how she had helped her unlock some of her past. So, this disciple had hoped Etta could enlighten him about Marah's life and person … tell him what kind of woman she had been … anything she knew of the family… even her age! … and had been particularly concerned that the modest wealth from which she had been helping to support them, was in a secure place. He knew that women were easily taken in by unscrupulous men, and would hate to see this happen to a worthy woman like the Magdalan – but of course, he had too much delicacy to suggest this to her himself. Was there any way Etta thought he could assist? He knew some very trustworthy bankers, and had some experience of managing money himself.

Etta, though mightily astonished, was not able to be very helpful. She had little more knowledge than he of Marah's situation, and it was her private opinion that Marah herself was the one to give the answers, regardless of convention. Without father or family, and with her own means of support, her life was at her own disposal, after all. If she wished this man to know more of her, she would have invited questions to her face. Etta was aware that Marah had some money bequeathed by her foster father, (contrary to the Dabab's conviction that he had left her only debts). She also knew that Marah had worked hard for many years in order to conserve it intact and safeguard a lonely old age; but any more detail about her friend's money or where it was banked, she did not know, and would not have cared to tell a stranger anyway, no matter whose disciple he was. Of course she did not say all that.

"Do you think he means to offer her marriage, Auntie?" Dan asked in surprise. "Isn't she a bit old for that?"

Aunt Etta gave him a Look. "She is not too old for childbearing, if that's what you mean, and even if she was, no woman is ever too old to be appreciated!" she said with a touch of frost. "They would be of similar age, I think, and a man who is on the move as much as the Teacher's men are, may be glad to have a strong woman like her – a sensible and capable wife who would make the best of an unsettled life. Clearly she is as dedicated to following the Teacher, as he is."

"Very well then, he came here to ask you some private things he didn't want to ask Marah, for his own reasons," Dan summed up quickly, not sure that he approved of this proceeding. "But now I know *why* he came, tell me what happened about your back! I know the Twelve cure people sometimes – did you ask him to?"

Suddenly his eye was caught by the sight of a dusty clay flask standing on the deep window sill – there was definitely something familiar about it. Aunt Etta followed his eyes, twisting herself easily around to see, as she had not done for many years.

"Ah! You have spied my good talisman!" she chuckled. "Of course, I praise and bless the Eternal, and the power of the Nazarene, Dan – praise and bless them evermore! – but you know, that dirty old thing was what began it!"

Not knowing the exact route to the Shepherd's House, the disciple had attempted to strike out for it before he had reached the village. Not surprisingly, he had missed the well beaten track from Banayim, and had pushed through the scrubby hills instead. He had stubbed his toe on this very flask, which was hidden in the undergrowth, and fallen into a prickle bush. His sudden furious exclamation of pain was what had startled Aunt Etta into attempting to spring from her seat – and falling over disastrously, as she explained to Dan.

"What a fright he gave me!" she said, pressing her hand to her heart for emphasis. "Leaping out of the scrub like a wildcat with that old jar in his hand! I thought he was a robber, about to crack my skull! Instead, I broke my own hipbone in the fall – and got a nice collection of splinters in my poor old legs."

"Oh, Auntie!"

"It's all right, now, Dan – and oh, how kind and gentle he was! As if he was my own son!" Which was rather ingenuous of Aunt Etta, whose brief moment of incredulous bliss as he held her in his arms, had nothing particularly motherly about it.

"He realised at once I was seriously injured, Dan, when he tried to help me up – oh, my hip! And my jarred back! I thought I would never walk again! I could not even feel my fingertips or my toes, and I'm afraid I went all to pieces then." She took a deep breath. "But, my dearest boy – never did my foolish moans and cries and tears call from anyone such a response! He cried passionately to heaven that *he* had caused this pain by his own impulsiveness,

393

and for my sake he begged God that it be undone. Then he told me to hold still, and asked if I believed in the Nazarene.

"*Of course I do!* I panted. *"The Baptiser himself said he was the Lamb of God! I heard him, I was there!"*

"Then in that name," he pronounced quickly, "the name of Jeshua of Nazareth, the Anointed of God, may this believer be whole and free of pain!"

Dan was holding his breath. Aunt Etta trembled at the recollection, which was still so fresh.

"I can't describe it, Dan," she whispered shakily, mopping her eyes and blowing her nose. "I just can't describe it. It was like waking up – and dreaming – all at once. The agony vanished, and I felt so light I thought I would float from his arms like a feather – me! Fat old Etta! I sat up, as easily as a child in the morning, and he jumped to his feet, and gave me his hand, and I positively *sprang* up beside him – not only my broken hip was miraculously mended, but my back, Dan! My burden, Dan, my constant load! My poor, dreadful, crooked, painful back! Straight! Whole! Free of pain!"

Overcome, she burst into sobs again, while Dan sympathetically flung his bony young arms around her and hugged hard.

"I was so stunned, Dan, I stretched, and moved and looked up – straight up into the sky over my head! I gasped and cried – and I ran to the door to measure myself against the mark I put there for you … I was so tall and straight again! I even bumped my head on the wineskin as I ran around the kitchen – as crazy as one of Hanoch's chickens with its head chopped off … then I rushed outside to thank my benefactor! But he brushed my gratitude aside with a smile, righted the bench and sat there kindly with me, interested only in asking about dear Marah. Afterwards

I ran in to fetch some refreshment for his journey – but when I came out he was gone! Only that filthy old flask he had tripped over was still sitting there … and I feel disgraced that I did not give him better hospitality. Oh, but Dan! I feel like a young slip of a girl again!"

Dan felt there had been quite enough crying for one day, and wiped his nose on his sleeve with a decided sniff.

"Well, Aunt Etta, praise and thanks to the Eternal and Lord Jeshua! But you're wrong there, anyway – you're still old, and you're still fat."

Aunt Etta gasped – and then they laughed and laughed and laughed, though Dan's behind got a very smart slap in the midst of it all, which was only fair.

By the time they were sensible again it was already dark. They lit the lamp, and made up the fire, and it was hard to say who found it more strange – Dan or his aunt, that she could stretch and twist and reach up and bend and cook with a smile and a buoyant step, and a pain-free light in her eye. So they sat chattering and eating – making merry and praising God as they had not done alone together for a long while, and it was quite like the old days, only better.

Crunching on shattered honey cracknels (his scrip having been crushed in the excitement), Dan licked his fingers and said stickily, "Two things, Aunt Etta! You were so intent on your story, you never once told me which one of the Twelve was here!"

"Did I not, Dan? Ah, I'm sorry – perhaps because in my mind I kept calling him my hero, and was determined not to let it slip out!" she laughed, and scooped up some sesame paste with hard stale bread from yesterday. She had been too scattered even to think of grinding more barley.

"Well? No, wait, let me guess – didn't he say he had experience handling money? And Uncle Louki said that Levi's the one who was a customs man in Capernaum, so it must have been him! I'd be surprised if he knew any trustworthy bankers, though!"

"No, you're quite wrong, Master Clever-Clues! It was the Kerioth – Jude, his name is. What a good and humble man, too – to do such a wonderful thing for an old woman – then only ask how to help someone else – and disappear! And I never even gave him a cup of cold water." She sighed. "So sensitive – so remorseful at causing me injury, so anxious to undo the harm! An anxious type of man anyway, I think, forever worrying at his nails. Well, if he really is setting his eyes on Marah, I don't think she'd be able to resist him! I know *I* wouldn't!"

She was still chuckling over her own daring, when Dan snapped his fingers. "The other thing! That flask, Aunt Etta! I'm sure I've seen it before somewhere."

"Yes, I think I have too. Jude must have snatched it up to see what it was, just before I screamed. I brought it inside as a keepsake – wash it off, won't you, and let's have a closer look. It's heavy and too dirty to use for food or water – but if it's still uncracked I will use it as a doorstop."

"A doorstop!" Dan's eyes took on a faraway look. He plunged the dusty vessel into the wash pot outside, and rubbed it clean with his fingers, bringing it back dark wet and dripping. "Uncracked, by the looks. Still has a stopper in it – wonder why it's so heavy?" He pulled out the leather plug with a jerk, swept a place clear with his elbow and poured out the clinking contents. The old woman and her nephew stared at the table. They stared at each other.

"It's my old shell collection, isn't it?" Dan cried. "Don't you remember? When Bukki left! He snatched up my shell collection and marched off with it!"

"So he did, Dan, I had almost forgotten. Yes, I was using it as a doorstop, and Bukki just swiped it up as if he'd done something clever, and off he went."

"I wondered at the time why he did that!" Dan was feasting his eyes on the treasures of his childhood, fingering gently each shell and polished pebble gathered over many walks and jaunts of exploration, every one watered smooth in the Sea, and lovingly brought home to share with his family. "Actually, I still wonder!"

"Well, Dan, my guess was that he mistook it for one of his own wine flasks. They were all from the same batch Ittai made, and he was in such a hurry he probably didn't even notice it rattled instead of sloshing."

"Ah! Then he soon realised he'd got the wrong one," Dan conjectured gleefully, "and of course he dropped it or threw it away – and it's been there ever since!"

"Waiting for a man to stub his toe on it and scare me silly … with a miracle to follow! Praise the Eternal! Extraordinary!" Etta marvelled, shaking her head incredulously. "A miracle waiting to happen from way back, eh, Dan?"

"Miracle of miracles!" Dan agreed, giving her another hug. Oh, wouldn't Anna get a shock when she came home! And Loukanos – and Marta next morning too – and everyone!

He ran into the courtyard for more fuel and looked up thankfully at the frosted stars which spoke of the Promises. A long time ago he had began to understand about them, about being blessed, about the new and good things which came to you – not happening to you, but formed inside you. And yet, here it was turned around again to be something given, and today the blessing was indeed something new and good – and all for dear Aunt Etta. *God is good!* Yes, out of all the thousands of people who had been set free – Aunt Etta had surely deserved her turn! As he had often done in times of great emotion, Dan bolted to the top of the hill behind the house where he could felt closer to the sky, to the stars, to the Master of the Universe.

"Thank you!" he shouted, opening his arms to embrace the heavens. "Thank you! Thank you!"

Early next morning, as a road-weary Ittai finally reached the village after walking half the night, he was overjoyed to spy his beloved Marta down the end of the street, just setting out for the well. He shouted to her eagerly – and she was waving back excitedly with a happy cry – when suddenly both of them stood stock-still with astonishment. Down the path from the Hollow two figures were striding along towards the well, each carrying a water-pot. The smaller was Dan with the borrowed jar on his shoulder, laughing up at his companion, a straightbacked old woman whose hips swayed with free and easy movement, whose steps swung along measure for measure with his – an old woman with erect carriage, whose straight arm steadied the pot high on her uplifted head, whose eyes and face shone with joy.

Marta dropped her own empty pot and it smashed unheeded at her feet.

"*Etta!*" she screamed at the top of her lungs, and the Dabab instantly tumbled out of her door, and people came running from everywhere. "*Etta!* Glory be! It's Etta!"

The healing power of the Nazarene had reached out and touched little Banayim at last.

Chapter Thirty-eight

JOHANAN could not help it. He had been grinning at Dan ever since he arrived, and was still at it even after the mutual cavorting and what Aunt Etta called 'playing giddy goats' were over with, and the boys had settled down enough to talk. Not that you could really call Johanan a 'boy' these days, with his neatly combed, stick-straight little beard and his broad shoulders and hairy, short-fingered hands. He was a young man now, though a *very* young one still, and until he turned forty, able to retain that youthful title by a figure of speech – unlike girls who ceased to be young barely ten years after they attained womanhood, and at forty were already old.

How young a man he still was, Johanan clearly demonstrated when he looked sideways at Dan yet again and began to laugh. Dan gave him a dark look – he knew quite well what was so funny. The auburn smudge over his lip had given place to a bright feathering of real whisker, and was now at work on his still rounded chin.

"Laugh all you want," he said sarcastically. "I told you it looked ridiculous, didn't I? But remember, you'll probably go bald first and then I'll be laughing at you."

Johanan threw back his head and gave a husky shout. "Well, at least you don't have pimples, and the Frog is croaking nicely! Poor old Dan, you have to admit midnight curls and a sunrise beard is an interesting contradiction. You'll never be able to commit a crime, you know – your face will be too distinctive!"

And he laughed again with a commiserating whack on Dan's slender shoulders. Dan whacked him back, and for a while the giddy goats were at it again, but eventually they broke off, panting, with mutual grins. The fact was, they were ecstatic to see each other again after many months, and letters could only say so much.

The new year's Feast of Trumpets had come in with the stirring blare of the ram's horn but not every man in the land could journey to the capital to hear the *Shofar* call. This year, Samuel and Ada took their three eldest, which of course included Eli; staying in Jerusalem for the solemn Day of Atonement ten days later, and returning just in time to release Dan for *Succoth*, the Festival of Booths. This meant that for more than two weeks, their two youngest boys, two hirelings and Dan had been busier than ever under Caleb's benign leadership. Fortunately Caleb knew how to handle the dogs, as without them it would have been impossible, and Ada had trained her boys early in life to milk both ewes and does, but they were all still so busy that it was a wonder Dan found the time to complain. Even so, weary Dan had groaned to Caleb only a week before, that it seemed the Festival of Booths would never come, and that after all the madly exciting days when amazing things had been happening, and people being lost and found and baptised and converted and cured and almost betrothed, and who knew what else … life had become very flat and dull.

He said as much to Johanan, who scoffed, "*Almost* betrothed? Who? You and Rhoda?" and laughed at him again.

"Well Thaddeus and Judith *would* have been, except she turned him down," Dan retorted, annoyed at feeling himself blush at his friend's quip. "But Eli says he'll get her before Thaddeus yet and I believe him. You just wait till the Festival of Lights. The moment that first lamp is lit, he'll make it sure – you'll see! When he said he didn't care how she looked, he really meant it."

"Good for him!" Johanan replied with genuine respect. "Better not change his mind later on, though."

But it was not likely that he would. Already Judith's face was healing better than anyone had expected. Her teeth were no longer loose, the red scar on her mouth was flattening, the bruises had faded and her nose, though still rather swollen, was *almost* straight. There was indeed a distinct lump high on the bridge, and she would never be beautiful, but then, she had not been so to begin with. Undaunted, Eli had begun to resume his visits, and as everyone knew the absent Thaddeus intended to renew his offer of marriage after the first rains, the villagers nudged each other about the interesting situation which was bound to develop. Already Old Zack in the privacy of his grubby storehouse had chalked up private wagers from men whose names were not written down but whose bets were somewhat revealingly recorded as so many eggs, onions, or earthenware dishes, to his figs.

Working south east of Tiberius with his new master, Thaddeus remained ignorant of any competition from the young shepherd. Only Widow Shana sent him any news, (deliberately saying nothing of Eli), from time to time revealing amusing little things about Thad, and reminding him what a comfort it would be when he exchanged the hired servant girl for a proper wife and mother for his boy.

About Ittai and Marta there was little to tell. The potter had his dusty head down and his mud-caked feet kicking the flywheel under his throwing table as fast as he could treadle. He had a lot

401

of lost time to make up, orders to fill, and taxes to pay so the whole family was busy. Marta seemed to be everywhere at once – mixing slip in the workshop and stews in the kitchen, pounding pigments one moment, grinding barley the next, checking special orders and counting out batches of popular pieces – lamps, dishes, bowls and jugs – for the Magdala market days.

Placid Shuni was now freed of swaddling bands, but to Marta's relief not yet able to sit up and tip himself out of the basket. He lay gurgling and babbling happily wherever his mother tied it … watching the play of shadows and clouds and leaves … listening intently to the sounds all around him … the chirruping of crickets, the wail of geckos, the buzz of insects – the sound of birds, voices, laughter, song, slap of clay, clack of the wheel, and wind in the scrub.

Their father declaring that four years of age was the end of babyhood, little Isaac and Abigail proudly helped with mixing and knocking down the clays, often joined by young Tirzah, and even Huldah, who wisely foresaw that bare-limbed girlish freedom would not last forever and she'd better enjoy romping while she could. The energetic twins were surprisingly consistent in their efforts, doggedly stamping and squashing very small quantities of the cold sticky clay with their calloused little feet – helping to glean stubble and dead grasses for packing, and gathering fuel for the never ending appetite of the kiln. All the village children, even fearless Isaac, had learned very early on to respect the firebreathing monster Ittai called 'Moloch', and no line scraped on the earth was needed to keep them at a safe distance, so Marta's constant fear of burns and the Dabab's dire predictions of disasters were thankfully never realised.

Widow Shana in her cunning had found yet another useful outlet for Thad's tempers, and hardly a day passed without the heavy-browed child tearing down the street to the workshop, snatching up his stout stick and obligingly smashing any dried pots which Ittai rejected as too faulty to put to the furnace. Pounded small, back to the water they would go to dissolve back into formlessness ready to be reshaped; and back home Thad would go, his temper similarly dissolved. Even Sabba Zimri stopped pottering so much at his daughter's house, and began 'pottering' with Ittai – cutting and carting clay from the pit, straw-packing the finished products – and so they were all very industrious and content, and Marta's only worry at the moment was Shuni's habit of sucking his big toe until it was as wrinkled as a half-soaked fava bean.

Uncle Joseph had been busy too, and with his usual energy and decision, had begun creating a new base for himself over Jordan in Pella, almost on the border of Decapolis and Perea. Comfortable in this Greco-Roman environment, he did a little business, but had more interest in resuming the charitable works which gratified him; succouring the poor and supporting the synagogue, in which he advised young men helpfully on many matters and discussed scriptures energetically and respectfully with the old. From here he was readily able to visit Anna and Loukanos from time to time, as well as keeping a watchful eye on the Nazarene's activities, ready to join the crowds when the Teacher came near enough, alert for the message he was sure must come, concerning the way to ensure salvation.

He knew quite well that it was not enough to be one of the Chosen People, that there was more to attaining eternal life than physically being of the Seed of Abraham – and so he waited to hear the vital word which would provide the key, and was not concerned

403

about the disillusionment which many felt regarding the restoration of the Kingdom. High above the Jordan valley, breathing the crisp air of Pella, he could almost have been back in the mountains of Cyprus, and there was little in the city to remind him otherwise.

In Cana, thanks to Mordecai, Sobek had found a safe haven with the Chattering Lamechs, and was painstakingly learning from her new mentors. The mother and daughter patiently taught her the routine skills of womanhood even as the father and son instructed her in the art of broom making. They found in her an eager apprentice, and a never-tiring listener who shared with them the new thrill of speech, the glorious freedom of easy communication. In the evenings she went to Mordecai, who lit the lamps, closed the shutters, and opened his schoolroom, teaching Sobek to read, write and figure, and encouraging Rhoda to improve her own limited skills, though he had not resumed his public courtyard classes for men and boys. He spent his days roaming the city and countryside with insatiable eyes, ministering to poor and beggars alike as he always had; and long hours devouring the parchments he had not been able to read for twenty years. Undecided about what he should do next, Mordecai recognised the irony that as a sighted man, he was still feeling his way.

Being aware that his first attendance at synagogue may cause some sensation, he had arrived very early on the first day of the Festival of Trumpets, and stood in the shadows half-hidden under his prayer shawl. He stayed long after most had left, and slipped out almost unnoticed. But when came the Day of Atonement shortly afterwards, Mordecai walked in with his face exposed like any other man, feeling the significance of this day as he had never felt it before. He stood in the fasting crowd, all of them equally hungry as beggars this once in a year, inhaling the warm press of fresh-washed clothes and bodies, of dust and wax and ancient leather, watching the soft stream of weak sun drifting through the high windows, seeing the mellow lamp-lit faces and the dedicated furnishings, the orderliness of it all just as he remembered – hearing the prayers, being part of congregation as they supplicated the Eternal that the gulf between God and man caused by 'Judgement' might be closed by the granting of 'At One-*ment*'. He felt the sense of mourning, he felt the depth of confession, and he felt that at last the Eternal had indeed blessed him with this sense of being 'At One' not only with his God, but with his own people again. Voicing the *Amens*, singing the plaintive cadences, and feeling the solemn benedictions vibrate through his very body, it seemed his heart would burst with sheer fullness of joy.

He thought unavoidably of Anna, how they had talked many a time on Joy and what it was, what it wasn't. Anna! Whom he hardly dared to face again. Among a pile of Loukanos' old medical drawings in the schoolroom Mordecai had found one of a disfigured, dreadful face, with observations scribbled beside arrows pointing to the crushed nose, and the burned eyelids. Beneath it was a neat sketch of a bandaged beggar, and he did not need to read the scrawled inscription 'Blind Corner', to know it was himself. It was a hard thing to see, but on this day of repentance and the national affliction of soul, Mordecai firmly reminded himself afresh that true joy did not require that a man felt merry, neither was it extinguished by sadness. With great thankfulness, he recognised that it existed independently in the soul, above the plane of earthly affairs, a trusting, glad response to the Creator of Heaven and Earth. *Yom Kippur* was a day of fasting, but it was also a day of new beginnings. Wherever that new beginning would take him, he was content to be led. As a blind man who now saw, he recognised more keenly than most, that it was not in man to direct his own steps.

But the Day of Atonement passed, and the Festival of Booths was quickly upon them. All the plans of Asa and Johanan to celebrate it as usual in Banayim were suddenly overturned now that so much had changed for them all. Instead, Aunt Etta, Anna, Loukanos and Dan would take themselves off to Cana where Asa's capacious house could easily accommodate all of them together, including Mordecai. Of course everyone knew that the Festivals were ideally celebrated in Jerusalem, but the whole nation could not fit in one city, and a family gathering was the next best thing.

Dan had a slight melancholy tinging his pleasure – recognising that this was the last year he would have such freedom to come and go. His formal schooling was finished, and after Pentecost he would be shepherding in earnest, celebrating the holy days wherever he happened to be at the time, just as Caleb was doing right now – and Eli too. Dan knew that he had been unusually blessed in the co-operative arrangement Samuel and Caleb had begun after Ammiel's death. There was always someone to share the load, and no single man had a relentless burden of care which could never be set down. Of course, eventually Dan's flock would be his sole responsibility, but meanwhile, he would just enjoy the holy days which made up for many a cold, wakeful night or parched, exhausting day. He hugged Moses, and set off with a light heart. The only disappointment was realising that his plan of building with Johanan a permanent shelter on the housetop, would now have to wait. They had already exchanged several letters about it, and his clever friend had even drawn interesting diagrams to explain how it should be done. But they would have it done by *next* year – he was determined!

A donkey had been hired for Aunt Etta, but she was having none of it, and so the fortunate beast walked beside them carrying all the packs, which were somewhat lighter than Etta. Not a great deal lighter, though, because Etta was not all the woman she *had* been – her unbounding delight in renewed activity had begun slowly to melt the lard from her flesh. So here they were, in Cana, the whole family – all except Aunt Mari, who rarely left Jerusalem, no matter how many times she talked about doing so. Having visited Banayim once, she had no great desire to repeat the experience, and Cana too could wait. In any case, she was busier than ever with her own hospitality, housing other pilgrims from the countryside who had come for *Succoth*. In particular, Mari had decreed that her house must always be open to disciples of the Teacher, whether associated with the chosen Twelve or not. Perhaps even the Teacher himself might stay a night at some time – and she could not be away from home with such possibilities before her! Mari's servants were kept busy collecting branches and poles for her visitors, who began constructing their little tabernacles at once. In the city they built booths everywhere they could fit them and by the time Johanan and Asa had recklessly followed Rhoda's example and mounted camels to Cana, Mari already had leafy huts springing up like mushrooms by the street gate, and on the rooftop – and although Johanan said nothing of it to Dan, there was even a large palm-thatched shelter taking shape on the paving three floors below, over the very place where Ammiel's body had lain broken.

In and out of the woods and fields around Cana, Dan and Johanan ran to and fro gathering armfuls of greenery, old hands by now at constructing their frameworks, but they had little help from Rhoda, happy as she was to see them again. Mordecai had suspended the girls' evening lessons for the Festival, so they did not see much of her, or Sobek. Dan was not sure if he liked this or not. He eyed Rhoda's new womanliness with great alarm, and felt unaccustomedly tongue-tied as she chattered, but every time she giggled at him and ran off, he kicked himself for not saying something impressive enough to make her stay.

However, Rhoda was not around to confuse poor Dan for very long. Asa having released her for the holiday, she tripped off to spend the week with her widowed mother Charron, who had returned to Cana in disgust after her old master in Sepphoris divorced the mother of his large brood, for a nimble new wife not worn down by constant childbearing. Charron was now preparing endless cheese bags in the efficient, sour-smelling shop of a quiet little Roman cheesemaker, himself a widower with two vapid daughters who had faces regrettably like his own cheeses. It was this man she was to marry after Pentecost, and whether they would stay or go abroad was anyone's guess. Rhoda was inclined to wring her hands over the whole situation, but she loved her mother, and was grateful to spend such rare and precious time with her, whatever happened later. Meanwhile Sobek was so happy she sang all the day long, and though she ran in to visit whenever she had a chance, she was very busy building her own little tabernacle with the Chattering Lamechs.

Loukanos, Mordecai, Anna, and warm-hearted Asa all were busy – Dinah too, brewing up storms of steam in her kitchen – but who laughed the most often, stretched up for the highest branches, thatched with the most enthusiasm, and almost skipped along the tracks into the orchards and thickets, but Aunt Etta. And where was Uncle Joseph? Not with them. He was a man who liked to be a host rather than a guest. He was delighted to hear of Asa's glad reunion with his stepson; he knew his family's hearts were light and their house was full; and he felt no need to add his presence to the clan gathering in Cana. He would see them all at Passover, no doubt, and if by then that vital key to Life had been revealed by Teacher Jeshua, he would return to Cyprus rejoicing. Meanwhile in Pella he made it his task to warm and fill and make glad those who had no-one else. His gracious house was a haven for the poor and needy to come to – and go away from – feeling blessed. He encouraged booths to be built in his garden, and moved among his poor, giving and receiving comfort, and hopefully, acquiring merit.

The folk back in Banayim felt that their own Festival was rather subdued by contrast that year – there had been so much excitement lately – but Malachi paraded his best vegetables, Old Zack his best figs (olives being notably absent) and the women their best clothes and ornaments in keeping with the spirit of the week. The booths were strung about with decorative vines and garlands of shells beloved by the little girls, who had been making them for weeks. The drums and pipes and finger-cymbals came out of baskets and down from their hooks, and there was plenty of singing, dancing, eating, visiting and storytelling – and goodwill. The argument about a Certain Person's chickens getting into a Certain Other Person's vegetables simmered in the background as usual, but more out of habit than rancour.

Widow Shana's visiting family again filled the Travellers' House where their petulant quarrels and unfortunate language could not offend anyone, especially Rachel (who was sure to be listening hard with a shocked look at the ready). Poor Shana was self-reproachfully aware of their shortcomings, and solemnly warned Judith that trying to discipline a family, before a woman had learned to discipline *herself*, was not a good idea.

"I didn't learn that till I was thirty but I was almost a grandmother by then, and it was a bit late, so you take warning, Judith, my girl. The children come when God wills, and not you, so a woman should set her mind to it early. Every time you let something slide because you are too tired or sick or sad or lazy, you thicken the rod for your own back." She sighed. "Of course my husband very inconsiderately died just when I needed him most, so he was no earthly use at all, may he rest in peace. My sons learned only to be quarrelsome and ungrateful, and alas, they all married sulks – so what could anyone expect of the poor grandchildren? Don't you repeat my mistakes when your time comes, my dear."

Judith privately rolled her eyes over all this moralising, but whatever her previous shortcomings Widow Shana *was* quite wonderful – and firm – with that wearisome little Thad, so perhaps she knew what she was talking about. Certainly the boy had never behaved as well as he had since the Widow appointed herself their guardian. But she could ignore all this worthy advice for the present. What was more interesting right now was whether Eli would be visiting during the Festival …

In Cana, the streets were lively with the gaiety of families enjoying the holiday, laughing and talking together as they wove their shelters and lived outdoors, the town's peaceful mood furthered by the forest-like sound of rustling leaves. The breeze wandering softly around and through the sociable streets, refreshed the air with fragrance from hundreds of booths – all overlaid with boughs of pine, plane, willow and myrtle, palm, quince and apple, terebinth and bay, pomegranate, vine, olive, pistachio and juniper – and a delicious, heady combination it was, especially in contrast to the usual pungent odours of township refuse.

There was an unusual sight at Blind Corner that year. Mordecai, obeying some inner compulsion, chose to build his shelter on the same spot where he had for so many years, had none. It seemed fitting to him to do so, and though he passed the evenings with the friends who were his family, late each night of the Festival he rose and walked across the street, to sleep in his booth – or rather, to lie awake and wonder, and pray. He still rarely slept soundly; twenty years of the light beggar's doze was a habit not easily broken.

The courtyard at Asa's held two separate booths, which exuded their own fresh clean scent of pine and willow and olive, but in deference to Anna, no vines were used, as even a fragment of the plant accidentally falling into her food could nullify her Nazirite vow. As, according to custom, the women only ever slept outdoors for the first night, Anna, Etta and Dinah had cheated a little by forming their shelter with the help of the large shade tree in the centre, while the men's was more orthodox.

So the second night of the festival saw only Loukanos, Asa, Johanan and Dan in their leafy, spicily-scented courtyard. It had been a squeeze for the four of them in the one tabernacle the night before, and now Johanan and Dan had decamped to the women's vacated booth which pleased all concerned. At last there was room to stretch out, and those who wanted to could sleep, leaving the others (meaning the boys) free to whisper half the night without waking anyone or being shushed. However, a fair bit of talking went on in both booths both before and after everyone split up, nonetheless, especially as Mordecai and Loukanos had their own private miracles to relate and be questioned about over and again. Johanan was very sober when he heard all Loukanos could tell of the Baptiser. He had been a great follower of the Prophet, even after the announcement of the Messiah, and had been baptised himself not long before Johannes was imprisoned. Dan had heard all about it during his last visit.

"What sins did *you* have to repent of? Have you ever had to offer a sin offering?" Dan had asked him incredulously, half in fun, but Johanan answered him seriously.

"My sins? Not the kind *you're* thinking of. See, Dan, the trouble with sin offerings is that you can't offer for *every* sin, so you save them for the big, rare, ugly ones. Then anything smaller or more common doesn't seem as bad. If they're not as bad, they don't seem as important to worry about either. Soon, we stop calling them real sins, they're excusable, even acceptable. That's how they become invisible to ourselves, as well as to others."

"Such as?"

Johanan shrugged. "Bearing grudges, meanness, pettiness, greed, pride, dishonesty, rage, lust, hatred, ingratitude, envy, cruelty … where do I stop?"

Dan bit his lip thoughtfully. "They *are* invisible, aren't they? All on the inside … you can nurse any of those without anyone knowing."

"Yes, but it shows in the end. Because how you think makes a difference to how you act, doesn't it? Like Heber ben Heber at school, who hated me. He'd punch me even if the rabbi caned him for it. Of course he knew it was wrong! But then he'd go off to synagogue and sing like an angel, and still punch me again the next day."

"But what if Heber *didn't* punch you, if he *acted* friendly even while hating you? If you have the right knowledge, can't you still keep doing the right things, even with evil thoughts? You'd be acting rightly *because* you had the right knowledge, wouldn't you – so is that wrong?"

412

Dan had once thought that acquiring knowledge was the most important thing, and would give glory to God, but Mordecai had disabused him of that idea.

"Knowledge has a seductive beauty, Dan. Like a miser's treasure – it gives a man a feeling of possession, of private pleasure, of power, of glory. A man can feel rich and fat as he yearns to hoard more and more! But no matter how many times it is counted and polished and held up for admiration – as I've said before, of what use is it, eh? Feeding nobody, clothing nobody, sheltering nobody."

"But the learned men!" Dan had protested. "All the scribes, the lawyers, the Pharisees, the rabbis ... they all have so much knowledge, and you can't say they hoard it because they preach it to others all the time. Isn't that useful? Doesn't that give glory to God?"

"Unfortunately, Dan, even preaching your knowledge, is not the same as acting on it. It is those who act on their preaching who are the most convincing."

But now Johanan was saying that even acting out one's knowledge was still not enough! He shook his head firmly at Dan.

"Even if you did just that (as if God didn't know the difference!), you'd be living a double life, wouldn't you? One outside for approval, one inside for pleasure, both quite opposite. The Law can't touch that, but it's thumbing your nose at the Eternal. That's why the Teacher is so fierce about hypocrisy. And anyway, like I said, nobody could keep up such an act forever."

"That's all very well," Dan felt his world again grow more complicated. "But if obedience when I'm not in the mood for it makes me a hypocrite; and *dis*obedience condemns me, it doesn't leave me much room!"

413

Johanan scratched his beard absently. "That's a good question for Mordecai tomorrow," he admitted. "I think it comes back to learning more of a *spirit* of obedience. You know, like acting in the spirit of the Law, not always the letter."

Dan rolled his eyes with exasperation. "But honestly, nobody *wants* to do the right thing *all* the time. So what hope is there for anyone, then?" he added crossly.

"None."

"What? Then why are we bothering at all? Or is that why we need to acquire merit?"

"No hope on our *own*, don't you see? But there's baptism now, and there's still the Day of Atonement ... both God's mercy, not *our* doing."

"Yes, but if one is enough ... why do we need both? And what about the merit?"

Johanan frowned. "I'm still working that out."

Chapter Thirty-nine

WHAT about earning merit, indeed? Dan and Johanan argued their way around the subject without any satisfactory conclusion. In Jerusalem Johanan had listened intently to the Teacher many times by now, and as he had told Dan, obviously the Eternal wanted His people to respond to the spirit of the Law, and not the letter. However, that did not answer the question of what to *do* with the letter, or more pertinently, all those *other* letters, meaning those which a scathing Mordecai (taking a big breath first) once dismissed as *pragmatic and contradictory interpretations-of-analyses-of-footnotes-to-expositions-of-all-explanations-added-since-the-Exile.* "As if the Law itself wasn't complicated enough in the first place!" Dan said glumly.

Small wonder that the learned men grimly claimed that Jeshua the Nazarene was a blasphemer and anarchist bent on extinguishing it – for to them, letter, spirit, Rabbinic precept, faithfulness to Moses – it was all one. It was *their* cherished Law being set at nought by an unschooled upstart. *Their* Law – their own esoteric knowledge of which defined them, and justified their position above the ignorant rabble; *their* precious Law, which was to them so supreme that some held that the Eternal and His angels pored over it with holy Rabbis of the past – Rabbis who *also* had been given miraculous, though often bizarre, powers!

Dan merely spluttered rudely when Johanan told him this startling piece of information. He scowled up at the bright sparkle of stars insinuating themselves through the whispering leaves, as if they were all the host of Rabbinism themselves.

"The Eternal studying their ideas about what *He* wrote in the first place? And as for their powers, did any of those old Rabbis, who supposedly made people's eyes fall out – or whatever you said – did they actually do anything *useful* like curing lepers, like the Teacher does? Well, I don't believe a word of it, I don't care *what* they say in Jerusalem. And they can sneer at our accent and tell all those jokes about *The Rabbi, The Roman and The Galilean* – but it takes more than a mincing accent and phylacteries the size of a camel's hump to impress *us*, so who *are* the stupid ones?"

Johanan grinned admiringly at his friend's withering comments.

"Go on, Dan, I like a man who speaks his mind, even in a clumsy dialect with an ugly peasant accent! (Ouch! don't hit me! *I* don't care how you speak! Here, take that! And that! Ow! Fight fair! All right, you win! You speak with the tongue of oracles and angels!) Yes, you poor old Galilean yokels *are* sneered at – but one of you is baffling Masters of the Law and the country's applauding, so of course they're frantic. Why *isn't* he an ignorant peasant? He ought to be! How *can* he know the Scriptures better than they do? How *dare* he scorn their hedge around the Law? They're panting to catch him out but there's nothing to take hold of. Not even when they set traps. Everyone's wondering if he'll be in Jerusalem for the Festival. Hope he won't, they'll try anything to shut him up. Have to do it by force, I think – words are no use on him – but maybe force isn't either. Nobody's had his kind of power for over eight hundred years –"

"How do you work that out?" Dan asked in amazement.

"Well, it's that long since Prophet Elisha, isn't it? He's the nearest person I can think of who had the same powers, and even *he* only did about ten miracles – strange ones too, only not like those old Rabbis. So how much power must Teacher Jeshua have then, when you think how many *hundreds* of miracles *he* has done?"

"And what else *could* he do if he wanted to?!"

"Well, restore the Kingdom with a miraculous word, maybe? It doesn't look like it's going to happen with swords, not so far. But here's a queer thing – Elisha's miracles … some were the same as Teacher Jeshua's – raising a boy from the dead, curing leprosy, making an armful of bread feed a hundred hungry men – so what do you make of that?"

"But wait!" Dan interrupted, ignoring the question in his eagerness. "Didn't he give out some stiff curses as well? Striking his servant with leprosy, for instance – and what about bears attacking the youths who mocked him! Maybe if the rulers thought about what Elisha did with *his* power, they'd be more careful of mocking the Teacher."

"Lucky for them the Teacher preaches peace then."

Dan snapped his fingers. "Wasn't there another miracle to do with Elisha's tomb? Something which scared some grave-robbers …"

"Grave-robbers!" Johanan burst out laughing and flailed Dan with a spiky palm leaf. "Go to the bottom of the class! No, you ignorant Galilean, you've got it all back to front. Or did I mistake what you said? Perhaps it's just your accent, or your dialect mangling the – help! mercy! –"

There was a brief and lively pause filled with scuffling, grunts, yelps and husky guffaws and immediate sleepy grumblings from the occupants of the other booth, whereupon Johanan, slightly out of breath, condescended to tell (more quietly) the true tale of Elisha's grave.

"This is what happened. Moabite bandits frightened some men going out to bury a corpse, so they threw the body into the nearest tomb and ran away. The tomb was Elisha's, and when the dead man touched the prophet's bones –"

"The man came back to life! Now I remember."

"That's it. The Wisdom Book of ben Sirach says, '*in Elisha's life he did great wonders, and in his death he wrought miracles*'. That saying fits the Teacher too, the first half anyway, though I'll bet some of the rulers would like to test the second half!"

"Do you really think they want to kill him? But they couldn't. He's the Messiah!"

"Of course not, but they can make life difficult for him and everyone else. Who wants to be threatened with being expelled from the synagogue? Well, in Jerusalem they're already hinting at evil reasons for his powers. Saying it's the work of Beelzebub not the Eternal! It would be funny, if it wasn't blasphemy. Even the silliest folk tale doesn't have demons freeing people from their own clutches."

"You know, we're all witnesses now, aren't we?" Dan said thoughtfully as he wriggled himself into a more comfortable position and picked off the last of the vegetation which had landed on his face during their 'discussion' about his accent. "Everyone knows someone who has been cured of something. Such as Aunt Etta, or Mordecai or Sobek and Thaddeus!"

Already their individual stories had been told over and over in the district, and many another of the same kind eagerly exchanged by friends, relations, visitors. Some were *so* amazing that Dan secretly wondered how much they'd been embroidered. As they

418

wound themselves deeper in their blankets Dan laughingly related to Johanan the most recent example going around – an unlikely tale of an official demanding tribute money from Fisher Shimon of the Twelve. At the Teacher's command, he threw in his line, instantly caught a fish, and in its mouth was a four drachma coin – exactly enough to pay the tax for Shimon and Jeshua together!

Johanan chuckled sleepily. "I like that one."

Dan, who was now of taxable age himself, thought it would be more helpful to be able to find a coin in the mouth of a sheep. A gleeful idea struck him that with the help of Moses, he might be able to try just such a trick on Johanan some day, and his eyes danced with anticipation as he tried to work out how he would manage it.

In the shelter on the other side of the courtyard, Loukanos lay on his back, with an arm under his head, also staring at the stars which glinted through the loosely thatched roof. His stepfather snored comfortably beside him, but Loukanos could not sleep. He was remembering the Festival of three years ago, when he lay wakeful with aggravation, anger, exasperation, irritation – and a lot of other things he dared not define. Never could he have imagined that he would one day willingly sleep in a booth he had built himself, with a heart full of wonder, and gratitude. A shadow was still there, though – an apprehension of what would happen next.

He knew of the mood in Jerusalem – all who had been close to the Twelve were well aware that things did not look good for the Teacher there, and yet Jeshua had chosen to go up for at least part of the Festival. Loukanos had heard the men talking one night and knew even they were divided about how 'safe' they were from the displeasure of their rulers.

Fisher Shimon was confident or cautious by turns, one moment declaring that the people would let nothing happen to the Prophet who gave them so much, the next, urging avoidance of conflict. Levi considered that expediency would guide both Romans and Sanhedrin council members. He reasoned that the Sanhedrin didn't care how much mud Jews slung at Romans, and *vice versa*. Such a state of affairs was the *status quo* in any occupied territory, so that was all right. On their side, the Romans didn't care how much mud Jews dug up and slung at each other, as long as they didn't create political potholes for the governors to step in – and Jeshua was clearly disinterested in rabble-rousing, so *that* was all right.

But religion was another matter, Levi pointed out. The Sanhedrin would not even have cared about mud being slung at Rabbinism had Jeshua been yet another hollow-eyed, ranting fanatic to be pitied, shrugged off or ignored, but he wasn't and he couldn't be. They could discredit him all they liked, but eventually their own popularity and respect and honour was everything, and must be held on to at all costs! So Levi's opinion was that regardless of how they gnashed their teeth, the rulers would not dare to displease the masses and provoke outright rejection of their authority. "They will keep barking, but they will not bite," he decided.

Lebbaeus frowned. "You're all being too clever for me. I think it's clear that he's a threat to the spiritual powers that be, and once he begins the push for the Kingdom, he'll pose a real threat to Rome. They will join forces one day, and try to dispatch him quietly, and that means us too. We had better watch each other's backs."

The Kerioth shook his head, as he picked the tattered skin around his pulpy fingernails, and in the firelight the blood did not show. He hardly noticed the sharp stabs as the quicks tore, he was used to it, and so his affectionate smile did not waver.

"O ye of little faith!" he mocked them gently with the Teacher's own words. "This is the man promised of God from the beginning of the world. This is the man who has power over death, who has banished it from corpses! How many times has he already escaped the grave? They could offer an assassin a king's ransom and the money would never be collected! Even when they tried to throw our Master off a cliff – true to the prophecy, the Eternal kept him even from dashing his foot against a stone. No – they may do what they like to him, but nothing will harm God's anointed – and we are under his protection. Have we not already had a taste of the same power? He has said himself, we will reign with him! Banish your fears, my brothers – neither he nor we are destined for death, regardless of futile plots and schemes. We are destined to rule over those same envious men – with honour, with shared glory, and great riches! Look to the reward set before us, and take courage!"

Lebbaeus grunted. "Well said, Jude. You put us to shame." He glanced into the shadows where the other faithful followers were sleeping, and accidentally caught the steady eye of a wide-awake Loukanos among them. He kicked Shimon softly to warn him they could be overheard by those who were not of the Chosen.

The burly fisherman gnawed his beard eagerly, mistaking the kick for a prompt.

"Courage!" he nodded firmly. "Yes, courage and loyalty are everything! The loyalty to die in cold blood, the courage for the heat of battle! Of course nobody can harm God's son! But things may get worse before they get better, so we must be ready to take up arms and fight, whenever he puts in the sickle and begins the harvest of which Johannes spoke."

Levi frowned into the dying fire as if hoping to read the future in the glowing coals.

"Every harvest is taxed," he said grimly.

This almost furtive conversation was one of the last things Loukanos had shared with the Magdalan before he left, urging her to stay alert as the Teacher's company went into Judea. She promised to remember and he was absurdly comforted to know that some of his words would stay with her because of it. Now, his nightly devotions finished, he allowed himself the luxury of retrospection. He sent his thoughts of her winging out to the stars, lifted on prayer, lit with love, soaring into the skies as if in search of her very soul ... somewhere in his half-dream he met her, burning to say all the unspoken words ... so real was it that he opened his lips to speak – and nearly choked on a juniper berry which dropped straight into his mouth at that very moment – and that was the end of that! He propped himself up on one elbow until he had finished coughing, then looked irritably at Asa's peaceful form rumbling away obliviously beside him. Some people could sleep through anything! There was some scuffling going on (again) in the boys' shelter though, and they were still quietly chattering away together.

"Go to sleep!" he barked, and after a stifled snort, two exaggeratedly quavering voices cried, "Oh, yes, master! So sorry, master!"

There was a burst of smothered laughter, and Loukanos' face relaxed into a grin despite himself. He turned over, pulled up the blankets resolutely, and drifted off to sleep.

In his tiny booth on the corner of the street, Mordecai was sorting carefully through the untidy jumble in his mind. A blind man needed clear corridors in his head, everything must be neatly in its place, and memory must be kept fine and sharp. But now that the floodgates of sight were reopened, impressions poured in from every side. Long forgotten incidents were provoked at the sight of a leaf, a look, a lamp. New sights had to be absorbed and understood. And the blending of his mental image of familiar things with the way they really appeared, was another task. People, for instance. Some were elegantly perfect matches with the picture he had carried in his head – such as Loukanos. What a treat it was to see that brilliant young man, looking exactly as he knew he must! Of course, he was already familiar with the physician's face – Loukanos used to have him pass his hands over it in illustration as he discussed eyes, or ears, or bone structure, and he understood how Mordecai saw with his fingers.

Rhoda, too, was much as he had imagined her – only nobody could have imagined those impossibly long eyelashes – though it was almost as much of a shock to him as it was to Dan to see how the girl had suddenly blossomed into young womanhood. Dan himself was thinner than he expected, and he had not thought of him as having such unusual reddish lights in the black, thickly curling hair – or a scruffy little red moustache bravely struggling to assert itself. He liked the boy's frank gaze and wide grin. Sobek was no more of a surprise to him than she was to anybody else, so changed was she from what she had been. Mordecai looked on her alert, eager face and coltish-awkward frame with delight – and a touch of sadness, as he knew how she must struggle to first recognise and then subdue her unselfconscious, rapturous child-like demeanour ... and become muffled in respectability if she was ever to win the security of a husband. Poor Sobek! Was it *her* fault that she was a woman before she had the chance to understand childhood?

Mordecai had a whole gallery of faces and bodies to compare with his before-and-after impressions – enough to last him for many a sleepless night. But he was aware that he was holding off the thoughts which were demanding to be recognised, about the woman who was a Nazirite. Too late! He had thought of her, and here she was in his mind's eye before he could stop himself. Tall – he already knew that. Her odd eyes – yes, he knew that too, though he had not reckoned on the disturbance which assailed him on meeting their gaze. He knew about her strange, bound hair, and was accustomed to her rippling, gurgling laugh. He had pictured her as beautiful, and she was not, with her level brows, her crooked smile glimpsed under the gauzy veil, the lines of care etched on her forehead and traced about her eyes. But she held a different kind of beauty about herself like a cloak, a beauty which transcended how she looked. The texture of her skin, its fineness, the olive glow of her thin cheek, the intrigue of her brown and hazel eyes, the tapering length of her large-knuckled fingers, the narrowness of her slender wrist encased in a single heavy bracelet, the graceful sway of her walk, right down to the curve of her pale instep, and the turn of her dusky ankle … all these were sights which affected him as any man is affected by the smallest details of a woman he loves … but it was the compassionate expression of her patient face, the wisdom in her eyes, and the calm resolve written on her brow – these made her beautiful to him. They made her beautiful, and unattainable. They drew him to her, and held him distant. They were the impress of years of loyalty to a man who was not, and never could be hers.

Youthful, golden Ammiel was gone, and part of her had gone with him forever, and could never be given to another. Especially not another so much older, who had been hideous, deformed, pitied, an unwashed beggar trading in foolery and living off his wits, and who had eaten kitchen scraps at her hand like a pet dog. Only one thing could he give her – and that was an understanding and cherishing of the vivid intelligence of her mind. Well, please God, perhaps this unspoken empathy might stand. Mordecai had always suspected that her vow held something of Jephthah's daughter about it. She was not for him, but perhaps, at least, she would not be wasted on another, and that was a guilty comfort.

So he thought, and so he whipped himself, and so he forced himself to clear the overgrown paths of his dreams. He feasted his perfect eyes on the stars – oh how staggeringly distant they were, how bright, how beautiful, and how they shouted of the handiwork of the Creator of the Universe! *So shall thy seed be!* Pain and longing were not forever – there was joyful eternity before those who were truly Abraham's offspring! Dwelling on the impossible made a man's heart sick, and he must not waste his new life – the glory and the blessing of sight – the experience in his own flesh of the power of the Messiah!

Abruptly, Mordecai sat up. The Messiah! The Deliverer of Israel! But he was not delivering Israel as a mass, as a lump, as a single entity, as a nation. He was delivering men from *individual* bondage – one by one … releasing the physical burdens, releasing the spiritual burdens. *Proclaiming liberty to the captives.* He was the Saviour promised from the foundation of the world itself! Then how had they come to think of him as 'the Nazarene'? Or even 'the Teacher'? There were Nazarenes and Teachers in droves, and although he was *The* Nazarene, *The* Teacher – it was a diminishing of his purpose to refer to him only in this way. Had people become so used to miracles? Did they no longer believe he was the true Messiah? Did they now see him as a kind of outdoor Haggadah exponent – the anecdotal lesson giver, who entertained congregations in the synagogue with sometimes the slightest and most tortuous of connections to scripture, under the guise of teaching spiritual truths? Was this man to them just a healer, just a travelling miracle show?

Never let that be said! Why, the royal blood of kings flowed in his veins! Never let it be forgotten that had the Kingdom not been wrested from the wicked hands of Israel and Judah hundreds of years ago, this workman, who had been born in obscurity, would have been born in a palace – a prince royal – heir to the throne! Mordecai as a blind man had better ears and memory than most, and Nazareth was not so far away that talk did not get around about people's ancestry – *he* knew that the skilled woodworker was not only born in the same town as King David, he was a direct descendant, no matter which side of the blanket gossip placed him. It was no arbitrary matter that this Jeshua was solemnly ordained and appointed by Heaven as a King! As *The* King.

Suddenly Mordecai did not need resolutely to push away his thoughts of Anna – for the moment, they simply dissolved in the greater mission before him. He must make sure that people remembered, that they realised, that they respected all that their lord Jeshua was, and all that he would be.

He must to go up to Jerusalem this very Passover, and beard in their dens all the old lions who had long since forgotten the fiery young scribe Mordecai. Perhaps Rabban Gamaliel or Rabbi Nakkai would remember him, but no matter if they didn't. Oh yes, the very day after the Feast, they would hear from him, all of them! They may even listen.

He bowed his head to pray – but it flew up again with a sudden thrill of excitement as it struck him – he would see again the Temple in Jerusalem! See it! *See* it! Oh! God was good!

Chapter Forty

THE Festival of Booths had passed, and the countryside was busily preparing for winter. The brawny Lake fishermen overhauled their craft ready for treacherous storms, patching sails and mending nets, ropes, bags and baskets, while across the spent-summer landscape, moulting orchards and exhausted vegetable gardens were thinned, pruned, hoed, or replanted. Throughout the Galilean hills, ancient sheepcotes were strengthened, and new folds built, wells were cleaned, and underground cisterns inspected and restored ready to receive the blessing of the rains. Stocks of slingstones were laid in by shepherds bragging to each other about their best shots. Blear-eyed beekeepers with smouldering dung shovels hovered smokily over their clay pipe hives, ensuring they were mudded tightly in dry-stone orchard walls, not easily dislodged by weather or reckless intruders; whereupon they cheerfully boiled up quantities of grape-must syrup and satisfied themselves that they could sustain their little workers through the coldest winter.

On the well-drained slopes, vinedressers were hard at work. Free of the constant strain of nurturing their bedraggled plants through to harvest, they tilled and trained, fed crackling bonfires with useless, twisted ropes of diseased or unproductive vines, picked stones, repaired watchtowers, props and trellises, cleared water channels and rebuilt walls. Over the red-soiled fields, farmers with iron wrists and steady eyes tramped patiently behind their oxen, the shallow ploughshares kicking under their hands, scratching up the rich, softened earth. With widely swinging arms they broadcast their seed, reploughing across the furrows to cover the precious grain without delay, setting their children to chase the greedy birds and mice which hovered and scampered in their wake. Draughty barns were stopped up, leaky stables made secure – the last figs were gathered to be mashed into cakes or threaded in garlands. Women and girls were salting, preserving, and stringing up produce from the beams of their dim kitchens to slowly dry in its warmth, distaffs spun and shuttles flew to weave warmth for rapidly growing families. On every hand were the hope-filled and satisfying occupations of late autumn.

Asa and his nephew were still in Cana, and therefore so was Rhoda, whose bright presence lightened both the household work, and everyone's spirits, with the exception of Johanan's (so he said) whenever she reminded him crossly that he was there not to play jokes on servants but to improve his schooling. A quick learner, Johanan was in fact not at all reluctant to work, but Asa and Mari had long since agreed that the young man had been so taken up with studying the Teacher during the last few years, and spending his school time arguing about him with fellow pupils, that his formal education had suffered deplorably. Mordecai was the man to keep him hard at his books, and in Cana there would be fewer distractions. Now that the blind scribe could see again, there was no question but that Asa should stay until Passover, and employ him to ensure that Johanan caught up. This suited both Mordecai and his pupil. It gave Mordecai work, and also spurred Johanan along smartly. Asa had demanded that by the time they left Cana, the young man would have made a decision about his future or be

428

shamed, for although his family's wealth could support him, every man must work for the glory of God and his own self-respect.

"Riches are fleeting, a trade is forever." So Asa declared, and while Johanan agreed with him in theory, in practice, it was the very idea of pursuing *any* trade 'forever' which was not so appealing. What if he went to all the trouble of learning something and hated it after ten years? Or two? The thought made him shiver. Entering his Uncle's business was clearly something which did not tempt him but he knew if he did not make up his mind, that was the path he would be obliged to take. So, he scratched his head long and hard over the choice of his future occupation, and every week found him with a different ambition. Groaning inwardly, he envied Dan, whose schooldays were over, and whose occupation was fixed. Right now it seemed to Johanan that higher learning was superfluous, and a carefree shepherd's life must be the simplest, easiest, and most delightful in the world. Dan, Caleb, Samuel and Eli could have told him otherwise in extremely plain language, but Johanan had the sense to keep his opinions to himself, knowing that few young men had any choice at all in the matter of a trade. Meanwhile he continued to hesitate. Mordecai urged him to take his time, Asa urged him to hurry up, Mari wrote urging him to take care not to adopt uncouth Galilean expressions and habits, and Loukanos simply told him to shut up.

"It's no good just talking and moaning about it," he said firmly. "Go and see what people are doing, how *they* like it."

Morose and excited by turns, his cousin obediently began his quest but it was not a success. Johanan the coppersmith (too noisy), Johanan the astronomer (what? Even Abraham couldn't count the stars!), Johanan the baker (early mornings!), Johanan the physician (blood!), Johanan the beekeeper (stings!), Johanan the blacksmith (too hot), Johanan the banker (responsibility!), Johanan the weaver (too tedious), Johanan the carpenter (too hard), Johanan the apothecary (might poison someone). The list went on and on – everything from a gardener to a silk merchant.

"What about joining the army and becoming a Cornicen?" Dan jeered. "Your grandfather Marcus was half Roman, wasn't he? And you're good at trumpeting orders … Aha! So the truth hurts, does it? Ow! Ow! Stop!"

"Oh, very funny!" Johanan puffed, rubbing the wrist which he had almost sprained in their tussle. "Why don't I just run a gymnasium and be done with it!"

"Good idea," Dan retorted rudely, having won unexpectedly. "You could do with some wrestling lessons."

"Rhoda's mother says her cheesemaker is looking for another apprentice." Johanan brightened up. "Could be a tasty job!"

"A smelly one," Rhoda put in disdainfully as she stuck her pert nose around the door. Dan's New Moon visit was over, and she had brought him some honey cakes to take home to Anna and Etta. She regarded Johanan seriously. "Master Johanan –"

"I told you not to call me that," he interrupted with a touch of annoyance, and she blushed.

"Your mother is my mistress …"

"You're a family servant, Rhoda, not a slave. You're one of us. Now, go on."

"Very well then. I was about to say, you are good at all your studies, not just the holy books. I have heard your mother boast of your skill with numbers, with geometrics, with history, and writing. But you will never choose if you have too many ideas."

"She's right," Dan said admiringly. "Take your tablets and write them all down. Yes, like that. Now strike out half! But which half?"

"Well, clever Rhoda?" Johanan drawled.

She tossed her head. "You are blessed with education. Why take a trade from someone who has only his muscle with which to earn his bread? Strike those."

"Done. But what's left is just as confusing. And there are so many more I could add."

Rhoda tucked the bundle of honey cakes into Dan's satchel with a loving little pat and perched herself in the broad window, peering over their shoulders at the list.

"What gives you pleasure?" she asked thoughtfully.

"Being useful," he answered promptly. "Starting something new. Seeing new places. Understanding new ideas. Making them work. And whatever I do now, I want to be able to do it in the Restoration, too!"

"People will still eat cheese ..." Dan taunted slyly, prompting his friend to whisk an arm around his neck and clamp his head down before he knew it was happening.

"You have money and can undertake a long apprenticeship without loss," Rhoda persisted, swinging her bare feet carelessly, as she used to, forgetful that she was now a young lady. "You have good health. Are you also strong?"

"Enough. Not powerful, but I'm clever." He let Dan go with a grin.

Dan rubbed his neck ruefully. "He's stronger than he knows!"

Rhoda hopped down from the window. "Strike the whole list," she said airily. "I know the answer."

"You do? It's a public scribe, isn't it? Or a notary or something like that. Mordecai said I could be good at keeping records, but I don't want to spend my days reading and writing letters and documents and contracts – ploughing through legal jots and tittles, and trying to explain confusing details to cross-eyed customers. Too many words! I want to *do* something where I can see the fruit of my labour before me."

"Oh, any scribe has great respect, which is sweet fruit for most men," Rhoda said coolly, "but of course, you have not the patience and skill with people that Master Mordecai has."

She took her ever-present broom and began quickly to sweep the flagstones, hearing Old Dinah returning from the market and clashing pots in the kitchen.

"You're not going without telling us your answer?" Dan cried, leaping to bar her way as she hurried to the door. Accidentally Rhoda bumped into him with an interesting bounce, and frowned severely. Covered in confusion, Dan let her pass, but Johanan only laughed.

"Tell us, or I'll have you beaten!" he shouted after her, but a giggle was his only answer.

The young men clattered into the kitchen shortly afterwards and sat down with Mordecai and Asa, while Rhoda served, without waiting for Loukanos. He was holding his monthly clinic at Parosh the Tanner's where he would be well fed. Then he would suddenly appear, demanding that Dan be ready to leave at once.

"Hear me, my uncle, and hear me, my tutor! My future is decided," Johanan announced with his mouth full. "After Passover, I will humbly seat myself at the feet of some new master, and begin. I don't know *what*, but Rhoda does. Don't let that dove-like innocence fool you, nor that Galilean accent. She has become as wise as a serpent since she went to live in Jerusalem."

Rhoda maintained her aloof look for a while, but relented at last, since nobody could guess.

"Well, young woman, what is this aimless fellow to do with himself?" Asa asked with amusement and considerable interest. Rhoda might be easily flustered and often shy, but he knew her from a child – she was quick, observant, and intuitive.

The girl handed Johanan the pitcher of grape juice and watched his broad, firm hand begin to pour. She drew an important breath and spoke proudly.

"With all his abilities – why, he should be a man who designs great things! Buildings, houses for rich men, synagogues, public baths, aqueducts … I have seen them at work in Jerusalem, measuring, ruling, and sighting the sun, striding round with their plans, directing their men … they have great respect, and when they are not scowling they smile to themselves."

Johanan looked up at her in wonder and sheer admiration, and his cup ran over. He put the pitcher down with a thump while she patiently mopped up the mess, but he hardly noticed that it was still trickling off the table into his lap and onto the floor.

"Yes! Of course! A Master Builder – or even an *architect*! Oh, yes! Uncle?!"

Asa pursed up his lips dubiously, and thought aloud.

"H'm, well thought, Rhoda! An interesting idea, though it is a long journey to attain such accomplishment. A lot of work, young man. A *lot* of work and training – and you would have to learn much about tactfully dealing with men both above and below you. But rewarding. Head-work, heart-work and hand-work – yes, perhaps it would suit you if you had the stamina to finish. Finishing things is not your strong point, you know. What do you say, Mordecai?"

"A demanding choice, indeed, Johanan, but as your uncle says, rewarding. As you learned you could travel – observe – record what you see. You are blessed, and would not feel the loss of any commissions which your conscience would prohibit. Well, why should Rome have all the best buildings?"

Johanan leapt up from the table excitedly, elbowing his bread into the small puddle on the floor, where it obligingly soaked up the rest of the juice.

"Rhoda, you are a pearl of great price and your value is far about rubies! Think of it – one day I may even design and build synagogues for our newly restored nation! Or a palace for our King! Ambitious, but something to aim for! Uncle Asa, now you can stop despairing of your useless nephew, and Loukanos will leave me in peace. I'll write to mother at once. What, Dan, you going already? Tell cousin Anna and Aunt Etta, won't you?"

Dan had heard the wicket gate rattle and now he jumped up, stuffing a final lump of bread into his mouth, knowing what came next. Here it was – a shout of impatience.

"Dan! The sun is high! Where are you, boy?"

"The women will be very proud of you," Dan promised Johanan, scrambling his satchel and cloak from the corner.

"H'mph!" commented Old Dinah, who had been tongue-tied till now. "I don't know why. He hasn't done anything *yet* except make a mess of my kitchen. Let's see how enthusiastic he *still* is by next Festival!"

The next one was *Chanukah*, the Festival of Lights, and Johanan, Mordecai and Asa were all going to Banayim to celebrate there. Dan and Johanan exchanged parting grins. The tangle of Judith, Thaddeus and Eli would soon be unravelled! Now that *was* going to be interesting!

Chapter Forty-one

HEAVILY weighted with evening cloud the sullen early-winter sun was dragged below the horizon. But all over the land, from the grandest to the most humble dwelling, mothers stood poised with servant-lights, ready to begin the *Chanukah* ritual which united them in witness to the gracious hand of their God. From ornate polished lampstands of precious metals which glowed with the steady clear light of finest virgin oil, down to crude and sooty pinch lamps with greasy rims, sputtering with cheap second pressings; and even reluctant smudge lights of tallow, or brave sticks defiantly stuck in earth by vagabonds and beggars who must borrow their first flame – tonight all would burn together in witness, like fiery gems heaped and strung across the dark velvet of the Eternal's own hills and valleys.

In the absent hireling's small mud house where Widow Shana nowadays spent most of her time, the comfortable middle-aged woman ceremoniously lit the first lamp in a row of eight. She smiled encouragingly to young Thad, who was perched uncomfortably on Judith's bony knee. They had been teaching him a somewhat tedious story-game which in years past had always fallen flat with the Widow's bored children, but it was all new to Thad and now he was eagerly waiting to do his part. He squirmed impatiently.

"Look, Thad!" Judith gasped, pointing with exaggerated surprise. "Tonight a special lamp is lit!"

That was his cue. He scrambled to his feet and held up both hands with the thumbs carefully turned in.

"But there are eight lamps. Why do we light only one, today of all days?" he asked proudly, in his best, sing-song recital voice.

"Good boy!" Judith whispered loudly, and he wriggled, hoarsely whispering back, "Ssshh! Now the story!" and the Widow began.

"Child, this is the story. Come and hear what the Eternal did for His people!"

She held out her arms, and Thad dived into her lap, grinning in anticipation of the fun to come.

"Once, long, long ago, bad King Antiochus came to our Land. He killed our people, and tried to stop us serving God −"

"But! We! Wouldn't!" Judith and Thad finished triumphantly, with three sharp claps.

"He took Jerusalem, and spoiled our Temple and put out the Holy Lamp and said we must worship idols −"

"But! We! Wouldn't!"

"Brave old Mattathias and his sons tried to take back the temple −"

"But − they − couldn't …" they replied woefully, shaking their heads and softly tapping their breastbones.

"But did the Maccabees give up?" *No! They! Wouldn't! (the claps came back fiercely).* "For two years everyone prayed and fought and when anybody asked, 'Should we stop?' everyone shouted − *No! We! Shouldn't!* One cold winter they camped around Jerusalem and could anyone inside get out? *No! They! Couldn't!* When the enemy was feeble with hunger the Maccabees attacked *(warlike noises*

436

and much arm-waving). They saved the city and cleaned up the mess in the Temple! *(cheers).* Oh, where was the oil for the Holy Lamp? *Nearly All Gone! (more breastbeating).* But they lit it anyway, and did it go out? *No! It! Didn't! (cheers again).* A miracle from the Eternal! *(more cheers from the tiny chorus).* How many days did it last? One? *No!* Two? *No!* Three? *No!* Four? *No!* Five? *No!* Six? *No!* Seven?"

"No, no no! – EIGHT days," shouted Thad triumphantly, jumping off her lap and running around the room, thrilled to think that they would go through this exciting performance every night for the next seven days as they lit each new lamp.

Judith and Widow Shana exchanged expressive looks. Their ears were ringing from the shouts and the clapping, and there was another week of it yet! Patience! Children must be taught their heritage pleasurably, with love and diligence – that was a mother's job, and if there was no mother, there must be those who took her place.

"You remembered everything, Thad," the Widow said, catching him for a hug as he spun past. "Your *Abba* will be proud of you!"

"When is he coming home?"

"When we get to the eighth lamp, I promise!" she answered. "See, here is today's – can you count how many are left?"

No sooner was the boy asleep after supper, than the two women, who had worn an air of suppressed excitement about them all day, sprang into action. Judith crammed mint leaves into her mouth and chewed busily, while hurriedly washing her face, ears, neck and arms with a damp cloth. Meanwhile Shana combed the girl's hair with perfumed oil, urging her to check that her nails were clean, and there were no dirty spots on her gown. Finally Shana put her head cautiously out of the door and nodded – Rachel was nowhere in sight! – and the two of them took a light and slipped across the courtyard to the Widow's house, where they recklessly lit more lamps, not forgetting the symbolic one in the window for the Festival.

"Quickly, Judith, put this on. It is fitting that you cover your face."

"Oh, this is beautiful! May I really wear it?"

Over her smoothly combed hair went Widow Shana's finest veil which she had herself embroidered as a very young woman. Shana draped and folded it expertly back over the girl's face, pinning it securely in place. The bump and the slight crookedness of Judith's nose, the purple scar on her lip, her sallow cheeks – all were hidden, and Judith's whole face was now only a pair of dark eyes, suddenly beautiful and mysterious, glittering with excitement in the lamplight.

"I have assumed nothing, as you warned me. But do you really think he will still come?" she faltered nervously.

"*Pouf!* Is Herod a fox?" Shana replied airily, meanwhile thinking grimly, *If he doesn't, I'll have to find a new song to sing in a hurry!* She dug her nails into her palms at the thought. Anyone would have thought it was her own betrothal she was so agitated about.

There was a determined rapping at the door! The women's hearts pounded! Pray Heaven Eli had not come to say he'd changed his mind! That Thaddeus could have her after all!

"Oh, Shana! I feel sick!" Judith gasped, quailing, her eyes enormous with fear. "I think I'm going to faint!"

"If you do I'll stick your head in the cistern!" the Widow snapped ruthlessly, and snatched the door open. She rapidly rearranged her face and said sweetly, "*Shalom*, Dan, blessings and peace to you, young man! You come on a good day."

She was surprised, for she had thought Samuel might have come with his son, but Samuel, always quietly finding ways to further Dan's maturity, had already encouraged him to take the position of the prospective groom's man.

Dan replied in kind, and explained formally that he had come on behalf of his friend Eli ben Samuel, who craved an audience with the Widow and her charge Judith, in the absence of a father or brother who could speak for the young woman. He was feeling very important about his part and intended to do everything correctly. Eli was ushered in. Judith, with dropped eyes, greeted them humbly, washed their feet, and placed drops of rosemary-scented oil on their heads. Despite the calm ceremonial behaviour, there were four fast beating hearts, and four dry mouths in the room, though each one of them was sure he or she was the only one feeling so flustered. In a way it was true, as each had come with very different reasons for anxiety. Judith was afraid of ending up with Thaddeus after all, Dan was worried about forgetting his lines, Eli was agitatedly hoping youth would outweigh an older man's home and security, and Widow Shana was acutely aware that in a week's time she may have a very tricky interview with Thaddeus, depending on tonight's outcome!

It was over. It was done. The offer of marriage was made and accepted. The right words had been said on both sides with the correct demeanour. Dan raced to the door and flung it open, waving Loukanos' thumbs-up sign into the twilight. Lo and behold, there were Samuel and Ada and their other boys who had been lurking at Zack's, awaiting the signal! Now they poured through the door, bearing with them a tame notary captured in Magdala and enticed with promises of Festival feasting. The contract was written! Dan's entire household, which this week included Johanan and Asa, had all been let into the conspiracy that morning, and were hovering at Marta's with food at the ready. Now they basely left Ittai to settle the sleepy children and swept into Widow Shana's, swirling out again and collecting the rest of Banayim like flotsam in a stream until Judith and her young man were surrounded by the chattering hamlet who stood excitedly to bear witness. Nearly bursting with importance, Dan took Eli and Judith's hands and joined them together. He stepped back, just as Ittai managed to squeeze through the crowd to find his wife. The potter slipped his strong arm around her waist, and they smiled at each other affectionately. Five years ago, it had been their turn. It seemed a long time ago, and yet only yesterday. They watched the ceremony sentimentally.

Eli carefully pinned a mesh of three silver coins to the borrowed veil which trembled over Judith's glowing expression, and held the document aloft.

"Judith, daughter of the late Fisher Amram ben Kenaz and his wife Idra of Magdala, may they rest in peace – by this document you are betrothed to me, in accordance with the laws of Moses and of Israel."

"So be it," responded Judith obediently, and felt she could let out her breath at last! Oh that her parents were here to see this day! But their bones had lain deep in the grey Sea behind them for so many years that the tears in her eyes were fleeting.

"Amen," agreed Samuel and Ada, and "We are witnesses!" answered Banayim, and the noise broke out at once – the clapping, the kissing, the laughter, the competition of who had seen this coming first.

Dan was momentarily tripped up by memories. It was the second time he had witnessed such a contract of betrothal. He met Anna's eyes steadily and she smiled at him.

Yes, Dan, she wanted to say. *I do remember that day. But I no longer spoil it with sorrow. Joy must not be forgotten.*

Old Zack and three of the men suddenly disappeared into his dusty, cavernous workshop which also served him as a storeroom, where the glow of a lamp wobbled for a while through the half open door. There was some chuckling and groaning and more chuckling, and let it only be said that nobody could get any eggs out of Hanoch for a week – while Zaccheus grew positively bilious with them. Now the Festival became even more festive – torches were lit and flared drunkenly, defying the cold in the dark street. Children crept out of their beds at the adult noise and laughter, the instruments came down from hooks and shelves again, the feet began to tap, the hands to clap, congratulations and merriment were flying everywhere. Now that the solemn part was over, Dan strutted about, proud of his part in the whole thing, and Samuel and Ada smiled damply as they warmly kissed the tremulous girl, knowing their family would never be quite the same again.

"Mind you make him happy!" Ada warned her, only half in fun. Vastly relieved, Eli couldn't stop smiling and laughing. He positively soaked up the jokes and the mock-punches and the rude asides of the married men, beaming so broadly that the light in the street almost seemed to come from his shining face.

As she was hugged and kissed and fluttered over – even by the Dabab, who kindly hoped she would remember this happy day to help her through the *many* sour patches of marriage! – Judith could hardly believe that she had risen from abject misery, through so much pain, to triumphant joy in less than a year. The spectre of exhausted poverty and loneliness which had loomed in far flung years ahead had vanished like a wraith. She had a family now! She would be married! She would have a home! And a strong, good, *young* husband, a shepherd with prospects, with friendly

441

and generous parents who did not reproach her poverty, her plainness, her insignificance. And he even loved her! Praise the Eternal! Surely, surely, in taking on this lifelong bond, she had been made free! She began to cry with sheer relief.

The celebrations grew noisier, as Zack brought out his wine, and the women brought out more delicious dishes, whispering to each other that despite it all being such a surprise, how *sensible* to have a betrothal at Festival time, with so much food already prepared! Johanan thought so too and helped enthusiastically. Loukanos began to teach an odd little dance which nobody knew but he and Anna, and they were demonstrating it to gales of laughter and stumbling feet as everyone tried to follow. Busily exchanging their own favourite betrothal stories, Widow Shana and Rachel were trotting back down the street to check on Thad and fetch more cups, when suddenly into the light who should step out of the scrub but – Thaddeus! – weary, hungry and muddy from travelling, but with an expectant look in his eye.

"Mercy on us!" gasped Rachel in fright. "What are you doing home already?"

"Why, Thaddeus! We didn't expect you till the eighth day!" stammered Widow Shana.

"So I see," he answered, surprised. "My master released a few of us early for the Festival. But this is unusual gaiety – even for the Lights. What is it? A wedding? Whose – Old Zack's?" he laughed.

Shana drew him away quickly. "No, no! No wedding ..." she murmured evasively and perhaps less than truthfully, for a betrothal was just as binding, "... only some extra visitors. But what man wants to listen to women's chatter when he is hungry! Here, my friend, you must be very tired, and quite famished – and eager to see your son. Come in and I will give you a bite to eat while you put down your bundle, wash your feet, and kiss your boy. After that you will be refreshed – and must join everyone in the feast. Loukanos is here, you know. Asa and Johanan too, from Cana. They will all be so glad to see you."

She motioned pleadingly over her shoulder to Rachel, into whose eyes suddenly shot a ray of dawning comprehension. With a cackle of glee, she hurried back up the street to join the crowd and called loudly, "Now, friends, music to go with this new dance! Huldah and Tirzah – you must sing with your mother!"

The little girls protested, the adults laughed and coaxed, and nobody had even noticed the little scene down the dark end of the street.

Oh, what *did* Widow Shana say to Thaddeus! For years afterwards it was fiercely debated in Banayim! What words she used she never told and nor did he, and neither did his son who turned as he woke and held up his hands to her, and snuggled peacefully into her familiar arms. As she gently passed him to his father, surely the boy heard something! But how could anyone expect a sleepy child to remember?

Exquisitely curious as they were, Banayim did not need to know and never did. All it knew was that hard-working Thaddeus had come home as promised, ready and willing to take Judith to wife, not even knowing he had a rival – only to find her snatched away from him at the eleventh hour! But he came out of his house almost with a look of relief. He had his sleepy boy draped easily over his shoulder like a little lamb, and beside him the Widow Shana walked with eyes modestly downcast – could it have been to hide an exultant gleam? Ah, such patience, such cunning, such sense, and such understanding – surely her reward was just!

Into the suddenly-silent crowd they walked, everyone exchanging looks which were almost guilty. Eli clenched his fists nervously, Judith drew an apprehensive breath – the four gamblers looked at each other uncertainly. Anna gave Loukanos an urgent push, and he stepped forward instantly.

"Welcome home, Thaddeus, my friend," he said genially, while the village held its breath. "You come on a day of gladness for Banayim, and I beseech you to open your heart and be generous in disappointment. Rejoice with us, brother, for the debt you so honourably planned to discharge has been paid in full by another."

"Yes," Thaddeus replied evenly. "I have just been told of it."

There was a general buzz of amazement, with just the faintest note of disappointment. What? No anger? No ravings? No punches?

Thaddeus held up his free hand for quiet. "Is the notary still here?" he demanded.

Silence! Would he attempt to declare the contract invalid – if that was even possible? Thrilled to her marrow, Rachel piped up, "Yes, he's still here!" She flapped her hands frantically at Malachi who detached the man from Zack's wineskin and hustled him forward.

The little notary was much happier now than when he had arrived. In fact, after the friendliness, food and drink which had been pressed on him from all sides, he was very happy indeed.

"Yes! Yes! I'm here … Ha ha! Greetings, blessings and peace to you, and all yours, my friend. *Hup!* Excuse me. Ha ha! Now, what can I do for you? Another betrothal? Ha ha! *Hup!* Ez'cuse me again."

Thaddeus stood sleepy little Thad on his feet and straightened up suddenly. "Yes!" he replied boldly, and everyone gasped. "Take

444

your pen and write! When the almond blossoms, the kind and loving woman who stands beside me will become my wife, and the mother of my son."

More gasps! Then sheer Babel broke out! Loukanos put his head down and began to shake silently until Anna dragged him away and told him to behave himself. Hugging his aching ribs, he looked up at her impishly, eyes streaming with tears of laughter.

"Well caught!" he choked delightedly. "Oh, well caught indeed!"

Around them clattered rapid tongues almost tripping over themselves with excitement and disbelief as people clustered together, puzzling it out, arguing over who could see it coming and who couldn't – well, the fact was, nobody could have, and all but Rachel had the grace to admit it. Thaddeus had created a sensation in the street by his violence months ago, and then another sensation when he was cured – and now here he was creating yet *another*, almost as marvellous. Incredulous laughter was everywhere, but it was all good-natured, even on Rachel's part. To tell the truth, she was breathtaken at the Widow's audacity, and full of admiration. She didn't think Shana had it in her! Well, Thaddeus might be nearly fifteen years younger than the Widow, but who cared? He had one son, and did not need more, and he never wanted another love to replace that of his cherished Naami. All he wanted was his occupation, his boy, his home and a welcome to return to. Now this would be provided by a capable, generous woman who would look after them all, without ever whining that he was never home to discipline his son, or that she was lonely, or that her life was hard compared to more fortunate friends.

Again a parchment was written with solemn words of promise. Again two hands were joined by the friends who were also their family, the document held aloft as a man made his vow, and a woman affirmed, "So be it" and a massed chorus went up happily,

445

"We are witnesses!" A slender chain of coins which had once graced a smooth young forehead was now laid across a furrowed brow, but it was a matter of form which offended nobody. Shana brought to Thaddeus a dowry which was worth far more than this symbol. Even aside from her house, and her ability to support herself frugally, she brought the riches of her maturity and experience which were unseen, yet understood by all.

Was ever such a winter's night in Banayim! How they laughed and sang and danced and ignored the cold, and not even the mist could dampen their spirits.

Dan and Johanan snatched at Huldah and fat little Tirzah, who had been drinking in all the details. There was no doubt but that playing at *Betrothals* and soon afterwards, *Weddings,* would supplant their previous favourite of *Funerals* for a long while to come.

"Come on girls, come on everyone! Let's dance The Victory!"

"How appropriate that is!" Anna laughed to her father, following him into posiition, leaving poor Loukanos to dance with Rachel because Malachi pretended he had the bone-ache!

The exultant Widow – her pardon! – the exultant *Bride* (for so she was considered from this day) once more lost her hold on propriety, and abandoned her demure poses, dragging a laughing Thaddeus into the circle, throwing up her head and ululating so joyously that all the women and girls joined in, until the men were half-deafened, and the noise could be heard halfway to Magdala and way across the black, choppy lake.

So The Victory was danced, and danced again, and this week of Lights looked fair to outshine any other in the village's memory. Meanwhile, over in Pella, comfortable Uncle Joseph, no longer quite so comfortable, was struggling for a victory of quite a different kind, and continued to do so for many more weeks.

446

Chapter Forty-two

THE snow on the high grounds had been washed away but in the far blue northern distance, aloof, hoary-headed Hermon remained as firmly wrapped as ever in his dazzling prayer shawl, while closer to the west Mount Carmel spread her deep green skirts under trailing scarves of mist, and closer still, all the subordinate hills of the Jordan Valley clustered like imitative bridesmaids, their delicate leafy veils decked out with the snows of almond blossom. It was a heart-lifting sight, but wasted on Joseph of Salamis, who had been staring only at the winding road far below him. It was well trodden, enabling fastidious Jews to travel all the way from Judea to Galilee and back on the east bank, thus relieving them of the distasteful alternative of the western route through 'unclean' Samaria. The great Roman spider kept its web in good repair, and even now a knot of road menders could be spied at work, and the faint, far-away chinking of their hammers floated up to Joseph's ears. A reliable route to major trade centres, the road was a corridor to many places – *and how swiftly it would take me to Seleucia and a ship to my beautiful Island!* So Joseph's wistful thoughts drifted idly, and thinking of Cyprus had his mind wandering naturally to Salamis and his little kingdom there – the estates, the grounds over which he had been sole ruler and lord, the workers who looked up to him for fatherly comfort.

He wondered how his life might have turned out had he taken up his Levitical heritage, lived in Jerusalem and become a Priest, learning the Law and Temple services instead of business. Then he could have ruled more than lands, more than a handful of grateful hearts – he could have been a spiritual leader as well, which might have earned him great merit. As the prophet Malachi declared, *'The priests' lips should hold knowledge, and the people should seek the law at his mouth, as the messenger of the Eternal!'* An honourable position, no doubt, but hard and often dirty physical work – all that butchering of animals and cutting up carcases ... and to be rigidly tied, his service no longer a free gift, but an obligation, a strict duty regimented by the calendar on every hand? No, it was far better this way, and his solitary life was his own. Perhaps too much his own, at times ...

His sigh changed to a little smile as he cheered himself with the thought of all his charitable arrangements for that night, the start of the Feast of Casting of Lots. More simply referred to as *Purim*, this celebration of national deliverance by the girl-queen Esther and her uncle Mordecai of old, was not a religious festival, and though commemorated in noisily enthusiastic synagogue services, there were no strict obligations; nothing but fun and laughter, eating and drinking, and giving of gifts all round. Children of the city's beggars and poorest families had been invited to Joseph's beautiful home for a party, and it would be held under the large portico so there was no need to be concerned about dirt and smells or damage in the house. His servants even had instructions to provide lavers and wash the children's faces, hands and feet as they came in. It was a stunningly hospitable gesture for such youthful riff-raff – it would make them feel like royalty, give them a rare taste of respect, and touch their hearts.

It was customary to abstain from food the previous day, in recognition of the Queen's fast before she begged the Persian King to foil the plot of his Grand Vizier to kill the Jews; and Joseph's capacious stomach was growling a protest. However, he reminded himself that these children of poverty had little choice – most of them were hungry every day of their lives. Tonight, when the new day began, all of them for once would be able to eat their fill, and even to dress up to play just as the wealthier children did. Sporting new black felted caps, some boys would be evil Haman, casting lots to determine the best time to kill the Jews, some would be the righteous Mordecai in striped linen sashes, and all the little girls would be given pretty kerchiefs either to veil themselves with, as modest Queen Esther, or wave imperiously, as disobedient Queen Vashti. Joseph himself was going to dress up as King Ahasuerus, and tell the story as he was wont to do each year in Salamis with the children of his workers. How he loved watching their excited faces receiving the gifts, and stuffing themselves full of delicious sweetmeats for at least this once in a year.

And what a hilarious time they had as he would tell the story. Every time he mentioned Haman the children would stamp and hiss and roar, "Cursed be Haman!" and every time Mordecai was mentioned, there would be cheers and applause and shouts of, "Blessed be Mordecai!" He smiled again as he thought of the pleasure they would all share tonight – he knew that the children and their families were tingling with excitement at the rare and novel prospect of such generosity to those who had nothing. But even as he warmed and filled himself with this anticipation, he had not ceased to study the stony highway far below.

At last, he saw what he was looking for – what he had been waiting for ever since he heard that the man he wanted would be passing through – there it was, emerging from the last twist in the road, a dark cluster trickling southwards and about to enter Pella. Immediately Joseph left his high vantage point and headed down the steep path towards the city centre. He should get there at just the right time if he walked briskly. He did so now, without effort. He was not as breathless, or as plump, as he had been when he first came to this place. Climbing up and down hills kept a man fit, and he never went to enjoy the warm spring waters of the public baths without feeling compelled to make a detour to the lofty spot where he could watch that road. As he reached the town a sudden moment's panic clutched his heart – he must be there quickly enough to get to the head of the crowd! – and almost he felt as if someone had elongated the distance on purpose to frustrate him. Striding with increasing pace through the colonnaded streets, he saw people already gathering in the open market place ahead, and his heart beat faster. He began to hurry even more, until he was actually running.

For the last few months Joseph had been wrestling with a sense of dissatisfaction which felt disturbingly like disloyalty – and he was alarmed by his failure to overcome it. For many weeks he had vainly manoeuvred his anxiety through an internal battlefield, seeking the victory of an answer which would quieten his fears. He tried to soothe his conscience by more spiritual devotion – prayer, reading, good works, synagogue attendance – but the vague sense persisted that the Eternal, or the Messiah, or both, had somehow let him down. In the past, he had upon many occasions paid close attention to the Teacher's discourses, and he had never yet picked up that key, elusive phrase; and no matter how deeply he dived into the sea of new ideas, and prised open its gritty shells eagerly one by one, he had not found that single priceless pearl which would outweigh all other gems – *the secret to securing eternal life*. Where was it, the mystery which the Messiah had surely come to reveal? Why preach for so long, yet omit the most vital thing? Could he be waiting until he had greater acceptance from the spiritual leaders, first? No, it was not likely.

Of course, there was a burning directness in the Nazarene's manner which blistered the skins of the religious hierarchy – but such was not new. Had not the prophet Samuel thundered plainly at hapless King Saul, *'Obedience is better than offering sacrifices!'*? The Baptiser had been equally forceful in demanding respect for the spirit of the Law. The Doctors of the Law might be enraged, but Joseph did not find the clarity of the Nazarene's teachings as novel, or as shocking as did many other rich men such as openly worldly Sadducees, or secretly worldly Pharisees (whether they had wealth or merely coveted it.) Cypriot Joseph may have spent most of his life outside the Land, but he had never been one for the hypocrisy of cleansing rituals which masked unclean thoughts. He had never been a man who accepted contradiction and confusion between belief and action, and he certainly did not subscribe to the Pharisaic thinking which held that a man's private thoughts were his own affair as long as he kept the traditions of the elders.

Joseph honestly rejoiced that the Son of the Most High pointed an accurate finger of accusation at such spiritual flaws, and required rather that a man act from his heart; and he thirstily drank in the lessons and the admonitions which came from the mind so close to the Eternal. Yes, he understood a great deal more now than he ever had – but where were the safeguards and assurances and guarantees? Since the beginning, all Divine dealings with men were bounded by laws and promises, by warnings and rewards, and recompense of both good and evil. Where were the *promises?* Naturally he realised the importance of invoking the spirit of the Law, but – as Dan had asked Johanan – what did you *do* with the letter? How did you measure merit, or chart your course in a trackless ocean? He could only conclude that it must be by doing as much of the letter as possible, *and* doing it with the right spirit.

Thus Joseph of Salamis continued as he had always done – he prayed and read and observed his rituals with care and thoughtfulness, conducted his business diligently and honourably, murmured kindly to beggars, visited the poor, comforted the afflicted, gave alms in private as well as in the street, shared all the rejoicings and sorrows of his acquaintances, in synagogue spoke humbly and wisely to young and old, and every night escaped to his comfortable home to give thanks for the prosperity which enabled him so easily to be generous.

There he wrote crisp decisive business letters to his bankers, and long directives to his steward Linus, amusing missives to Anna about life in Pella, reassurances to Mari and Asa about his welfare, and well-meant exhortations to Loukanos to keep following the way that the Teacher had set; though he was uneasily aware that even apart from his own disquiet, he was at a frustrating loss to know how to encourage a non-Jewish believer. If Louki was not a Jew, what forms or rituals could he, or should he adopt? Outside the Law how could he worship – in a kind of primitive manner without rules to gauge himself by? How did Loukanos atone for sins committed since baptism, how did he accumulate the merit which led to Sonship with God? Once Joseph even took up his pen to ask Mordecai's opinion, but the ink dried on the poised reed's neatly cut nib – and he laid it down in defeat. Why was he agitating himself over Louki's position when he felt increasingly disturbed about his own?

Unlike many, he was not disillusioned with the lack of tangible preparation for restoring Israel's rightful Kingdom, but he was restless – confused as to why the Nazarene, the Teacher, the Son of the Highest, had given his followers so little to grasp hold of that was *measurable*. And so Cypriot Joseph – homesick Joseph – determined upon three things. One, that he could not stay in Pella forever; Two, that he must not return to his beloved island without the answer; and Three, that the answer could only come from the Teacher himself. Joseph would patiently continue good works in Pella, but if the Nazarene did not come near the city before Passover, it would be time to take to the road in search of him.

And so he had listened to the talk in the streets and the market places and the synagogues, and he had stalked up to the highest places to watch the road, and now the moment had come at last. Joseph did not preen himself with vain ideas that the Teacher would remember his face out of the thousands in Israel, or that a loose association with disciples in the past would grant him an audience or give him any preference. He would have to come before him just as any other supplicant. Well, so be it, but now the crowd in the Pella market was thick and selfish and with Joseph's chance for enlightenment being swallowed up before his anxious eyes – for once, the crippled and the curious, the sick and the sceptical alike would find that he could behave like the rest of them if he had to!

And this was how it came about that the large richly dressed man who hid his baldness under beautiful turbans and conducted himself with the utmost urbanity, on this day of opportunity became almost a man possessed – panting with increasingly grim determination – pushing, shoving, struggling – forcing himself through the crowd – ignoring the petitioning hands, the indignant looks, the muttered wrath – oblivious to all but the lean-muscled, spare figure speaking in clear, carrying tones in the midst ... a man with an air of great stillness about him despite the restive throng, a man with compassionate, care-furrowed eyes, and

453

sensitive lips in a sooty beard. It was still a young man's beard, only lightly brushing the strong cheekbones, thickest around the firm jaw of the keenly intelligent face, but like his hair, the short black waves were already well threaded with silver – and there were sleepless shadows smudged around the clear dark eyes, a waxy pallor beneath the drawn, deep olive skin.

Had one of his own servants betrayed such signs of mental strain and physical exhaustion, compassionate Joseph of Salamis would have noticed instantly, but in the passion of his own need, he was curiously blind to them now in the man he longed to serve faithfully, and of whom he had such a weighty thing to ask. The answer could change his whole life! Could *give* him life! So as he fixed the Teacher with his desperate eye, he did not see a man, but a prescription.

Ahead of him, the Nazarene was turning his back, was already moving on his way, was being swallowed up once more – Joseph ploughed his way frantically – he must not lost this chance!

"Teacher!" he shouted in the voice usually reserved to be heard across whole vineyards, and those he was elbowing so recklessly shrank away in shock. "My lord! Stop!" He stumbled forward, losing his turban – staggered on – threw himself into the path of the Nazarene – and dropped, gasping, to his knees. There was a ripple of laughter as someone obligingly tossed out from the crowd the dislodged turban, which landed in the dirt beside him. Joseph snatched it up and jammed it on his balding head without even glancing at it. Smeared mud obscured the rich brocade, and there was a tail of fabric flapping down in front of one ear.

The Teacher had stopped – a warm smile flitted over his weary face.

454

"Teacher! Wait, please wait! Your pardon! Good Teacher!" Joseph panted, his mouth dry. "Please tell me plainly! What good thing will ensure me Sonship with the Eternal? What is it that I must do to gain His inheritance of eternal life?"

The smile faded. Jeshua squatted beside Joseph and looked at him seriously. "Why are you calling me *Good Teacher*?" he asked quietly. "Why do you ask about what *Good* thing *you* can do? There *is* nothing Good in men – only in the Eternal One Who is Goodness itself, and its only source."

Joseph looked confused. Jeshua sighed and stood up, motioning to him to do the same.

"You know what Moses says – that if you want life, you must keep the commandments. Do not commit murder, adultery, theft, perjury, fraud – honour your parents, love your neighbour like yourself."

"Yes, my lord!" Joseph replied humbly, scrambling to his feet. "And I have done this ever since childhood. I have heeded Moses all my life, keeping the commandments in spirit *and* letter – but now that you have come, the Anointed of God, the Chosen One, I know there must be something more! What is it? What am I missing? What else must I do to secure my salvation?"

"Ah!" The smile was back, just faintly. "Yes, there is one thing."

"Oh, my lord, thank you! Thank you! I knew there must be! Please – tell me, I beseech you!"

Jeshua looked him straight in the eye.

"Eternal life is not a business transaction. Shed all that keeps you safe, and learn to trust in that Goodness of God, which is not of yourself. Just as Esther and Mordecai did."

"I – beg your pardon, my lord …?"

"Sell everything you possess. All of it. Give it to the poor. Wherever your treasure is, your heart is tethered. So exchange that earthly wealth for heavenly riches and be secured from above, not below. That is true faith, my friend. Then you will be free – to join me."

He put out his firm, warm hands and grasped the cold, sweating fingers of Cypriot Joseph, who trembled mightily.

"Join – *you*?"

Join the Son of the Most High? Out of all these people? Like one of the Twelve – actually *asked* to follow Jeshua as master and lord? Oh, what an honour! To be judged so worthy! But … what about …? Oh, surely …

Joseph looked around wildly, seeing nothing. Give it away. *All* of it. Not just a part. Not just half. Not just most. Sell *every* thing. Give away almost a king's ransom! Surely Esther and Mordecai still kept their wealth and positions? But without *any*thing … what then? No more estates, no more private kingdom, no more wealth, no more security. No more helping his family. No more bestowing gifts on the poor. No more organised charities. No more quiet miracles worked with money, no more freedom. No more thankful words and grateful tears, no more easing of his own distress when faced with those suffering pain and injustice.

"How much do you really care?" the quiet whisper came. "Enough to take their place?"

The steady eyes burned into his. Joseph's chest was in a vice – he was suffocating. All he had done! All he had! All he could do with it! His whole world shifted under him like quicksand! The universe whirled! Could he do this? Should he? Was it right? Was it responsible? It was the word of the Son of God! But – even so …

The warm hands holding his, squeezed gently in silent encouragement. His throat was so tight he could not speak – he looked desperately and imploringly at the man from whom he had so eagerly sought the answer of years – and with a great choking sob he dragged away his hands, covered his face – and fled.

The people parted silently to let him through. How had the mighty fallen! Benevolent Joseph of Salamis had lost face today, and they were sorry.

As the shattered man ran home to begin scraping belongings together for his escape back to Cyprus, Jeshua watched him for a moment – could it be, lovingly? – and his eyes filled. He looked around at his stunned disciples.

"Entering the realm of heaven is not easy for a rich man. It costs him far too much."

Even before the indignant, lengthy discussion that this provoked was finished with, Cypriot Joseph had already flung out his orders and was being jogged in a closed litter northward along the very road he had watched so eagerly, only a few hours ago. And in only a few hours more, the glorious fun that was *Purim* would be celebrated in the elegant home without him. The party would be his final benefit, and as soon as it was over the house would be stripped bare, and the Sadducee in Jerusalem who owned it would rent it to the next rich man who was looking for a desirable residence in a good area, with cool fresh summer air or his money back.

The generous man who so freely gave to those who had nothing to give back but gratitude, did not comprehend that Sonship with the Eternal was a similar free exchange of loving gifts. All the while he had striven so earnestly for an inheritance guaranteed through obedience and righteousness, he had forgotten that the Master of the Universe, who might extract slavish obedience from any man, chose not to compel but instead to invite faith. Deliberately to give up his security was something Joseph could not imagine, but without helplessness, how would he learn dependence?

Perhaps later he would see what Jeshua had shown him – that the joyful trust of one who chose to be powerless of himself, was a priceless gift – the only true gift any man could dare to offer his Creator. For such who held up faithful, empty hands in grateful humility, would the Almighty God ratify his inheritance and bestow His gift of Sonship, which alone would lead to righteousness, and eternal life. Cypriot Joseph did not yet realise that he had it the wrong way around. All he realised at this moment was humiliation, grief, rejection, fear and panic.

He had no intention of detouring so far out of his way as Banayim, or Cana, for his shattered confidence to be picked over by his family, and so he went straight to Antioch, taking a berth on the first passage out to Cyprus from Port Seleucia, and did not write to them until it was almost Pentecost. He could hardly believe it of himself, but in his most wretched moments he was miserably aware that he was now doing exactly the same as Loukanos before him – running away.

Chapter Forty-three

NOBODY in Banayim could have had any idea of what had just happened to the wise, kind, self-assured and benevolent man they all called Uncle. Pella was miles away on the other side of the Jordan, and it would take time for any news to travel. All they knew was that it was the *Purim* holiday at last and everyone was happy to the point of silliness – which at this time of year was positively encouraged. Almond blossom was everywhere, whirling like snowflakes in the fresh gusts which blew off the Sea, and the tiny petals danced gaily wherever you looked. The heavy rains were over, and green shoots were flush in the fields, limes were ripening in the orchards, the baby-talk of turtledoves murmured in the air, and the optimism of Spring abounded.

In the tiny village by the Sea, the holiday was only part of the reason to celebrate, because true to his word, Thaddeus was marrying the Widow – with as much ceremony as if she had been a bride of fourteen. The affectionate looks exchanged by the oddly-matched pair no longer astonished anyone. Shana herself had seemed to grow younger by the day, and Thaddeus looked positively smug to have landed a capable woman who had some very modest means of her own; who had grown genuinely fond of the now-cheerful boy she had once called a bad-tempered fat little menace; and who would not be likely to overwhelm her comparatively youthful husband with family additions to drain the uncertain income of a hireling shepherd.

Little Thad had indeed flourished under her care, and so had Judith. With Shana already assuming so maternal a role of them both, Judith had turned her attention to learning from her as much as she could about managing a home carefully and faithfully, instead of in the undisciplined, slipshod manner which was all she had achieved in the past. Come the next *Chanukah*, it would be *her* turn to be wed, and meanwhile, she had a lot to absorb.

When Shana was married, they had agreed, she and Judith would literally exchange places across the courtyard. Judith was ecstatic – she would not have to leave Banayim or her motherly new ally before her own wedding, and until then she could housekeep at Shana's all by herself with Banayim supporting its resident orphan as befitted a God-fearing community.

Judith knew she would miss Shana's kindly advice and ready ear once she joined Eli's family – but she would worry about that when it happened. Perhaps Eli might even be gradually persuaded to live in Banayim ... but that would depend on how the in-laws saw it, of course ... well, it was good to have things to dream about! Judith tinkled the coins on her headdress with a happy shake of her head, and got back to work.

"Amma Shana! How do you make that fish soup? I've forgotten whether you said use the heads or the tails ... and do I have to scale them first or not?"

A visitor to the village might have been extremely puzzled to hear the Widow being addressed as 'Amma Shana' by the young woman and the little boy, both before and after the marriage, but it pleased all who heard it especially Thaddeus on his rare visits. It was dawning on him that little Thad was already finding in

460

mature Shana far more of a mother than young Judith could ever have been, and so Thaddeus was a thankful man. It was going to take time before people stopped calling Shana 'the Widow', but everyone knew her sons would always be prepared to remind her, long after she had forgotten it herself. Nobody, not even Shana herself, was sorry that they had refused to come to the wedding, even if it *was* deemed the darkest social insult a person could give, short of a slap in the face.

"It would be hypocritical to be insulted," their mother said resolutely, "when I am profoundly relieved to hear it. Now we can enjoy ourselves without having the milk turned sour by their looks. One day perhaps they'll be happier themselves, and then they won't grudge it in others."

Since her own house was practically on top of her prospective husband's, Shana and her attendants at Anna's insistence were installed in the Travellers' House early in the day, and great preparations went on within, with much scurrying, laughter and giggling. Everyone contributed to the feast – two of Hanoch's chickens accompanying Malachi's vegetables in the stewpot just as closely as they had in the garden – then with a great many preparatory washings and combings, the villagers pulled out their best clothes and decked themselves in finery to honour the occasion. Marta shook out the heavily embroidered festive dress (so rashly made with tightly bound seams) which nearly four years ago she had hastily let out and prinked up ready for Anna's wedding. Mercifully it still fitted, and she had resisted the temptation to make it over for Abigail. A busy mother with limited means had little hope of ever having another, and it would have been a disgrace to attend a wedding in everyday garments.

Since the fishermen had moved on, the village had shrunk to a mere handful of neighbours with no common occupation but their quiet existence, enlivened only by the Festivals. But today there was a Feast – *Purim* at that, the most fun of all! – *and* a Wedding. Never had the central street of Banayim and its tiny alleys seen such a display of embroidery, of fringing, of tinkling ornaments and shining bracelets, of colourful sashes and soft veils, of spring flowers, and fresh palm leaves. Baskets and boxes and secret places alike were plundered of their rare and special treasures, and such a lot of perfuming and oiling went on that Old Zack got the sneezes. But mothers cast approving eyes over daughters and smiled proudly at the activity in the street. Yes indeed! Today, drab little Banayim looked as gay and prosperous as Magdala on a high market day.

Three days before the wedding, Anna and Marta sent Ittai to Magdala for fresh limes while they patiently pounded and sifted and ground dried henna leaves in one of his sturdy little pestles. Once the lime juice had been stirred in to create the paste and fix the colour, they spent the whole day while the mixture rested, in pestering Loukanos to help them, reminding him that as a physician, he had inspected many ladies' hands and feet without scandal, and that as an artist, he had the skill. Eventually, rolling his eyes and warning them sarcastically to keep an eye out for frowning Pharisees, Loukanos consented to defy convention *("only if you promise not to tell anyone else!")* and use his artistry to apply the paste to the Widow's plump hands and feet. So thrilled was she that she sat rigid for nearly the whole day while it took, lest she spoil the beautiful red brown patterns. When the crumbling paste was finally scraped and washed off, the result may not have caused any henna artist in Jerusalem to hang up her tools in despairing homage, but Loukanos was privately quite proud of it, and so were Shana and her bridesmaids.

Dan had a fleeting, unworthy thought that it was just as well Uncle Louki stuck to a neat design of swirls and dots, and did not attempt to recreate anything realistic, like a picture of pomegranate, for instance. Meanwhile, Banayim's younger bride-in-waiting ran errands dutifully, excited to think that before another year was out, it would be her turn for all this glory. She was almost glad Eli and Samuel were stuck out in the field lest the novelty and impact of her own wedding be dimmed, but there was no chance of them being present today since Caleb and Dan were here to support Thaddeus. However, Ada had come, treating Judith with a pleasantness rare among prospective mothers-in-law with eldest sons, so that was something to be grateful for.

The day's fun and bustle kept the minds of the more dedicated off the emptiness in their fasting stomachs, but strictly to observe the custom in the midst of so much cooking and preparing of food would have been more than flesh and blood could bear, and much surreptitious nibbling took place. Even Rachel said little about this clear breach of etiquette except to sniff to her husband (caught munching a pistachio-stuffed date ball), "All the more sweet, no doubt, for being *bread eaten in secret*, as the Wise Man says!" Fortunately for the peace of the day, Malachi's mouth was too full for his retort to find utterance. Instead he comforted himself mightily with the daring thought of replying (with meek yet cutting expression), *"Well, my dear, you ought to know."* And indeed she ought, for not only was this a fair comment on the Dabab's scandal-mongering, but she had quietly eaten two of those date balls herself while she was preparing them.

At sunset there was a shout of, "The Bridegroom comes!" and lo, a well-scrubbed Thaddeus appeared, resplendent in a bright striped robe made gorgeous with an ancient beaded girdle – on loan from Old Zack, who mumbled that he had last worn it maybe fifty years ago on a special occasion ... which he refused to name, thus provoking a gratifying amount of wild speculation thereafter. Around the bridegroom's muscular neck (more accustomed to being draped with kids or lambs), hung a creamy garland of heavily perfumed spring lilies, cloaking the pervading wool-fat odour which usually clung to his garments. Ceremoniously he marched up the street to the Travellers' House, with Loukanos, Dan, Johanan, Caleb and Old Zack in noisy attendance. There they collected a dazzlingly arrayed Shana and her bridesmaids – Anna and Judith with little Huldah, Tirzah and Abigail, who trotted out proudly with their lamps. Of course, the tiny girls were far too young for the job, but then Anna, Caleb and Old Zack were really far too old (and so was the bride) – and nobody cared. They were determined to have a wedding with all the trimmings, *and* they combined it with *Purim* without turning a hair – which was unorthodox but a great success. Banayim had always done things its own way, after all.

With laughter and songs the whole village joined the procession back to Thaddeus' house, its doors and windows open wide so that all who could not cram inside might press themselves close and hear as much as possible. It was not every day there was a wedding, still less with such as Asa from Jerusalem conducting the ceremonies, and nobody wanted to miss out. So the prayers were made, the holy writ recited, the vows confirmed and blessings pronounced, the affirmations witnessed, the heavy veil lifted, the contract put in Shana's henna'd hands, and the marriage cup solemnly drunk ... and now the psalms of praise rang forth, the dancing began, and gifts tumbled out of every hiding place. *Purim* gifts for all, not just for the nuptial pair – what a double celebration!

Out came the food, out came the wine, the instruments – pipes, cymbals, Dan's tattered drumskin, the gourds of seed which shook out the beat. They sang every wedding song they could think of,

464

and then made up some of their own. The children reminded them – It's *Purim! Purim!* Where's Haman? Where's Mordecai? Esther, and Ahasuerus? Why of course, the bride and groom were the Queen and the King! Rachel took the part of Vashti, with a glint in her eye. Caleb consented to be Haman, to be booed and hissed and jeered, enjoying it as much as anybody. And tall dark Loukanos was shoved to the fore to be cheered boisterously as the hero Mordecai.

So the *Purim* play became part of the wedding entertainment, and everyone shouted themselves hoarse, applauded till their hands hurt – played jokes on each other, ate too much, drank perhaps a little more than necessary ("Encouraged at *Purim* by some of the best Rabbis," Old Zack solemnly assured Loukanos), and danced themselves breathless. Rachel laughed so much she got a stitch in her side and thought she was having a stroke like Nabal of old, and while gasping in vain for Loukanos, anxiously promised the Eternal to mend her gossiping ways – until Asa hilariously made her drink from the wrong side of her cup and her resolution somehow faded away with the stitch.

Once the new bride and groom had been tactfully shut in their chamber, the wedding guests, who had filled the house, courtyard, and half the street, became increasingly noisy, until the singing and dancing shook the shutters. Straight-backed Etta outdanced most of the younger women and when she and Dan energetically danced The Victory together, both glowed with the knowledge of just how great a victory she had been blessed with.

Finally the laughter and hubbub dwindled, children slept where they dropped, and Malachi and Hanoch were arguing as dreamily as if talking under water. When chief bridesmaid Anna discovered Loukanos sitting bolt upright in a corner with a full cup in his hand, not spilling a drop but nevertheless fast asleep, she decreed

465

that the party was over. She was relieved to have made it through the affair without being accidentally compromised by any stray raisin, vine leaf, vinegar or splash of wine. Everyone drifted off happily to bed, supposedly to sleep, but there was a lot of drowsy chattering for a long time. What a wonderful start to *Purim!* What a wonderful outcome all round! What a wonderful year it had been! What wonderful things might happen next? Praise the Eternal, and now let's plan for Passover next month!

Dan and Johanan made many such plans. It was to be Dan's very first Jerusalem *Pesach*. He was of age now, both in Caesar's eyes, and the eyes of the law, and it was high time he went. So Loukanos declared, Asa and Anna agreeing. Besides, Loukanos had also determined to take the entire family – and in this, he included Mordecai and of course, Etta. It was a thrilling prospect, but sad too, as they all knew that a family Passover in Jerusalem was to be Louki's parting gift, before he left the Land and took up the task he had set himself – to bear witness back in his homeland, of Jeshua the Messiah, the Son of the Most High God. In all the heady excitement of that week, nobody really thought much about Uncle Joseph, unless to imagine that no doubt he was having an exuberant Purim in Pella, loved and respected by everyone.

As Joseph made a lonely escape north towards his island refuge, the man who had so painfully prised open his heart was on a lonely journey south. He was not fleeing, but steadfastly setting his face to Jerusalem. He was not alone, for he had his chosen men with him and the band of women who followed, and he was explaining to them not for the first time, where he was going, and why, and what would happen to him when he got there. But he was deeply alone in spirit, because the men who knew full well that he was the embodiment of Truth, somehow, neither believed nor understood a word he said.

466

Chapter Forty-four

LAMBING was over, and Dan was now released from the fields in readiness for the adventure of his first Jerusalem Passover. First there were important things to see to at home, such as digging the new privy pit. Anna was a firm believer in 'the warmer the season the deeper the hole' and by the time she was satisfied, Dan had toughened the callouses on his hard palms into shiny brown plates like the flat whorled shells he used to collect on the sea shore. Aunt Etta had explained carefully to Loukanos, who pretended to be aghast at the thought of helping, that they had always dug in the same wide stretch of ground, but since it took years before a previous patch was returned to, except for the darker coloured soil in the porous sandy limestone there was 'never a trace' of its previous use. Dan grinned to himself over this – it was not quite true, because one day they would get back to the same spot where he had angrily disposed of Uncle Bukki's wine flask – which would be quite a surprise for the next hole-digger! There was a sudden, slight niggle in his mind as the thought passed through his head … something to do with Aunt Etta? … but it was so faint and so fleeting that he dismissed it almost at once – likely it was her already half-forgotten concern that the flasks for their journey had fresh stoppers since the old were cracked. He would see to it as soon as the wretched digging was finished, and meanwhile, tease Uncle Louki again about his laziness.

As it happened, Loukanos (who in his travels had actually dug more latrines than he wanted to remember) was too occupied with his regular physician's circuit of the district to take part in the heavy labouring, but with Dan's help he moved the wooden shelter and set it up again, had Sabba Zimri make a new wooden cover and earth scoop, and even filled the first barrel of dirt himself from the sandy heap which Dan had dug out of the hole. That was his noble contribution to sparing Dan's tender muscles, he told him with a wink, since filling the barrel was usually Dan's task. With the basic necessities of living thus attended to for another season, Anna and Aunt Etta heaved a sigh of relief and turned their attention to the annual repairing of walls and roof where the hard winter rains had done their usual damage.

To see Aunt Etta crawling around on her hands and knees on the roof, warbling happily while she packed and rubbed the mixture of cow-dung and mud into weak spots, and rubbed them smooth with a polished stone – who would have thought it! She positively exulted in hard work and every task was to her a gift.

"All those years I had to put up with the drips when Bukki did a waster's job and I itched to do it myself! Don't try and stop me now, my dear!" Her shaggy grey eyebrows waggled teasingly when Anna begged her to do less. "I mean to work hard while I can – for not being *able* to work is far worse."

So there was Aunt Etta above, with her wide sleeves pinned up behind her neck and her veil twisted into a turban, while below, long-limbed Anna and Loukanos patched and painted the walls. This year Anna had bought the limewash directly from Ittai, who while experimenting with additions to his clays, had hit upon the idea of reselling a large quantity of lime from a kiln in South Galilee. It was not the highest quality but it was good enough, and people would improve on it or not as they saw fit – deciding for themselves how long to rest it after slaking, and whether they would add oil, ochre, or fibres, according to their own pet methods or the tightness of their purse strings. Ittai had astonished himself with his business acumen. So much lime was cheaper to transport in a single wagon-load of barrels, and Banayim was delighted to be able to buy it without stirring from home or paying extra cartage. Old Zack kicked himself for not thinking of it first, but Ittai had been still more enterprising. At Marta's suggestion he had also taken to selling very fine clay paste – the residue of his slip pot, scrapings and the sludge which fell from re-soaked unfired work. This paste made a thick, creamy, slightly greasy paint which covered fine cracks in the mud walls, and was soon in great demand, especially for inside work, the more so because though it was inexpensive, it was not plentiful. Shabby little Banayim smartened itself up, as it must every spring, or dissolve back into the earth from which it sprang.

Inside, Dan was undertaking a seasonal task he had made his own for the last few years – one which had been his father's custom – to scrape and mend and limewash the dingy walls of the kitchen corner where Etta's polished shelves were set in the stained plaster. In the new house, there was no hiding place behind them such as Ammiel had made to secretly store his savings, but it gave Dan a feeling of completeness, of rightness, and of manliness, to do as his father had done. Although heavy cooking could be done outside in fair weather, a small, low fire was lit on the stone hearth most days, and its smoke painted the dim room even darker during winter.

Dan stepped back to admire his finished work and was satisfied. He ran his eye with pleasure over the freshly-brightened plaster, once more a clean white background to the beautifully crafted shelves which had survived the razing of the old house. Hanging on a neat peg beside them was the elegantly curved and polished walking stick which had been made by the same skilled pair of hands – a stick which Aunt Etta no longer needed, but prized more than ever.

Finally all the spring tasks were completed and Jerusalem beckoned. The house was in order, the women had packed their bundles (all flasks now tightly sealed with newly bound stoppers), Loukanos was making his final rounds of the village – and Dan ran to spend his last night with Samuel and Caleb at the district fold outside Magdala. The next day they would be off – and there were sure to be various small commissions from fellow shepherds to be undertaken, either in Cana, or the great City.

"You must make the most of your special holiday, Dan," Samuel said kindly, after Caleb had finished counting his sheep and their giddy little lambs through the gate. The aged Queen of Sheba plodded through last of all, coughing resignedly. "It will be the end of your boyhood. When you come back you will take up your father's mantle in earnest."

Dan nodded thoughtfully, watching the other shepherds as they took their turns. Ephraim with his rough mixed herd, Eli and his brother Shaul counting in Samuel's goats and their kids, and finally the Magdala hireling – a jobbing shepherd paid to tend the handful of beasts owned by individual families in the town. By banding together they could afford a shepherd, and profit from the extra income of wool and milk, perhaps raise an animal for sacrifice, or a future family celebration. Unfortunately the casual nature of such arrangements meant that communal sheep or goats were rarely trained as well as they should have been, and many were the farmers' shouts and threats which followed their straying footsteps in the growing seasons.

Dan had once thought it must be a very fitting thing for a shepherd to raise his very own sacrificial beast – but as each of the tiny rams and ewes slithered helplessly into the world, some

470

surviving only because of his own hand, his own tender attentions, the thought of slitting its soft throat began to appal him. It was one thing to raise perfect kids and lambs and sell them off to the market, even knowing their fate. It was quite another to be the direct instrument of death. For this reason, the men in Dan's group usually exchanged their animals at Passover or feast times, so that none of them had to kill their own 'children'. Dan hugged Moses and scratched his shaggy red-brown head.

"I'll miss you, you silly old boy, you," he said lovingly. "Don't you get into any trouble while I'm gone, or I'll give you such a whacking with my rod!"

Moses nuzzled his master's ear affectionately, understanding only the familiar, teasing warmth in the young shepherd's tones. The last time he'd felt Dan's rod was as a yearling, when the short knobbed stick continually nudged him on one side then the other, as he was learning to keep to the narrow path between two cornfields. As for Dan's tall crooked staff, he had felt that only once – when it hooked around his tiny newborn body, and dragged him to safety from the rocky crevasse which had killed his unlucky dam. Dan nuzzled his pet in return and pulled his long ears gently – ears which had heard many a private confidence over the last few years. Dan was sorry for anyone without a Moses.

The Magdala hireling was having trouble – he barked orders at the confused little flock, and half of them ran the wrong way, and then he had a chase on his hands. Samuel patiently shut the fold's door until he should regroup the animals, lest his own should be unsettled, and whistled to his dogs. The eager yellow and pied-black bodies flashed into action, rounding up the tiny public flock almost before their shepherd had finished swearing. Samuel opened the door, and they ran inside. The hireling crashed it closed behind them, giving Samuel a dark look.

"When I want your help I'll ask for it," he said rudely.

Samuel shrugged but made no reply. He didn't see why the sheep – or their owners – should suffer for the man's attitude, and he wasn't going to aggravate it. Well, tomorrow Thaddeus would be here to stand in for Dan – and Heaven be thanked that there was one hireling who had compassion on the helpless creatures who depended on him, whether they were his or not. When this Philistine's stint was over, Samuel thought, he might just have a quiet word to the Magdala owners about their choice of shepherds. Ephraim caught his eye and raised his hands expressively. The hireling's sheep were anxiously milling around, and the other flocks were becoming restless. The shepherds moved among their charges, murmuring soothingly as they made their routine inspections. Dan was gently rubbing Golan's weak leg when he heard deep, harsh, urgent coughing from the back of the large fold.

"Dan!" Caleb's voice called sharply. "Samuel! Over here! Quickly!"

"No!" Dan cried, as he dropped beside the panting, rasp-winded Queen of Sheba. "Oh, Caleb! Can't you do something?"

The old ewe's flanks were heaving, her pale tongue protruding, her yellow eyes staring uncomprehendingly at the shepherds who had loved her for so long.

"No, Dan. Death comes to all creatures, you know, in the end."

"We did not expect her to last the winter, my boy," Samuel said quietly. "But she has seen in her last spring."

Sudden tears rushed to Dan's eyes. He flung his arms around the old creature's neck, and was shocked to feel how bony she was beneath her winter's coat. Caleb pulled him away gently but firmly.

"Let her breathe easy, Dan boy. That's the way."

472

The three of them sat on the ground with the dying animal, tears slipping unashamedly from their eyes. They stroked her head, her coat, her ears, and they murmured to her their own words of comfort, as her rattling breaths were drawn heavily, further and further apart.

"Sheba! Dear Sheba! You were father's darling, his favourite!" sobbed Dan. "You were his queen, his beauty!"

"Yes, old girl," murmured Caleb, smoothing her tangled coat, "such a good mother you were! So many lambs, and never one dropped beforetime."

"And even triplets, hey, Dan?" Samuel tried to smile.

"She led the flock so well – didn't she, Caleb?" Dan wept. "The first out, the first in, until she got too slow – and always so obedient! Father loved her – he loved her, and I love her … I don't want her to die!'

"We all loved her."

The panting body began to quiver, the eyes trembled, the narrow bar of their pupils dilating and then shrinking, as the cold long ears and the worn out hooves twitched. Pulling himself together, Dan put his young face close to the old creature's ear, and stroking her sunken grey, almost toothless muzzle, he sang to her the shepherd's call which she had heard every day of her life. In his voice at last was the little burr which had been so long coming.

"Queen of Sheba! Come on, my darling! Come to Abba! Come on, my darling! Come to Abba!"

Sheba sighed, the twitching stopped, and she grew still, as the last breath of life escaped. The lips drew back, the slack tongue became blue, the gentle eye glazed. Now Dan hugged the motionless body, and cried. Caleb sat with tears trickling into his scraggly grey beard, one weathered old hand on the boy, one on the faithful old sheep which had been a companion through so many bleak and lonely watches over many years. Twilight was approaching, and there was no more to be done for her tonight, except to cover her sadly staring face with a scrap of tenting, for Dan's sake. They would keep her safely in the fold, this one last time, and bury her in the morning.

Samuel quietly returned to his goats, wiping his eyes on his sleeve with a sniff, clearing his throat. The Magdala hireling lifted his flask to his teeth, swigged deeply, and chuckled.

"Someone's grandmother die?" he asked insolently.

Samuel turned on him a look of such wrath that the hireling flinched.

"Pardon me for living," he muttered, and that was the last they heard out of him.

At sunrise Dan heard the scrape of the gate, and an impatient voice calling unfamiliar names.

"Tobias, Suzannah, Bel and Daniel! Shadrach, Meshech and Abednego! Nebuchadnezzar, Belshazzar! Come on, you lazy beasts."

It had to be admitted that the sheep owners of Magdala had done their best to create a coherent flock out of their unrelated purchases, and in this artful way, they made it easier for any hireling to remember their names. But the sheep remained unimpressed.

"Why so soon? They have not been inspected yet," Dan asked Caleb quietly, as they went about this task with their own animals. "He didn't even look at them last night."

"Do you think such a man cares about a thorn in a hoof, a canker on an ear, or a sore teat? He needs them in the town pasture by midday if he's to get paid," Caleb replied, with a shake of his head. "He wants his money daily or he won't stay. But it takes him so long to get them anywhere he has to start very early. He has only had this job for three days, and he usually ends up chasing them out of the fold."

"Tobias! Belshazzar! Suzannah! Come on!" The voice became sterner, but the sheep did not follow. They lay chewing the cud, or stood patiently feeding their lambs, oblivious to the voice which commanded them. The hireling marched back into the fold and lifted his clubbed rod.

Suddenly there was a little rill of notes piping like birdsong outside the fold, and a familiar voice called cheerfully,

"Tobias, Suzannah, Bel and Daniel!" The sheep pricked up their ears, and four of them trotted towards the gate. "Shadrach, Meshech and Abednego!" Three more, as willingly as their namesakes entering the fiery furnace. "Nebuchadnezzar, Belshazzar!" The last two rams plodded forward, leaving the hireling dumbstruck, and fearing some devilish spirit.

Thaddeus stuck his head around the gate with a smile and waved his double pipes. "Good morning, I hope that helps! You'd better go after them now before they get scared."

"How did you do that?" growled the hireling, putting his rod behind his back, and hoping uneasily that this man was not one of the owners he had not met. Thaddeus laughed.

"Oh, I've had the Magdala Persians before – scruffy, scatty, but sweet-natured. They know my pipes and my voice from way back. Nebuchadnezzar wants watching, my friend. He has no morals and is prepared to ruin every herd he meets with crossbreeds, so don't let him alone for a second, and Suzannah is a tearaway, not a good mother at all, so keep an eye out for poor little Bel – she gets a headbutt as often as a teat."

475

A moment's conversation revealed that Thaddeus had in fact been the first man asked by the Magdala owners to take this very job, but he was already tied at the time, and then would be going straight to Samuel's employ. Dan appraised him indignantly of the way the hireling treated his animals, Samuel made a suggestion, and Thaddeus winked. He then went and offered to help the man bring the sheep down to the town pasture, where he met the owners; and by the end of the day, the harassed Magdala Persians had joined Samuel's animals for the time being and everyone was contented, especially the hireling, who now could go off to Tiberius and liquidate his assets, in a manner of speaking.

The interlude had distracted attention from the sad task of burying Sheba, but as soon as the fold was clear, it had to be done. There was no question of skinning her hide, neither Dan nor Caleb would have countenanced it, so the Queen of Sheba was buried intact in her wool robe, as befitted a faithful friend.

Mournful as he was, Dan was thankful that he had come back for one last night. It would have been terrible to have returned in several weeks' time to discover she had gone in his absence. Caleb too, as distressed as his apprentice, was glad they had been able to bury her together.

As Ephraim and his herd moved off to the waterhole, Dan took detailed instructions from Samuel concerning the purchase of certain shears only to be found in the Street of the Coppersmiths in Jerusalem's Tyropean Valley, and a solemn reminder from Eli regarding some bridal jewellery Anna had promised to find for Judith. He bid them all farewell, they bid him God speed, Caleb with sorrow still in his eyes … and then Samuel stepped forward.

"Caleb, my friend – how long is it since *you* were at Jerusalem for Passover? What? You can't remember? Have you no respect for the Law, man?"

Shaking his head, Caleb smiled. He knew Samuel must be teasing, but it hurt him to realise that he would probably never see the Holy City again this side of the Restoration – or the Resurrection.

"I won't have heathens working for me," Samuel said severely. "Take your pack, old man, and be off with you."

Caleb paled – Dan looked from one to the other in horror – then Eli and Shaul gave a shout of laughter. "Stop that, father! How dare you be so cruel! It's all right, Caleb – father arranged this with Loukanos days ago, and even Extra Pressings knows about it! She's even packed a bag for you and left it with Anna. That's why Thaddeus has come. We didn't need him just to replace Dan!"

Caleb sat down suddenly, and Dan frowned at Samuel angrily. Samuel hastened to embrace the trembling form of his faithful flock-master.

"Old man, I am so sorry! I repent in dust and ashes! My humour is too heavy for a gentle heart like yours – forgive me!"

"*Hi-yi!* Samuel! Another shock like that might carry me off like poor Sheba! Well, I do forgive you, and bless and thank you too, most heartily." Caleb's wrinkled face worked in vain to hold back the tears. It was too much in one day. "I never thought to see the Temple again! And we may see the Messiah! And what if the Restoration should come while we are actually there! Praise the Eternal for my kind and generous friends!"

Arm in arm the old man and the young strode gratefully back to Banayim, walking and talking out their emotion-charged morning until they were quite themselves again. They commented on Thaddeus's immensely improved moods, manners, and motivation, not only since his healing, but particularly since his surprising marriage to Shana. Dan didn't think he'd ever seen him quite so full of benevolent good humour as he had that morning.

When he and Caleb reached Banayim, they found out why.

"What?" Dan cried, aghast and entertained all at once. "But – is that – um – possible?"

Anna laughed. "Oh yes, it certainly is. Unusual, but not impossible."

"Indeed, Dan," Aunt Etta nodded confidentially. "It's the very reason your father was *not* called Amos."

"Aunt Etta," Dan said firmly, hoping his juvenile whiskers were bristling with indignation, "I have been promised answers for far too long. The year is nearly out, and the beard is growing!"

"Very well, my boy," she chuckled. "I will tell you on our journey. Now you run round and congratulate dear Shana in the proper manner. She has been rarely blessed, and declares her name should be changed from Shana to Sarah! As for young Thad, a brother or sister is exactly what he needs and nobody in their right mind ever thought he'd get."

"It's very early days, Etta," Loukanos warned gently, "and this is a precarious business at Shana's age."

Etta covered Dan's ears at once. "That's quite enough of that, Doctor Louki," she said stoutly. "We will pray the Eternal's blessing continues to be showered on Thaddeus and his family, and leave the details to the angels, if you don't mind."

Dan shook his head free of her muffling hands and continued to shake it in disbelief – another miracle of miracles – would they never cease?

478

Chapter Forty-five

WITH so many delays and surprises it seemed they would need a miracle themselves to get on the road at all. But eventually, of course they did – rising very early and setting out to Cana, where they met up as arranged, with Asa and Johanan and Mordecai *and* Rhoda. Why Rhoda? Simply because Aunt Mari had declared she *could* not be deprived of her any longer, especially with all the visitors she was expecting for Passover. However, the girl would be allowed to return with them to Cana until her mother's marriage after Pentecost. Then she would be free to go back to Mari, that is, if she did not have to leave the Land with the enterprising cheesemaker and his new wife.

What a glad group they were as they made the three day journey to the Holy City! Scores of others were on the same pilgrimage, and as they journeyed southwards, more and more small tributaries of such wayfarers from all directions flowed into the main river of travellers, some like themselves with a well-laden donkey or two, but most on foot. From time to time a wealthy family might sway past in richly decorated hand-litters borne by expressionless, wiry Nubians, their sweat-glistening, purplish-black skin chalk-powdered from the road like ripe olives dusted with flour; and at least every few hours a string of camels would overtake them – much to Rhoda's dismay. Her uncomfortable, queasy rush to Cana with Shalal and his post some months ago had only confirmed her loathing of these lofty beasts of burden. Dan secretly rather looked forward to the camels. They gave him a chance to stand protectively between Rhoda and her biggest fear, and show how unconcerned he was.

With so many people on the road, the way was safe, and never wearisome. There was always someone to share a joke, a story, an argument, a song, or a moment of wonder. Then, as she had long promised, Aunt Etta finally revealed the story of why the name of Amos had not been handed down to Dan's father (or Dan himself) according to the established family custom.

"As you know, my father – your grandfather, Dan – was an Amos, and so were his father and his grandfather and so on, for who knows *how* far back. The men in our family had all been proud to bear and pass on to their eldest sons the name of the holy prophet Amos, especially as he was a shepherd like themselves. They even adopted for themselves his saying, '*Surely the Eternal God will do nothing without revealing it to His servants the prophets*', as a sort of play on words – because they were each an Amos who was also a servant of God, you see?"

"Well, this was all very fine until my father married, and I was born – but *only* me. Though my mother was not young, she was a stout woman who looked as though she should bear him many strong children, but though she grew fatter and fatter with the years, there were no more little ones, and being devout people, they sadly accepted it as God's will. Finally the manner of women was passing from my poor mother and that was that – until one day she was taken very ill with terrible cramps – her pangs so severe that we thought she must be dying and so did she, and the apothecary was useless. Father ran for a Rabbi to pray over her –

I ran for a physician – and by the time we returned, my shocked mother was holding in her arms, a slippery, squirming, squalling baby boy with a thatch of hair as red as his fat little face.

"It's hard to say who was more stunned! The neighbours talked of nothing else for weeks. Oh! the jokes that went round! The rude remarks and the rib-poking, with friends and family laughing that *this* Amos was 'no prophet', as God had done a thing which he had *not* revealed to his servant. Father didn't even care about the teasing, he was so jubilant – and he decided that in honour of this miracle the child's name must break the old chain. Well, the family always believed they were Danites, though of course since the Exile who could say, so he had the Rabbi search the genealogies of Dan in the books of Moses, and out of all those names he chose *Ammiel* – 'people of God', which was close enough to 'servants of God' to give a nod to the family tradition. Then when *you* were born, Dan, *your* father turned it neatly the other way, so *Ammiel of the tribe of Dan* became *Dan of the tribe of Ammiel*. Except that poor Ammiel would have no tribe – but of course he wasn't to know that, the dear man, may he rest in peace. So that is the whole story!"

Amid the burst of laughter and applause which followed the gratified Etta's complicated history, Dan heaved a sigh of total satisfaction. Yes, that explained it. That explained a *lot*.

From Cana they passed through Sepphoris and Nazareth, which being on the Via Maris trade-route was usually busy and today was even more so with Passover caravans, and a company of priests called from their various homes in Galilee, who customarily gathered in that town before going up together to serve their Course's turn in the Temple. Almost unintentionally Dan's family slowed as they passed the small woodworker's shop with its faded

481

sign 'Ben Netser'. It looked still and empty, no hammering or sawing, singing or chatter came from within. In the rather shabby house beside it a loud argument was going on – gruff male voices protesting with a note of belligerence, piping interruptions from tearful young women, and a stern older voice overriding them all.

"She is in Jerusalem with him, and that's all there is to it. Yes, she likely *is* as touched as he is, probably as bad as our dear deluded aunt, who's gone with her, but she's old enough to please herself, and you're old enough to have more sense than to cry about it. You girls, go back to your husbands, and leave this to us. As for you, Joseph, it's time you and Shim stopped complaining and pulled your weight. You can't leave everything to me – or Judah! Isn't it bad enough that –"

The voice broke off as Dan's group was spied through the window, and the door was wrenched open. A dark, sturdy man in a sap-stained, scarred leather apron and sawdust-sprinkled clothes glared angrily at the folk who were dawdling outside silently wondering about many things.

"No, we don't know anything!" he barked impatiently. "No, we don't agree with him. No, we don't have special powers. Yes, he always was a thoughtful child and none of us could live up to him. No, I've never heard him swear when he hit his thumb, and No, you can't have any keepsakes! Satisfied?"

He was in the act of slamming the door when Dan sprang forward. "Jacob? Wait! You *are* Jacob, are you not?"

The door opened reluctantly a little way. "Well? How do you know my name, young fire-beard?"

"I was here four years ago, with my father. Your brother got sawdust in his eyes and you smacked your face into a plank when you went to help him. You sold us a beautiful walking stick for my Auntie! Because of your brother – she no longer needs it!"

There was a snort. "Hah! – *If* you say so – but you don't expect your money back, do you?"

"No, of course not. But it was a great help to my Auntie for a long time – and thank you."

"H'mph!"

"Wait!" Dan turned back impulsively just before the door banged again. "*Did* you get black eyes, by the way?" he asked curiously. "From that plank?"

Stocky, black-bearded Jacob stared at him through the half shut door. The things young people asked their elders these days!

"What? How should I remember? Oh yes – no I didn't – everything was blurred for a while, but then I was all right – unlike my precious brother who seems to have stayed rather one-eyed about many things – thank you for asking, and *not* that it's any of your business! Now go away, I'm busy – this Passover is already causing me enough grief."

The door crashed closed, and with a grin Dan ran lightly back to his family.

"I always wanted to know whether he got black eyes!" he laughed. "Too bad he was so cross, but I'm glad I thanked him anyway." He stroked his chin proudly. "H'mmm … *Fire-beard!* I like it!"

The adults had been listening without smiles. Asa caught his daughter's eye and shook his head, his lips compressed. If a man's own family could turn on him, what might his own followers do? Or his own nation? They kept their thoughts to themselves, and the journey south continued. During the last month, roads had been mended, public cisterns repaired, and the country prepared for the regular holiday onslaught. Even so, the way was not easy, often steep and slippery, by turns dusty or miry, and Aunt Etta's newly-granted health and strength was well tested; but she never faltered.

Asa's group passed into the hill country of despised Samaria without a qualm. Something of a mixed multitude themselves and living proof that Galilee was certainly 'of the Gentiles', they had no interest in returning the occasional spats of outright hostility shown to them as Jews, though others on the road could not resist trading insults. There was safety in numbers, and just as well. The Sabbath fell that night and there they must stay, and there could be no more travelling till the morning of the First Day. What a strange and heart-warming interlude it was – the gathering mass of Jewish tents huddled outside the Samaritan city like a wandering flock – and everywhere, lights glowing, campfires dying submissively, Sabbath prayers and meals shared, and a great humming sound hovering over them all as the Sabbath songs were sung. In the morning the sleeping camp gradually came to life again, with families and neighbours wandering from tent to tent, meeting friends old and new, sharing food and water and travellers' tales; all sojourners, feeling akin to Israel in the wilderness of old.

At first light on the First Day they strode out again – through the city of Samaria, on to Marbartha, Sychar, then – *Ah – Judaea at last!* – overnight again at Lebonah, Bethel, Ramah, struggling over the mountains of Ephraim, down over the Valley of Jehoshaphat, with Jerusalem's hustling din and dust already hanging in the air – great swards of pilgrim tents on the slopes outside the city, springing up like mushrooms wherever you looked – past the Royal Tombs – *Yes! We are really here!* – plunging into the bazaars of the northern quarter – busy, clamorous, full of bright sounds and dazzling colours, pungent smells and dirt, and bleating animals;

484

braying youths swaggering boldly and oh, so casually! in front of shy, tittering girls who pressed close to their mothers, daringly casting sideways glances over their intriguing veils; shrill women of all shapes and sizes disgustedly declaring the worthlessness of the goods so lavishly spread before them; shouting sellers of all complexions, coaxing and bargaining, throwing their hands in the air and calling on heaven's witness to their poverty, chuckling to each other with winks as they swept coins into their laps. Occasionally at street corners could be seen the pale, rigid faces of fasting Pharisees, large phylacteries extravagantly lashed to foreheads and wrists with long, trailing black thongs, hands raised high in ostentatious prayer. They might appear motionless in the heavily-bordered gowns which proclaimed that they walked more deeply in the blue circle of heaven than others, but their surreptitious glances betrayed that some had one eye open for the admiration of the less holy, from whose touch, nevertheless, they fastidiously shrank.

The city was crammed with Jews from all over the Land and the Empire, camping in public squares and gardens, on rooftops and under porches, wherever there was room to throw up a bit of canvas. Passover drew them like no other Festival, and no wonder, when tradition held that just as the newly forged nation of Israel had been wrested from the Iron Furnace of Egypt by the hand of Moses, so would the Messiah arise to free his people from the Iron Rule of Rome on Passover Eve. Who would not be in Jerusalem at such a time! How they all fitted was a miracle in itself but every overflowing house and inn gave hospitality freely, as befitted those who might soon be sharing the spoils of victory over their oppressors. The increased presence of leather-clad soldiers did nothing to improve the wary, touchy mood in the overcrowded city, and the Roman administrators remained grim-faced. Governor Pilatus, the Prefect, did not enjoy Passover. Quite apart from the difficulty of keeping these unruly Jews in order at any time, the Festival heightened the intensity of warring religious factions, particularly with the seditious Zealots sowing discord. With the annual Deliverance fever, especially with a controversial prophet drawing the masses unchecked, even a whisper might start a disastrous riot. The Prefect did not care much what Herod thought, but Caesar's opinion would be quite another matter.

Dan's party pushed their way determinedly across to the steep Tyropean Valley and the lower city where the merchants both humble and well-to-do lived and traded. On the other side of the steep ravine beckoned all the glistening tiers of the glorious, gilded Temple, and a surging tide of busy humanity responded, ebbing and flowing to and from the holy precinct, pouring across both its high narrow bridge and the broad way beneath it, while all around the noisy city seemed to bubble hotly with anticipation.

Ancient Shefi, Mari's Egyptian handmaid, opened the gate, her kohl-rimmed eyes lighting up to see them all safely arrived at last, and Rhoda flew into her dark skinny arms without ceremony, babbling excitedly, asking about all that had happened in her long absence. Two menservants unloaded and stabled the patient donkey, as Aunt Mari came hurrying out to sweep everyone into her large house with a haste bordering on anxiety.

"My dears, how glad I am — how wonderful to see you all. Johanan, my darling, did you miss your mother? Of course not! Well, I missed you enough for both of us so I suppose that makes us even. My dearest Etta! Why, your hair is becoming quite white now, but you see I am catching up with you, alas. So many years since — but how wonderful you look, and praise the Eternal for your lovely straight back! and Dan, how you've grown! give your

Auntie Mari a hug, what a dear little colourful beard, and you too, Anna. No, Anna, not you, I mean not you with the beard, the hug, I mean, oh well, you know what I mean – Ah, Asa, oh, don't squash me, you don't know your own strength, my dear brother – well, well, Loukanos! What wonderful things I've heard of you – and this must be Shepherd Caleb – I rejoice to meet you at last – and – Oh!" She gasped a little and actually blushed.

"Mordecai of Cana. Greetings, Lady, blessings and peace upon you and your house, and may the Eternal reward your kind hospitality."

"You might have warned me!" she hissed at Anna, wide-eyed behind her hand. "It isn't decent for a man to look so handsome at his age!" She looked around in confusion. "Rhoda! Where is she? You haven't left my pet behind have you?"

"I'm here, mistress," laughed Rhoda, and ran forward to be embraced, for what Johanan had said was true – she was one of them and no slave.

With Shefi and the servants flitting around like efficient shadows, Mari settled her guests quickly on cushions and couches in her capacious reception room. Bowls were brought, hands, faces and feet were washed, and she urged the men to take advantage of the bath in the basement as soon as they had refreshed themselves from the trays of food and drink she had prepared for them. The women were promised the attentions of Shefi in their own chamber. Rhoda jumped up, impatient with being waited on, and ran off to the stable to find her pet dove, anxious to know whether he still remembered her enough to fly down from the beams and perch on her shoulder.

"I must warn you, my dears," Mari rushed into speech again, "that you may not be my only guests this Passover – oh, dear, so much has happened and I don't know where to start!"

Asa took his sister's hands in his and said reassuringly, "Now, Mari, don't get in a fluster. Start at the beginning, go on to the end, and then stop."

"No, no, there's no time! But I have so much to tell – you must be patient and hear me out without confusing me with questions. So please, eat, drink – but don't speak whatever you do or I'll lose the thread."

Obediently the weary travellers drank their cool grape-must or watered wine – pomegranate juice for Anna – crunching on pistachios and almonds and dried figs, while Mari talked incessantly in her quick, polished accents, scarcely drawing breath, her bracelets jangling on her fluttering hands, fanning herself rapidly with a woven palm leaf.

"The most extraordinary things have been happening! The very day you left Cana, the Teacher was greeted – oh, no, I must go back ... You have heard of the raising of Bethanite Lazarus – of course you have, everyone has – why, he was not only dead but corrupting and nobody can brush *that* off as a death-like faint, let me tell *you*! The word is, the rulers want to assassinate the poor man so they can deny he ever lived again – too wicked for words, and I don't know if I believe it ... but it has raised everything to fever-pitch here. Hundreds have been milling around in Bethany hoping to see and touch this miracle man for themselves – or gathering in the temple surrounds hunting for the Teacher – or going to and fro trying to be in both places at once ... and of course you know there's always singing of *Hallal* psalms and responses and lots of waving of palms and so on as they come in for the celebrations, but on that day, just before Sabbath, you know – the Teacher himself came from Olivet over the way into the Temple – actually riding a little colt and of course it would have to be significant, wouldn't it because he has *never* done such a thing before and people had draped the creature with their own cloaks – in homage, I am sure of it. You know, willingly putting themselves under him, so to speak …

"Well, everyone else was sure it was all very significant too – and they thronged him with shouts of praise, and the *Hallal* songs and went completely wild! Right under the noses of the Temple priests and everyone – imagine! – hailing him publicly as the promised Son of David, praising his miracles, cheering for the coming Kingdom, shouting *Hosanna in the Highest!* – waving victory palms as if he was one of the Maccabees delivering Jerusalem – throwing their branches and even their coats in his path. Their coats! What poor man – or rich, for that matter – parts with his precious *coat* and lays it in the mud to be trodden underfoot by a donkey, tell me that? – not to speak of its dam following to complete the damage! Oh, my dears, at Passover too, you know – the time of Deliverance! – what else *could* it be but the entry of a King!"

Dan and Johanan gaped, and Anna felt the hairs on her arms standing up.

"Hosanna in the Highest!" croaked Caleb. "So the angels sang at his birth!"

"*Rejoice and shout, daughter of Jerusalem!*" Mordecai repeated the scripture softly. "*Behold your King is coming, righteous, having salvation, gentle, and riding on a donkey's colt!*"

"Has the time come?" Aunt Etta demanded faintly, even as Asa's awed voice echoed her question.

"Is the Restoration really happening at last?"

"But I don't know!" Mari replied agitatedly, taking a quick sip of water and motioning to Johanan to open the tightly closed cedar shutters of the nearest window. "We are all very confused! You see – our beloved Teacher was so sober, so solemn, wasn't he, Shefi? There was nothing warlike about him at all. And then he stretched out his hands to the city and broke down completely – crying bitterly, wearily, like a man whose only child is dying … Oh dear, I'm afraid I'm all choked up now – you tell them, Shefi, you were with me. Tell them what happened!"

The old Egyptian handmaid shook her head, the heavy earrings clanking and dragging at her stretched lobes. "Aiee, Mistress! There were tears, but not of joy or victory. Such painful sobs! Such lamentable cries! Such deep grief!"

Mari's voice trembled. "He entered the temple still weeping and looked around with searching eyes that would break your heart. He said nothing – then left with the tears still streaking his face."

Shefi raised her hands helplessly. "Who can say what it means?"

"The next day he was back, in a very different mood," Mari continued more firmly. "Of course, we'd run there early, panting to see what would happen next – and he was neither sad nor triumphant but *angry* – furious! He was everywhere at once, blocking people carrying goods through the courts, shouting that they had turned God's house into a robbers' den! He simply tore through the place, overthrowing money tables and flinging benches – oh, to see those traders leaping out of the way, scrabbling on all fours with their rumps in the air squabbling over their scattered coins like dogs over a bone! and hopping around snatching at escaped doves! Oh, it sounds so funny, but it wasn't – he was truly terrifying! Of course, they *were* trading on the Sabbath, but it's winked at because worshippers need exchangers, and sacrifices, and if you're a temple worker or Levite you're exempt, aren't you, and he never mentioned *that* anyway. After all, they rob you blind on every day, not just the Sabbath. Oh dear! Mordecai, I'm so sorry ... I didn't mean ... Close up that window, Johanan, your mother is frozen."

Asa scrubbed his head agitatedly. "It doesn't follow, does it?" he said apologetically. "It makes no sense at all."

"Of course it doesn't! It's driving us to distraction, but I haven't finished, have I, Shefi? You see, the next thing was that with all the merchandise swept *out* of the public court, the cripples and blind and so on swept *in* to see him – and right then and there – right in the Temple courts, under the priests' noses, on the Sabbath, as if to say *This is what should happen in my Father's house!* – he healed every single one, as calm as ever!"

"Calm as ever, mistress," Shefi nodded emphatically, reasserting her narrative, "and all the young boys, so excited they were – running around crying out and singing *Hosanna to the Son of David!* Singing it to *him* and not as part of their choral service either, and those lawyers and priests spitting at him to shut them up."

Mari herself was at a high pitch of nervous excitement – words streaming out of her in a whirling torrent of information and dismay.

"The Teacher never turned a hair – just asked if they'd read the scripture about God perfecting praise in the mouths of children! That shut *them* up in a hurry. But, oh, dear, it looks very ill for him! Yet he was back again the First Day, that's yesterday now, teaching again ... despite being challenged by those terrible men who have knives in their eyes ... and everyone just *watching* them like a play at the hippodrome ... which seems so wrong. Didn't he once say if you hate your brother you are a murderer? Then he was *surrounded* by murderers in my opinion – you could fairly *taste* the hatred in the air! – and he feels it too, because he told a story of a man being slain by his tenant farmers, and talked about a rejected building block becoming a capstone which would fall and crush people ... and another story about a wedding which ended in weeping and teeth-grinding ... all very dark and desperate ... not at all joyful and triumphant and kingly ... No, no, don't interrupt me, Asa, I haven't time, I'll explain later, you must listen!

"All yesterday they were heckling and baiting him – first the Pharisees about loyalty to the Emperor – with some pet Herodians as witnesses of course. *Pharisees* caring about loyalty to Caesar? Don't make me laugh! Then Sadducees piously asking about the Resurrection which they don't even believe in – yes, *Sadducees!* Posing a ridiculous case of a woman who died after seven husbands. Seven! No wonder! As if surviving one isn't hard enough for most women! The only relief was a lawyer who asked an honest question with no tricks – and actually agreed with the answer. Rabbi Jeshua even commended his wisdom, in fact he said he was 'not far from the Kingdom of God' – so does *that* mean he *is* close to restoring it after all?"

She shook her head quickly and hurried on. "And now that brings me to the next thing I have to tell you, my dears. You see, the man is utterly exhausted, but he is simply hard-driving himself to be at the Temple constantly, instructing everyone, pilgrims and all, as if his very life depends on it. All that weary trudging up and down to Bethany and back again, and sleeping under trees on damp Olivet and so on ... and ... he has such a look about him ..." Her voice broke, and she stopped.

Nobody spoke, they were hanging on every word. Aunt Mari drew herself up with a determined breath and continued firmly, clasping her jewelled hands as if to give herself courage.

"I mean quietly to offer him and his men the use of this house. The mood out there is as menacing as the heat before a thunderstorm and I can tell you I don't like it. I mean to be a Shunamite and comfort myself that a prophet of God has found my home a refuge in a difficult hour. How can they hold their *Pesach* supper in quietness if they are in the public view every hour of the day and worrying about knives in their ribs or accusations of disturbing the peace? I wouldn't put anything past the Sanhedrin and I don't care who knows it. This house is large enough for us to keep downstairs and not disturb them, but first he must be asked with great tact and discretion. Patience! I have nearly finished, and no, Asa I will *not* tell the end of my tale first as you always demand. Working backwards only muddles me, and you never wait to hear it anyway and don't get the full story, and then you get cross later. Johanan, do open the window – it's very stuffy in here.

"Well! I have been very brazen, my dears. I clutched hold of one of the Twelve, the nice round one they call The Twin and asked where they would be tonight. At first he didn't want to tell me, which is understandable, but he knows I follow his Master sincerely, and I begged hard enough, and I have been running around ever since, making arrangements, and not even been near the Temple today, though I know the Teacher is *still* up there teaching and I hope I'm not missing anything vital. Cleopas my steward has been stationed there on duty – sending me reports all day through his dear little wife Miriam – only fifteen and the swiftest pair of feet I've ever seen in a woman, I can tell you, it must be all that running up and down to Emmaus they do to visit his family – well they're

493

both back now, and oh, dear! they tell me that brave Rabbi Jeshua has been freely attacking the rulers again, and *all* his lessons hint of death and destruction and judgements.

"Surely some battle is imminent and these are momentous times! But if Elijah and Elisha could call down fire and mobilise the hosts of heaven, what will *this* prophet do but still greater things? We must be fearless if there is war, but so far the Romans are mere bystanders, so perhaps it will be civil war, Heaven forbid! but who knows what will happen? Now do wash and change quickly, we must soon be off or keep our host waiting – not that I'm even sure he knows we'll be at his dinner tonight. I'm afraid I was rather underhanded about that … I had to recall a few old favours to get us in with the steward."

"What, Mari!" astonished Asa managed to ask. "All of us?"

"No, no, no, that would be far too many. I have wheedled invitations with the utmost bare-faced boldness, but for only myself, my son and my brother. I'm sorry it means another long walk after your tiring journey, but we must get ourselves to Bethany before sundown. The rest of you stay here – do talk to Old Pagiel if he comes in, he's very concerned about everything and especially for the safety of his young wife and children – and Nathan Hill-and-Dale might visit too. He's very strange, and you must pay no attention if he either laughs hysterically or broods, because he's really a very clever man – but whatever else you do, someone must keep an eye on what is happening at the Temple."

She clapped her hands impatiently. "Come *on,* Shefi! I look like a fishwife, and Simon is a man of standing. Guests who invite themselves owe it to their host to look as respectable as possible – Johanan, look sharp, my son. Has anyone seen my fan? Asa, do stop bumbling around – we have things to do!"

Chapter Forty-six

BEFORE long, Mari, Asa and Johanan had gone – freshly attired and respectable enough to satisfy Mari's exacting taste. A flurry of animated discussion followed their departure, with tongues loosened at last after Mari's flood of news, and it was clear that nobody would be content just to sit around waiting for Passover – or a revolution – or a riot in the streets. Before long it was settled that they would go in pairs for security and find out whatever they could. Loukanos would take Dan – the pair well matched for speed and sharpness of eye – and Mordecai, with his old connections to call on, would escort Anna, who refused to be left behind, especially as her knowledge of the city was far more recent than Mordecai's.

Mordecai firmly agreed with Mari's opinion that something momentous must be about to happen – the Teacher from Nazareth *was* the Messiah, wasn't he? And now he'd been acclaimed as the Saviour of Israel, on Mount Olivet, no less! His clear eyes alight with excitement, the scribe recited from the scroll of Zecharias.

"Then shall the Eternal go out and fight against the nations, even as in the battle-days of old, and in that day his feet shall stand on the Mount Olivet …!"

Poor Rhoda began to tremble tearfully, and Anna hugged her with a warning glance at the men, who were already gathering a certain warlike air about them.

"Don't be afraid, *dodi*," she encouraged gently. "I for one am not sure how we can comfortably put one passage about *a gentle Saviour proclaiming peace* alongside the other about *going out and fighting nations as in battle days of old* – even if Zecharias *does* also mention a colt and a donkey and Olivet. Nobody knows what is going to happen, and it may all blow over. What can possibly happen at Passover, with a High Day following?"

Aunt Etta nodded. "Everyone will be too busy with his own affairs, my dear," she said, patting Rhoda's smooth cheek reassuringly. "But whatever happens, I am sure that the Teacher will protect his own, like a good shepherd does his sheep. And that he has full power to do so, I am certain. After all, a man who can restore life to the dead can surely shield those who are loyal to him!"

"And remember," Anna continued cheerfully, "Adonai God saved His son from wicked swords as a child, and He will do so again if it comes to such a pass. So be comforted and put your trust in Him. We must go now, but you won't be left alone, and you'll have so much to do we'll be back before you know it. Etta will be here with you – and this brave Caleb, who has fought bears and wolves in his lifetime and lived to tell the tale, as you see!"

"Ah, yes, little one!" Caleb patted her shoulder with a comical look, "What's a Roman or two to a warrior like me! Look here! Do you see these scars?" He drew her away towards the kitchens, where Shefi and the cook were creating clamorous echoes. "Now, let me tell you about the time …"

496

Bidding the others to take care, and God speed, Etta followed the two briskly. With the possibility of thirteen extra visitors to prepare for, there would be no time for anyone to fret.

Loukanos, Anna, Dan and Mordecai stood looking at each other for a moment. Then out they went, into the labyrinth of dirty, crowded, marble-paved streets, into cold shadows thrown from dank stone walls; where the gloom was stabbed with narrow bands of late afternoon light which flashed across the housetops; and the lowering sun gilt-brushed the intense faces ascending and descending the steep steps of the restless city.

They did not go directly to the Temple, their ultimate destination. First, Anna and Loukanos had a private promise to Dan to fulfil. They led the way to a hilly garden a little way out of the city; a garden creeping through a kind of irregular low ravine with paths criss-crossing over the top and down throughout its floor, where small entries were cut in the rock-face, and covered with slabs of sandstone.

The rock above these little caves, at their sides, and over the doorways – wherever the solid surface was exposed – was all freshly whitewashed, glowing brightly in the mellowing light. Here and there were piles of round stones, mounded up into heaps both small and great. Other visitors could be seen walking soberly along the winding paths, or cautiously adding a stone to one of the little cairns. Away in the distance, a gardener was pretending to work, dabbing intermittently at a patch of thistles with his pruning hook.

Anna did not enter this garden, and she warned the others to take care where they trod.

"The sepulchres have all been whitened in the last few weeks, Dan," she told him. "Not to make the garden beautiful, but to show visitors where the graves are. Be sure not to render yourself

Unclean by treading on or touching any of them, if you want to go inside the Temple. I will wait here – Louki knows the place – but you must take as long as you want to and not hurry on my account. Who knows when this chance may come again?"

Dan hugged her gratefully but Loukanos looked disapproving.

"We will be out of sight, Anna. You are not sitting here alone under a tree in such a place, it is getting too late. You will be taken for a loose woman and may incur unpleasantness. Mordecai, will you remain with her? I will feel easier in my mind. Come on, Dan."

"I'll place a stone for you, *Amma*. And you, too, Mordecai."

Walking briskly, the two of them disappeared around a curve in the path.

Anna sat down, leaned back and sighed. "Thank you, Mordecai, for staying. I confess I did not relish being on my own. Of course, it's not as if you really knew him yourself."

"What little I did know makes me glad that Dan is placing a stone for me. It is good you have brought him here. He has not been since the burial?"

"No, they left for Galilee almost at once. Etta has not been here at all. But I think she should come before we return, though I know it will distress her."

"The Nazirite vow keeps you out of the garden, I know – but does it distress *you* to be here, Anna?"

She paused before replying carefully, "I hardly know the answer to that, my friend. I can only tell you that I feel ... disturbed."

She tucked her feet up inside her robe, tugging the hem straight automatically.

"You have heard the saying *You can only die once!* But when Ammiel died, I found it was not true. The death of others kills something in oneself, and so does the death of hopes, and there is even the death of thoughts and impulses which we deliberately strangle, and the death of things which die naturally. But each leaves behind it a process of corruption which takes time to dry up and blow away as dust, and some leave rattling skeletons forever. I know now that life is a series of inner deaths, to be feared, endured, and grieved through. It is true that after each one the soul revives and grows again, until next time, and the next time. But how long before a soul is exhausted?"

"Lady, these are morbid words from a sensible woman. You see that gardener? He could tell you that each time you prune a tree it brings forth more fruit."

"But what if I don't *want* to be pruned into a lavish harvest? Don't you think sometimes the forced growing itself causes as much pain as the pruning? What if I want to stay safe in my isolation and my memories, and beg only for contentment with a modest crop? Is that not enough? Oh, don't answer – I know it is not honourable to protest what the Eternal does for our good."

"What is it, Anna? What is disturbing you?"

She shook her head and stared into the distance. A single tear trickled down the side of her nose and slid under the veil she quickly drew across it. Mordecai said nothing. Then, with deliberation, he untied the linen girdle at his waist, folded it narrowly, and began to bind his eyes. Thus blindfolded, he sat back, crossing his legs in the beggar's pose, holding out both hands with the palms upward.

"Alms for the blind, Lady? Not money, not bread – only your burden. Give that to me and it is enough."

Anna struggled for composure. Yes, when he was blind she *had* talked freely, and she had never seen that as giving him a gift. Perhaps it was? Yes, of course it was! To be needed *was* a gift, and nobody had needed Mordecai for twenty years. *Except Sobek*, she thought with a sudden jolt. Sobek *and* all the others like her, she hastened to remind herself – but perhaps that was more of a practical need – not an emotional or spiritual one. Anna shook herself crossly – now she was doing what everyone did – reducing the needy to a loaf of bread, a bandage or a dry corner. Was poor young Sobek not as much a woman as herself, with needs beyond bread and shelter?

She jumped up impatiently and drew a deep breath – she could not even keep her mind still for a moment! – and here was Mordecai calmly waiting for an answer. Loukanos and Dan would be back shortly and this rare time of quiet would be over. Smoothing her gown, she sat down again and spoke quickly before her spirit failed her.

"I am disturbed, Mordecai, because I can sit here, in the graveyard where he was buried, and *not* weep over Ammiel. The agony which nearly killed me, but which I dreaded losing, has passed."

"The pain was because of your love. Now you feel disloyal."

"Yes. Does not the intensity of sorrow echo the intensity of the love behind it? Oh, the sadness is always there – but the passion of my grief has left me … Am I really so shallow?"

"Anna, love which is one sided cannot sustain passion. It must have stimulus. One small store of half-realised hopes is not enough to feed a lifetime, and you cannot light your life with an extinguished lamp. Would Ammiel *want* you to live so feebly?

500

Did he not turn to you – joyfully! – when the pain of his wife's death had also faded?"

Anna blinked. Of course he did! Why had she never realised it?

"Joyfully!" she repeated numbly. "Living joyfully! You showed me that was what mattered – that was your milestone. I took it for my own – but somehow, lately, I have taken my eyes away from it."

She leant forward and slid the bandage from his eyes with fingers which shook as they accidentally brushed his bearded face.

"See here, my friend?" She showed him the fringe on the hem of her mantle. There was a gap where a blue tassel had been torn away.

"This is the same one?"

"No, I have three. I even tore them all alike, so I would not forget. And yet I did forget."

"I did not. And I did pray for you ... I still do."

Mordecai pulled from his clothes, the silken blue decoration which hung on a cord around his neck, and saw her eyes flicker in response. She compressed her lips firmly with a half-impatient shake of her head, but they still trembled as she hesitantly replied.

"And I ... I may have forgotten to live joyfully, but I did not forget my promise ... I prayed for you too ... and still do, my friend."

"Still? But now I am healed, and my whole life is changed! What more is there to ask for me?" he asked, with half a smile, though his heart was anxious.

"You would have me stop?" she flashed.

Their eyes met briefly – hers, brown and hazel, filmed with tears; his, clear and dark and carefully expressionless. He looked away quickly. *You might bare your soul to a man who cannot see your eyes, but if you see what is in mine you may regret it.*

"There is more," she said abruptly, "but turn your face or I shall never have the courage to finish."

"Very well. Should I cover my eyes again, Lady?"

"Don't call me *Lady*, as if you were still a beggar, Mordecai!" she cried. "The formality is all very well for my aunt, but between us surely it is not needed! I am not above you now, nor ever was, even when you were on the streets."

Between us! If only that had meant something!

"Say on. I will not stare at you." *Ah, Anna! You may have stared at my ruined face, but you always spoke to the man behind it.*

"It is a miserable confession, but I can bear it unspoken no longer, and whom can I tell? It is simply this – I … I am … lonely … and very ashamed of it, when I have so many good and loving people around me. It seems so ungrateful, when I think of others who have so much less than I, and nobody at all to care about them. I have my family, of course – father and Johanan and Aunt Mari – but they will stay in Jerusalem once I have returned to Galilee. My Dan is still young, but he is almost a man now and already he is away more than he is at home. My beloved Louki, so recently found, and who understands me best, and with whom I can ask or discuss anything freely and know we will both be the richer for it … he will soon leave the Land altogether. Dear Etta and young Marta are close to my heart … but …" her voice broke, "unworthy and unwomanly as it sounds, it is not enough!"

"Ah, so you need Ammiel more, even while you need him less. I perceive your conflict."

Anna took a deep breath. There was no point in stopping now. She spoke almost coldly.

"Do not misunderstand me, Mordecai. He was a rare and generous man who stirred my senses – loving, and respectful of a woman, even one more educated than he. But it is not Ammiel himself I hunger for – it is the consolation of a like mind."

"I see. And if you found such a mind?"

Again Anna sprang to her feet. She leant back against the tree, tapping the gnarled trunk impatiently with one foot.

"Oh!" she answered sarcastically, though her voice was unsteady. "We would fly to great spiritual heights together – and then I would crash to earth, starving for want of tenderness and shivering for lack of warmth. And should he be a man of strong affections and delight in natural beauty, would he choose an old virgin such as I, unless he was in his dotage?"

She swallowed a betraying sob. "I was not made to be an Abishag."

That is enough! She stopped herself in alarm. *Are you mad, Anna? This is a man you are speaking to! Take hold of your senses at once!*

She dropped her eyes, and rubbed her arms wearily, attempting to smile.

"There, I have finished my self-pitying little confession, and now you need fear no more 'morbid words from a sensible woman'. The Eternal knows what is best for me, better than I do myself. He taught me twice that I must live without the man I wanted. As for the man I need now – he does not exist. Therefore, clearly, I must *not* need him." She bit her lip to stop it trembling.

503

Mordecai stood up slowly, retying his girdle, his face set, his dark eyes dilated beneath their strong black brows. Strange, neither of them had noticed before that he was the taller. Now he stood over her. Now he looked her in the face. He was in Jerusalem the Holy City after years of exile. The Messiah was here. The King was preparing his throne. The rulers were in an uproar. The people were defiant. The whole world was on edge. But there was only this garden, this moment.

"He exists, O blind one," he said quietly, holding her eyes with his. "He knows full well that you are both a soaring eagle and a nesting dove. And you do need him. He only waits to hear that you also want him."

The world stood still.

There was only a sharp intake of breath, the pounding of two hearts …

"Anna! Mordecai!"

"We're ready to go!"

Dan and Loukanos strode into view, waving as they called. Dan ran up, chattering.

"We were really careful, we didn't touch any graves, but it's just as well they're marked, isn't it, Uncle Louki? We put a stone for each of you on father's grave. There is quite a little heap there, where Johanan and Uncle Asa and Aunt Mari have been putting them – even Rhoda and Shefi, she told me – Oh! and of course, you too, Anna – at first … anyway …"

His voice trailed off. Loukanos was looking oddly at the others. Anna had been crying.

"I'm sorry, *Amma*," the boy said repentantly. "You must be sad that you can't put your own stone there …"

"It's all right, Dan!" his mother answered hastily, snatching him for a hug and sniffing bravely. "I'm better now. We'd better hurry, hadn't we, Louki?"

She looked at him as if daring him to say anything.

"Yes, we had," he replied, obediently neutral. "It will be dark soon, and we should be getting back to the Temple where there are lights … and people … and split up to find out what's happening there. Mari said Old Pagiel, and Nathan Hill-and-Dale may visit the house, so perhaps by the time we get back, Etta and Caleb will have news as well."

"Dan! Whatever is wrong?" Mordecai asked sharply.

The boy's face was stricken – his jaw dropping, his hand pointing with a shaking finger.

"The gardener!" he gasped. "The gardener!"

They swung around to see the gardener in the far distance, having finished his efforts for the day, wearily dragging off his headcloth. He wiped his face and neck with it, and began stumping off with a curiously familiar gait.

They were all frozen for an instant – all but Mordecai, who had never seen the man before.

"Surely – that's not – those ears! – he looks just like – Bukki!" Dan hissed. "Oh, Anna! It is! It's *Bukki!*"

Loukanos drew breath to roar at the man to stop but Anna clutched his arm frantically.

"No! No! He'll run away if he knows it's us! Quickly, Mordecai – he won't know you!"

Mordecai nodded. "Stay together – do what you need to do – I'll meet you back at Mari's house!" he flung at them.

And he began to run as fast as he could after the figure retreating along the narrow, shrub-crowded path towards the end of the twisting, graveyard garden.

Chapter Forty-seven

IT was very late when, weary and cold, Asa, Mari and Johanan finally returned home from the dinner at Bethany. Expecting that the household had retired to bed, they were amazed to find the large reception room full of people all talking at once, and before long they had forgotten their tiredness and were soon as wide awake as everyone else. Asa, as the head of the house, took charge, holding up a hand for silence.

"Brethren, please sit down, and let us save confusion by exchanging our information in an orderly fashion," he advised courteously. "Shefi, will you bring spiced wine and hot water, and more braziers? Rhoda, some extra blankets – and a fleece for Old Pagiel's feet – yes, sir, your hands are blue too and your wife will be angry with us for neglecting your comfort. Cushions, Johanan, that's the way. Etta, take a blanket too, if you please. Nathan, my friend, do mind that brazier, a cheery heart is a good thing, but burns are nothing to laugh at – remember the last time … Anna, don't sit in that draught, you are very flushed, and may take cold. Now Shefi and Rhoda, you have done enough for one night and must be exhausted. Off to your beds, and thank you."

Finally everyone was as settled and comfortable as Asa's hospitable heart could wish, and the news of the night was exchanged. Dan told of the visit to Ammiel's sepulchre, and everyone was astounded at hearing that they had seen none other than Bukki – the lazy, the perfidious, the thief – whom nobody had seen since he stalked out of Banayim four years ago. Mordecai had run him to ground in the lower city near the rank warehouses for salt fish … in a sour little shop crammed with noisy travellers from all over the Empire. Bukki had scuttled in to this veritable Babel, clearly late and much out of favour with a massive, ferocious and moustached woman – who seemed to have six brawny arms at once, swiftly serving Cretan beer, Galilean wine, Idumean vinegars, dried fruits, pastries and soup, with grim efficiency. Bukki was at a loss to understand most of the insults that were flung his way by the multilingual patrons, but those hurled at his jug-shaped head by the mistress of the establishment were pretty clear, even to an ignorant Galilean, judging by the way his prominent ears glowed red at the sound. He slunk out to the kitchen, sullenly bailing heavy dippers of liquor from great firkins, with hands still grimed with graveyard mud – and it was there that Mordecai finally accosted him. Now at last they would know what *had* happened to Bukki. They listened intently as Mordecai told them what he had found out.

"After he left Banayim, Bukki went to Tiberius but left in a hurry after suspiciously winning too often at *Basilius*. He wandered aimlessly around various garrison towns for a while, ending up in Jerusalem because the cost of living here is so cheap. He was robbed of the last of his money while he was drunk, so he had to find work, like it or not. Parah – the big woman – employed him two years ago, to serve during busy times, feast days and so on, and he helped himself to the bag when she wasn't looking. Bad luck for Bukki, she realised what he was up to, so she placed witnesses and let him do it several times more, before she pounced. She said he could face a Roman tribunal on a charge of *furtum manifestum*, or be beaten to a pulp by her four large brothers. If he didn't like the sound of those, she'd generously give him another choice. Being ignorant of the penalty and terrified of being sent to the galleys, he shrank from being taken to court, neither did he want to risk being crippled or killed by a beating from four big angry men at once. He took the third choice. So now Bukki spends his days working as a labourer in the graveyard – he's not a true gardener of course – and his nights slaving in the food and wine shop. No, Dan, he can't run away, I don't think he'd have the spirit for it any more. But more than that, not only does she hold all the money, the condition was," here Mordecai's fine eyes twinkled, "he had to marry her to take away her reproach." There was a collective gasp, and he added casually, "Oh, and by the way, she lied about having brothers."

The room erupted! Aunt Mari went into a peal of giggles and frantically flapped her fan – Caleb chortled quietly to himself – Dan crowed and Asa roared! Johanan laughed till he hiccupped – Loukanos laughed till he cried – Aunt Etta laughed and then cried – Anna laughed and cried at the same time. It was justice for Bukki, but somewhere deep down, the women felt for him too.

"What is *furtum manifestum* anyway?" Dan asked once gravity was salvaged from the waves of hilarity. "*Would* he get the galleys for it?"

"*Open theft* – caught in the act, as it were – and the penalty is the same as the Law of Moses," Mordecai answered with a half-smile. "*Repay fourfold*, which would have been more honourable, and no doubt preferable. It would have been a shorter sentence, anyway, even if he had to work it off! Unluckily for him, guilt and ignorance – and fear, their inevitable offspring – pushed him to make a poor bargain."

Dan's rumpled spirit where Bukki was concerned was soothed considerably on hearing that the wicked had *not* prospered like a green bay tree, and suddenly the answers he had once determined to choke out of him could wait. Finer details of Bukki's story would have to be more fully explored at a later time. Now they must get down to the more serious matters. Caleb and Etta had been talking with Pagiel and Nathan, who now gave their opinion that with the doubling of military presence in the city, and the volatility of its overcrowded inhabitants at Festival times, any disturbance would incur instant and severe retribution.

The Judaean Prefect was always in attendance during the Feasts – anticipating trouble from the massive influx of pilgrims who swelled the population of the city three times a year. That expectation, thanks to his heavy-handedness, was often realised. His insolence towards the Jews' religion extended even to assuming custody of the ceremonial garments of the High Priests, (the office of which he changed at will). The holy vestments were now released only for the Festivals – restricting religious autonomy was a useful tool in maintaining control. Because of this, the Prefect also had sole power to endorse or reverse a death sentence passed by the Jews' Council according to Moses' Law. Not that he cared who lived or died, but he did care about maintaining order. Down he would come from Caesarea with the pomp befitting the Emperor's Procurator, bringing extra troops, coldly demonstrating his readiness to use the swords which clanked at their sides. Nobody made the mistake of assuming this threat was idle. He was the man whose disguised soldiers had mingled with thousands of Jews protesting his misuse of Temple funds to build an aqueduct. When the swords came out, blood had splashed the temple itself. Most of that blood was Galilean, but some of Herod's men had got in the way, and deepened the rift between the two politicians. The

Prefect's self-serving decisions, arbitrary judgements, and indifference to the people he ruled, made him a dangerous person to provoke. If Herod was a fox, Pilatus was a weasel – all the more ferocious for his smallness, stubbornness, and spite. This Passover, Herod was in residence himself, and the ill feeling between the wary rulers did not ease the city's tension.

But now Mari was itching to have her say. She, Asa and Johanan had arrived at Bethany respectably early, the two men humbly taking the lower seats at the dinner into which she had cleverly insinuated them. Several years ago she and Johanan had been to a wedding in Jericho and there she had made acquaintance with the host's sister-in-law, subsequently giving hospitality to Rebekah during her various trips to the big city for the purchase of presents and gowns and such-like female missions. Mari had shared her friend's distress over Simon's leprosy, and rejoiced wholeheartedly when the Prophet of Nazareth restored him to health. Now her sympathy was being rewarded. Having obligingly arranged matters with her brother-in-law's steward, Rebekah tugged Mari out to where the servants waited. "They're coming in – quickly, if you want to ask him something, now's your chance!"

Mari snatched the towel and basin thrust at her and hurried. So it was that as the servants did their duty by the guests of honour, she knelt at the feet of the Teacher himself and washed his dust-caked feet with her ringed fingers and braceleted hands, the bright gold and gemstones blurred in the muddy water, and his clean wet footprint dark on the lap of her expensive gown. The woman kneeling beside her, washing the splayed and hairy feet of Fisher Shimon, looked sideways and smiled warmly.

"My lord, I know you are the Anointed of God, and imbued with His power," Mari whispered quickly, drying his instep with her dress instead of the towel, so flustered was she, "but I can see that you are also a man in great need of rest. Would you accept the hospitality of my house in Jerusalem for Passover, and as long afterwards as you wish? You *and* your men. You will be quite private. I have a large upper room, and it is being made ready as we speak …" The foot twitched suddenly and she looked up apologetically. "Oh, I'm sorry, have I …?"

"No, Mari – not at all," he whispered back with amused eyes. "Your rings are tickling my foot." The smile faded and he added soberly, "Thank you for the room – one night is all we need."

Mari sighed with relief and hastily began the other foot, being more careful with her jewellery, and this time remembering the towel. "I am honoured, sir," she said gladly. "Now, to get there, you –"

"No need for directions, Mari. Did you need to tell me your name?"

Simon hailed his guest enthusiastically just then, and Mari's snatched moment was over. She slipped away swiftly before anyone could ask awkward questions about the bejewelled servant, and bent down beside the others, shaking with reaction as she told them of her success. Asa and Johanan squeezed her hands admiringly.

"Well done, Mari!" "Well done, *Amma!*"

Her eyes glowed. Johanan did not call her *Amma* very often now that his beard had grown. Mari pressed their hands in return, and thankfully joined the women's table in the adjoining room.

The evening was long, but they did not feel it so. As well as Jeshua himself, and his twelve in attendance, there was the very man half of Jerusalem had been desperate to see – Lazarus! Looking,

512

at first glance, exactly like any other middle-aged man in the room, except for the energy which characterised his every movement. Even in repose, reclining at the table, he looked eager, as if everything was a new experience. Waiting on the men were his two older sisters, Miriam and Martha – quiet, plain, dumpy. Almost they could have been described as unattractive – were it not for the sensitivity of their time-written faces, and the tenderness in their crinkled eyes. Miriam in particular had an intense air about her which Johanan observed closely. He noticed that their loving looks were as much for their younger friend Jeshua as they were for their beloved brother – and that Miriam had a strange expression on her gentle face which was somewhere between fear and grief. The dinner was a good one, generous and varied, but there was a subdued atmosphere which they could not fathom.

In the women's room, the conversation quickly turned to the extraordinary day when Lazarus had been raised from the dead. He was definitely dead, Martha assured them grimly. Those who doubted it, and who inspected his sepulchre immediately afterwards, came out smartly. There had been no other body in that tomb, which still held the unmistakeable stench of death. As they hurriedly tore off the face cloth, and unwound the wrappings which bound their brother's awe-inspiring, shuffling body, the sisters had held in their hands linen stained and soiled with the swift putrefaction of the unembalmed corpse. What they could not understand was the pristine state of the white linen grave clothes beneath. Miriam lifted her veined hands expressively. A miracle was a miracle, why quibble about details? She seemed preoccupied, watching the men through the doorway, continually touching a bulky leather pocket tied at her waist, as if reassuring herself it was still there. Meanwhile, Mari reached for her ever-present fan and plied it vigorously. Most women had a remarkable ability to discuss graphic details of gruesome topics in the middle of eating – but perhaps this was carrying it a bit far.

In the feast room there was a lull as the women cleared dishes before replenishing the table, and this was the moment Miriam had waited for. She entered quickly, pulling from its protective pocket, and cradling in her hands, a sealed alabaster jar. As the lamplight caressed it, the translucent pinkish stone glowed like living flesh. Johanan thought perhaps it was a gift for their host, but suddenly Miriam struck the narrow neck against the table with a sharp blow, snapping off the top. Everyone stared, but without a word she stood behind Jeshua, and gently swept back the short thick curls from his forehead. Lovingly, like a mother who protects her child's eyes, she held her hand cupped there, and slowly inclined the jar over his head. Under her breath she was reciting disjointed fragments from the ancient parable of Solomon the wise.

My King …
Your love-tokens are more praiseworthy than wine …
Fragrant and beautiful your perfume …
Your name is as oil poured from vessel to vessel …

A dark golden brown stream flowed from the broken edge – and a strong perfume filled the room, pushing out the mundane smells of fish and bread, spiced lentils, burning lamps, hard-working bodies and the herbal pomades of the guests. Even Mari's expensive oil-of-roses was overpowered, rendered pale and sickly in comparison. An insistent, musty, spicy, pine-tinged, smoky effusion was this scent, with its overtones of wood and old leather. It was distinctive, it was unmistakeable. It drew the women from the other room into the doorway, and the dinner was forgotten as the essence distilled from the crushed roots of a small, rare mountain plant seemed to take over the house.

514

This was no heavy scent imported from Rome, no sweet oil of Arabia nor sensuous potion of Egypt. This was a perfume which came from the highest snow countries of the far, far south east; a robust, pervasive incense, the pure product enhanced with compounds guarded jealously by the perfumers, such as were named by them 'Blameless' and 'Joy of the Mountains'. It was an incense most precious – an incense of royalty. It was Spikenard – but not the essence of the hardy mauve flower commonly given the same name in the village markets, a cheap perfume for pomade and linen. This was the original, the true, the rare, the real thing – harvested in a cold, lofty, mysterious land; carried thousands of miles on the backs of camels; prepared by master perfumers – and priced beyond comprehension for the average man.

While my King is at his table, my spikenard breathes out its scent . . .

The rich oil poured into his hair and slid behind his ears, down his neck, down his back – some flowed down the side of his face to his beard, through its strong black waves, dimming the white threads within it, slipping over the bare skin of his neck, and sinking into the crisp hair of his chest. He sat still, his eyes were closed, and he seemed to inhale the scent deeply. Miriam smoothed her protective palm back from his forehead, gently raking her creased fingers through his hair, combing the oil evenly through its dark curls, stroking it into his beard.

"The King leaves his bride," she murmured. "She will seek him and not find him."

Everyone was paralysed. What *was* the woman *doing*? A few drops of such precious stuff would suffice for an honoured guest – and she was almost bathing him in it! But she had not finished. The decisive way she had ruined the jar showed she had no interest in saving any of it for herself. Her face sober, she bent over his feet, which were tucked up on the bench behind the next guest, one of the thunderous ben Zebedees. The fisherman made room for her quickly, unsure of what she might do next. Just as deliberately, she poured the remainder of the broken, pink-veined jar on to the calloused feet which Mari had recently washed. Kneeling down, she threw off her veil, revealing her straight, hip-length hair – hair which was almost white at the roots, streaking to grey for much of its length, and yet for a wide handspan at the very ends, it still held a faded reminder of the rich brown it had once been. Miriam reached behind her head and with a swift, practised movement, pulled the whole mass forward, and wrapped the ends around her hand. The hair grown long ago by her younger self thus became her towel. Silently, tenderly, thoroughly, she wiped it through the dripping dark-gold oil and so all over the feet which had walked so very many exhausting miles. She then sat back and watched him, almost as if she were praying. She held his feet with both hands, leaned forward and said quietly,

"Love is stronger than death, and many waters can not quench it."

Jeshua opened his eyes slowly, and a few silent drops brimmed and fell. He looked full into the earnest face before him, taking the woman's wrinkled, oil sticky-hands, pressing them gently, with a deeply grateful smile. For a moment she could have been his mirror, reflecting the same look, the same smile, the same tears. She stood up, twisting her hair back to its place, resuming her veil.

The perfume had produced a potent effect on the whole room – the tension, anxiety, and strain on all the faces began to melt away. Nobody understood what had happened, but nobody cared any more. Except, strangely, the Nazarene Prophet's own men. Suddenly a knot of them clustered together, whispering, almost hissing. The Kerioth's face was a study in righteous indignation.

516

"This is outrageous!" he said agitatedly. "Teacher! Master! In your company have we not been at pains to live frugally, without selfish extravagance, as befits holy men? How can you condone – how can you *accept* this luxurious waste?" He picked up the empty bottle and ran his bitten fingertips hurriedly inside it, as if to scoop out the last viscous drops, but succeeded only in cutting himself. He dropped it with an impatient exclamation. He turned to Miriam, looking almost sick.

"This could have been sold for a full year's wages, Lady! And you have wasted it in a meaningless gesture to draw attention to yourself! Don't you realise what all that money would have meant to the poor?"

Suddenly Jeshua sat up straight, his hair and beard and skin gleaming with the clinging oil, his clothes damp with it. "Leave her alone!" he said sharply. "Why are you reprimanding her? If you really care about the poor, give them *your* money, not someone else's. Be charitable to them whenever you please – they will always be around. But I will not. Tonight, this good work was done for me, out of everything this woman has to give – not the money you think she has wasted on me but a precious gift of love, care, touch, compassion – and profound understanding."

Understanding? Nobody was understanding any of it! Not the Kerioth, not the ben Zebedees, not anyone in the room – except the Prophet Jeshua, the quiet old woman standing behind him, and perhaps the other woman who had knelt beside Mari to wash feet; watching closely, as if she too might understand.

"This woman has truly *heard* my words. She has poured this perfume on my body to prepare it for my burial," Jeshua said clearly. "And mark this truth, my friends – wherever the good news is preached in the whole world, this action of hers will likewise be a powerful, lingering incense, and that will be *her* memorial."

Mari sighed as Johanan finished the story.

"We have no idea what he meant," she said confusedly. "We can only wonder if he was referring to the burial of his humble life – as he is raised to the throne – the anointing of a king's body to bury the common man's, or something like that. Miriam was too upset for us to ask her what it was all about. But whatever it meant, we could see that the one they called the Kerioth was simply fuming – chewing his nails like a cannibal, he was. Anyway, everyone soon calmed down – spikenard does have a soothing effect on people, I'm told, though if we hadn't had so much fresh air blowing through the room I'm sure we would all have got headaches, it was so strong. Perhaps the Kerioth had one, he stepped out shortly afterwards and we didn't see him again."

"So, that was our night," Asa managed to get in edgeways, and shrugged.

Everyone shifted in their seats and drew breath and stretched and sighed and then looked expectantly at Loukanos, who also shrugged.

"For all our good intentions, we found out nothing more," he said resignedly. "We loitered about in all sorts of places – even near the High Priest's quarters. There was some kind of gathering called there, priests, Sadducees, Pharisees and various grim-faced men coming and going but with guards and torchlight around the gate we couldn't get close enough to find out anything. Had Mordecai been with us, he might have managed to slip in somehow, but running that wretched Bukki to earth put an end to that. Apart from nearly breaking our necks when some fool ran out of the light and shoved past us on some Stygian steps, it was

518

otherwise uneventful. Queer, I thought something about him was familiar for a moment … I just couldn't put a finger on it."

Loukanos mentally kicked himself. To talk about dark steps and breaking necks just after mentioning Bukki's name was painfully unfortunate, especially considering where they had been just that afternoon. He yawned noisily in the hope of distracting attention from his clumsiness. Old Pagiel took this as a hint and politely dragged Nathan Hill-and-Dale away with him as he said good night, promising to let them know if he heard anything else the next day. Etta, who was almost asleep in her chair, gave in too, and slipped thankfully off to the women's guest chamber.

"Well, I suppose we had better get to bed, as well." Asa rose reluctantly. "It has been a long night, with another long day tomorrow – especially with the Teacher and his men here for Passover. We must be sure to have everything arranged discreetly, and keep out of their way. They won't want crowds collecting, so be careful not to mention anything ahead of time, even to the servants, about who we are expecting."

"Yes, my dear," Mari replied obediently. "And even if that spikenard didn't give me a headache at dinner, a late night certainly will, so let's disperse now and get some rest. Come on, boys."

Loukanos suddenly sat bolt upright. "Wait! What did you say about a headache?"

Mari stared. "Late night? Spikenard?"

"No, no, before that! At the dinner …"

"Oh – ah – oh yes, I said without so much fresh air in the room we might all have got headaches … and that perhaps the Kerioth had one, because he went outside …"

"And you didn't see him *the rest of the night?*"

"Well, no, I didn't – we didn't. Goodness me, Louki, why should you care if the man had a headache or not? From what you've told me, you didn't even like him very much."

Loukanos leapt to his feet and slapped his hands together. "It *was* him! Jude! Jude the Kerioth! He was the one who nearly knocked us over by the High Priest's palace! He was so preoccupied I doubt he even noticed."

"Louki! That sleek young man in a hurry? Are you sure?"

Mordecai, Dan, Asa and Johanan all repeated variations of Anna's question but the more Loukanos thought about it, the more certain he was.

"I think the only reason I didn't recognise him at the time was because I believed him to be in Bethany! But of course it was him – savaging his fingernails as usual – and that settles it for me!"

Mordecai frowned. "The question is," he said uneasily, "not just why did he leave the dinner without a word – but what in the world was he doing anywhere near that den of lions, who are just slavering to devour his master?"

Dan piped up sleepily. "Perhaps the same as us – trying to find out more so he could warn the Teacher."

"Ah!" Asa nodded approvingly. "Very courageous of him."

"Not a bad thought," Mordecai agreed slowly, determined to worm his way into a Council meeting himself, the first chance he got.

"Good or bad, it's as far as we'll get tonight." Anna stood wearily and dragged the boys to their feet. "To bed, everyone, before we drop where we stand. The leaven search first thing in the morning, too … and preparation for our own Passover as well as the Teacher's. Tomorrow will be quite a day."

Chapter Forty-eight

MARI looked around with satisfaction. It had been a frantic day, with everyone so tired from the previous night, but now everything was almost ready. The servants had scoured the house from top to bottom and then Asa had taken his lamp, said the correct prayer and in perfect silence ceremoniously inspected every corner for leaven. There was a moment's panic while Rhoda tried to remember whether a stale barley cake put aside for Noah, her dove, had been made with fruit juice or water, but water it was, so the cake was left alone, and if there *had* been a fermenting drop or two within, well, that would be covered by Asa's ritual declaration as he snuffed his lamp.

"All the leaven in my house, which I have seen or which I have not seen, may it be nothing, may it be counted as mere dust of the earth."

Caleb and Dan were wide-eyed at such additional ceremony embellishing the prescribed search for leaven, but once it became clear that any prohibited foods so discovered were not to be disposed of by eating, they disappeared to a sheltered pen at the stable end of the courtyard, where they lovingly tended and inspected the young ram which Asa had bought with such keen-eyed care at the sheep market the week before. It was a satisfying feeling to go about something which was their normal business,

521

and though they were glad to find the small creature as sound as it ought to be, its pre-determined end was something they preferred not to dwell on. Dan picked up the heavy little body, settling it easily across his shoulders just as he might do in the field, comforted by the familiarity, missing his pet Moses, and trying not to think about the ever-nearer fate of the innocent animal which lay so trustingly against his bare neck, raising its head occasionally to chuckle gently in his ear and nibble curiously at the red whiskers which sprouted on his chin. Dan put him down reluctantly. Sometimes he wished the Eternal had asked people to sacrifice something cold-blooded – like fish.

Now someone was calling, and he had to go. Loukanos and Johanan were taking him to observe a ritual he would not see at home. In the valley over the fast-rushing Kidron Brook, white-clad priests were striding importantly through a barley field, carefully selecting and tying up bundles of uncut stalks in preparation for the first day of the Unleavened Bread festival which would start after Passover Day. With the festivals interlocking, and drawing in the start of the barley harvest, this was one of the busiest times of the year. Although a High Day, and therefore a ceremonial Sabbath, the first day of Unleavened Bread still required that the first sheaf must be ceremonially cut and waved before the Eternal, accompanied by even more sacrifices – but it would be followed by a boisterous feast which nobody wanted to miss, especially after the relative solemnity of Passover.

Dan thought the field looked very comical with all its bunches of barley standing up like the shaggy plumes on a soldier's helmet, or some of the strange hair-dressings he had noticed among the ebony-skinned Ethiopians who sprinkled the city's population. He and Johanan tore up bunches of grass and fashioned similar head-dresses for themselves until they were in kinks of laughter.

Finally Loukanos – wearing the Very Patient Face which he produced at such times – eventually dragged them away, reminding them that the serious part of the day would soon begin. They returned home without further delay and after some last minute flurry from the kitchen servants, everyone assembled in the courtyard. The small pen was opened, a rope put around a woolly neck, and the eager, fat tailed lamb trotted out, looking up at them with trusting eyes. They all silently put their hands on the warm, rough coat, then Asa and Mordecai led him away.

Old Caleb immediately took himself off down the street, to become involved in a head-whirling argument with Nathan Hill-and-Dale about the complications of the Festival calendar which had frayed the original observance dates at both ends. Nathan tried to explain that the difficulties had been caused first by the Babylonian Exile, then by the bizarre Roman system of beginning days in the middle of the night, and later compounded by the sheer impracticalities of a whole nation trying to kill their animals on the same day in the same place. When he began to hold forth on how the moon and the sun affected the months, and tried to tell Caleb that every now and then there must be extra days in a year, Caleb was outraged. Sunset and sunrise, the early and latter rains, the time of almond blossom, lambing, shearing, ploughing and harvest … with all their moons waxing and waning sensibly, (not messing about with the calendar) … what more did a man need? He refused to believe that the Festivals were as moveable as Nathan claimed. The old ways were good enough for him, he said darkly, as if suspecting Nathan of sorcery.

Nathan's intense lecturing began to escalate into forcefulness, and he shook his head crossly at Caleb's ignorance, advising him to heed the saying *When in Judaea do as the Judaean!* As Caleb left, Nathan shouted after him that he would be joining with Old

Pagiel's family for their *Pesach* meal on the following evening and he was sure Caleb would be very welcome if he changed his mind …! However a bemused Caleb just shook his head, shivering at the unorthodox idea of eating two Passovers only a day apart. He was thankful that Asa and Mari – whatever they usually did – would for their guests' sake proceed as rustic Galileans, and engage in the prescribed ritual tonight. He was glad that *he* would not be queuing with a poor little lamb tomorrow for hours in the Temple; holding its precious, perfect, frightened body in the crush – just so that he might slit its throat before the priests, and see its blood pouring into a basin and flung against the altar by a practised flick of a priestly wrist! Then for its carcase to be hung on the flaying hooks and its entrails cut out and washed, the fat salted and slapped on the burning altar, along with thousands of others … all while singing joyful *Hallal* songs!

It would be far too much for Old Caleb and he knew it … and there would still be the matter of carrying it all the way home – the pathetic waxy shell of flesh wrapped up like a dead baby, to spit-roast and eat! He was glad Mordecai and Asa were despatching their lamb quietly at the first shades of twilight, not among the oppressive crowds of the next day – it would be less distressing for all of them, especially the helpless little animal.

Caleb's tender thoughts did him credit, but Asa and Mordecai did not see before them, as he did, a happy, lively youngster which might have lived abundantly, providing wool and siring offspring until it grew too old and calmly died a natural death. They were talking seriously of many things, merely scratching the lamb's ears and stroking his coat without thinking, until the time came, and even then, as they laid their hands on him and prayed, and stretched his tender neck for the swiftly plunging blade, they saw only a sacrifice, accomplished as a necessity.

524

The women were busy in the upper room used for guests and large gatherings. It was the same room where the whole family had shared their last supper the night of Ammiel's untimely death … so neither Etta nor Mari commented on Anna's absent look. The low table was prepared, the floor made comfortable with thick flat cushions for a leisurely night of lounging on an elbow. No longer was the Passover celebrated with families standing up to eat in haste, shod and clothed for an immediate journey. Since the Exile, the Rabbis had insisted that as dwellers in their own land, Jews should modify various details of the remembrance, and such changes had been adopted for so many generations past that they were now established custom; even when the Passover instructions were read out from the Second Book of Moses in synagogue, few remarked the difference. As decreed by the learned ones, Jews must now dress in festive garments – because they were no longer poor wanderers and outcasts. They ought not to stand, as though they were still slaves who may not sit and must quickly be away. Now, they should recline to eat with leisure, in the manner of men who were free. Therefore, as Mari's upper room was prepared for Passover supper, the best and thickest cushions were brought, with the most comfortable put at the centre of the long table, where the Head would sit, with his most honoured companions on his right and left. Bedding was neatly stacked in the corner of the large room, so the men could unroll sleeping mats and blankets when they pleased.

Up and down the stairs the women ran, bringing basins and generous towels for the ritual washings, Uncle Joseph's best wine and Mari's finest cups, bitter herbs, salt water, freshly-baked unleavened bread, vinegar, and compounded dried fruit. The foodstuffs they placed discreetly to one side under a cloth, Mari having been too flustered to let the Teacher know she would provide them, and having no idea whether the group of the Chosen would be arriving with all their own food for the supper, or bringing only their lamb ready for the fire. Whichever it was, they must not find anything missing!

Rhoda carefully placed a large crumb in the window sill beside a tallow candle, according to custom, so everyone would be assured that the room had been properly examined by the leaven search. It was an unleavened crumb, just in case their guests did not notice it – but if they did, they would throw it out of the window as a matter of form, and know that all was as it should be. A small brazier with a large brass kettle stood ready to warm the room and supply hot water with which to cut the wine if required. Mari's bracelets jangled energetically as she polished with her own hands a precious silver-coated menorah of many lamps, and the women counted off last-moment tasks on their fingers.

"Are there extra lights for the length of the table and the window embrasure? What about spare oil? Fuel for the brazier? Did you have those knives sharpened?"

Yes, all was done! While readying the upper room, Mari had not forgotten her own family's requirements, and it only remained for her to check Rhoda's work downstairs. The young woman was glowing with the honour of overseeing the preparation for such a special occasion. All the finest furnishings and dishes and other items had gone to the upper room, but there was no lack of respect or beauty in the arrangements which Rhoda had directed so well. A steady, clear fire was burning in the large stone-flagged kitchen, and soaked pomegranate-wood spits stood ready for the lambs. The small and tender carcases would not take long to roast, and a whole night stretched before them. Had it not been for the fear of their guests arriving too early, Mari would have been quite calm.

Now the dusk was rushing upon them, and here was Asa with the meat to roast at last. Quickly, on to the spit with it, careful, break no bones, mind those little ones in the neck and the tail. Where is Mordecai? Ah, Mordecai – a sentimental man at heart, Asa was sure. He had been taken by the sight of a beautifully decorated water jar in a late-closing market, and waving Asa on, had stopped to buy it for Mari – a gift for his hostess. It would be bad luck to bring it to her empty, so he would have it filled first, but he would not be much longer. Rhoda! the gate! Rhoda, laughing at the tall man who cautiously carried the elegant glazed jar unsteadily on his shoulder, instead of easily on his head – clearly unused to a woman's task! Anna – appearing so suddenly anyone would think she had been watching – hurrying to take the burden from him. Wait! Two strangers at the gate, with baskets and a heavy bundle – they had followed Mordecai – asking for the head of the house. Father! You are wanted here!

"This way, sirs," he replied. "All has been made ready upstairs. First let me show you where your lamb can be put to the fire."

Mari! They're here! Anna – run up and light those lamps! Gather around, everyone, the Teacher will soon follow, and they must not be disturbed. *Hi-yi!* May the good God forgive me – I forgot the water! Such a disgrace ... Mordecai! Quickly, take your lovely new pitcher-full up to them – oh, thank you! What a relief! Thank you!

The lambs are roasting over the fire, there is a continual running to and fro to turn the spits, but the religious preparations are complete, and now for the social – a time for washing, careful dressing, more fussing – the smells from the kitchen more enticing

527

all the time, until finally, the honey-brown, shining crackled carcases, dripping juices, seared by flame, are cooked right through, tested and ready. Down come Shimon and the younger ben Zebedee – catching sight of Loukanos – mutual glimmers of recognition, could it be they look abashed? – but no remarks pass.

Shrouded with a cloth, the roasted lamb goes upstairs on a tray – there is a murmur of men's voices at the gate – in they come, eleven more of them, quietly, the leader intense and silent. Loukanos whispers their names to the boys as they pass, and a heady smell of spikenard hangs in the air. The gate is closed, the family steps out of sight and retires to take their Passover in the kitchen with the servants. Dan, the youngest male, will ask, "What mean ye by this ritual?" and the answer will come, "A Syrian ready to perish, was my father ..." and, "Many years ago, when we were slaves in Egypt ..."

Asa will say the words as usual. But tonight, nobody thinks of him as the head of the house, not even Asa himself. For tonight, this house is only the Teacher's. Once he himself was the youngest son in a little household, observing the lamb slain, asking, "What mean ye by this ritual?" How old he was before the answer echoed yearly within his boyish heart – "*This means that I must die, so that death will pass over all men!*" – only his Father in Heaven could tell.

Who is the youngest in the upper room tonight? Perhaps it is the Kerioth, perhaps Johanan ben Zebedee, perhaps the clear-hearted Nathanael – whichever of the Twelve it is, now he will dutifully ask the Lamb of God the same question. But he has already told them the answer, time and again, and they could not hear it, so tonight he will reply like any other household head, and only later will they understand.

528

And so it was, that on two different levels of Mari's spacious home, the Passover was celebrated. Of course, it was not according to the customary manner of one dwelling, one meal, one animal. But everyone in that house knew by now that ritual was not everything, it was the spirit of God's law which gave life and meaning – not the outward observance.

Downstairs Asa's Passover proceeded as usual – the benedictions over the wine, the hands washed, a blessing on the bitter herbs dabbled in salty water, the bread of affliction broken in half, held up in invitation and shared, the wine lifted up again, the ritual question, answered with the Deliverance story, the *Hallal* psalms, another cup lifted up, a prayer, the wine sipped by all except Anna, and hands washed once more.

Now the meal itself was begun. Asa wrapped a morsel of the lamb in a piece of the flat bread, and dipped it in the bitter herbs, passing this sop to Mordecai, who looked at him with a veiled expression, and thanked him for the honour. Mordecai passed his sop to Old Caleb, Caleb to Dan, Dan to Johanan. Johanan in a fit of unprecedented daring, passed his to Rhoda, who flushed mightily and quickly passed hers to Anna, and so it went, to Etta, then Mari, to Loukanos, to Shefi, and proceeded on to the other five household servants, the last of whom handed his respectfully to Asa. Mari began to fan herself suddenly and looked imploringly at Johanan, who grinned at her and slipped over to the window to open the thick, weatherproof shutters. He knew in a few moments she would be wildly motioning to him to close them again, but it kept her happy, and he didn't mind. Johanan paused – was that the creak of the main door? Surely not. He reached for the shutter latch, glancing out curiously.

Bars of light fell across the courtyard, and a shadowy figure was briefly illuminated – it was the man Loukanos called the Kerioth, slipping through the gate into the street. Greatly wondering, and not easy in his mind, Johanan returned to the table – but it was not his business. Who knew what private commissions the Teacher had given his men? No doubt he would return soon. His mother gave him a puzzled look, but he only winked at her and she flapped her hand at him laughingly. All of them being hungry, they ate heartily, but there was a thoughtful mood around the table. The Anointed of God was upstairs, eating the Passover under their roof, and had he and his men looked cheerful the family would have sung with noisy joy. But there was an air of strain, of tension, which did not sit well with merriment.

In the large kitchen, they finished the feast, sang their psalms soberly, put the carefully-picked lamb bones in the fire and finally went quietly to bed. On the third floor lamps were still burning in the guest room, voices still murmuring, but Asa's household was almost asleep on its feet. The servants vanished into their various quarters by kitchen, storeroom and stable, and the family retired to the second floor; the boys to Johanan's room, the men to Asa's, the women to their chamber.

Dan – too tired even to undress – thoughtlessly blew out the lamp and dropped into bed, where he fell asleep almost instantly, even as the more elaborately dressed Johanan was still struggling out of his best clothes. He was undressing as fast as he could, dragging both brocaded coat and under-tunic over his head as one, with a single hearty yank from the back of his neck, impatiently unlacing and trampling off the hated breeches he wore on holy days. But thanks to that selfish Dan, suddenly the room was pitch black, and his *comfortable* things were invisible on the other side of the room, probably still in a muddled heap on the floor where he had stepped out of them earlier. Well, too bad, it was cold, and he wasn't getting back into those scratchy things again, even if he *could* find where he'd kicked them in the dark. Bare as the day he was born, he slid into the linen sheets which still astounded Dan with their luxury, dragged the thick warm blankets up around his ears and dropped off to sleep almost as quickly as a country boy himself.

Something woke him, suddenly. Perhaps it was that the low murmuring on the floor above had stopped. Perhaps it was the very belated singing of their *Hallal* song which vibrated through the beams. Perhaps it was a wretched jackal howling in the far off smouldering valley where the rubbish was flung, or a fox barking in the Potters' Field close by it – a pit-gouged ugly wasteland of muddy dens where wild dogs prowled and bayed exasperatingly at the moon. Whatever it was, Johanan's eyes flew open. Dan was still fast asleep, but Johanan was instantly, very wide awake. There was the muffled rattle of a wooden latch and a creak from the door below. He leapt up and put his head out of the window. The men were filing silently out into the courtyard – *why?* – and there were only twelve of them. So the Kerioth had not returned.

Johanan's feeling of unease increased – something was not right. They had come to the supper looking sombre – the Teacher appearing pale and drained, though intense and sharply alert, his resolute eyes lit with a strange elation. The men were quiet, self-absorbed, almost sullen. Even later on there had been no laughing, no loud talking, no cheerful hubub as was usual at any feast when the solemnities had passed. But there had been what sounded very like a quarrel in the upper room – Johanan had tried all evening to pretend he hadn't heard it, or had misunderstood the import of the raised voices and injured tones, but it *was* a quarrel, shocking as that seemed. And the Kerioth *had* been lurking around that mysterious gathering at the High Priest's house only the night before – having slipped away from that special dinner given for his master *(deserting two feasts in a row – why?)* – and everyone knew the Priests' vicious hatred – and they were foot-in-sandal with the Sadducees, and with Herod ... and to their disgust and fury Jeshua had been publically glorified by the common people in the Temple ... and it was all happening at once ... and *now?* ... what was going on ...?

All this passed through Johanan's head in a lightning flash of stark alarm. He snatched up the sheet from his bed, and on noiseless bare feet flew down the stairs and into the night, not even pausing to shut the door after him. Darting through the gate, he tore into the street after the faint slapping echo of their footsteps and the low, tense voices, clumsily wrapping the sheet around him as he ran, holding it tightly in one fist. Ahead of him trailed the unmistakeable scent of spikenard, and this he followed, his heart hammering with anxiety, with a skin-crawling sense of perilous adventure.

Chapter Forty-nine

THE room was in disarray. Soft flat tapestry cushions, piles of blankets, oil-smudged menorah, kettle, bowls and ornaments, baskets, unused platters, a large cold brazier full of greasy ashes and burnt bones, an empty decorative water jar … all had been pushed into a jumbled corner; and the long table which had been surrounded by men only three days before, was now surrounded by women. Ashen faced, stricken women, with grief-burnt eyes, women who moved as if struck in the head, who worked relentlessly with shaking fingers at a task they need not perform. They worked in silence, broken by only occasional sobs, for they had wrung out almost every tear they had left in the world. Mari had brought into the room a treasured, gilded, greenish-glass bottle which had caught the family tears on the death of her parents, her husband, her three stillborn daughters, her two dearest friends – and in latter years, her sister-in-law Helen, and finally, Ammiel. Other memories were held there too, the mingled joys and pangs of her wedding night, of Johanan's birth. She had touched it to the cheeks of the women in turn, and their collective grief was added to the precious contents. Now it stood on the window sill, the bronze rays of a dying sun infusing the glass to cast a glowing patch of dull, sea-coloured light over a mass of white linen heaped on the low table, and the cold hands of the women at work.

Mari, Anna, Etta, Rhoda, Martha and Miriam Bethany, whose hair still whispered of spikenard, little Miriam Cleopas, Salome, the Magdalan, Bina, Jael, Shoshana, Joanna and a wisp-thin woman with purple-hollowed, haunted eyes – Mariah, who worked with a sword piercing her side, because her firstborn son was dead. A firstborn who was precious above comprehension, wholly hers as no other child could ever be to any woman, because no man had fathered him, and he had emerged from a wholly innocent girl-body. And yet he was far *less* hers than any other child, because he was the offspring of the Eternal Creator, and could not be owned by any man or woman, not even his mother. Who could describe the bitter grief she felt; the anguished, guilty sense of betrayal by a God who had given her a son in a shame-shadowed birth, and now took him away by a disgraceful death? The brief period of joy and hope and adulation, which had only brought her boy's downfall, was meaningless inside such agony. Still, her mute cries for answers from his Father went unvoiced, because the woman who had once been overshadowed by the power of the Holy Spirit, knew that she did not need to understand; it was enough for her to accept. *Faith!* Without it, life was death anyway. But none of this washed away the pain, the confusion, the reaction, the shock.

Now she and all the women were silent, holding themselves as carefully as if they might crack … as if they might shatter at a sudden move … all of them cried-out, raged-out, talked-out … working, breathing, working, bleeding … working, breathing, bleeding …

There was only the harsh scraping of mortar against pestle, the sharp cracking of seeds under wooden rollers, the rhythmic pounding of dried bark, the gritty sweep of spatulas blending spices in dried gourds, the heavy, dismal sound of ripping cloth, the sibilance of thread dragged through linen in stitch after stitch after stitch. They worked as if in a dream or a nightmare. The High Day Sabbath had held their hands, and they had not managed to complete all their laborious preparations on the Sixth day. Today, the enforced rest of the Seventh had nearly drained their hearts' blood, and the news that the tomb's stone door had been mortared in place, and a guard posted, had them quailing.

Now that the Temple's triple trumpet blast had finally pierced the gathering gloom to announce that the weariest of all Sabbaths was over, they were free to work, but still they could not leave until the first glimmers of daylight – and meanwhile the dark hours must be endured. As for the sealed stone, they must just get themselves there, and trust to the Eternal to show them a way. *When we do what we can, the Eternal will do what we can't,* they reminded themselves again and again. He would not deny His son their last ministrations! And so they lit lamps and finished what was needful, but they could not stop – regrinding, resifting, remixing, pulling out stitches and restitching, packing and repacking their loads, folding and rerolling their bandages, and stiffening their nerves to the grim task ahead.

What did it matter that the bloody, mangled body of the bright Hope of Israel had already been wrapped in a rich man's linen, with a ruler's spices? Full well they knew the haste in which it had been done, and what would a fastidious pair of wealthy men know about preparing the dead? Oh, dealing with the elemental was women's work – yes, the bloody, the hidden, the unclean – the birth, the bridal and the death!

What did it matter to them, that the body which had vanquished corruption in others, would itself be corrupting? They would open the unstitched shroud, would scrape aside the heaped

535

layer of spices and begin again, ignoring the stench as only women could; and they would lavish on the tortured corpse the time and devotion to detail which had not been possible till both Sabbaths had passed, and they would not be hurried. They would sponge and dry the mottled, heavy limbs, the lacerated, suppurating torso; clean and oil and comb the matted hair and beard and gently pick out the thorns snapped off in his scalp; wash the ears free of darkly crusted blood, close the bruised lids of the glazed, staring eyes, draw down the blue lips over the bared teeth and mercifully cover the inanimate face with a fresh napkin.

They had not looked on his nakedness when he hung with agonised, heaving chest on a vicious wooden *Tau*. All but his own mother had stood afar off, respecting his manhood, even while they inwardly died with him. Now it would not matter; in death the waxen, clay-cold body would be as a child's in the loving hands of many mothers, and they would wash him, anoint him, and dress him in the clean linen clothes they were stitching now, before they swaddled him limb by limb, strip by linen strip, with all the beautiful, costly materials which a King deserved. The rich men's spices would be mingled with theirs, and he would lie meticulously shrouded, neatly bandaged, white and perfumed; and the angels would see that this was a man greatly beloved!

Mariah methodically tore and rolled her linen, just as she had done nearly thirty-four years ago. Then, it was only a small piece, just enough to enfold a soft tiny body anointed simply with oil and salt. She had tied him with swaddling bands so joyfully stitched, and placed him in a feeding trough dug from the rocky walls of a cave where animals shared their shelter. So was he who was the Bread of Life presented to the world! *Eat of my flesh, drink of my blood*, he had told his followers, and lost many of them. Who

knew what he meant? But now – oh, the sword stabbed deep and sharp! – her son was dead. As if the dying echoed the birthing, there had been cries and blood and water. Once more his body had been anointed, again wrapped and bound, and laid on rough-hewn stone … the Bread of the World, on a table, in a cave! But strangers had tended him and not herself … and like all the women, she refused to be denied that last act of love. It would not be until she was satisfied, that she would give the word, "It is finished." Only then would she leave him.

While the women were thus occupied with their thoughts and their determination, the rest of the house was littered with dazed and shaken men. The eleven Chosen ones were closeted in the downstairs reception room, and only the occasional outburst of despair, guilt, misery, argument, or bewilderment, escaped through the thick door. In a corner on the second floor, ink block and parchment at his elbow, Mordecai with furrowed brow crouched over a pile of scrolls, rolling and unrolling with impatient twists of his wrist, scratching furiously with his pen. Johanan and Dan were whispering argumentatively and miserably together in a window, Asa was staring blankly down into the drizzling courtyard where Caleb sat in the sodden straw of the empty pen, heedless of the wet, head in his hands like a drunkard. Only in the stable was there any sign of life. Asa's donkey and Rhoda's dove watched warily as a wild-eyed Loukanos paced the cobbles, whirled round and paced the other way, and then the other again, up and down, flinging question after unanswerable question at a vigorously working and increasingly angry Lazarus, who continued to sweep the immaculate stalls, and spilled half the donkey's feed in his agitation.

A low rumble threatened the darkened air, perhaps a thunderstorm was brewing. *It would be fitting!* thought more than one, *the sky crashing, and crackling with savage lightning!* Had not the heavens frowned blackly as the most righteous man on earth hung dying with common criminals? Had not the earth itself shuddered mightily in revulsion — had not the very rocks of Jerusalem split, and the great lintel of the temple cracked through, shearing the massive holy curtain from top to bottom as easily as papyrus? Even as the hair on their necks rose at the memory, the rumble deepened and again the whole city shook violently. People cried out, goods toppled and crashed from shelves and tables, new cracks flashed across plaster, and those from three days ago yawned wider.

In the upper room the spell was broken, and the women wailed with one voice. Surely it must be the end of the world! What else was left them now that God had allowed His own Holy One to be wickedly executed! But the walls gradually stopped undulating, the floor steadied, until only the people were still quivering. In the upstairs window, the bottle of tears had somehow stayed upright. Anna forced the stopper more tightly into the neck, wrapped it in its leather cloth, and putting it safely in a basket, went drearily down to the kitchen where Shefi kept the fire, her sad, ancient eyes darting questioningly from one to another like a dog who does not understand his whipping. Anna looked at the food with distaste, but people must still eat, even if they would sleep where they dropped this bitter cold night. She must also be sure that there were enough blankets and braziers to keep everyone warm.

Many were the nightmares and black were the dreams and fitful was the restless sleep of the frightened household that night.

Dan and Johanan caught their breath as they heard shuffling footsteps on the stairs in the dark, but when they peered out it was only the women, burdened with their grave goods, who would not be held back any longer and meant to steal a long march on the sleeping sun.

"Can't we help you?" Dan whispered anxiously.

"No, no, *dodi*!" whispered the Magdalan, her hair streaming loose, tears fresh on her face, cradling her heavy bundle like a baby. "Best leave it to the mothers in Israel to tend the dead." She put her free arm around him as if he was still a little boy, and kissed his hair gently, murmuring with a choked sob, "We who would have died for him!"

Like shadows, the women flitted down the stairs and crept out, leaving Dan trembling at a sudden memory which leapt out clearly before him … the grey pre-dawn of a long ago shearing feast – and a savage, mad Marah All-Alone, with wild hair and pouring tears, cradling a dead baby made of earth, bewailing the slaughter of innocent life with screams and whispers, shaking him by the hair, hissing, "Does your mother love you? Are you her *dodi*? Would she die for you?" … and he wondered to think this was the same woman.

Shivering, he and Johanan crawled back to bed and fell into an uneasy sleep. Every noise, every raised voice in the street might be a self-righteous deputation to haul in the followers of a blasphemer, every passing tramp of feet the captain of a legion sent to deal with treason, to imprison the followers of a Jewish pretender to Herod's throne!

But what could be a woman's shriek at the first glimmer of sunrise? A frenzied shaking of the gate, a battering of hands on the door, a woman pushing past the alarmed servants, screaming for

Shimon, for Johanan ben Zebedee! Neighbouring households yelled alarmed or irritable or sleepy protests, but the two men came tumbling downstairs barely dressed, with everyone else scrambling fearfully after them.

"It's been moved!" she cried wildly, her mouth dry with panting, her breath coming in heaving sobs. "The stone! That huge stone as big as a man – rolled clean away! But there's no *body!*"

"Calm yourself, Magdalan! It's scarcely light – did you look properly? You went to the wrong one!"

"Do you think we didn't mark the place? That grave is new-cut, bare and unweathered! Why, it still reeks of myrrh and aloes! He's gone, I tell you – vanished! Would I run the length of the city to report such a cruel thing without being absolutely certain?" She began to wail noisily, heedlessly. "Why would they do it? Why open a grave they sealed and guarded so carefully? Don't you see? They've stolen him – hidden him to thwart us! And now we'll never be able to tend his body, or even lay a pebble of life on his grave!"

Sobs racked her, so violently that she never even noticed that Etta and Anna had their arms about her, murmuring comfort. She dashed the tears from her defiant eyes and snatched at the drink Loukanos ran to fetch her, gulping it down like a man and glaring at him.

"This had better not be a sedative, Loukanos! You all think I'm hysterical, I know. Well, with or without your help, I'm going back until I find out what they've done with him! You wait till the others return – they'll tell you the same story!"

She wrenched herself from them and flew angrily out of the house and through the gate, her feet pelting down the street. A furious discussion broke out in the courtyard, until Loukanos said tersely, "If she is hysterical she should not be left to herself."

Mordecai quietly agreed. "And if she is not, her words should be verified – what if it is some cruel trap devised by Herod, or the Sanhedrin? Either way, it's a lonely graveyard with hostile sentries … and remember the other women are still there, burdened with all their goods."

"You're right," Shimon said gruffly. "We had better follow. Come on, Johanan – no, not you, boy – ben Zebedee I mean. You others stay here and keep your heads down. Until we know what mood the city is in today, we'd best be careful. We'll be back before the third hour."

The two pulled on coats and sandals and left at once, striding into the dark, silent, empty street with a purposeful pace, as men who go to do a disagreeable duty. But before the sound had died away, the Nazarene's followers at Mari's house heard those steps quicken, and quicken, until they had become a race.

Almost silently, people wandered back inside to throw themselves on their beds, restlessly thinking. Wrung out with sorrow, they were reluctant to fully face a day which had barely dawned, but the Magdalan's commotion had left them too unsettled to sleep, too numb to pray. Anna and Mari gave up, and rousing themselves to take the household in hand again, and busied themselves in the large kitchen beside the servants. Mordecai and the boys did not go back to bed, instead they occupied the whitely scrubbed table, poring dully over various parchments by lamplight, oblivious to anything else. The others worked around them. With so many in the house, there was plenty to do, and they must see that everyone was fed and warm, no matter how sorrowful. Anna knew full well how easy it was for the grief-stricken to fall ill through neglect of the body, and the women who had gone so early to the grave would be cold and hungry when they returned – even if nothing evil befell them. She was thankful that the two men had gone in search of them. Two brash, bold and brawny fishermen would be a force to be reckoned with. ... perhaps ... if their courage did not fail them ... again ...

Mari and Anna said little as they worked, each silently wondering what would happen now. It was clear that soon the men and women who had sought refuge there would have to disperse to their own widely scattered homes and gather up the fragments which were left of their lives, their families and their occupations. For most of them this meant returning to Galilee, but until the seven days of mourning were over, there was no hurry. The heart-searchings, the recriminations, the fury towards the vanished betrayer, began to give place to reluctant thoughts of the future which stretched so confusingly bleak before them all. No Messiah! No Teacher! No deliverance from Rome! No restoration of the Kingdom! It was totally unthinkable that God could have mocked them – if Nazarene Jeshua had not been the Messiah, who would be? Could any man do more than he had done? Could any man have received greater approbation?

Anna sat down between the boys with a sigh, and massaged her aching temples. Johanan patted her back and she smiled at him sadly.

"And what will *you* do, Anna, with your shattered hopes?" Mordecai seemed to have read her mind, asking her quietly, his fine eyes clouded with exhaustion. She returned his look with eyes scarcely less weary, but pensive with growing resolution.

"I will bury them and build new ones," she replied slowly, putting her arm around silent Dan to hug him in an absent-

542

minded gesture of comfort. "I do not understand how we could have been wrong. Teacher Jeshua was endorsed by the Almighty Master of the Universe. No trick, no lie, no doubt."

"And endorsed by the scriptures!" Mordecai tiredly pushed away the pile of parchment and papyrus in front of him. "No, I don't understand either. It just seems to be all wrong, that's all I know."

Johanan sat up straighter. "Dan!" he said eagerly, reaching behind Anna to joggle his friend's arm. "Wake up. Do you remember when we were so sure the Baptiser was the Messiah? And then we found out he was a Levite, and we couldn't understand it?"

"Mmm?" Dan mumbled, and yawned sleepily, rubbing his face against Anna's shoulder to scratch his wispy cheek. "I never seem to understand anything at first …"

"Yes, that is my point! Don't you remember what you said? You said *maybe we just don't understand it properly.*"

"Yes, Dan," Anna tapped her teeth thoughtfully with a fingernail. "You said *sometimes I think something is wrong just because I don't understand it all yet.*"

"Well, it *was* wrong that time, wasn't it? Because *we* were wrong. The Baptiser wasn't the Messiah, he said so himself. So what do you mean?"

Loukanos had come in and was rummaging for food. He threw them each a few dates and Dan snatched them gratefully – his stomach was waking up. His uncle swung his long legs over the wooden bench by way of joining the conversation, and said firmly,

"Look, your facts were wrong then, but your reasoning, O thou Daniel, was astute. Let's apply it to the patient – our Hope, which is sickened almost unto death. So, were we wrong about our Lord

Jeshua? Let's see. Was he announced by angels? Yes. Did he come according to the correct times of the prophets? Yes. Was he announced by a voice crying in the wilderness? Yes. Did Eternal God *tell* us plainly that this man was His beloved son? Yes."

Mordecai quickly caught up the interrogation. "Did he preach peace? Yes. Did he proclaim liberty to the captives and give eyes to the blind, legs to the lame, and so on, according to the prophets? Yes. Was he a prophet greater than Moses? Yes. Did he demonstrate the power of God? By his signs and miracles and wonders – Yes."

"Did he come as a King to Jerusalem, riding on a donkey's colt, according to prophecy? Yes!" Anna said breathlessly.

"Was he of God? Yes!" Johanan thumped the table with his fist.

"Was he betrayed and tortured and killed?" Dan demanded morosely. "Yes. Did he do anything to save himself? No. See, those two don't fit!"

"Right, Dan!" Mordecai's eyes were intense with concentration. "They don't fit. *But everything else does!* What are the odds of that? So, what is the only logical conclusion? Say it again, your own confession."

Dan blinked. "Sometimes I think something is wrong just because I don't understand it all yet?"

"Right, Dan!" Anna echoed quickly. "Then if everything else is right, and it *must* be! – the fault is not in what happened! The error is in us – in our understanding – we have missed something!"

"Dead is dead is dead," Dan shook his head. "That stops everything. Why would God allow that? Even when Abraham was commanded to kill Isaac, an angel stepped in at the last instant to stop it. So why wouldn't the Eternal would do the same for His own son?"

Johanan was worrying his date stones into the deep knots in the wooden table. "Could we have been mistaken about the Baptiser? That he wasn't the wilderness voice after all? Could it have been Jeshua himself who was the fore-runner of Messiah?"

"No, no, and no," Mordecai said firmly. "Don't play around with the facts to make them fit the scripture, it's just as bad doing the opposite. Your cousin is right – we have missed something. Let us not invent what that might be …"

"Miriam Bethany – surely *she* knows something we have missed – the Teacher said she was anointing his body for burial! But she is as shocked as we are – did she know what would happen? Did *he*?"

Crash! The gate bursting open in the courtyard! Cries and frantic female voices! Chaos at the door – and even more chaos as once again people started from their beds and tried to calm a wild-eyed woman – no, *women*! Empty handed women, with fear and glory on their faces – who had crept out to a darkened tomb, dropped their burdens with shock, and fled back again. Yes! They'd found it empty – smelling of myrrh and aloes, just as the Magdalan had said! So she was right, not hysterical after all … no she's not here now, she was going back to the graveyard … of course the myrrh was yours … Not so, brethren, we knew there was enough myrrh for a king already! We took oils, perfumes and other spices, yes – sandalwood, cassia, stacte and such – but never mind that now – please listen! … Oh – what! – now you are *all* overwrought! Shining men? Angels? The Messiah risen? Yes, we would all like to think so. The temple guards in their white garments, surely, sneering at you, telling you to run to Galilee – take the troublemakers out of Jerusalem … Did you see a body? No. Did you see a risen Teacher? No. Never mind, we understand … it has been a great strain … Loukanos, can't you do anything for these women?

This time nobody returned to bed, and men went outside to wash and remained in muttering groups. The women, badly shaken, were folding, packing, cleaning the upper room in a kind of ostentatious silence. Loukanos refused to interfere. Traumatic grief – its hallucinations and reactions – should not be sedated, he snapped. Let them alone, and let them talk if they wish. Just listen. The more you contradict, the deeper you will drive their pain.

Oh, that gate, again! This time it was Fisher Shimon, puffing and blowing, followed by panting Johanan ben Zebedee – striding rapidly in to be surrounded by the other men, the women watching in agitation from the upper window.

"Gone – she was right – no doubt of it." Shimon had the grace to look abashed.

"Just as well – they are *all* saying it now, you know!" the Twin told them nervously. "But they've added angels!"

Mariah leaned out and called urgently, "Shimon! Did *you* see the angels?"

"Angels!" Shimon eyed Johanan ben Zebedee accusingly. "She is *your* mother now, Johanan, your special charge! What do you mean by allowing her to run around the city and a graveyard in the dark and get in such a state! What would *he* say to that?"

"Mother!" the young fisherman called kindly. "Come down here to us. No *malachim* – no angels – but everything else is as you say!"

546

She came down, with the others, and he put his brawny arms around her thin frame and rocked her as she wept on his broad breast.

"There were angels, son. There were. They said he has risen!" She lifted her head and looked directly at Shimon. "*Malach* Gabriel was not there, Shimon, but do you think I don't know an angel when I see one?"

People shuffled their feet nervously. Of course! Thirty four years ago, Mariah had been visited – they had all heard the tale – and though a host of angels had proclaimed to men the birth of her miraculous son, it was *Malach* Gabriel himself who announced his conception – the angel distinguished with his own name, the very same, very special angel who had instructed Daniel the Prophet. This woman had spoken to him face to face! No, she could not be deceived about angels.

Johanan ben Zebedee looked over her head and met their baffled looks one by one.

"Well? What else could explain it?" he demanded. "We saw for ourselves it was the right grave. It would take strong men to shift that boulder, and a few weary women wouldn't have a hope. But it was pushed clear, the mortar sheared clean off, and no guards in sight. The linen was there, the head cloth was folded neatly. *Folded!* If this was some perverted plot by the rulers or the Romans or anyone else, to drag him out and throw him in Gehenna with the criminals … would they have unbound him? Still less *neatly folded* his face shroud?"

There was shaking of heads and thrusting out of lower lips. Murmuring and muttering and avoidance of eyes. Dan's family stood at a respectful distance, tensely watching and listening. Again the gate! It swung open slowly, triumphantly, and in walked

547

the Magdalan, with her veil awry. Loukanos felt his heart turn over – never had he seen her so radiant, so lovely, and never would she be further from him than she was today – and she was singing, holding out her hands, tears pouring down her face – singing a weird melody all her own, the words a bizarre twist of a passage from the book of Job.

"I know that my Redeemer is alive!

I know he stands in these last days on the earth!

And though after death corruption may come

Yet in my flesh too, I have seen Divine Power

I have seen for myself, my own eyes have beheld.

I know that my Redeemer is alive

And standing now upon the earth!"

She broke off, smiling, elated, glowing – they were all so silent! She flung her arms around Miriam Bethany and fiercely kissed her wrinkled cheek, whispering exultantly, "Dear Miriam, you were right! Love is stronger than death! He said he must die, you and I heard it. But did we imagine *this?*"

She turned jubilantly to the others – and somehow she could speak firmly though her voice shook violently with emotion. "He *is* alive – oh my dearest friends – he is *alive!* The stone was moved and the tomb was emptied because He *lives!* Don't you see? Jeshua lives!" She gave a sudden sob. "I have seen *angels* at the tomb."

The other women nodded to each other with satisfaction. "And we saw them too!" they encouraged her eagerly, watching the men's faces …

"And – I have seen - *him!*"

Everyone shifted – ever so slightly – away from her. She laughed.

"You are right to wonder – I hardly knew him at first, I thought he was a gardener. So tall and dark and upright – so clean and free from that terrible blood from his flayed back and the thorns and the nails and the cruel spear! Oh to see him with all the heavy lines of pain erased, looking so calm, and young and glad! No wonder I was confused. But he called me by name! He told me so gently to stop crying! And then I realised who he was!"

Etta's grip tightened on Anna's hand and she bravely stepped forward, speaking the words on everyone's mind.

"Marah, dear – your brother, you know ... so you used to describe meeting your – dead – brother. Are you feeling quite well, my dear?"

The Magdalan flinched as if she had been slapped. She looked frantically from one to the other and her pale lips trembled. "You are all afraid of this, all of you! Do you think the Lord Jeshua fixed my mind with a piece of sealing wax? And it has now dropped out? I knew him, I tell you – and he knew me!"

"Where is he now?"

"He told me he was going to God his Father – God *our* Father."

"So we can't see him for ourselves – he's gone? Like Elijah? Or Enoch!"

The Magdalan tossed a scornful look over her shoulder as she whirled around and marched over to Loukanos, snatching off the bedraggled veil to reveal her whole face. She gripped his hands and her passionate eyes burned into his.

"Louki," she said softly. "You know me. You know these women. We all saw angels. But did I alone see our Lord, our Teacher, the Master of all teachers? Are miracles still happening? Or am I mad?"

He turned her hands over and lightly laid his fingertips on her wrists. Her pulses throbbed – slow, strong, steady. Her pupils were neither dilated nor pinpricks. She did not sweat, she was not drily feverish. The pallor of her skin was grief and exhaustion, not shock. She was uplifted, excited, but not illuminated by any morbid, icy fire in her soul. He dropped his eyes to her imploring lips.

"Tell me, Louki! *I* know, but tell me."

He released her hands, unwillingly. "You are not mad." He looked up at the tense faces around them and raised his voice deliberately. "I, Physician Loukanos of Philippi, disciple of our Lord Jeshua, say – she is not mad."

The look she gave him then, was itself a kiss.

He would remember it all his life.

Chapter Fifty

A STIFLING sense of foreboding was oppressing the household, particularly the Eleven, whose names were known to the authorities. The women's illogical reports aroused fresh fears of some elaborate plot to flush them out and entrap them. They demanded to be locked in. The women would have none of it and they left. A few would first retrieve the costly bundles abandoned in the graveyard, but their course was clear. Hadn't the angels said Jeshua was going to Galilee? The last woman paused by the gate, and with the faintest glimmer of a smile, tightened her sandals. She turned.

"Go with God, Loukanos."

"Go with God, Magdalan."

She was gone.

Hard on her heels went Fisher Shimon – miserably restless and reckless, peering suspiciously from an enveloping mantle which almost covered his face – stalking off to the reassuring smells of the lower Fish Market to trawl for any news. Next went Twin One. His devoted Twin Two, having faithfully followed him to the City, dragging with her the whole family, was now struggling in a rented bakery in the northern markets. Well, she needed him and his family needed him, and his bakery needed him and he would not be held back. The authorities would arrest him if they must, but he'd be hanged if he didn't bake some decent bread first. Young Cleopas was of the same mind. His precious Miriam had already left with the other women, determined to farewell her mother in the street of the Tailors on the way, and now he stormed off as well. He would go and see his own family before *he* was arrested, just see if he wouldn't!

"Wait!" Loukanos snatched up his thick cloak, bag and staff. "Only a madman walks the roads alone in a festive season – there'll be bandits at every bend!" He embraced Anna hastily. "I'll go mad myself if I'm cooped up any longer. Don't worry, with two of us we'll be all right, and you'll still have father and Mordecai, and Lazarus too – with his sisters secure in Bethany he won't stir till he knows more, no matter what the others do. I'm sure you're safe, or I'd never leave you. We'll be back tomorrow night, please God."

Lazarus barred the gate after them, and took himself to the stable, to be alone with his thoughts and prayers and the comforting presence of warm and trusting animals. He disliked being shut indoors. But the nine remaining Chosen closeted themselves upstairs, and once again began the endless threshing out and confession and agonising over every detail of the last several days, with the impossible claims of the women only confusing them the more. Faithful Shefi and Rhoda took them food, and then were packed off by Mari to rest. The two had been running around after everyone since early morning, and with the men all on edge, the day, still barely half spent, would probably run well into the night. Only the menservants were on duty, guarding gate and door, warned to admit none but familiar faces, or family of those within. Uniforms and phylacteries must not gain entry! But none tried – only a few breathless women returning with the salvaged grave-goods, shakily claiming that they too had met the risen

552

Jeshua. Yet even Mariah's passion could not convince the stubborn men, and so the baffled women left them to their misery and went away in silence.

In the kitchen Dan's family, with Caleb and Mordecai, slumped mutely at the well scrubbed table, exhaustedly eating a scrappy meal. Dan rubbed his stomach, then his chest, but the weird sensation he was feeling was still there. A strange kind of hollowness was hovering somewhere inside him – or around him – an anticipation of something, whether good or bad, he could not tell. The others seemed to be restless too, though not with anxiety. Aunt Etta and Asa both kept looking sharply at Anna, whose colour was a little heightened. She lowered her eyes quickly every time she caught her father's glance. Dan looked with impatient curiosity at them all. There seemed to be some invisible conversation going on to which he was not privy. Johanan was casting odd glances left and right himself. It was no good looking to Aunt Mari for clues – she kept jumping up and down to close and open windows. Caleb was munching morosely, lost in his own world, desperately missing his open fields, his contented sheep, his hard bed. Only Mordecai seemed to be behaving at all normally – apart from a rare clumsiness when he upset a polished wooden bowl of shelled almonds and sent them scattering all over the table. The peculiar tension was eased as everyone gave a shrug at the mishap and began scraping up the brown kernels within their reach and tossing them back into the bowl.

Perhaps the slight scuffle of this activity had prevented them from hearing the knocking at the gate or the low tones of servants dutifully asking the right questions. Neither did they hear them give entry to the white-garbed stranger, first into the courtyard, and then into the house, and then into the kitchen, where the first pale smiles were emerging because a distracted Mordecai, just as

553

he dropped the last almond into the replenished bowl had somehow knocked it over *again* and deserved a little sympathy.

The stranger stood silently in the doorway looking at the family scene before him. So noiseless was he that nobody had heard him, and how it was that they began to look up from the table and over to the door, was hard to say. But one by one, they did. And one by one, they were turned to stone where they sat. The last to turn around was Anna.

The stranger was looking at someone else. He was looking first at Dan, with his black curls, lean young face and sparse bright moustache. He looked at white-haired Etta, at deeply wrinkled Caleb, at Asa's beard, almost silver now, at Mari's streaks of grey, at Johanan's neat dark whiskers. His bright eyes passed over Mordecai without curiosity, and it was only then that he looked at Anna, at the seven bound braids which told of her Nazirite vow, at the fixed, dilated gaze from her odd eyes, one brown, one hazel.

He smiled. A warm, slow smile from the depths of a generous heart.

He spoke. A warm, slow, Galilean voice from the depths of a generous, curling, auburn beard.

"Caleb – my friend. Anna – my love. Dan – my son!"

It was Ammiel.

For the rest of his life Dan could not have said what happened next or who said what – who slid under the table in a dead faint, who laughed hysterically, who gasped, who screamed, who cried, who shook until he could not stand, and who looked sick – and neither could anyone else, except Mordecai, deathly calm, who seemed turned to ice, seeing everything very clearly, but as if from very far away.

What – who – when – *how?* As soon as order was restored, Ammiel told them all he knew. The earthquake which had cracked walls last night, had opened tombs. The faint warmth of the pale morning sun had fallen across his face, and woken Ammiel in his cold cell. He sat up, greatly astonished to find himself there, believing he had only been knocked unconscious by the fall from Mari's roof, until a mass of old bandaging lying all around him, and dusty ossuaries stowed in the cave showed in what dread place he was and why. He trembled, believing it was the Day of Judgement, but heard no angelic summons. He had stumbled out into the light to find others in a similar state, both men and women, wandering in their graveclothes. Together they came across an open, fragrant tomb where two white-robed young men sat as though waiting for them, their clothes and bodies shimmering with light. With glad faces they said, "The Messiah is risen! Go in to the City and witness to the power of resurrection!"

He obeyed as if in a dream, very slowly making his way to Mari's house, greatly confused – and here he was.

To ask *Why?* was simply beyond them. Everyone around the table was in a daze – staring at the unmarred face, once so bloodied – their hearts racing, bodies shivering in shocked reaction. Ammiel searched them all with his eyes, puzzled by the sudden changes in the family he had left – so he felt – only the night before; confounded that Old Caleb had so quickly come from Galilee – perhaps to pay respect to his grave? How had he never noticed how fast little Dan was growing! And Johanan! And what extraordinary thing had Anna done to her hair? And – and – ?? Slowly it sank in … he must have been dead for months! But he felt so alive, so – normal! To imagine, even now, that he could have lain cold, ghastly, rotting … *ugh!* He shuddered, and then the tears came, and Dan, forgetting he was a young man now, threw himself into his lap, burying his face in his beloved father's neck, clinging as if he was still only ten years old. It was some time before the storm of emotion abated, eyes were dried, and they were all ready to talk, even laugh.

They could not stop touching him. Dan, Johanan, Etta, Caleb, even reserved Anna, though she seemed more fearful than the rest. Stroking his hair and beard, squeezing his arms, feeling the warmth of his fingers, the ripple of muscles in his back. Suddenly Ammiel reached out, swept up a handful of the scattered almonds from the table, and tossed them into his mouth. He crunched gratefully, and looked at their dropped jaws and blank faces.

"I'm hungry," he said apologetically. "I haven't eaten for – how long?"

"More than four years," replied Anna – and then she laughed, incredulously, with only a touch of hysteria. There it was after days of silence – her rippling, skipping, hiccupping, dizzy laugh. Ammiel glowed to hear it; yes, this was his Anna! But – *four years!* He tried several times before he dared to ask the question which trembled on his tongue. When she answered quietly with downcast eyes that no, she had not married, and Ammiel gave a great shout of relieved triumph, Mordecai prayed nobody had seen him flush, but the shepherd's next question swept all else before it.

"Where's Bukki?"

There was a sober moment as the tale was haltingly told.

"I didn't even see him," Ammiel said slowly. "Perhaps he tripped. I was knocked off my feet before I knew it." He paused. "It's hard to understand, how that fall seemed to last such a long time. So

556

much flashed through my head, though it can only have been a matter of heartbeats ... *delaying the wedding yet again!* ... then realising, *No! all was finished! ... I would miss the Messiah* ... then *Oh, my Dan! My boy! Fatherless! How much I had meant to teach you!* ... and just at the last, strangely, came the words of that carpenter with the sawdust in his eyes, *He is already well taught, friend. Let that thought comfort you.* I felt a moment of deep gratitude – then a fierce blow to my head, with no time to feel pain – and suddenly I woke up, surprised to have no headache ... and with those same words still on my mind."

There was a moment's awed silence.

"But, *Abba!*" Dan hugged him excitedly. "You *didn't* miss the Messiah! He was there all the time! The Messiah was – *is* – or was – the carpenter himself – that very same man, and he has been working miraculous cures everywhere – just look at Aunt Etta! Haven't you noticed?"

More astonishment, questions, explanations! Ammiel's outburst of praise was something to witness; and when Asa's rich voice shakily led them in heartfelt prayer it seemed that the tears they had run out of only the day before, were freshly springing from a deep fountain of life. Their distilled joy was added to Mari's glass bottle, while the afternoon hours sped by as if to make up for the agonising slowness of the dreadful days they had just endured, but of which none would speak just yet. Let Ammiel steady himself in his newborn world first.

"There is still so much you must tell me," Ammiel despaired, "and I with more questions than you can answer in a week! Caleb, the sheep! Anna, your vow? Dan – you are almost a man! What of your schooling – what of Banayim – how have you fared – oh, and a thousand things!"

557

Ah, but where to start? Dan caught Caleb's eye, and an understanding crossed between them that this was not the time to tell Ammiel about the loss of his cherished Queen of Sheba. So they began with the finding of Loukanos, which only called for even more explanations.

What a tangled skein of words criss-crossed that table as they threw and caught or even snatched their narratives hastily from one to the other, trying to relate everything at once! Only Mordecai was almost silent, though he too wept when the man who had once shared his beggar's mat in the street embraced him tenderly and marvelled at the restoration not just of his sight, but of his face, and indeed, his whole life. From what mingled pure and bitter waters did those tears of Mordecai well up, even he dared not ask himself in the face of life from the dead. Not *all* in the graves had risen – this man was the Eternal's choice.

"But in all this amazement, I do not forget that I have been spoken to by messengers of the Almighty God," Ammiel continued seriously as Mari lit the evening lamps. "Incredible, miraculous, unbelievable as it seems; though you say miracles are almost common now that Messiah is here! But tell me what they meant by *Messiah is risen.* Is it that he has gathered his army and has even now risen to the throne? What *does* it mean?"

Oh, how would they ever explain what they themselves did not understand! And who would attempt it first? But at that moment, the meaning of what the angels had said to his dear master began rapidly to dawn on Old Caleb until suddenly it was as clear as the sun! His wrinkled old eyes lit up – of course! Why had they not realised? He stood up and spoke as boldly as a rabbi. It was so simple!

"It means that though the Messiah was dead in that tomb, yet he has risen to life again!" He nodded emphatically at the others. "Just as the women said! Yes! This is no longer merely a time to hear, to wonder, to doubt or to guess what has happened! *This is a time to see it for ourselves!* So, look! my friends! The all-wise Eternal in His loving compassion for our foolish, disbelieving hearts, gives us even more than the faithful witness of others – He has sent to us, and to many others in this city, one of our *own* dead, *risen* – to prove to us all that His son has also walked out of his grave."

Ammiel staggered to his feet. "The Messiah – dead? Buried? Risen?" he gasped. He gripped the old man by the shoulders. "Is this true?"

"Yes, my friend! As true as you also were dead, buried and resurrected!" Caleb flung himself on his master's breast, hugging him with his stringy arms, crying, "Truly, truly, God is Great! You were dead but He has made you live again! Therefore we can be *assured* that by His command our Lord Jeshua *also* lives again!"

Just as they all were beginning to realise the force of Caleb's words, there came an impatient shouting at the wildly shaken gate, flurried apologies of harassed servants, feet pelting over the dark courtyard – and in bolted Loukanos and Cleopas, panting, mud-splashed, incoherent, yelling like madmen, dashing upstairs to the Chosen. There was an excited babble of voices above, suddenly turning argumentative and lowering to muttering growls, protests, and exclamations of disgust.

A door shut smartly and down stamped the abruptly-returned travellers with flushed faces to the astounded family in the kitchen. Loukanos opened his mouth to explain, but at the same moment – yet *another* commotion outside, and yet another crash from the

559

long-suffering gate – more feet slapping the moonlit cobbles – the heavy door smacked open with a whack that shook the lintels – a mighty three-step bound up the stairs – massive fists hammering on the door of the upper room – and the thick Galilean accent of Fisher Shimon bellowing with the full force of his lungs.

"I've seen him! I've seen him! The Magdalan was not deluded! The women spoke truth! Truth! Praise the Eternal! Praise and exalt Him! Jeshua lives!"

From overhead came a chorus of stunned exclamations, a cacophony of incredulous male voices and a storm of heavy sobs torn from overcharged masculine chests. Loudly and feverishly demanding to know what was happening *now*, Lazarus came tearing in from the stable to be swept up in a stampede as thundering down the stairs came Jeshua's ten men together, yelling, pushing, recklessly leaping – roaring victoriously and calling out praise. They poured into the kitchen, jostling and jumping dementedly, still all shouting at once. The small smoked fish which Shimon had bought at the market with the only coin he could find in his belt, was tossed exuberantly into the air from one to another, until rescued from the chaos by a bewildered Aunt Etta.

"It's true! Loukanos, Cleopas, forgive us for doubting you!" Laughing and crying all at once, Johanan ben Zebedee was ecstatically hugging and rocking and thumping his grinning brother. "Almighty God has called forth His son from the tomb, even as Jeshua summoned Lazarus! He lives again! I *felt* it must be so when I saw the graveclothes, but I couldn't understand it – and everything he told the women has not yet happened because he is still here, praise God! Still with us – close by! – and now he has appeared to Shimon – *and* to these two!"

"Yes!" Cleopas barked hoarsely, gratefully gulping water from a cup plucked from astonished Mari's hand even as she was passing it to thirsty Loukanos. "And to us! That's why we came racing all the way back at once!"

"Tell everyone!" urged the ben Zebedees, anxious to make amends.

So jubilantly, eagerly, tripping over each other's sentences, the two told how they had met a stranger on the road who asked why they were so dejected, seeming to be sorely ignorant of what had just turned Jerusalem upside down … but when they told him he had rebuked them.

*"What fools you are, and so reluctant to believe the prophets! Don't you realise the Messiah **had** to suffer these things before entering his glory?"*

"It's all so clear now!" Loukanos cried exultantly. "He went right through Moses and the prophets and explained every single prophecy – and it was all *there*, all of it! We've been incredibly blind!" He grabbed Dan and shook him ferociously. "You were right, Dan! – it only seemed all wrong because we didn't understand it."

"The trouble with the obvious is that it isn't always obvious," agreed a deep voice behind him. Loukanos turned and froze to see a man who was wearing plain linen – what? – *graveclothes*? His mouth went dry. He had felt the life-warmth drain from that body himself, settled pieces of skull back in their place, straightened the broken limbs, shouldered the bier …

"Yes, Louki! It's him! It's true!" Anna whispered, tears pouring down her face, clinging to her brother, feeling she was in a kind of delirium. "Yet another surety that Messiah has risen – Ammiel is proof! And he is not the only one – there are many others

561

witnessing even now to their families – witnessing to the power of resurrection!"

Ammiel opened his arms, and wonderingly, tremblingly, Loukanos embraced him, holding him tightly, feeling the swelling of the broad chest, the air rushing in and out of the lungs, the throbbing of his heart, the vibration of his voice … yes, this man was real, alive, solid, no phantom, no hallucination. Oh, what wouldn't he give to understand *how* a corpse was restored!

Cleopas was plunging on with the story of how the stranger had finally revealed himself as the risen Teacher, their Lord Jeshua himself, and how they had dropped everything to fly back to Jerusalem. They had pounded excitedly on the door of the Twins' bakery as they passed it but found only weary, dogged scepticism within. Chastened to realise how the women must have felt earlier, the two ran on, resolving to be far more insistent than their humble sisters if they met with more disbelief. But in Mari's house disbelief was now cast out like the Magdalan's demons.

Nevertheless, there was still reason to be cautious, and at a nod from Asa, Johanan and Dan ran outside and locked everything up tightly again, the gate, the door, even the downstairs shutters. With all the uproar in this house today, trouble from outside may arise at any moment, and nobody could be sure of their safety, people rising from the dead or not. Everyone was exhausted but they could not stop talking. Would the Restoration now begin in earnest? After all, what could stop it – who would dare try to kill the Messiah again! That there were now two men present in this very kitchen who had lately corrupted in a tomb – one for four days, one for four years – but were this moment standing here warm and breathing among them, was irrefutable proof that the Lord Jeshua must live! Would Adonai God raise commoners and *not* His own princely son? Of *course* he lived! Shimon, Loukanos, and Cleopas had seen him – *spoken* with him – yes, and the women too! Why had they ever doubted it?

But what would be expected of them now, and what would happen next? The rulers would never forgive this insult to their power, and the danger may not be over yet. Meanwhile, where should they go, and what should they do? The kitchen was impossibly full, the noise was tremendous, people were talking, arguing, laughing, gesticulating and crying – even singing – and anyone would have thought there were several Purims and a wedding all happening at once. Rhoda and Shefi had long since squeezed themselves back in, and since nobody had been out to market for days, were anxiously trying to discover whether there was any decent food left in the house apart from Shimon's rather inadequate little fish.

"Blessings and peace be with you!"

A wave of stricken silence crashed through the room and rippled to the edge.

In its wake were strong men with knees turned to water, faces turned to ashes.

Men who had been laughing and shouting were dumb with terror. Women who had been joyfully singing had the notes frozen in their throats.

Before them was a man who had risen from the dead. Yet they had seen resurrected men before, had spoken with them, eaten with them; yea, two were even with them in this very room. But those were merely mortal men, raised to continue a mortal life.

Before them was a man who now drew aside the veil which until this moment had hidden a new reality from their reeling minds.

Before them was a man who was not just *revived,* as Lazarus, as Ammiel – here was a man who was a creature no longer mortal, *no longer wholly human*, but imbued with the Divine Spirit of immortality! It glowed from his perfect skin, it radiated from his shining eyes, it vibrated in the power of the still, quiet voice which could subdue the very storms of nature.

Small wonder that they trembled! Small wonder that they shrank! This was a man who had been one of them – and now was like one of the *Malachim.* Yes, some had seen angelic beings before, divine creatures of light, ambassadors of the Almighty. But never before had any mortal man who breathed seen his own kind – *changed* – transformed – re-fashioned into a new creation!

Lovingly he held out his hands. "Don't be afraid, my friends, it is really I, the same Jeshua and no other. Here, touch me – I'm real – flesh and bones, and no illusion. Look at my hands and feet."

He showed them his beautiful hands, and the feet which were ever swift to bring the gospel of peace to the mountains of Israel. The raw, bleeding flesh which had been ripped ragged by iron spikes only four days ago, was healed, and the skin radiant as a child's – but even in this immortal flesh was preserved for all time, the evidence – pale, deep, perfect scars.

Still they held back in fear, and he chided them for their lack of faith and for rejecting the reports of those chosen to bear witness, while they remained speechless in his presence.

He shook his head at them. "Do you have anything here to eat?"

564

Trembling, Etta took Shimon's smoked fish and handed it silently to Johanan who handed it to Dan, to Caleb, Asa, Ammiel, Anna, Loukanos, Mari, Mordecai. Through the press of them all it went, until Jeshua took it from Shimon's own hand, pulled off the flesh and ate it, with evident enjoyment. He dropped the bones neatly in the empty almond bowl, licked his fingers and smiled at them affectionately, gladly, triumphantly.

Then the noise broke out again ... quietly at first ... gathering in courage until the whole room overflowed with joy and singing – cries and tears of overloaded hearts pouring forth like the bursting banks of the Jordan in flood ...

Then the risen Lord Jeshua put his arms around his men, and breathed on them – and they breathed in the life force of a spirit-driven creature who needed neither air nor food to live.

Nothing was ever the same after that ... for any of them.

A new life was beginning for Dan and his family too – and for the scores of others who had been affected by the resurrection of their own dead, as well as their Lord – how could it not!

Three days later Anna slipped quietly out to the Temple. There she purchased a strange assortment of offerings and entered a special chamber in the Court of the Women. A sharp bladed knife flashed again and again, the lengthy sacrifices and rituals were performed, and finally, Anna walked away, her razor-swept, bare head swathed in a soft new veil, never again to be called *bath Netzir*.

Her Nazirite braids had been burnt with the offerings, she was free.

Epilogue

ANNA wept when Asa forbad the wedding until her hair should grow.

"Are you are ashamed for your daughter to be a bride with a shaven head?" she cried passionately. "*I* am not ashamed!"

"I would be ashamed to give only part of my daughter in marriage – and the part which is missing is not your hair."

"The Eternal gave him back to me! I will honour that gift."

"You will dishonour that gift if it was not meant for you. Was he not given back to his son?"

"We are betrothed!"

"No, Anna. You *were*. Like it or not, Death severed the bond, life healed the wound, and time has cauterised it. While your hair grows, all these high emotions can settle, until you – and he – can be sure there will be no regrets, and that you truly know your own heart. Then I will gladly give you to the man you love."

"But what of Dan? My precious Dan – how will he remain my son?"

Dan had been eavesdropping unashamedly. Finally he understood. Now he walked in and fondly kissed the stubble on her pale scalp.

"Grow your hair, *Amma*, and choose with your heart, not your head. I have my father back again, and whatever happens, you will always be my mother."

He wrapped his lanky arms around her shoulders and rubbed his soft auburn whiskers against her tear-stained cheek, like a yearling lamb. Straightening up, he pulled a new knotted cap from the folds of his girdle and fitted it on her bare head, tidying the rumpled silken fringe proudly. He had bought it himself only that morning. Anna obediently arranged her veil over it, and they both smiled with satisfaction. She smoothed his curls gratefully and hugged him, closing her eyes with a resigned sigh. Relief warmed every joint in her cold body. She looked up, to see Mordecai and Ammiel standing quietly by her father in the doorway, watching her with deep compassion.

Abruptly, in strode Loukanos, rubbing his hands, hardly noticing them as he barged through. He clapped his hands together and grinned round at everyone.

"What are you all moping about in here for? Come, rouse yourselves! Messiah is with us – and He has work for us to do! This is only the beginning!"